WORLDS APART
THE SHADOW REALM

FOUR FRIENDS. TWO WORLDS.
ONE DESTINY.

WORLDS APART

THE SHADOW REALM

R.J. WALLER

The Book Guild Ltd

First published in Great Britain in 2022 by
The Book Guild Ltd
Unit E2 Airfield Business Park,
Harrison Road, Market Harborough,
Leicestershire. LE16 7UL
Tel: 0116 2792299
www.bookguild.co.uk
Email: info@bookguild.co.uk
Twitter: @bookguild

This work is entirely fictitious and bears no resemblance to any persons living or dead.

Typeset in 11pt Adobe Garamond Pro

Printed on FSC accredited paper
Printed and bound in Great Britain by 4edge Limited

ISBN 978 1915122 100

British Library Cataloguing in Publication Data.
A catalogue record for this book is available from the British Library.

*For Jess: thank you for your belief,
encouragement and enthusiasm.*

PROLOGUE

"I don't want to go," cried Lenara. *She held on tightly to Taegan's hand, wishing that this terrible nightmare would end, that she could stay here where she belonged, with her husband.*

"You have to, Len," Taegan shouted back, raising his voice above the howling wind that was buffeting the chamber. *"This is for the good of Sunea."*

"I just don't think I can do it," she cried, letting her head fall against his chest.

"I wish there was another way, Len, but there isn't. You're our last hope to stop this madness." Taegan began to dig around in his pockets, scrabbling around before pulling the Star out.

"It's unthinkable what will happen if he gets his hands on this. You must take it; it can never be used again." Taegan placed the amulet in Lenara's hands, the small golden star at its oval centre vibrating gently.

The storm outside the Mages' chamber was raging wildly, tearing the place apart: the walls began to crack; large chunks of stone and marble were smashing down on to the floor around them. Lenara looked around, wild-eyed, as the world fell to pieces.

"What about you?" she yelled. *"What happens to Sunea?"*

"I don't know," said Taegan. *"But I do know it will be worse if we*

lose the Star." Their eyes locked, his full of stern sacrifice, hers awash with fear. He guided them to their feet, then kissed her tenderly.

"Do you believe the prophecy can still come true?" she asked.

"I have to," he said. "It's all we have left."

She began to cry, holding on to him tightly.

Just then, the door to the chamber crashed in, showering them in fragments of wood. In the shattered doorframe stood their enemy; he'd found them.

"Give me the star," he commanded, his voice reverberating around the chamber.

There was no time to waste: they had to act, or the world was doomed.

"Go, now," Taegan ordered urgently, before turning to launch himself at the figure. The man in the door could not block the flying tackle, and they both went sprawling back outside the chamber. At the same time, Lenara placed the golden chain around her neck, turned the amulet three times and awoke the Star from its four thousand-year-long slumber. Taegan smiled ruefully.

"It's over, Gregovir," he said triumphantly, before a massive explosion erupted behind them, sending them both hurtling through the air.

Taegan landed in the trees, gasping and struggling for air like a fish flung from its tank. As he groped the wet leaves beneath his fingers, a strange noise began to emerge from the ringing in his ears — a creaking, splintering noise, like the slow spread of a crack across glass.

Through the blur of his vision, he could see a huge crater where the chamber had been obliterated. In the centre was a huge, dark cloud, hovering just above the ground, pulsating, like a blackened lung. The dark energy cloud growled and buzzed, growing larger and louder with each pulse of its beating heart, until, with an incredible crescendo of shattering noise, it exploded outwards. Taegan was devoured by pain as the darkness consumed him; all he could hear were countless screaming voices as the black cloud tore through the world, leaving nothing in its wake.

Lenara landed with a bump on wet, muddy ground, in the middle of the forest. Rain was streaming down around her, and it took only a few seconds before she was soaked through, her long hair plastered on her face.

She had no idea where she was, what had happened or what to do.

All she knew, with a gnawing certainty, was that she was totally, and utterly, alone.

CHAPTER 1

As the glass began to make its slow, scraping way across the Ouija board, Ben Freeman looked carefully at his friends. Which one of them was doing this? Who thought it would be a laugh to pretend they'd made contact with a ghost? Jake still had his eyes shut, his spiky-haired head tilted up, humming an incantation to bring forth the dead. To his left was Sam, who looked panicked and scared behind his thick-rimmed glasses. To his right was Heather, whose pale complexion appeared to have whitened further in fear. *It must be Jake*, he thought. *This was his stupid idea in the first place.*

"Anyone for a little Ouija?" he'd said, with a cheeky grin. Before any groans could turn to protests, Jake had whipped out the board, an ornate hand-crafted piece of wood, painted a glossy black with blood-red letters, and set it up. The dying light of the fire bathed the tent in an eerie shade of orange, and they had pulled their sleeping bags tight against the rising chill.

Instructing everyone to rest their fingers lightly on the small thimble glass, Jake Walker had asked for silence, bowed his head and begun talking in a slow, monotonous voice.

"We are calling the spirit world. If there are any spirits present, please make yourself known."

Heather started giggling, stifling it quickly when Jake shot her a look. He repeated himself.

"We are calling the spirit world. If there are any spirits present, please make yourself known."

The torch lamp that lit the inner tent flickered, as if it were a candle blowing in the breeze, and a coldness replaced the warm atmosphere they'd been enjoying only a moment before. The glass began to shake a little.

"We feel your presence, oh spirit," intoned Jake. "Can you hear us?" Ben shivered.

"If you are there, move the glass to 'Yes'," said Jake.

And then, slowly but steadily, the glass had moved, coming to a stop on 'Yes'.

"Who pushed that?" squealed Sam. Jake gave him a furious look, quietening him with his eyes.

Jake shut his eyes and looked up again. "Please, oh spirit, tell us your name?" he intoned.

The glass began to move again, this time a little quicker, finally settling on 'No'.

"No?" exclaimed Heather, tucking her long, ginger hair nervously behind her ear. "Not quite Casper, is he?"

Jake ignored her and carried on. Ben and Heather shared a smile.

"Where are you from?" he said slowly, putting on a deeper voice than normal.

Again, the glass started to move around the board. Letter by letter it spelt out the word: *S-U-N-E-A*.

"Sunea?" said Ben. "Where on Earth is that?"

"Ssh," Jake hushed him. "Do you want them to go?" The question hung over the other three, who were by now thinking that perhaps they did.

"Can you tell us what's it like where you are, oh spirit?" called Jake.

The glass moved and spelled out the word: *D-E-A-D*.

An owl hooted right above them and made them all flinch.

"Someone's pushing the glass," said Ben. "Come on, who is it?" No-one owned up.

"Maybe we should stop," said Sam.

"No way," declared Jake. "This is amazing, we have to keep going." Before another objection surfaced, he pressed on.

"Do you have a message for us, oh spirit?" he asked sombrely.

The glass stayed still for a moment, time hanging as they waited for a response. Then it was off again, quicker this time, almost too quick for their fingers to keep up.

H-E-L-P.

Ben's eyes widened, his heart giving a little flutter. This was getting a bit much.

"Who's pushing this?" he demanded, his voice rattling a little. The scared looks he received from the others finally convinced him of the frightening truth. None of them were.

But for Jake, despite his fear, this was exactly what he wanted. He pushed on.

"What help do you need, oh spirit?"

They all seemed to stop breathing as the glass traversed the board, their fingers racing along on top of it, the dying crackles of the fire outside the only noise. Finally, the glass came to a rest, having spelt out its message.

F-O-L-L-O-W.

Ben had seen enough. He lifted his finger from the glass, Heather and Sam followed his lead immediately.

"No!" cried Jake. "We can't break contact."

"Nothing's going to happ—" Ben's words were interrupted as the glass flung itself across the tent and out of the flap at the front. Heather shrieked. The boys looked on in shock.

"What... was... that?" said Sam, breathless with fear.

Ben was up first, following the glass out of the tent. His frame was lanky and slim, the result of a recent growth spurt, and he had thick, brown foppish hair, which was ruffled and un-styled. His face was handsome, although his chin was pointy, giving him a slightly elfish look, and his brown eyes were round and innocent.

The glass was rolling away a few feet from the tent, as if pushed by the wind, although the air was still. Ben felt an icy chill go through him. He picked up the glass and flung it as far out into the forest as he could.

That was when he sensed it.

A tug, a pull, an irresistible call from the forest urging him out towards the trees.

Jake popped his head out of the tent.

"That was amazing!" he cried. "Have you ever seen anything like that?"

"No," murmured Ben, continuing to look out into the forest.

"Have you found the glass?" Jake said brightly. "Shall we have another go?"

"No, not yet. Just going to… look over here." Ben said, his thoughts and words slow.

Dark clouds were gathering in the sky, a gust of wind whipping up loose leaves and dust around him. A feeling of electricity hung in the air: the promise of a storm to come.

His feet began to move independently of his brain, marching him slowly, zombie-like, further and further into the forest. Soon Ben found himself in a small clearing, no bigger than a tennis court. Through the opening in the tree canopy, Ben could see the clouds racing across the moonlit sky. He felt rooted to the spot, unable to move as if he were in a dream and had no control of himself. He stumbled forwards, and as he did so, something changed.

The temperature dropped suddenly, as a freezing cold wind rushed through the clearing. His skin felt like it was being pricked by a thousand icy needles. Colour drained from the world, with everything washing to a pale, pastel shade. He began to choke as if he'd just been transported to the moon and there was no atmosphere, the air sucked out of the world.

Panicking, he opened his mouth to scream, but no sound escaped his lungs. He tried to run but it felt like his legs were stuck in a vat of glue.

Then, almost as abruptly, the sluggishness was replaced by a swift whooshing sensation, his vision blurring and the faded colours jumbling together in a crazy mosaic, before merging into a brilliant white light. An intense pain jolted through his body, like he'd been hit by lightning and then squeezed through a mangle.

After a second that seemed like an eternity, the pain subsided, ebbing away almost as quickly as it had come on. He was lying on the floor, panting hard. His eyes were open, but it was completely and utterly dark. He listened intently, but there was nothing, no sounds from the forest at all. It was as if he were just floating in a dark void. Ben Freeman had no idea what had just happened, or where on Earth he was, but he did know he felt very, very scared.

CHAPTER 2

The smell of rotting mulch filled Ben's nose, the loam underneath his fingers soft and damp. Pine needles pricked his hands as he moved them across the ground.

He sat up, careful not to make a sound, and fished his phone out of his pocket. It wasn't working. Ben shook it, trying several times to turn it on, but it was lifeless. He sat there, alone, afraid and confused.

Through the startling quiet he suddenly heard voices, and he froze, his instincts telling him to keep quiet and stay down. The voices were strange, rough and yet melodic, and definitely not from around the New Forest.

"I told you it wouldn't work, Akmar."

"Well, it's never been tried before, so how would you know?"

"It just seems a bit desperate, chanting an invocation for divine assistance."

"Come now, Manatang, don't you want the prophecy to come true?"

"Of course I do, but this isn't going to help. It's just a waste of magic."

Ben listened to the argumentative voices, confused about where he was and what they were talking about. He cocked his ear towards the voices to try and hear better.

"Anyway, if the prophecy were to come true, it should probably have happened by now, don't you think? We don't have long left."

The other person grunted. "I have to believe we still have time."

Ben's eyes were beginning to get used to the dark, and he was able to make out a few shapes of trees around him. He slowly stood up, trying to get a view of the disembodied voices, but as he did his foot snapped a twig, the sound reverberating in the darkness.

"What was that?" said one of the voices.

"Someone's there."

Ben instinctively stepped backwards, as fear and adrenaline pumped through him. Suddenly he was struck by an incredible pain, as if his heart had been grabbed by invisible, icy hands and squeezed until it was ready to burst. He screamed as his vision blurred, his ears popped, and then he found himself back on the floor in the New Forest, light from the moon spilling down onto the ground around him.

He realised he was still screaming but quickly stopped as the pain evaporated. He sat up, his vision swimming, feeling dizzy and disorientated. His friends burst into the clearing then.

"Dude, are you OK?" asked Jake.

"Um… I think so," replied Ben, patting himself down just to make sure.

"We heard you scream. We thought that ghost had got you!"

Ben gave a hollow little laugh. "No, I just suddenly felt a bit odd," he said, unsure he wanted to share his experience with his friends.

"OK… and you've just been here," said Sam, looking around, "in this bit of forest? We were getting worried about you."

"Sorry," muttered Ben. "I don't really know what came over me."

"Well, now you're back, how about we have another go at the Ouija?" asked Jake enthusiastically.

Ben shook his head vigorously and started marching back to the tent. "I think I'll just go to sleep now, if it's all the same to you."

The trip hadn't really panned out the way Ben had hoped. He had imagined long bike rides deep into the forest, games of 'nine-nine-in' whilst basking in the warm evening sun, and toasted marshmallows around the fire as they gazed at the stars.

Instead, Ben had suffered a restless night, with dreams of the pain he'd felt waking him up several times, sometimes screaming in anguish. He felt a flush of shame as he remembered Heather, who was two years younger than him, having to calm him down on a couple of occasions, deepening his embarrassment.

The events in the clearing the night before had started to feel unreal, like a dream. *Perhaps*, Ben thought, *they were a dream*. It made more sense than it being real.

The heat from the morning sun was beginning to make the tent stuffy, so he leant forwards and unzipped the door. The others murmured and moved in their sleeping bags like squirming maggots but didn't wake. Ben emerged from the tent into the fresh morning air, stretching his arms out wide. Compared to the tent, it was still quite chilly, but a beautiful crisp blue sky raced away overhead, as mist rose from the dewy forest floor.

Ben looked around at the trees, and a weird sensation of déjà vu came over him, as he looked in the direction he had walked last night.

And then he felt it. The same urge, the same desire to go and walk out into the woods, beckoning him deeper into the forest. He tried to dismiss the notion, but he found his feet beginning to walk the way they had last night anyway.

Scarcely believing what he was doing but morbidly curious, Ben walked out past the blackened remains of the fire towards the trees. With each step he became more nervous; what was he walking into? What did he think he was doing?

A shiver went down his spine as he reached the clearing. The trees gently creaked in the breeze, but Ben heard only his own breathing, his heart hammering against his chest.

He took a deep breath and stepped into the clearing. Nothing happened. Ben exhaled, feeling silly. Of course nothing was going to happen. It must have been a dream, so what had he expected? He inched his way closer to the centre of the clearing, stopping suddenly as he sensed something, and the hairs on his arms stood on end, as if electricity were coursing through him.

A gust of wind picked up, and then he heard his name sung softly on it. He looked round, startled, wondering where it was coming from. Then he heard it again and realised it was Heather, calling out for him. He took one last look at the clearing, shook his head and ran back to the campsite.

After a breakfast of a cereal bar and banana each, they packed away their things and the tent, and began the walk to their favourite hangout – the tyre swing. They'd discovered it by chance one day, hanging off a branch over a river, and for Jake, it was like a red rag to a bull. He had instantly run up to the tyre and jumped on, flying out over the water, whooping and yelling as he sailed through the air. A moment later and Sam had lost himself, running up and trying to jump onto the tyre whilst it was still in motion. He failed but held on as he was dragged out over the water, before plunging into the cold river below with an almighty splash.

Jake laughed hard and had then jumped in after him, bombing into the river and covering Sam with a wall of water. When Jake surfaced, they were both laughing.

Since that first day, whenever the weather had been good, they'd gone back to this spot to cool off and have some fun. As they made their way through the forest, dodging horse muck and ploughing through thick ferns, their chat turned to the night before.

"So, crazy stuff last night, right?" began Jake.

Sam shuffled uncomfortably, folding his arms across his plump chest. He clearly didn't want to talk about it.

"I don't know, it was pretty scary," said Heather, one hand

clasping a skinny wrist. "I barely slept a wink. Ben's screaming in the middle of the night didn't exactly help either."

"Yeah, sorry about that," Ben said, going a little red.

"If you want to know what I think," said Jake, not stopping to check whether anyone actually did, "I think there can be no doubt that what we witnessed last night was a ghost: a spirit from another world."

"Oh, come off it, Jake," snapped Ben. "I'm not so sure about that. Any one of us could have been pushing that glass around."

"Well, was anyone?" Jake demanded. None of them said anything, which only spurred him on. "And I didn't see any of us throw the glass out of the tent, did you?"

The question hung in the air like a bad smell, before Ben conceded that he hadn't.

"So, ipso facto, it must have been a ghost," concluded Jake, a smug grin on his face.

"I'm sure there could be any number of rational explanations for what happened."

"What do you think, Sam?" asked Jake, his strong square jaw jutting out as he spoke.

"There was definitely something spooky going on. The whole thing, what with Ben marching off and then screaming half the night, has put me a bit on edge."

"Maybe we should do it again," enthused Jake. "See if we can get back in touch with the spirits."

"*No!*" shouted the other three in unison.

"Just an idea," muttered Jake to himself.

The talk of last night had made Ben think of his experience in the clearing again. It was easy to believe, whilst here chatting carefree with his friends in the warm light of day, that it wasn't real, that it was all in his head. The idea that it could have been real – well, it just seemed a bit deranged.

The day was heating up nicely, and they were able to spend a couple of hours at the tyre swing, flinging themselves out across the river and diving in, time after time. As Ben dried off on the riverbank, he closed his eyes for a moment, feeling the warm sunshine on his skin, the wind feathering his face, and wondered if this was true happiness. After a while they bored of the swing and headed to the knotted tree for a game of seeker.

"Last one there's a rotten loser!" shouted Jake.

Ben groaned but started running anyway, a silly competitive instinct kicking in to avoid coming last. The knotted tree was one of the oldest trees in the forest: a big, gnarly oak that looked like a twisted gargoyle. Local legend had it that it would come to life after dark and look for children to eat.

Sam was, somewhat predictably, the last to reach it, much to Jake's delight.

"Right, Sam, you big loser, you can be seeker," he jeered.

"Must we really play that game?" moaned Sam.

"Yeah, come on, it'll be fun."

"Fine," he sighed, agreeing to seek them out whilst the others hid.

They tried to catch their breath after the dash, but Sam was having none of it. He covered his eyes with his hands, faced the tree and began his count immediately.

The others exchanged a quick glance, then scattered.

Ben already knew which way he was going to go. He ran into a dense area of trees that stretched along the north side of the knotted tree. The forest thundered up around him, trees splaying out their long branches like bony fingers that clawed their way towards the sky.

He slowed down, looking around purposefully, trying to find somewhere inconspicuous, a hole or bush he could drop into. He knew he only had a few moments left before Sam would stop counting and start looking for him.

Skidding to a halt, he realised that he had wandered into the clearing that he'd been in twice now, once last night and once this morning. He groaned inwardly but tried to force his mind to concentrate on the game, to look for somewhere to hide, but there was nowhere in the sparse clearing. *I must get out of here*, he thought, but then he froze.

The hairs on his arm stood on end as his skin flushed with goosepimples, and a familiar pain gripped him and compressed his body and soul into the size of an atom, squeezing him through a pinprick in space. He saw nothing but blinding white light and felt only pain, until it was suddenly all over and he fell to the floor, gasping for air, unable to see nought but inky blackness.

CHAPTER 3

Slowly, but surely, a very dim, faint light began to filter into Ben's eyes, and shades of grey began to emerge from the gloom. Shapes of trees and branches lifted into view, glistening a soft silver against a moody black. It wasn't the forest like he'd ever seen it before.

A dense, impenetrable fog made it impossible to see very far, and above him there was only darkness; there were no stars or moon to be seen. Despite the lack of illumination, there was still somehow a little light, almost leaking out of the trees. It lit the world a smoggy grey, a winter scene that was hewn in ash, rather than snow.

For a moment Ben wondered if he'd died, and this was hell.

He knew he couldn't sit on the floor doing nothing for much longer, so he stood up. As soon as he did, a calm, soft voice spoke from the edge of the clearing.

"Stay right where you are."

Ben panicked and turned to run, managing only a few steps before tripping and flying headfirst into a coarse thorn bush, his face scraping through the sharp talons.

Shocked and hurt, he turned to see where the voice had come from. He saw a figure had entered the clearing and was slowly pacing towards him. It had short legs and long arms. *A bit like a monkey,* thought Ben, but he knew there were no monkeys in the New Forest.

The weird monkey-figure was pacing backwards and forwards now, grunting an occasional awkward sound and keeping its eyes firmly on Ben. Ben propped himself up on his elbows and held his arms out to the creature in what he hoped was a reassuring manner.

"It's OK," he said, sounding like he was telling a snarling dog to be a 'good boy'. "I won't hurt you."

The animal stopped and stared straight back at Ben. Its face was distinctly human, but its body looked a lot like an orangutan. "And why do you suppose you can do *me* any harm?" the monkey-human said, with a slight Scottish twang.

Ben's mouth fell open, his eyes widening in shock.

"Rude as well, it would seem," said the creature, after a few moments of Ben gawping at it.

"Sorry," he said automatically, before catching himself. *This must be a dream*, he thought. *I'm not talking to a monkey.* He pinched himself, then hit himself in the leg, but he didn't wake up and the monkey-man was still looking at him intently.

"I... I... I'm just having some difficulty believing that... are you talking to me?"

"Of course I am, who else would I be talking to?"

"I mean... It's just I can't believe you're talking." Ben frowned. He'd never seen anything like this creature in his life. "Um... are you a monkey?" he asked, plainly.

The thing looked at Ben quizzically, cocking his head. "What's a monkey?"

"It's... well, it's..." began Ben, struggling to explain. He shook his head violently. "No, I'm dreaming, that's what's happening, I'm stuck in some awful dream I can't wake up from."

The thing pursed its lips together. "It doesn't matter. You're not from around here; I need to know who you are and what you're doing here."

Ben looked around, apparently deciding that if he was going to start talking to animals, he may as well throw himself into it.

"I'm... Ben," he said, slowly. "I don't know what I'm doing here. Or where here even is. What is this place?"

The creature looked at Ben, his eyes narrowing slightly and his face darkening. His tongue darted nervously around his lips. Finally, he leant forwards and whispered softly, "This is the Shadow Realm."

A cold shiver crept along the nape of Ben's neck. "The Shadow Realm?"

"Yes. The Shadow Realm," he repeated, less than helpfully.

Ben sighed. "And where, exactly, is the *Shadow Realm*?"

"Not where, rather what," came the cryptic reply.

"OK then, *what* is the Shadow Realm?"

"Just a pale imitation of what we were before..." said the monkey-man, trailing off.

"Look, you're not making much sense," said Ben, his voice rising in irritation. "Who are you?"

The creature gave Ben an appraising look, before giving a little smile and a nod.

"If you must know, I'm Manatang."

"A Manatang?"

"No, not *a* Manatang. Just Manatang. And where are you from, Ben?"

"The New Forest, I was just here... I mean there... oh, I don't know what's going on," Ben wailed, throwing his head in his hands.

"Ssh," Manatang whispered urgently, putting his finger on his lips and looking around with a look of alarm on his face. "He might hear you."

"Who might hear me?" he whispered back.

"Lord Blackwood." Manatang cringed as he said the name.

"Lord Blackwood?"

"Yes, Lord Blackwood."

Ben felt a flare of frustration. "Who is Lord Blackwood?"

"Wow, you're really not from around here, are you?" Manatang's face turned to one of deep suspicion. "I have to ask you a question, and it's important you don't lie to me. Have you been here before?"

"No!" protested Ben, but then, "Maybe, I don't know. Something weird happened last night, and…" Ben trailed off as he realised something. "Your name," he shouted. "Manatang. That was you! You were here last night."

Manatang looked around wildly again. "Firstly, please keep your voice down, we really could do without him turning up. Secondly, I wasn't here last night, it was a couple of hours ago. But that was you we heard, hiding out here?"

"I wasn't hiding out here," said Ben. "That's what I can't explain: one minute I was in the New Forest, then I was here."

"Well, this is a forest," said Manatang, gesturing to the wood around him. Ben looked at the barren and blackened trees around him.

"Not like mine," Ben moaned, suddenly feeling hopelessly lost.

"Listen to me, Ben, we may not have much time. Tell me how you came here."

"I just told you, I don't know how. One minute I was in the daylight, playing with my friends, the next minute I'm in this godforsaken place."

Manatang tapped his chin, considering Ben with a cool expression. "This could be important – you wait here, I'll go get Taegan."

"*No!*" shouted Ben. "I need to get back, please help me."

Once again Manatang looked around, scared that Ben's shout may have been heard. "You're really not getting the need to stay quiet, are you? Look, we can help you get back, but first I really need to tell Taegan about you coming here."

"I just want to go home."

Manatang helped Ben to his feet.

"Is it always like this?" asked Ben. "Dark and foggy?"

"The fog comes about once a week. We call it Galle's fog. But it's always dark in the Shadow Realm, hence the name," Manatang said matter-of-factly. He stroked his human-like chin, apparently in deep thought. "Where did you say you were from?" he said eventually.

"The New Forest. In England."

"Never heard of it."

"But you're speaking English," Ben complained, pointing out the obvious. "How can you be speaking English if you've never heard of England?"

"I'm speaking Sunean," Manatang said forcefully. "And I had wondered the same about you."

"Sunean?" repeated Ben, forming his mouth around the strange word. Why did it sound familiar? "Oh my, that's it!" he exclaimed, rather loudly.

Just then something in the atmosphere changed: the air became heavy with electricity and a wind rushed through the clearing.

"Uh-oh," uttered Manatang, wide-eyed with fear.

"What? What is it?"

"I told you to be quiet," Manatang cried, and dropped to the ground.

An explosion sent a thunderous blast ripping through the clearing, smashing into Ben and sending him flying against a tree. He landed in a crumpled heap at its base, groaning at the pain shooting through his back. Manatang ran to Ben as he tried to drag himself up from the floor, grabbing his head between his hands.

"Now would be a very good time for you to disappear," he hissed urgently.

A tall, dark figure was silhouetted at the edge of the clearing. Ben knew he should run, but he couldn't; he was unable to rip his eyes away from the giant figure in front of him. It was clad in armour, like a knight of the realm, and at least ten feet tall. The helmet had an open front, but there was no face there, just a dark void.

Then, exploding into life, two circles of bright fire appeared for eyes, burning with a ferocious intensity. Ben stared at them, mesmerised; his world got smaller as he felt inexorably drawn towards them, their fiery outline filling up his vision, his world. The flames danced higher, faster, hotter as they anticipated burning him up.

Manatang cleared his throat. "Good evening, Lord Blackwood," he said, before bowing low. "How can I be of service today?"

The voice that came back filled Ben's head without bothering to travel the distance between them. It was thunderous, powerful and infinitely chilling.

"*Out of my way, Manatang. I will take this boy with me.*"

"But he shouldn't be here," cried Manatang. "Can you not just… let him go?"

Lord Blackwood towered over Manatang, his flaming eyes burrowing into him. Manatang shrank back under the glare of the man.

"Do you really wish to stand in my way?"

Manatang's shoulders fell. "Of course not."

Blackwood pushed Manatang aside and bore down on Ben, who scrabbled backwards as terror took over. He prayed he would wake up from this terrible nightmare, that he'd just be back home, in bed. Blackwood reached for him, and as he did so Ben stumbled, his foot catching on something, and suddenly time slowed down.

It was the same sensation he had felt half an hour ago: a thousand icy needles pricked his skin. Lord Blackwood roared as he made a final lunge for Ben, but it was too late; his iron fist grabbed at nothing but thin air.

Ben screamed silently as his body was crushed and sucked through the eye of a needle. The incredible pain dissipated quickly, colour coming back to his world as he gasped fresh air into his lungs.

He was lying on his back looking up at a beautiful late summer's day. Dappled sunlight was filtering down through the leafy canopy, warming him as he lay on the ground. He felt a bit dizzy, his head in a spin, as nausea crept up his glands and tickled at his cheeks. He couldn't hold it back, raising himself up on all fours and vomiting on to the forest floor.

After emptying the contents of his stomach, he sat back and tried to catch his breath. He couldn't quite comprehend what just happened, his mind and body going into a mild state of shock. Was it real? The pain was certainly real, as he rubbed his stomach and massaged his temples. He focussed on his breathing, trying to calm himself down, to reduce the panic and nausea he was feeling.

His attention was diverted when he heard his name being called out. It was his friends, sounding concerned.

Ben tried to call back, but his voice was hoarse, barely carrying beyond the clearing. He lurched to his feet, clambering his way through the trees. Heather was the first to spot him.

"Ben!" she shouted, running towards him. "Where have you been?" She stopped short of him, looking like she couldn't decide whether to hug him or hit him. She turned back and shouted out loudly, "He's over here." Ben winced at the attack on his ear drums.

"Where have you been, Ben? We've been worried sick. You've been gone for over two hours."

Ben looked at her, not sure of the truth in what she was saying. Had he really been gone that long? He didn't know what to tell her – none of them would believe him if he told them the truth, or at least the only version of the truth he knew.

Sam and Jake came jogging over, Jake giving him a hard punch on the arm.

"Why didn't you come out when we started calling you?" asked Sam.

"I... I didn't hear you. I guess I must have strayed out of the boundaries."

Jake was enraged. "You didn't hear us? We've been shouting for two hours, wondering what on Earth has happened to you. Two hours! We were about to call your parents."

"Sorry, guys," Ben said, resigned to lying to his friends. "I must have lost track of time. I think I fell asleep for a bit. That's how bad Sam is at this game." His lame attempt at humour brought no laughter from his friends, but they smiled and seemed glad that whatever emergency they thought they had was now over.

"C'mon, let's go home," said Sam. "I think we've had enough excitement for one camping trip."

CHAPTER 4

As they walked home, Ben's mind kept returning to that dark world, and what might have happened if he didn't disappear when he did. He felt dazed and wanted only to get away from the forest. He tried to feel the warmth of the sun, but it was no use: he couldn't shake the cold he felt in his core. He trailed behind the others as they ambled along, so Heather dropped her pace to walk alongside him.

"Are you sure you're OK?" she asked, lightly touching his arm.

Ben toyed with the idea of telling her everything right then, just letting it all out. But what could he say that wouldn't make him sound mad?

So he just nodded his head, unable to formulate a sentence with all the thoughts swirling around his mind. Where was this Shadow Realm? Who was Lord Blackwood? What did he want with him? And what became of poor Manatang when he disappeared?

She looked at him, deeply dubious, but accepted his answer and, sensing his desire to be left alone, returned to walk with the others.

He still felt like his head might explode with the pressure of these unanswerable questions. He felt like he had to tell someone. Once they'd arrived back in their village and said their goodbyes to Heather and Jake, Ben turned to Sam, taking a deep breath.

"If I tell you something, Sam, do you promise not to tell the others? Not to tell another soul?"

Sam looked at Ben with trepidation, wondering what he was about to hear. "Of course," he said slowly.

"This is going to make me sound mad, but I have to tell someone. I didn't just stray too far when I went missing earlier."

Sam eyed him warily. "OK," he said finally. "Where were you then?"

Ben paused, searching for the words. "I think I... travelled... somewhere." He studied the dirt under his fingernails. "One second I was stood in the forest, the next I'm in the most incredible pain, and then it was just dark. Like pitch black." He paused to gauge Sam's reaction, which at this stage appeared to be mild confusion.

"Go on."

Ben tried to describe the Shadow Realm and what happened to him there: meeting Manatang and then the monstrous Lord Blackwood, and how he had nearly been caught.

Sam's face was slowly screwing up in disbelief. "This... Lord Blackwood," he began. "What do you think he wants with you?"

"I'm not sure, but I don't think it's anything good. I think he's evil."

Sam chuckled. "Well, how could anyone with fire for eyes *not* be evil?"

Ben frowned, disappointed his friend would make light of this.

Sam sighed. "Look, maybe all that happened was you hit your head when you were hiding and had a bad dream, and that's why you didn't hear us," he said, trying to reassure Ben.

"But what about the night before? I travelled there then as well. Once you could chalk up to my mind, but twice? And dreams might feel real at the time, but at least when you wake up you know it was just a dream. This still feels like it actually happened."

They had come to Ben's house, a detached mock Tudor house with neatly nipped lawns, one of many like it down 'Field Way'.

They hovered at the end of his paved driveway, not saying anything for a moment. Finally Sam spoke. "It's quite some story, Ben. Do you really think it happened?"

"I have to," said Ben, puffing out his cheeks. "Otherwise I'm going mad."

Ben's face suddenly went ashen as he remembered his conversation with Manatang.

Sam saw the change. "What is it?"

"Manatang. He was speaking English, but he told me he was speaking Sunean."

"And?"

"Don't you see?" Ben said, thrusting his arms wide. "The Ouija board – it spelt out Sunea when we asked who we were speaking to. Sunea. Sunean. That can't be a coincidence."

Sam didn't look so impressed. "It's hardly proof, Ben. Your brain could have taken that word from your subconscious and put it in your vision or whatever it was. It was a strange word in a very weird situation – it's not surprising you remembered it."

Ben only muttered defensively.

Sam's mother had come out of their house further down the road, calling him in for tea.

"I would suggest one more thing," Sam said, turning back to Ben as he walked away.

"What's that?"

"Don't go telling anyone else this. Don't want people to think you're losing it."

Ben smiled weakly in response, wondering if he was, in fact, losing his mind.

Ben went inside his house, taking his backpack off and slinging it into a corner. His mum came to the kitchen door, wearing a spotty blue pinny over her clothes. She had thick, wavy black hair that she wore naturally and dark, chocolate-brown eyes. In her youth she was quite the beauty, but the years had been a little unkind to her. Deep wrinkles were etched into her brow and crow's feet raked at her eyes, whilst a hollowness in her face hinted at a personal anguish.

"So how was it?" she said, attempting to sound light and airy, but her voice betrayed the concern that lay beneath.

"It was fine, Mum," sighed Ben. "We had a really good time." There was something in Ben's voice, though, a falseness that his mother picked up on instantly.

"What happened?" she asked, coming to him and putting her hands on his face, studying him intently.

"Nothing," Ben said strongly, squirming away. "I told you, we had fun. I'm sure we'll do it again soon."

Helena Freeman clucked her tongue. "I'm not sure I like the idea of you going away again too soon." She hugged her son. "I've missed you."

"Oh, Mum," Ben whined, embarrassed, but he gave her a little hug back.

They walked into the big kitchen/diner that acted as the family hub. His dad was sitting at a solid oak dining table, reading the Sunday papers. He peered over the top of them as Ben came in.

"Hello, son," he said happily. "Did you have fun?" He had small, beady eyes, but they radiated warmth. A few wisps of hair were all that remained on his head.

"Yes, thanks, Dad."

John Freeman seemed satisfied with this and went back to his paper. Ben carried on through the hallway and up the stairs to his bedroom, lying down on his bed.

Like any teenager's bedroom, it was messy: the floor covered in clothes, the desk with knick-knacks, his laptop adrift in a sea of paper. The walls were covered in posters of his favourite bands and video games, but nestled amongst these were a few environmental protest pictures.

His mind began to play back the events of the weekend, despite his best intentions. Everything had happened so fast: the game of Ouija and the glass thrown from the tent, the two trips to the Shadow Realm, ending with his meeting the terrifying Lord Blackwood. He tried desperately to think of something else, but the last image of Lord Blackwood towering over him kept creeping in.

Eventually the lack of sleep from the night before caught up with him, and he snoozed lightly on top of his bed sheets.

He was woken an hour later by his mum calling him down for dinner. Feeling a bit groggy, but at least with the Shadow Realm out of his mind, he trudged down the stairs.

"What's for tea?" he asked, as he rounded the hallway door into the kitchen.

"Lasagne."

"Yum. My favourite," he said, his mood lifting.

He pulled up a chair next to his dad and poured some iced water from the jug.

"So, tell us all about the trip," said his dad. "What did you get up to?"

Ben shrugged his shoulders. "Not much, really. We mucked around, played some games, standard stuff. We did cook our own dinner, though – a nice hearty round of beans and sausages."

"Well done, son," said his dad, in mock pride.

"Is that it then?" his mother enquired. "No hijinks?"

"Well, maybe some, but nothing special. Sam did tell us he wants to be a rock star."

His mum and dad both laughed at that, then stifled them, feeling guilty. Ben saw their faces and chuckled too.

"We're thinking of going to Stonehenge tomorrow," said his mum, completely changing the subject.

"Again?" groaned Ben.

"Now, come on, Ben," said his dad. "You know how much your mother loves Stonehenge, and it's an absolutely fascinating piece of ancient history. I think it's nice to spend some time there; you can feel connected to the past."

"Fine," said Ben, a little glumly. It wasn't that he minded Stonehenge itself, just the volume of times they'd been. This would be their third trip this year. Last year they went five times. There's only so much of standing in a rainy field looking at a bunch of stones that one person can take.

The next day was overcast, the pregnant clouds threatening rain at any moment, just as they always seemed to do when they visited Stonehenge.

He climbed out of the car and trudged over to the entrance gate with his parents. Having flashed their National Heritage life membership cards, they walked through the tunnel that led to the stones. That first sight still had the power to send shivers through Ben's body. The stones loomed into view, standing majestically in the same place they had occupied for over five thousand years. It was essentially just a circle of giant pillars of rock, some with one stone balanced precariously across the top of two other pillars, like rock goalposts. It certainly was quite an amazing feat of engineering for a primitive society. Ben thought they looked like a domino set made for a giant, mindlessly plonked down in the middle of a field.

Nobody really knew what the circle of stones was for or why it had been built, although hundreds of theories had been proposed. The most generally accepted was that it was effectively a giant calendar so that the druids could mark the passing of the seasons.

Ben was more convinced by burial ground theories or that the stones were used for religious and spiritual reasons. Perhaps even the centre stone was a site for sacrificial slaughter, as gruesome a thought as that was. It made perfect sense to him – a druidic tribe offering up bloody tributes to their god at a place of divine worship.

His mother, however, had her own theories about what the site had been built for. She'd read up on most of the theories out there and was more attracted to those with a supernatural flavour.

As they wandered round, she shared her thoughts with them for the umpteenth time.

"You know, some people believe that the druids built this place to communicate with the dead," she began.

"Uh-huh," muttered Ben.

Undeterred, his mother continued. "They believe that the site is built on an ancient energy store that, if harnessed at the right time, in the right way, would allow them to communicate on another spiritual plane."

"Right," said Ben. "Sounds like a lot of effort to say 'Hi' to Grandma."

A glint of mischief shone in his mum's eyes. "But I don't think that was it," she declared.

"Oh?"

"There is another theory…" she began, coyly.

"Do tell, I can't bear the suspense," said Ben.

She ignored the sarcasm. "This theory states that the stones were built to communicate with other dimensions. Perhaps even to travel to them."

This was the first time Ben had heard his mother suggest this one.

"Come on, Mum, that's a bit out there, even for you, isn't it?" he mocked.

"Well, what do we really know about what ancient civilisations were capable of?"

"OK, so they managed to put up some pretty heavy stones, which, give them their dues, have lasted a *very* long time. It's not quite in the same league as inter-dimensional travel, is it?"

"It's just a theory," she said defensively. "I'm merely relating what I read. It is believed that every equinox night the stones would align with ley lines in space-time, and portals to other dimensions would open."

"Ley lines in space-time," repeated Ben. "Whoever thinks of this stuff?"

"The truth can be stranger than fiction."

He didn't reply. He was thinking again of what happened in the forest, about him travelling to the Shadow Realm. What if alternative dimensions did exist? What if he'd travelled to one?

"What do you think, John?" Helena asked, turning to her husband.

"I'll refrain from commenting on this one, I think." John loved his wife, but she was best left un-indulged when on one of these flights of fancy.

They wondered around the cordon for another half an hour before it started to rain, and they called it a day.

CHAPTER 5

Too soon the summer holidays ended and the new school year started. It was a chilly September morning, the kind where you realise you can see your breath, as Ben sauntered up to the bus stop, where his friends were already waiting.

"Morning, mate." Jake nodded. "Feeling fit and fine for year nine?"

Ben chuckled. "As ready as I'll ever be."

"Did you see the Saints game on Saturday?" asked Sam.

"Yeah, great result. That new left back looks pretty good as well."

The coach pulled up and the kids got on, excitedly chatting about football and all sorts. Before long they were arriving at the school. It was a large comprehensive, pulling in children from lots of villages and the nearby town. It had several buildings of different architecture, most of them put up in the seventies and eighties: rectangular boxes of cheap steel, sheet glass and ply-board panelling, but the original building was older and made of brick. A new arts and drama centre stood out like a sore thumb, a modern oasis in an ageing desert. It was shaped a bit like an upturned clam, with a sweeping glass and metal structure intended to inspire.

Ben said goodbye to his friends and went off to his form room for the morning register. Receiving his timetable for the term, he groaned as he saw it started with double science. *Not a particularly friendly start to a Monday morning*, he thought. It got worse as he realised he was sharing the session with Fred, Danny and Joe, widely regarded as the roughest kids in the school and the biggest bullies in their year. They didn't particularly like Ben either, after a run-in or two last year.

"Oi, Freeman!" shouted Fred, as Ben entered the class. "Wanna sit with us?" That had the three of them laughing. Ben was now stuck in a little trap. To say yes and sit there with them would be terrible – they'd just take the mickey all lesson – but to say no would be 'rude' and they'd feel vindicated in bullying him further.

Relieved to see Sam on another table, he hurried past them. "Sorry, chaps," he began. "Said I'd sit with Sam, sure you understand." He knew he was in for a difficult lesson, though; he'd just have to grin and bear it, and wait for them to move on to another mark.

Sure enough, throughout the lesson, Fred and the others did their best to antagonise Ben: flicking little paper pellets, whispering and laughing at him; they even knocked his test tube of vinegar all over his book when they threw a rubber stop at his table.

Ben saw red. "That's it," he muttered. "I've had enough of this."

"What are you doing?" Sam started to say, but Ben had already stood up. He grabbed a baking soda tablet, walked over to their table and dumped it in a pot of vinegar. Instantly there was an explosion of foam. Almost as instantly, he regretted it when he saw the look of shock and anger in Fred's face.

"*Boys*," shouted the teacher. "What on Earth is going on?"

For once, it wasn't the usual trouble-makers' fault, and Ben was given detention.

"It'll be a lot worse for you when we catch up with you later," whispered Fred menacingly, as he left the classroom.

"What did you do that for?" asked Sam, as he walked with Ben to the next class.

"I don't know," moaned Ben. "I saw red and just... did it."

"Well, it was stupid; they're going to be after you now."

It didn't take long. Ben was with Jake, waiting at the back of the queue for the hatch at breaktime, when the three boys saw him. Their scruffy shirts were already untucked, ties barely done up and all had short buzzcuts.

"Oi, Freeman. We want a word with you," shouted Fred, as they approached.

There was no use running away; he wouldn't escape. He had no choice but to face the music.

"Yeah, we need to have a little chat about respect," thundered Danny. "Namely, you giving us some."

As they neared him, Ben held up his hands, trying to plead his case. "Listen, guys, what I did, I over-reacted. I'm sorry, I shouldn't have taken it out on you."

"Damn right," said Fred. "And now you're gonna pay."

"Yeah, and you know how you're going to pay?" Joe threatened.

"Interest-free loan with repayment holiday?" Ben said, before he could stop himself.

The three bullies looked at each other, smiling.

"Now he's a joker." Fred chuckled. "Got any more jokes there, Mr Funny-man?" His face became hard, suddenly severe.

"Erm…" Ben stuttered.

"No, didn't think so." Fred cracked his fingers. "Now we show you the error of your ways." He strode forwards and punched Ben hard in the gut. Ben dropped to the floor, clutching his stomach, the wind knocked out of him.

Jake leapt in front of Ben. "Whoa, guys, what are you doing?" he said, appealing for them to stop.

"Get out of the way, Jake, this is between us and Ben."

"I think not. You can't just take him on three to one."

"He deserves three on one. And if you don't get out of the way, we'll just go through you," Fred threatened.

"I'd like to see you try," said Jake, sounding braver than he felt.

Fred looked between his two mates and all three of them burst out laughing. It was meant to be humiliating, but Jake stood there calmly, waiting for their mirth to subside. Eventually it did, and Fred returned his attention to Jake. He thrust his head forwards as if to headbutt him but stopped short. He was trying to make him flinch, but Jake stood firm.

Angry, Fred went to push him, but in one fluid movement Jake shot his arms forwards and up, neatly deflecting the push before slamming the edge of his hand into Fred's neck in a hard, chopping motion. It was Fred's turn to drop to the ground then, holding his throat and gasping for air.

Jake looked at the other two, struck a martial-arts pose, and waved his hand in the universal language for 'come on then'. Now a full-on fight, Danny moved in to punch, but Jake deftly moved aside and grabbed his arm, twisting it round as he did. Danny had no choice but to follow his arm round, flipping on to the floor and landing on his back, winded.

Seeing all this, Joe decided to run in hard on Jake, to rugby tackle him to the ground. Jake caught Joe under his arms and rolled backwards, thrusting his leg up into Joe's stomach to throw him over his head. Joe landed in a crumpled heap, and before he could get up, Jake dropped an elbow into his groin. Joe's cheeks puffed and swelled as he rolled around, clutching himself in agony. Jake stood up, dusted himself down, and announced his terms of victory.

"I suggest if you don't want more of the same, you best leave us alone." Jake and Ben hurried away then, keen to put space between them and the three bullies.

Ben was flabbergasted. "Where... when... how did you do that?" he spluttered.

"You're welcome," said Jake, bowing.

"Seriously, where did you learn to fight like that?"

"I've been doing kung-fu since I was seven, did I never tell you?"

"No!" Ben exclaimed.

"I'll cite that as technically being self-defence. An attack on one of us is an attack on us all, eh, mate?" said Jake, slapping Ben on the shoulder. "You'd do the same for me."

"Yeah, of course," said Ben, unsure of his ability to do anything of the sort.

"I think that might not be the last we hear from those chaps," said Ben.

"Maybe not. But they'll think twice before messing again, won't they?" Jake chirped, and with a wink he set off for class.

That afternoon on the bus home, the four of them discussed the fight from the morning. The incident had gone round the school like wildfire, ensuring Jake celebrity status for the day. Due to the strict code of student silence, there would be no teachers or parents informed, and therefore no punishment.

Heather had sat next to Jake to get the lowdown on what happened. She wasn't best pleased.

"You shouldn't be using your kung-fu to beat people up, Jake," she said.

"I was saving Ben," he retorted. "Would you prefer I let him get hurt?"

"Of course not," she bridled. "I just don't know why boys have to fight at all."

"I still can't believe it." Ben grinned. "You were totally awesome. How come you never told us about this before?"

"Well, I don't like to brag," said Jake. Ben nearly choked. It was the first time he had heard any genuine modesty come from Jake.

"Yeah, that's so not your style," Sam replied sarcastically.

"Where do you do it?" asked Ben.

"It's just a class at Endon village hall." Endon was the next village over from Lyndshaw, where they lived. "It's every Thursday at six o'clock. I'm sure you could come along if you wanted to see what it's like."

Ben nodded. He liked the sound of becoming a martial-arts master, to take on bullies as effortlessly as Jake had.

"Do you really think they're going to let this rest?" Heather interrupted.

"Who?"

"The Archbishop of Canterbury," replied Heather sourly. "Who do you think? Fred, Danny and Joe. They're not going to be happy that they got beat, and they're going to be after revenge. Only they're not going to want to fight Jake, so they're going to come after you, Ben. Probably when you're on your own." She sat back sharply in her seat, upset at the prospect of her friend getting hurt.

"Don't worry about me," Ben said, trying to calm her down. "I can look after myself." Though as he remembered the punch that floored him earlier, he knew that wasn't true.

Jake was more buoyant. "Nah, they won't mess with us again. They took a good hiding today; they won't want more of the same."

Ben wasn't so sure, and deep down knew Heather was right. Trouble had simply been stored up for another day.

"Perhaps I do need to learn some self-defence," said Ben.

"That's the spirit." Jake grinned. "We'll make a fighter of you yet."

It was a bright and sunny afternoon, perfect weather to hang out and chill after the first day back at school. They headed to Jake's house, arriving as his older brother was leaving on his new motorbike.

The bike was Zach Davies' pride and joy; he'd spent hours with it since he bought it second-hand online. An old Gilera DNA, in a beautiful deep crimson red, he had polished it to within an inch of its life, and now it shone as if it were fresh off the production line. The wheels were small but had a lot of suspension; the elongated front looked like an ant's head, with one bold, menacing eye. Since Zach had bought it a couple of months ago, there was nothing else he would talk about, becoming quite the bore on the topic.

The younger boys lapped it up, though, and he paused at the edge of the driveway to talk to them now.

"Alright, ugly," he said, punching his brother on the arm. He nodded at the others. "Losers." They were all used to being greeted in this derogatory manner by Jake's older brother and would have thought it strange if he'd said something nice.

"Hi, Zach," said Ben, looking appreciatively at the bike.

Zach patted the bike. "Just going out for a ride." Heather rolled her eyes as the boys virtually swooned.

"Where are you going?" asked Sam.

"Just round the village."

"Do you think we could have a go?" asked Jake cheekily.

Zach sniggered. "I think not, young brother."

"Oh, go on," he pleaded. "We could just have a go in the field opposite the Youngs' house. Please?"

"No way, you'll break it. You can barely ride your bicycle."

Ben also really wanted to try out the motorbike, his young teenage mind yearning for a go. He tried a different tack. "You could teach us how to do it properly," he said, attempting to flatter Zach. "Show us how it's done."

Zach wavered slightly, the thought of being able to show off beginning to overpower his caution at letting anyone near his bike.

"I'm not sure…"

Jake picked up on the tactic and employed it as well.

"We'd only do exactly what you tell us. You'd be like… our guru."

Zach was unable to resist; the opportunity to look like the big guy was too strong. "Oh, alright…"

Fifteen minutes later, Ben was throwing his leg over the heavy bike, experiencing a daunting moment as he struggled to keep it upright under the weight. He eventually settled onto it and listened intently as Zach explained patiently how to get the bike moving, by slowly letting out the clutch, whilst applying a small amount of acceleration with the right hand. Not too much or he'd lose stability, but just enough to get going.

His heart raced as he started to release the clutch and the bike began to jerk forwards.

"A little bit of power," called out Zach.

Ben twisted his right hand down and the bike roared forwards, the burst of speed exhilarating. Adrenaline pumped round his body, and he laughed and whooped, building up more speed as he rode around the field. The wind rushed against his eyes through the open visor, and he felt free, like he was flying.

He sped round for ten minutes, until finally Zach was running after him, flapping his arms frantically to get him to stop. He spun the bike round and rode back to where the others were standing, skidding to a stop. His face beamed as he took the helmet off.

"Have fun, did we?" said Jake, his voice strained. Jake had only managed to stall the bike a couple of times before his brother announced his turn was over.

"A lot more than you!" He laughed back.

Zach slapped him on the shoulder. "You're a natural, Ben."

"Thanks."

His face darkened. "But when I say five minutes, I mean it."

"Sorry, Zach. I just got carried away."

Zach's frown broke into a smile. "Ha! I can't blame you. Right, who's next?"

The day's events played on Ben's mind throughout the evening, and he couldn't concentrate on his homework or his favourite show on telly. Later that night, as he tried to fall asleep in bed, images appeared unbidden in his mind of Jake and his smooth yet lethal motion as he took out the bullies. Then he was back on the bike, rocking this way and that as he raced around the field. Reality merged with the dream world as he drifted away, believing himself to be a kung-fu master riding into battle on a motorcycle, performing daring stunts as he took on all assailants before him.

The background to the dream swirled and changed, and he suddenly found himself standing out in the forest again. It was dark, but everything was lit by the lazy, pale glow from the full moon. The dim landscape was caked in mist, and Ben could feel an evil, pernicious presence lurking there, a madness in the shadows that spoke his name. The forest felt surreal, there but not really there, as if it were decaying around him. He kicked up dust as he went, which swirled around him in lazy arcs, causing him to sneeze and cough. Looking at the floor he could see it was made up of nothing but ash; he tried to pick up a rock, but it crumbled in a puff of dust.

Then, suddenly, the giant figure of Lord Blackwood was in front of him, arms crossed, laughing a deep, hollow laugh that gave Ben icy shudders. He turned to run but found he couldn't; his legs wouldn't obey his brain. Rooted to the spot, he tried to scream, but his mouth had disappeared; in its place there was only skin.

Blackwood reached forwards and grabbed Ben's head firmly between his hands and started pulling upwards. Ben felt his neck stretch, pain searing through his nerves as muscle and bone began to give way, ripping and snapping as his neck was torn off, his silent screams echoing in his mind.

Ben woke up gasping, clutching his neck, with sweat streaming down his face. The power and intensity of the nightmare was unbelievably strong, and it took him a while to calm down.

It was the first of several nightmares that Ben was to have about Lord Blackwood in the coming days.

CHAPTER 6

The dreams kept coming, so vivid and intense, and each one involving a horrible death at the hands of Lord Blackwood. The most recent one had him being skewered by Blackwood's sword and hoisted aloft like a limp flag. He had to talk to someone about them or he felt he might go insane.

He decided to try and talk to Sam again; they went to the local ice-cream parlour, and once they'd settled on a bench in the garden, Ben broached the subject.

"I didn't tell you this before, but I've been having nightmares about Lord Blackwood."

"Who?" asked Sam.

"You know, the one I was telling you about after I inexplicably disappeared for a couple of hours in the middle of the forest?"

"Ah yes. That Lord Blackwood."

Ben hadn't thought about the potential for Sam having forgotten his secret, for it to be dismissed, written off as nothing more than vivid imagination. He ran a hand through his hair, vaguely irked with Sam's forgetfulness.

"Well, anyway, they're horrendous. Really vicious and violent dreams, typically involving me being ripped from head to toe. I'm wondering if there's something wrong with me."

"There's nothing wrong with you. Maybe it's just part of puberty."

"Having violent death dreams is part of puberty?"

"Maybe for you." He chuckled. "Do you still think you actually went to this… Shadow Realm?"

Ben shrugged. "I don't know any more. The dreams fade quickly, but the trips there still feel real, you know? But it seems so crazy that I can't be sure I didn't just imagine the whole thing. I need to stop these dreams, though; I can't bear to keep having them."

"They sound like night terrors," said Sam. "My cousin used to have them. He kept a little diary of when he would get them and then wake himself up just before that time with an alarm. Before long, he'd broken the cycle and stopped having the dreams."

"That's really good advice, Sam," Ben said happily. "I think that could work. Thank you." He licked his black-cherry ice-cream and smiled.

"No problem," said Sam. "But honestly, mate, I really don't think it could have been real."

That same week, Ben decided to take Jake up on his offer of going along to his kung-fu class. He was a little nervous as they drove to the village hall, as he didn't really know what to expect. Would it be like a Wild West movie where the stranger walks into a bar and everybody turns to look at him? Would they all laugh at his pathetic attempts to join in?

However, when they arrived at the hall, Ben realised he had nothing to worry about. There were plenty of people stood around, some chatting, some sparring, but no-one paid him any special notice.

"Welcome to Wing-Chun," said Jake proudly.

Ben observed a couple of kids a year or two younger than him, who were sparring in one corner of the hall. Their arms appeared to be interlocked, moving with great speed and rotation, dancing with a graceful fluidity.

"That's called Chi-Sau," said Jake, noting Ben's interest. "It's what we do to practice. Each person attempts to land blows on the other whilst simultaneously defending against attacks made on them. It's good fun."

"It looks difficult," remarked Ben.

"It is, if you want to do it well," said Jake, smiling. "There's Sifu, let's go tell him you're new."

They trotted over to the man Jake had pointed at. He was a short man with a bald head and a friendly smile, but he looked as hard as nails.

"Good evening, Sifu."

"Good evening, Jake," the man replied warmly. "How are you?"

"I'm well, thank you. I've brought along a friend this evening. This is Ben – he's interested in joining up." Ben couldn't believe how formal and posh Jake spoke. He sounded like a completely different person.

"Excellent, excellent," he said, turning to face Ben and offering a hand. Ben took it and shook it as firmly as he could. "I'm Michael, but you can call me Sifu, which is our term for teacher."

"It's nice to meet you, Sifu," said Ben, as graciously as he could.

"So, you want to learn Wing-Chun Kung-Fu?"

"Well, I've only recently found out that Jake does it, and it looks like a really great way to learn self-defence."

"The usual drill for newbies is just to jump in and give it a go – do you think you'll be OK with that?"

"Sure," said Ben, sounding more confident than he felt.

"Great," said Sifu, clapping his hands and turning to the wider class. "Everyone," he said, raising his voice, "this is Ben, he's joining us for the first time tonight so I'm sure you'll all make him feel very welcome. Right, let's get going. Line up for the first form."

Everyone scrabbled around then, jockeying for position in the line-up, eight across and three deep. Uncertain exactly what was going on, Ben decided it would be best to move towards the back and watch. They started the form, which was a kind of warm-up. Ben watched and was mesmerised by the way everyone moved as one, like a flock of birds all wheeling and turning as one in the twilight sky. He tried his best to follow what the other students were doing, but he was hopelessly out of sync.

After the form, Sifu showed the entire class a couple of moves, apparently building on stuff they had learnt the previous week. Jake was assured and swift in his mastery of the new moves, whilst Ben struggled to understand what he was even supposed to be doing. After Sifu had shown the class how to practise this together, he took Ben and Jake to one side and asked whether Jake would mind taking Ben through some of the basics.

"Not at all," said Jake, grinning one of his mischievous smiles at Ben, who didn't share the same glee, only vague embarrassment at now being taught by his friend. But he quickly forgot that as Jake showed him a couple of basic moves and went through a simple block and strike routine with him. He was soon getting into it, practising the move with aplomb and learning more about the theory of the 'centre' and why it was such a crucial point in Wing-Chun.

"All power in the body comes from the centre," explained Jake. "The more you learn to find your centre of gravity and pivot around it, the more power you can produce." Jake showed him the correct stance to encourage stability and centrality.

"When I punch, block or do anything, I'm pivoting around this line going through the centre of my body."

"Right," said Ben, not really getting it but not wanting to look stupid.

"Try a punch," suggested Jake. "Straight out from your chest."

Ben made a fist and attempted to punch as Jake had showed him. Jake deflected the punch and attacked back.

"Simultaneous defence and attack, that's what Wing-Chun is all about."

Ben was fascinated as they worked on some simple routines for attack and defence, and keen to learn more. Time had flown by, and they had come to the end of the lesson.

"Do you think you'll come again?" Jake asked Ben.

"Yes, definitely. That was good fun. Next week?"

"You bet."

Ben smiled, pleased he'd made the effort to come. They made their way outside to be collected by his mum.

"Thanks for the lift, Mrs F," said Jake, as they got into the car. "I know my mum's pretty chuffed she won't have to do all the driving anymore!" he joked.

"Freeman's taxis, at your service," said Helena Freeman, doffing an imaginary cap. They spent the journey home talking excitedly about kung-fu.

It was a very cool, crisp night that evening, and as Ben climbed into bed, he felt a chill go down his spine. He shuddered as he remembered the last time he had felt like that – right after he'd travelled to the Shadow Realm.

Ben tried to bat the thought to the back of his mind and turned his light off, plunging the bedroom into darkness. His curtain flapped lazily in the breeze from the window, letting in the silvery light of the moon. Bathed in that pale light, his room looked like it had been transported to the Shadow Realm.

Stop it, he thought to himself. But controlling your thoughts, Ben was discovering, was a very difficult thing to do.

A bead of sweat crept across Ben's forehead as his pupils began to move furiously under his eyelids. He was having a nightmare about the Shadow Realm again. This time, though, Lord Blackwood was not involved; it was the land itself that was trying to murder him. The ground was soft, giving way under his feet; every step he took, he sank further into the earth. He struggled against the thick grey sludge, but there was no escape. He spluttered and choked as he screamed, inhaling ash with each lungful of air. Only his eyes were now still above ground, looking up into the inky blackness of the Shadow Realm's sky, an empty nothingness that reflected his departing life. As he suffocated in his sleep, his mind brought him back to the real world and he sat bolt upright in his bed, gasping for air.

"Nasty one," he muttered to himself, rubbing his neck. He made a note of the time – three am – and tried, unsuccessfully, to get back to sleep.

On Friday, Ben had geography with Jake, a class he wasn't looking forward to as it also contained Fred, the bully that Jake had decked with his kung-fu. Since the fight, Fred still hadn't said anything to Ben, but there was simmering tension that bubbled in the air whenever they saw each other, the resentment palpable. Fred wasn't the smartest cookie in the tin, so his revenge plan was likely little more than to 'smash Ben's face in', but that simplicity was Ben's painful future.

The classroom was in the older block at school, a rather dilapidated building that was in good need of demolition. The room itself looked tattered and dog-eared, with the wear and tear of fifty years of teaching evident on the walls and furniture. Each table was covered in graffiti, mostly the names of ex-pupils, with the likes of 'Dave woz ere' etched or inked into them. Ben sidled past the table in front of Fred, the briefest flash of eye contact communicating a deep loathing, and sat down next to Jake.

"Alright, Ben," Jake mumbled.

"Alright, mate," said Ben as he took out his books. He flicked his head backwards towards Fred. "I think he's getting angrier, you know."

"Let him stew in his own juices."

"Easy for you to say – it's not your face he wants to cave in."

"You worry too much," Jake said nonchalantly. "He's too stupid to hold a grudge for long. I'll look out for you until then."

At that point Mrs Hurrell, their geography teacher, came into the classroom and told them all to sit down and shut up. Mrs Hurrell always looked like she had been standing in a gale, with a big bouffant of wiry, grey hair, only semi-tamed. She ruled her classes with an iron fist, but her lessons were enjoyable as she had the knack of getting people to participate, and she always managed to make the subject matter interesting. Or at least Ben thought so.

She flicked up the first slide onto her white projector board, which simply said 'Climate Change'.

"Today," she said in a bold voice, "we will be talking about climate change, its impact on the planet and its consequences for the human race." She paused, as if studying the reaction to today's topic amongst the pupils.

"First, can anyone tell me what they already understand climate change to mean?"

A smattering of hands went up around the class, including Ben's, although he was overlooked for Jessica Parker, an intelligent, homely girl.

"Yes, Jessica," said Mrs Hurrell.

"Climate change relates to the impact on the world's climate of global warming, typically noticed in the temperatures and weather patterns that we see around the world."

"Perfect, exactly that, well put," said Mrs Hurrell. Jessica beamed back at her. "Can anyone tell me what the two biggest problems associated with climate change are?"

More hands, this time Peter Abram being chosen.

"Rising sea levels and drought?" he said, less than certainly.

"Yes!" exclaimed Mrs Hurrell. "Right on the money." She started flicking through some pictures that depicted climate change: ice melting at the north pole, desert land where few crops would grow, cities flooded, that kind of thing. "Warmer temperatures have meant that the ice caps at the North and South Pole have been retreating and melting, releasing more water into the sea. This not only destroys habitats for animals that survive at the poles, but it also raises sea levels, so that low-lying land around the world is in peril from being submerged. Conversely, despite there being more water around, it also means that areas on the edge of deserts and places that are already extremely hot will completely lose the ability to support life, and the deserts will grow." More pictures of animals likely to be affected were flashed up on screen, before she settled on a picture of a rice paddy field being tended by Asian workers. "It'll also hugely upset eco-systems that have built up over thousands of years, making it difficult to grow food in the kinds of places they have traditionally grown, and lots of animals will likely go extinct. Due to this, there is a strong chance there will be mass migration of humans to places where food can still be grown, and as ever, that probably means an increased likelihood of flashpoints and war over resources."

She looked around the class. "In short, not a very good thing at all. Can anyone tell me what the cause of climate change is?"

Plenty of hands this time. She picked on Ben.

"Greenhouse gases, Miss," he said with conviction. "CO_2 pollution from humans is causing a protective barrier in the atmosphere so that heat from the sun can't escape into space."

Another smile from Mrs Hurrell. "Couldn't have put it better myself." She was about to continue talking when Fred put his hand up. Mrs Hurrell noticed and said, "Yes, Fred?"

He coughed. "I heard, Miss, that climate change is just a big hoax."

"That's not quite right," said Mrs Hurrell. "The vast body of scientific evidence supports the fact the world is warming."

"Well, my old man reckons it's just a big conspiracy, that nothing bad is going to happen."

With a masterful stroke of expert facilitation, she pulled that point out to the floor. "Any thoughts on alternative climate change theories?"

Ben was grouchy from his lack of sleep the night before and wasn't going to let that one lie.

"I think watching some dodgy conspiracy theory on the internet doesn't count as quality research. It's a bit of a nonsense to say it's a conspiracy. Who's the conspiracy against? The idea that pumping out two hundred years of carbon dioxide won't have any effect on the climate is just obviously ridiculous."

Fred was fuming at him across the classroom, his thick jaw grinding his teeth.

But Ben wasn't done, clearly not knowing when to stop. "The only people denying climate change are those with something to lose if we stop polluting the planet. Doesn't your father work for the power station, Fred?"

Fred scowled at him. Ben knew he'd pushed his luck a bit too far, provoking him as much as he had. It was like tossing a balloon filled with petrol onto a barbecue.

The discussion moved on, but the bad feeling simmered, hanging in the air for the rest of the lesson. Outside afterwards, Fred grabbed Ben and pinned him up against a wall.

"You think it's funny to take the mickey out of my old man, do you?"

Ben struggled to get free, but before Fred could hit him or say anything else, Jake tapped him on the shoulder.

"I think you should be letting him go now," Jake said, ice-calm.

Fred turned to face Jake and then looked back at Ben. He raised his finger into Ben's face.

"One of these days, your little chum isn't going to be around to save you, and when that happens... *bam*, you're going down." Ben had no doubts about the sincerity of the threat. Fred let him go and he readjusted his tie.

"Thanks," he said to Jake, barely able to look at him for being saved a second time.

"No worries," said Jake, as they went their separate ways to the next class.

CHAPTER 7

The first week back at school had left Ben tired and weary: the fight with the bullies, and the nightmares that were plaguing him, were burdening his thoughts. The autumnal weather began to match Ben's darkening mood. Heavy clouds of iron hung in the sky, the wind whipping the loose leaves off the trees, where they twirled to the ground to form a blanket of red and gold.

But on Saturday morning, he woke up feeling great, for once not having a dream about the Shadow Realm or Lord Blackwood. He bounced out of bed, dancing to the bathroom to brush his teeth. A full English breakfast followed, lovingly cooked up by his mum, and Ben ate until he was stuffed. Life was good.

He skipped out of the house, hopping on his bike to head to Jake's for a solid session of gaming. Turning out of the drive, his heart missed a beat, as he saw who was on the street waiting for him. Fred, Danny and Joe were there, just a few yards away, loitering on their bikes. They'd obviously cycled over from the neighbouring town where they lived and had been waiting for him to leave his house, ready to pounce.

"Hello, Ben," said Fred, a dollop of playful menace in his voice.

Ben didn't hang around to find out what was going to happen

next, as it was clear he was in for a beating. He turned his bike around and scarpered.

The boys gave chase, whooping and shouting at him as they followed, the hunt now part of the fun. Ben fled towards the forest and, in the absence of a well-thought-out plan, decided it might be a good place to try and escape the three boys.

He cycled harder than he ever had before, pushing the pedals with as much force as he could muster. He hoped he was fit enough to outrun them, but by the time he had reached the forest edge he was already breathing hard, his lungs fighting and gasping for air. He stole a quick glance behind him and saw that they'd fallen behind but were still following intently. Thankfully the main road that ran along the edge of the forest was clear, and he ploughed straight over.

He went into the forest at lightning pace, his bike feeling like it might shake apart as it thudded across the cattle grid. He redoubled his efforts, fear and adrenaline driving him on. The road twisted and turned and started to go uphill. Ben struggled up it as fast as he could, but his pace was slowing and he was beginning to fear how much longer he could carry on. He looked round again and saw that the boys had gained on him.

He realised with a horrifying jolt that the forest was in fact an excellent place for them to dish out their revenge, unfettered by any watching eyes that might come to his aid. He headed off-road in the hope that they would find it harder to follow him cross-country. He rode over mounds and jumped ditches, went through bushes, and scraped past trees, but his strategy wasn't paying off: the boys were still gaining. His legs burned; his muscles groaned with every turn of the pedals. His lungs heaved, fighting for breath, but it was not enough; he could feel the fatal stitch growing in his stomach. They were still with him, showing no signs of abating, and he realised he was short of options. It was clear they really did mean to catch him and cause him some serious damage.

Then disaster struck.

He ploughed into a peaty bog, his wheel sticking in the viscous mud, and the sudden slowdown sent him tumbling headfirst over the handlebars. He landed with a splash in the mire, which at least afforded a soft landing. He could hear the three lads explode with laughter behind him, although they were so out of breath it didn't last long.

Ben staggered to his feet and started to run, still desperate to avoid the gang. He made for a thick set of trees so that at least they would be forced to follow on foot, and he could gain a few seconds whilst they laid their bikes down. He reached the trees just in time, Fred's grasping hand narrowly missing Ben's jumper by inches. The three pursuers were forced to stop and continue the chase on foot.

Weaving between trees and ducking under branches, Ben ran as fast as he could, but he knew that the others were faster than him, that they'd catch him eventually. The stitch in his stomach was growing more painful by the second, a dagger in his gut that kept on stabbing. His mind raced with images of what would happen to him when they caught him, none of them nice. The fact was they'd probably lay into him even harder as he'd made what should have been a simple beating so much tougher.

It was only when he reached the edge of the clearing that Ben realised which direction his forced fleeing had taken him. His legs, still desperately pounding the earth to escape his persecutors, carried him straight into the centre of the clearing before he could think any more about it.

He glanced behind him to see where the boys were; they were still giving chase, further behind now but coming up quick.

But then time stopped, perhaps only for a fleeting nanosecond, but it was enough for Ben to register every sense and feeling his mind was receiving. Paused in mid-air, he saw the world come into sharp focus, each leaf on every tree precisely defined, sparkling in the dappled sunlight and glowing with a radiant halo. The golden colours of the autumn shone with a wonderful brilliance for one beautiful moment, before all smudging into one another, like someone smearing their hand across a wet painting.

Then the pain came. That terrible, intense, prickling pain that felt like he was being stabbed in every square inch of his body, and the sensation of being squeezed through a keyhole.

As the world disappeared into nothing, and the pain built into an unbearable crescendo, there was a pop, a sudden whooshing as time started again, and Ben fell to the floor, gasping for air and clutching his head.

His temples throbbed and his body ached as if he'd just been through ten rounds with a heavyweight champion, but the worst was over. He knew where he was even though he hadn't yet opened his eyes.

He was back in the Shadow Realm.

The darkness of the Shadow Realm enveloped Ben in a cold, sinister blanket, shrouding his senses with its melancholic gloom. He peered through the murky, fetid air, but it was useless: he couldn't see a thing. Slowly, over time, his eyes began to adjust to the dark, and the soft shine that seemed to come from the earth itself lifted the world into view, like a slowly developing photograph. The trees and bushes around him swam into focus, and he realised he was lying in the same clearing as before.

He listened hard, but there was no sound at all. No wind, no rustling leaves, no noise from any animals. No sign of life whatsoever.

Here he was then, back in the Shadow Realm, and a mixture of emotions flooded his heart: a combination of relief that he wasn't mad, this place was real, and terror unlike anything he had felt before. Lord Blackwood was here somewhere, in this world, and Ben knew he meant him harm.

He weighed up his options. He could go exploring and try to find out a bit more about this place, but what if he got lost, or worse, if Blackwood found him? Or he could stay here and try to figure out how to get back home. In the intensely suffocating darkness of the Shadow Realm, he wasn't feeling all that brave, so it was an easy choice.

He heard a snort in the distance, the noise piercing through the quiet like an arrow, and his heart jumped. He was suddenly painfully aware he wasn't prepared to be here; he had no torch, food or weapon. He had to get home again. Perhaps then he could prepare for another trip here, if he could find the courage.

Ben assumed that what he'd been squeezed through, painfully, three times now, was some kind of gateway, a portal between his world and this one. He just needed to find it again to get home. He started feeling around, as quietly as he could, for anything odd, a hole, a warm patch, just something that was out of place.

Me, he thought, with a hint of irony. *I'm out of place.*

It was less foggy than it had been the previous time Ben was here but more haunting because of it. The grey, lifeless trees ran away into the distance, vanishing as the darkness took over. A monastic silence hung over the forest, unnatural and oppressive. It was chilly, but Ben was sweating with anxiety and fear. The longer he was here, the more he began to panic. What if he couldn't find the portal and was stuck here? How long before Blackwood appeared to tear him limb from limb?

Suddenly, a huge noise erupted out in the darkness of the forest, a crashing and creaking that sounded like a tree falling over. This was accompanied by a deep, menacing growl, that grew louder and louder until it was a howling snarl. It would have been heard for miles around. Ben turned around wildly, panicked and frightened, his heart racing. Then something came charging through the forest, branches snapping as they were pushed aside, bushes trampled, and whatever it was, heading straight for him.

Ben was rooted to the spot, mortally terrified and unable to breathe. A looming shadow appeared in the gloom, a shape that was rapidly advancing, until it broke into the clearing and Ben saw it clearly. A huge animal, a monster, a mix between a bull and wolf, with sharp, vicious teeth and slavering jowls.

Ben didn't even have time to turn and run before the beast ran into him, butting him hard. He flew backwards through the air, pain flaring throughout his body as he hit a tree, sliding down to its base. For some reason as he began to pass out, he reflected on the irony of escaping a beating from the school bullies only to end up being mauled to death by a hideous monster.

CHAPTER 8

Ben was brought round by a rough, hairy palm slap to the face. Manatang was staring intently at him.

"Quick," he shouted. "I can't hold a Kraw this size for long – you have to get back, now."

Ben was dazed and confused but nodded. He staggered to his feet and saw that Manatang had his hands outstretched towards the beast, which was snarling and snapping its teeth only a few feet away but apparently frozen on the spot.

"And I really don't think you should come back again," Manatang called over his shoulder.

"I didn't mean to…" began Ben, feebly, but realised perhaps now was not the time. He tried desperately to find the portal, moving around the clearing with his arms flailing like a windmill. It wasn't working; he couldn't find the way back.

"Just breathe," offered Manatang. "See if you can sense it," adding to himself, "Quickly."

Ben shut his eyes and took a deep breath, exhaling slowly and trying to ignore the sound of the monstrous animal nearby. And then the hairs on his arm stood up, and he felt it, sensed it towards the middle of the clearing. A tear, a rip in the fabric of space-time, a fizzing hole where the dimensions were connected. He felt almost triumphant as he moved towards it, touching it just as Manatang lost control of the Kraw.

A different kind of pain kicked in then: of being stabbed by tiny little ice axes, an excruciating chill like plunging into an ice bath. And it was familiar, and Ben knew then that he was travelling through the portal, that he was once again being saved in the nick of time.

Everything went pop, and he had the queasy sensation of falling off a cliff, before the world filled with colour, sounds and fresh air, and he was back on the New Forest floor.

Ben fell back, holding his ribs, pain from the animal's impact throbbing in his chest. Hysteria was bubbling up inside of him; the roller-coaster of this morning was too much, and he began to sob, curled up on the floor. The bullies, the Shadow Realm, that horrible... *thing* that had nearly killed him; the enormity of it all came over him in huge, crashing waves.

He stayed like that for a few minutes, before finally he began to calm down and get a grip of himself.

The clearing was still, the leaves on the trees swinging softly in the breeze, some of them detaching and fluttering down around him. Then he began to feel elated. He'd been able to sense the portal and touch it. He knew now he could travel through it at will, if he chose to. That changed everything.

He looked around. The bullies had gone, and he wondered what they must have thought. Did they see him disappear? How long did they carry on their search before giving up?

Ben fished out his mobile to check on the time and saw that two hours had passed since he left the house. That couldn't be right. To Ben it felt like no more than fifteen minutes. Surely he hadn't been in the Shadow Realm for that long?

He groaned as he reached the edge of the treeline. His bike had been completely totalled by Fred and his friends, looking as if a tank had driven over it. The wheels were completely bent, buckled and slashed. It had been slammed into the ground repeatedly so that the metal frame had stressed and bent, and the pedals and gears had fallen apart. Nothing had escaped their wrath.

Large raindrops started splashing down from the grey and heavy sky, landing on Ben's head with a sullen plop.

"That doesn't look too clever," said a soft, kind voice.

Ben was jolted out of his miserable reverie, startled that someone could sneak up on him out here. He looked round to see a woman regarding him with sympathy. She was probably in her early twenties, with shoulder-length black hair tied back in a ponytail and large, brown eyes. A small dog came yapping up behind her, eager to see who his owner was talking to.

"It, er…" stuttered Ben, unsure of how to relay the story of his bike.

"Fell under a tractor?" she said, chuckling.

Ben rubbed his head. "Something like that."

She smiled at him and he smiled back, and although she was much older than him, he felt quite giddy. He couldn't place his finger on it, but it almost felt like he knew this woman, like he'd met her before.

"Do I know you?" he blurted out before he could stop himself.

She laughed heartily. "I don't think so." She held out a hand to shake his. "I'm Natalie."

Ben felt like a bit of an idiot but shook her hand gratefully. "I'm Ben."

"Looks like you've lost your mode of transport," she said, pointing at the ruined bike.

He grimaced. It was indeed trashed beyond repair, and he wouldn't be able to ride it home.

"Yeah," he agreed, meekly.

"Perhaps I can help? My car is parked not far from here – I could give you a lift somewhere?"

"Oh, that's very kind of you," began Ben, feeling himself beginning to go red. "I don't want to be any trouble, though."

"It wouldn't be a bother," said Natalie. "I'd like to."

Ben hesitated for a second. The lady seemed very kind, although he knew he probably shouldn't accept rides from strangers. But at the same time, it was two miles home, which was a long way to go with a bike on your back.

"Thank you," he muttered, barely able to look her in the eye from his embarrassment. "That would be very helpful."

She touched him gently on the arm, to indicate it was fine. "You're welcome, Ben."

He sat nervously in the car, staunchly looking ahead at the road, unsure of what to say. Natalie was quietly humming along to the radio.

"Left or right?" she asked as they reached a T-junction.

"Oh, right," spluttered Ben. He felt like he should thank her again, but he'd already done that three times. He tried to think of something else to say.

"Do you live in the village?" he said eventually.

"Oh no, I was just having a long walk in the forest with my dog. I live near Southampton."

"What do you do?" he asked, trying to sound casual.

"I'm training to be a nurse at the uni. Not long until I qualify now, I'm mostly doing shift work to build up my hours at the hospital."

Ben was impressed. "Wow, awesome."

"Thanks." She laughed. "It keeps me out of trouble."

As they turned into his road, he asked Natalie to pull up a few houses short of his own. The small red Ford Fiesta slowed neatly to a stop at the side of the kerb. It was with a little trepidation that he turned to offer his gratitude once more.

"Please," she said quickly, cutting him off. "No more 'thank you's. I'm just pleased to help get you home." She winked at him, and his heart melted a little.

"Well, it was very nice to meet you, Natalie."

"And you, Ben, take care now."

Ben yanked his bike out of the boot and waved as she did a three-point turn and scooted away. He suddenly realised that he couldn't take this wreck home. There would be questions, awkward, searching questions that he'd rather avoid. But what to do with the bike? The only thing it was fit for now was the tip, but for now he decided to hide it rather inelegantly behind some trees and bushes.

Traipsing into the house in a melancholy mood, and suffused with questions about the Shadow Realm, he wasn't prepared for the immediate onslaught his mum greeted him with.

"Where on Earth have you been?" she barked.

Ben blinked, a little shocked. "I, er…" he stuttered.

"Your friends were worried when you didn't turn up so came to call. I, of course, thought that you were already with them. No-one knew where you were, Ben. That's enough to report you as missing. And your phone was off. Why? I was worried sick."

Ben had taken the few seconds of this outburst to try and think of what to say. "I'm sorry, I just decided to go for a long bike ride and lost track of time. I didn't think it would be a big deal, I'm old enough to be out by myself now."

"You should tell someone if you change your plans, Ben," she said rather icily. "It would have saved me a lot of worry. Your dad's out looking for you right now. I shall have to call him and let him know you're back."

"Sorry, Mum," he said, with as much conviction as he could muster. He did feel bad, but he was also extremely weary from his ordeal and just wanted to lie down. He left his mum's disapproving looks behind and went to run a bath.

His aching joints and tired muscles groaned with relief as he eased himself in, the steaming hot water relaxing him, evaporating the tension he was holding in his core. His mind was swirling with thoughts of the Shadow Realm, and his close encounter with that giant, snarling beast.

He tried to think rationally about what the Shadow Realm might be. It was clearly not his own world, given the types of creatures that lived there. But were they alien? Was the portal a wormhole to another planet or a doorway to another dimension?

There were many unanswerable questions, and Ben knew that the only hope for solving any of them was to travel back there and search for the answers, a thought that made him feel quite ill.

When he'd finished in the bath he went to his bedroom, took a new journal from his stationery set and started noting down all these questions as they went through his head – if he didn't, they'd never stop circling round and would send him mad. He made fastidious notes of what had occurred in the Shadow Realm and when, as well as jotting down the nightmares he could remember. He didn't want to miss any detail, no matter how small, in case it proved significant.

Ben finished his breakfast quickly on Sunday morning, not wishing to hang around too long with his mother. She didn't look very cheery. He cautiously made his way outside to retrieve his bike, vigilant for any signs of trouble. It was a nice day, sunshine cascading down through the September sky, split into spears of light by the puffy white clouds.

He was fishing around in the tree where he had stuffed his bike when he heard a familiar voice.

"Now, what have you been up to, young man?" It was Jake, looking mischievous and a bit dishevelled at this time in the morning.

Ben jumped, pulling back from the tree, looking instantly guilty. "Nothing," he said, clearly lying.

Jake peered round him to look at the tree. "What's in there?" he enquired.

"It's…" Ben said, pausing because he didn't want to tell Jake everything about yesterday. "It's my bike," he said finally, bringing it out from behind the tree. "It's completely totalled."

Jake took one look at it and whistled. "What on Earth did you do to that? Put it through a car crusher?"

"It got trashed by Fred and his chums. I was on my way to yours when they ambushed me. I was on my bike, so I thought I might be able to outrun them."

"But you couldn't?"

"Not quite, no. Turns out they're pretty persistent and really didn't want to let me go."

Jake studied Ben and his face for a moment. "But it doesn't look like they touched you?"

"No, I crashed my bike as they were giving chase but then managed to run off through the forest." Ben pointed at his bike. "They took their revenge out on this," he said, being economical with the truth.

"I see," said Jake, stroking his chin. "So why hide it in the tree?"

"So that I don't have to tell my parents what happened. I'm going to take it down the tip now and then tell them it got stolen."

"Quite the little liar, aren't you?" Jake smirked. "Anyway, why did it take you so long to get home? Where were you?"

Ben withered slightly under Jake's glare, before coming to the decision that he would tell Jake what had happened. He was his best friend, after all.

"OK, but you probably won't believe me. It's a little... fantastical. I didn't truly believe it myself until yesterday, but I'm pretty sure I'll be able to prove it to you. To all of you."

Ben wasn't making much sense, so Jake just nodded, encouraging him to continue.

"You know a couple of months ago, when we were playing seeker in the forest, and I disappeared for a couple of hours. Well, I wasn't quite telling the truth when I said I'd just been hiding and must have fallen asleep. I went... somewhere, and it was the same place I went to yesterday."

"Where?"

Ben gulped and carried on. "To a place called the Shadow Realm. I can get there through some kind of portal in the forest. I think it's another world. I don't know much about it, but it's very dark and grey – it looks a bit like everything's caught on fire and burnt to ash." Ben paused, noticing that Jake was looking at him extremely suspiciously. He pressed on anyway. "And, well, there are some strange, dangerous creatures there, and…" He paused, starting to feel rather silly. "And some kind of evil ruler called Lord Blackwood, who has fire instead of eyes. Oh, and a talking monkey."

Jake burst out laughing, guffawing long and hard. Eventually he settled down and looked at Ben, who still had a very serious expression and didn't look in the least amused.

"That's brilliant, Ben, very imaginative. But we're not eight. Come on, where were you really?"

"I'm telling you the truth," protested Ben, but he knew it was pointless. He would have to prove to Jake, to everyone, that it was real. "Look, I know you're not going to believe me, so why don't you help me get rid of my bike, we'll go and get the others, then I can show you all that I'm not completely insane."

Something in Ben's eye unsettled Jake, a glint that suggested perhaps he really was telling the truth, or at least believed himself to be.

"Alright, I'll humour you," said Jake. "We'll go and see this, what did you call it, '*portal*' of yours. And we'll all have a lovely day out in '*The Shadow Realm*'. It sounds like a really nice place."

Ben scowled, but it had felt good to tell another person, even if he hadn't believed him.

He would, soon enough.

Between them they carried the wrecked bike down to the local tip and spoke to the metals man, who took it off their hands. God knows what he was going to do with it after that. Melt it down, probably.

They picked up Heather and borrowed Jake's dad's bike for Ben, and then went round to Sam's house.

Sam came to the door holding a doughnut and regarded them quizzically when he saw them all huddled on the doorstep.

"Get your bike, Sam," said Jake. "Ben's going to show us a new world."

Sam looked bemused, as did Heather, who so far had not been told anything about the jolly they were embarking upon.

Ben looked at Sam. "I wasn't missing yesterday," he began. "I went to the Shadow Realm."

Sam rolled his eyes. "Not this again."

Jake looked surprised. "You know about this already?"

"Know about what?" asked Heather.

"Ben told me ages ago," said Sam.

Jake rounded on Ben. "Why wasn't I told?"

"Neither of you believe me anyway, so what does it matter?" Ben said defensively. "It sounds ridiculous, I know, but it's true. If the only way I can get you guys to believe me is to take you there, then so be it. Rather that than you think of me as crazy."

"We'll always think of you as crazy," chimed in Jake, grinning. "Especially after this."

"Woah there, people," said Heather, her thin, red lips set in a stern frown. "Would somebody please explain to me what on Earth is going on?"

Ben looked at her, then at the others, and decided it would be easier to start from the beginning with all of them.

"OK," he said, "but can we go to the den and talk it through there?"

They all muttered their assent and wandered round the back of Sam's house to the end of the garden, where a small cluster of trees stood. A couple of years ago they'd managed to convince their dads to build them a treehouse, which they'd used as their very own clubhouse ever since. It was actually pretty impressive, solidly made with good-quality wood, a reasonably spacious interior and a small terrace. The exterior was now somewhat hidden by moss growth and weathered so much that it was well camouflaged amongst the branches and leaves. With its gently sloping pitched roof providing protection from the elements, they often had sleepovers up there during the summer and had decked the place out with a few small comforts: a little table, beanbags and a couple of tatty old chairs. Some dog-eared posters of previously favoured bands and films adorned the walls.

They clambered up the rope ladder, each finding a place to sit or perch, and waited expectantly for Ben to speak.

"OK," Ben said, rubbing his hands and deciding how to begin the story. "I've given Sam and Jake abridged versions, but I think for your sake, Heather, I should start at the beginning and not miss out a thing."

So he laid it all out for them, starting with the Ouija board they'd played camping, and finishing with his most recent excursion, where he was saved from a snarling monster by Manatang.

"For some reason, and I don't know what it is, I'm able to travel to this place. I just feel like… like I'm meant to go there. That it's not chance that took me there, but, I don't know, fate… or something."

The others were sat looking at him in a mixture of disbelief and shock. Jake spoke first. "See, crazy!"

"That is quite some tale, Ben," said Heather, slowly. "You've got a great future in front of you as a storyteller. But you can't honestly expect us to believe all this?"

"She's right," Sam said, weighing in. "It is pretty far-fetched."

"I didn't expect you to believe me," said Ben defiantly. "I wouldn't believe it either, if it hadn't happened to me." He paused, frustrated at his inability to make his friends understand. Having told them, he wanted nothing more than to convince them of the truth. "Let me take you there," he said. "I have to show you it's real. I'll take you to the portal, and you can come to the Shadow Realm with me."

Heather looked up sharply, startled at Ben's suggestion. "But if what you've told us *is* true, then the Shadow Realm sounds like an extremely dangerous place. Do you think it would be a good idea to go there?"

Ben wrung his hands. "I know it's a lot to ask," he said. "But I can't deal with this by myself. We'll just go quickly to prove it's real – we wouldn't hang around very long, I promise." A feeling of extreme vulnerability swept over him. "I just need you to believe me."

The other three looked at each other, coming quickly to an unspoken agreement.

"Alright, Ben," Sam said, with a strong determination in his voice. "We'll come with you, and one way or another, find out the truth. We'll all be in this together."

Ben looked up at his friends, emotion welling in his eyes.

"Thank you, guys. This means a lot to me."

Jake slapped his thighs. "Well, what are we waiting for?" he said. "Let's go!"

And with that, they all climbed down from the treehouse, clambered on to their bikes and set off for the forest. It felt like a big adventure, the four of them cycling off on an exciting mission, chatting and laughing. It would be the last time any of them would laugh for quite some time.

CHAPTER 9

Their arrival at the clearing was hailed by a slight drizzle meandering its way down from the heavens. They stopped at the edge, peering in uncertainly at the unassuming space, an awkward disquiet settling on the group. The clearing looked tatty and miserable, like a shivering dog left outside in the cold rain.

"I can't see a portal," said Jake belligerently.

Ben looked despairingly at him. "I did say that you wouldn't be able to. I can't see it, but I've been through it several times now, so it's definitely there."

"What now?" asked Heather.

Ben plucked up some courage. "You guys wait here a minute; I'll go in and see if I can find it."

Ben gingerly put his bike down and wandered into the clearing. He felt it almost immediately – the prickling on his skin, the hairs on his arm rising.

The sensation got stronger and more painful the closer he got to the middle of the clearing. *Closer to the portal,* he thought. He was about to yell to the others that he'd found it, when he realised they were frozen, as was he, unable to move. The world dissolved around him, whooshing by as he fell through nothingness, to be suddenly replaced by the eerie dark of the Shadow Realm.

That time it had definitely been easier. The pain that had previously accompanied a trip through the portal had diminished, and he'd been able to stay upright rather than end up sprawled on the floor. He felt a flash of accomplishment at knowing the others would have witnessed his disappearance; they couldn't deny his story now.

He looked around, listening out for any sounds, but the Shadow Realm was quiet. No strange beasts or evil lords; just cold, quiet, inky darkness. His eyes widened to drink in the dim, silvery glow that emanated from the world around him, bringing the land slowly out of the dark. The eerie calm made Ben feel uneasy, and he decided to get back to his friends.

He sensed the portal in front of him, noticing against the silence an almost imperceptible fizzing and crackling that reminded him of a bowl of Rice Krispies. He stepped forwards, and the world went pop; he felt like he was being sucked through a broken window on an aeroplane, before the reddy-brown of the New Forest swirled into life around him.

The startled faces of his three friends were the first thing he saw, all gaping open-mouthed at him.

He looked at them triumphantly. "Now do you believe me?"

No-one replied. They were all too shocked.

Finally, Heather stammered, "You... you just... disappeared. How is that possible?"

"Great party trick, mate," added Jake.

"No trick," Ben said. "Just something I can't quite explain. There's something in this clearing that leads through to another world. A portal. That's what I've been trying to tell you. That's what I've been going through."

"You said it hurts to go through?" asked Heather timidly.

"It did, but that time much less so. Maybe my body is getting used to it, I don't know." He shrugged.

"This is incredible," exclaimed Sam. "If this really is a portal to another world, or another dimension, this is of huge global scientific importance."

Ben hadn't considered it like that, but he supposed it would be. That is, if he could prove it existed.

"Maybe," he said slowly. "I still have this gut feeling, though, this *instinct* that this is happening to me for a reason. I'm not even sure if anyone else can go through. Maybe we should try it."

There was a distinct lack of enthusiasm from the potential volunteers.

"I don't know about anyone else," Sam said eventually, "but what I just witnessed I found pretty damn scary. Given what you've told us about where you went and the pain you go through to get there, I'm not sure it's such a great idea, mate, to be honest."

"I have to agree," Jake admitted, uncharacteristically subdued. "I'm not really up for it either."

Ben's initial elation turned to disappointment. He knew his friends were scared, their fear palpable, and he couldn't force them to go; they had to come willingly or not at all. And so, he might really be alone in trying to understand this weirdness.

The silence was getting uncomfortable, but then Heather moved forwards towards Ben, taking his hand. "I'll go," she said, with a steely determination in her eye. "I don't want to regret running away from this moment."

Jake rolled his eyes. "Great," he blurted. "My little sister wants to go, so now I have to."

"You don't have to do anything, Jake," Heather said bluntly.

"I'll never hear the end of it if I don't, will I? And what am I going to tell Mum if you don't come back? Oh, sorry, Mum, Heather and Ben went off to a desolate world and have probably been killed by an evil lord?" He folded his arms, indicating the matter was settled.

Which just left Sam. He looked at each of them in turn before sighing with a resigned huff. "I suppose I ought to come along as well then. Can't have you all gloating forevermore that you've been to a parallel universe and I haven't."

"Attaboy," said Jake.

Ben looked proudly at all of them, his elation returning. "Thank you, guys, this means a lot to me." He resisted the urge for a group hug. "We'll just go through for a short minute and come back, so you can see what it's like. I don't want us to hang around there."

"Wicked," said Jake sarcastically. "I can't wait."

"Shouldn't we get some weapons or something, just in case?" Sam fretted.

"Well, there was no-one there just now. I think if we're quick, we won't need them. We'll just see if you can get there, and then if you can we can come back and have a longer think about what to bring with us next time."

"Let's just worry about this time for now, shall we?" remarked Heather.

"OK," said Ben. "If you edge a bit closer to where I am, we'll see if you can sense it."

The others moved forwards, oblivious to the portal, eventually passing right through it. None of them disappeared. Ben hid his disappointment that none of them had travelled through.

"Look, it's just here," said Ben, making waving motions around the area he could sense the portal to be, trying to avoid getting too close in case he got sucked through.

"We can't see anything," complained Sam.

Heather was again the first to put herself in the line of fire. She flung herself through the air with such force that the others jumped back in astonishment. Nothing happened, though, and she hit the ground hard, where she whimpered at a graze on her knee and a bruised elbow.

Ben went to her, leaning over and offering his hand. Their eyes met, and they exchanged a little smile, both grateful for the support the other was showing.

"C'mon, let's get you up," said Ben, helping her to stand. As they straightened up, Heather's eyes suddenly widened in shock and pain. Ben had touched the portal, and they were both being pulled through. He locked his arms around her middle just as his vision drained of colour and the world around them disappeared in a smear of grey. This time felt different for Ben, though. His body seemed to entwine with Heather's as they were compressed down to a small point and then re-inflated on the other side. They landed in a heap together on the floor, Heather on top of Ben. The second she regained her wits she rolled off, and even in the intense black, Ben could sense her embarrassment. It lasted only a second, though, as fear took over.

"Ben?" she hissed, dread and panic edged in her voice.

"I'm still here," he said soothingly, trying his best to calm her. His hand reached out and found hers, and she instantly clutched it.

"Is this it?" she asked, still whispering. "Is this the Shadow Realm?"

"Yes," replied Ben, as resolutely as he could. "You came through with me."

"It really hurts, doesn't it?"

"Yes. But you get used to it."

"I can't see anything," she said, waving a hand in front of her face, which she couldn't see, as if to prove her point.

"It takes a few minutes to get used to it, but there is some light. It seems to radiate from the trees and leaves."

She was silent for a moment, taking it all in. "I'm scared, Ben."

"Do you want to go back? I think I need to be touching you when we go through the portal."

"Give me a couple of minutes. I want to see what you described."

They waited a few minutes as their eyes slowly adapted to the oppressive gloom. Gradually, the world around them started to get some definition, the soft shine of the Shadow Realm emerging from the void around them, giving the world a silvery edge.

"Can you see now?" Ben asked softly.

"Yes," replied Heather, taking in the wonder of it all. "It's actually quite… beautiful."

Ben regarded the Shadow Realm from a new perspective. He'd never considered the alien world as anything other than a harsh, dangerous place, but the strange way the world was lit and the way it seemed suspended from life did have a haunting quality that, he supposed, could be considered beautiful.

All the same, it was a dangerous place, as well as cold, and Ben decided they should be getting back. Heather looked bewildered but agreed. He wrapped his arms around her and guided them both to the portal, which Ben felt he now had the measure of, and quickly went through. Heather gasped once again as her body squeezed itself through the tiny space, the life draining from her eyes momentarily, before rushing back when they popped through the other side. Fortunately, they landed upright this time, so they didn't repeat the embarrassment of earlier in front of the other two.

Sam and Jake looked frantic.

"Finally, there you are. We were worried sick," huffed Jake.

Ben raised his eyebrows quizzically. "We were only gone a few minutes," he said.

"A few minutes?" said Sam, louder than he meant to. "Try twenty-five. We've been going out of our minds here, not knowing what was going on or what we should do." He was pacing back and forth. "We tried going through the portal several times, obviously with no success."

Heather looked bewildered, but Ben had a grim smile on his face, as the meaning of this finally twigged.

"I had found it strange before but not thought too much about it," he began. "I think time passes differently in the Shadow Realm, slower somehow. We really were only a few minutes, yet twenty-five passed here."

Sam looked unhappy. "That's just weird, not to mention inconvenient."

Jake turned his attention to his sister. "What was it like, Sis? What did you see?"

Heather paused, reflecting on what she'd seen. "Ben describes it as a dead and harsh place, but something about the light, the way it gives everything a ghostly glow, it was just mesmerising – magnificent, almost." She paused to catch her breath, shivering at the image of the place still imprinted in her mind. "You've got to see it," she stated finally.

Ben looked round at them. "I think for whatever reason only I can travel through the portal, but I can take you with me if we're touching. So, what do you think, do you want to come and see it?"

Sam and Jake looked at each other, each gulping as they realised that this was it. They were going to have to go through to the Shadow Realm now. They certainly couldn't back out, not now that Heather, a girl nearly two years younger than them, had been through and seen it. They nodded at each other and walked forwards, both putting their hands onto Ben's shoulder.

"Let's do it," they affirmed.

Ben smiled. He looked at Heather. "You coming back?" he asked.

"Just try and stop me," she said with an impish grin.

"You're going to have to stand behind me and put your hands around me."

She did as she was told, moving behind Ben and wrapping her arms around his waist. It was a good job she was behind Ben, so he couldn't see the tinge of red that crept into her cheeks.

Now that he had hold of everyone, he started to walk forwards, towards the portal.

"Get ready for a little bit of a squeeze," he said, as they shuffled forwards with him.

"Ooh sai—" began Jake, cut off by the world and all its oxygen disappearing as he was put through a mangle. Ben felt like he was glued to everyone; the hold he had on them unbreakable as they were wedged through the rip in space-time.

They landed on the other side in a heap.

"…lor," finished Jake.

"Are we all here?" Ben whispered urgently.

All he got were three groans in reply, and he lay back, exhausted from having been through the portal so many times in quick succession.

"Is this it?" asked Sam loudly. "Is this the Shadow Realm?"

Ben was about to reprimand Sam and tell him to be quiet, but a cold, sinister voice sliced through the dark before he could answer.

"It certainly is, and it's so *good* of you to come back."

CHAPTER 10

The unexpected voice in the darkness caused pandemonium: Heather screamed out loud; Sam jumped out of his skin and fainted; Jake instinctively crouched, ready to strike. Ben kept enough of his wits about him to set about gathering up the others, to try and get back through the portal.

"Everyone come to me quick – we need to get out of here *now*!" he hissed urgently into the void.

"Oh, I don't think you'll be going anywhere," came the chilly voice, disembodied in the darkness.

Ben felt his muscles and bones seize up, frozen solid by an invisible force that wrapped itself around him and squeezed him tight. He couldn't move his arms; they were stuck to his side, drawn tight by unseen bonds. He tried to call out but found his mouth to be clamped shut. The only sound to escape his lips was a muffled groan. The dark shapes of his friends began to emerge from the gloom, and he could see that they too were stuck rigid. They were now prisoners, and Ben had walked right into the trap. He felt like an idiot.

He gradually became aware of a figure on the outskirts of the clearing, perched atop a boulder, watching the four of them. The figure rose and began to walk towards them, his gait halting and unnatural. He was an extremely thin man, ghostly pale and wretched, his face gaunt, with sallow skin stretched tight over harsh, pointed cheeks. He walked up to Ben and stared at him with cold, black eyes that swam with malicious intent.

"I'm so glad you popped back to see us again," he said, in a thin, raspy voice. "I was beginning to wonder whether you would." He looked round at the four of them. "And it looks like you brought some friends too… so good of you."

The man stepped closer, imposing despite his weak features, his command of them complete by the magic that kept them prisoner. *At least it's not Lord Blackwood*, thought Ben, although that seemed scant consolation right now.

"You'll be coming with me now," said the wraith-like figure pointedly. He turned to walk away, clicking his fingers as he did. The four of them looked at each other in terror as they felt a force lift them off the ground and push them through the air, where they bobbed along behind the man, like floating corks.

The four of them were curled up into the air with the slightest flick of the man's wrist, and then quickly stacked into the back of a small cart, limbs and bodies knocking painfully together.

Ben was on top of Sam, whilst next to him Jake was having to suffer the indignity of lying on his sister. Ben was slightly twisted round so that he could see up and out over the top of the cart beyond Jake. The silvery forest shone its pale, lazy glow, unwitting and uncaring of his fate.

The ghoulish man climbed up onto the seat at the front of the cart, clicked his fingers again and the cart started moving forwards, apparently all by itself. For a few minutes they rolled through the forest, the spindly, grey boughs and rotten branches of the corpselike trees crossing Ben's vision like a phantom cavalcade.

He became aware of stifled groans and screams coming from his friends, slowly getting louder as they trundled along. He tested his own mouth and found that he was able to move it, albeit only slightly. Ben tried to move his body, struggling against the invisible ropes, but it was no use: he was still held tight.

"Mmm... mmm... moo." He could feel his mouth and tongue loosening by the second.

The pale man turned to look at him, raising an eyebrow quizzically. "Trying to say something?" he whined. "I shouldn't bother if I were you, or you might find I can get quite nasty."

"Who... who are you?" he finally managed to stammer out, as his speech returned.

The man clipped Ben around the head. "What did I just say?" he yelled, suddenly ferocious, his pale face filling Ben's vision like a giant full moon. "You shut up or I will shut you up." A vicious glint twinkled in his eye. "You should save your chat for Lord Blackwood."

Ben's heart sank. *Of course that's where he's taking us – he works for Blackwood.* He looked at his friends, who were looking back at him with terrified eyes.

"Please," he ventured, figuring it was worth a go at reasoning with the pale-faced man. "We're not meant to be here – if you just let us go, we'll disappear and never come back, I promise."

Paleface sighed, clucking his teeth. He turned round again to look at Ben, giving him a stare of such intense hatred that Ben physically shrank back from it. "I warned you," he said calmly, and clicked his fingers.

A jolt of intense pain shot through Ben, his every nerve jangling in extreme distress as he was electrocuted on the spot. His body remained rigid throughout, but his mouth screamed in anguish. The others could do nothing but look on and sob.

"Stop it," shouted Jake, who immediately suffered the same fate as Ben, screaming in agony as the electricity coursed through his body. Once the pain subsided, they stayed silent, the harsh lesson learnt.

Ben continued to watch the terrain roll by, the pallid trees drooping alarmingly, many of them having fallen to the ground already, dead. Ben heard a hooting in the distance. The creepy feeling of being watched crawled across his skin, but there was no way for him to see if anyone was there. They rumbled on, the trees beginning to thin, replaced with grey, ashen ferns that were just as dusty and dead as the forest.

The road changed, and the wheels began to crunch on gravel. The heathland continued to roll idly by. Ben looked at his friends, at the dread plastered on their faces, and wondered if they were all about to die. He wished he could comfort them in some way, tell them that it would all be OK, but that would be a lie, as well as something that was likely to yield another painful shock from Paleface. He remained quiet as he and his friends suffered their terror in silence, their bodies remaining tightly bound by an unseen hand.

Every now and again the quiet crunching of the cart over the gravel road was interjected by loud, guttural animal noises: different squawks and trumpets, the occasional snarl. None of the noises appeared to bother Paleface as he drove the cart, though they frightened the life out of its passengers.

Eventually, the crunching gravel gave way to rocky road and progress quickened slightly. They began to pass decrepit shacks: scraggy, rotten-looking things that had been abandoned. Several of them had fallen down completely. As they continued, the shacks began to be replaced by larger buildings, sturdier-looking but just as filthy and wasted. Nobody seemed to be around; the whole place was uninhabited, a deserted ghost town. Ben wondered what had happened to the people who once lived here, what awful apocalypse had befallen this place to leave it so dead.

Some of the buildings were bigger than the others, larger houses or what might have been commercial premises, with charred signs that hung above blackened doors or jutted out over the street on metal arms. They were unreadable, scorched beyond all recognition and decomposing slowly in the pitiful silence. Ben pondered if perhaps there had been a nuclear war, such was the devastation.

And all the time the darkness and mist hung over them, an oppressive presence that accentuated the otherworldly feel of this depressing place. As the cart followed a sharp turn in the road, they were able to see their destination.

A huge castle guarded the edge of the town, a massive, imposing, frightening structure. Several turrets twisted off into the inky black sky where the hazy fog swallowed them up. Small arch windows were dotted all the way up and along the outer wall, gazing down lifelessly on the town below.

It towered above them and everything else, and the hopelessness of their position began to take its toll. Heather started crying. Ben could do nothing to comfort her, still unable to move his body.

The cart came to a stop by the portcullis. Paleface lowered himself slowly from the cart and hobbled round to the back. Not only did he look sick, but his manner and gait suggested failing health too. Hatred was etched in his face, perhaps disgust at the many years of living in a world like this.

"I'm going to release your binds now so that you can walk." He paused, looking at each one of them sternly. "Try to escape," he hissed, "and I'll lift you forty feet in the air and drop you. How many of your pathetic bones do you think will snap like twigs?" To prove the point, he clicked his fingers and a nearby rock went flying up into the air, before screaming back down and smashing into the ground, breaking into sharp fragments.

"Got it?" he thundered.

All four of them murmured their assent, Heather from beneath further sobs. They felt the invisible force that held them still begin to loosen, and for a moment they had a strange sensation of being lighter than air, as if they were rising. They stretched their aching muscles, which protested creakily after the ordeal of being clamped shut.

"Get up," ordered Paleface.

Jake got up quickly, eager to remove himself from on top of his sister. Ben struggled against his sore muscles and slid off the cart.

Heather then slowly sat up, flexing her stiff joints, and shuffled off the end of the cart. Sam took a bit longer, clearly in a great deal of pain from the enforced rigidity, eventually sliding off the cart, whereupon his knees buckled and he fell to the ground. Ben rushed to help him, supporting him as he regained the feeling in his legs.

"Follow me," said Paleface, turning abruptly and walking away into the darkness. The four stood there stunned for a moment, not wishing to set foot inside the castle. Paleface turned back to face them. "*Now!*" he demanded, clicking his fingers to administer a quick shock.

They yelped in pain, then hurriedly obeyed, shuffling into step behind him as they made their way into the gloomy mouth of the castle.

The already faint light began to fade the deeper they went. Paleface clicked his fingers and a dozen fires leapt into life, dancing on the wall, unsupported, drawing fuel from something unseen. The light revealed a long, wide tunnel, made from stone and marble supports, with many doors and archways leading off it. They followed Paleface through one of the archways, which began to slope down and turn a bend. For half a heartbeat, Ben swore he could hear screaming, but when he listened harder, all he could only hear were his own shuffling footsteps and the faint gurgling of water. Eventually they reached an archway which led to steps going down. Paleface stood by them and indicated for them to get moving.

Ben went first, driven by guilt that he had led his friends into this awful mess. He edged his way down the steps with great trepidation, the complete darkness swallowing him as he descended into hell. A couple of times his feet slipped on the slick steps, but he managed to retain his balance. Only the scuffled knock of heels behind him told him his friends were following.

After what seemed an eternity the steps ended, and the corridor levelled out. Finger-clicking behind him lit a small fireball to his right, and the corridor was thrown into sharp relief. It was small and squat with a heavy wooden door set into the rock wall a few paces from where Ben was now standing. Paleface scuttled past them and opened the heavy door, gesturing for them to go inside, which they obediently did.

The room was pitch black, currently only dimly lit by the fireball from outside the open door. It didn't take them long to see that it was a small, dank cell.

"But this is a dungeon," exclaimed Jake.

"Astute, aren't you?" snarled Paleface from the doorway, his voice cloaked in sarcasm. The backlight threw his face into shadow, adding to his menacing aura.

"I thought you were taking us to Lord Blackwood?" complained Ben.

"He's otherwise engaged right now. You'll wait here for him." With that Paleface closed the door, and the dungeon was cast into complete darkness. There was a clunk as the heavy lock turned, and then they were alone.

"Well, this is just marvellous, isn't it?" Jake cried out. "What on Earth are we going to do now?"

"We're going to die, aren't we?" bawled Sam.

From somewhere in the darkness, Heather started crying.

"Let's all just calm down a little, shall we?" Ben implored. "Try and think things through rationally. There must be a way out of here," he said optimistically.

"It's a friggin' *dungeon*, Ben," Jake huffed. "Of course there's no way out. Benefit of it being specifically designed to hold prisoners." Ben ignored him and started feeling his way around the edge of the walls, trying to find something, anything, that might present a way out. Jake found his sister from the whimpering and hugged her sympathetically.

"There, there, Sis," he said. "It's going to be OK." She just buried her head into his chest.

"But it's not going to be OK, is it?" Sam agonised. "We're stuck down here waiting for god knows what to happen to us. We could be left down here to die for all we know."

Ben finished his tour of the dungeon walls, which yielded nothing except slimy hands. "Look," he said. "I shouldn't have brought you all here, that much is clear." His voice was high and hesitant. "But I think Blackwood is only interested in me, so I'll try and reason with him, get him to let you all go."

Jake snorted. "Yeah, I'm sure he'll do that for you, buddy."

Ben's head dropped. "I'm sorry. I messed up; I never should have made you come."

"Nobody forced us to come," said Jake, pivoting suddenly. "We all came here of our own free will because we wanted to help you. So, there's no point feeling sorry for ourselves, we're all in this together. Right, guys?"

There was no reply. Jake spoke louder. "*Right, guys?*"

The others gave a muffled affirmative response, including Heather, who had stopped crying.

"We need to work out what to do when he comes back for us," said Jake.

"What can we do?" said Sam, defeatism plain in his voice. "They've got some kind of magic in this world, something that we can't fight against. You all felt it tighten around us, holding us fast." He paused, pinching his eyes together before gesticulating wildly. "We floated through the air, for god's sake."

They all remembered how it had felt to be constricted and lifted off the floor, a vomit-inducing sensation.

"We have to think smart," said Ben, trying to rally his friends. "We have to find a way to fight back, to get out of here and get back to the portal. Otherwise…" Ben let the word hang, wishing he hadn't said it, but it was too late. The unpleasant possibilities that lay within that incomplete sentence were endless.

"Why don't we rush the git when he comes back to get us?" Jake volunteered. "We'll hear him coming, it's dark; we'll just wait by the door and all four of us can take him down. Then we run."

Sam snorted. "Brilliant. That's the smart thinking we're looking for."

"I don't hear any ideas from you," Jake shot back.

"Where would we run to?" Sam continued. "We've no idea where we're going. We'll never find the portal, we'll get lost, then caught, then we'll get killed. Just a super, super idea, Jake."

"I think it's worth a go," Heather chipped in. "We need some kind of plan… unless you can think of a better one, Sam?"

"It may be our best chance of getting out of here is to comply with their requests, co-operate freely, and when they realise we're not a threat, they'll let us go."

"So lame," muttered Jake. "I think we'll count that as no, you don't have a plan."

"OK," began Ben, "so when Paleface comes back to get us—"

"Who?" Jake interrupted.

"That man. That's what I'm calling him. When Paleface comes back to get us, we wait for him by the door and pounce, give him as good a kicking as we can, and then leg it."

"Umm," murmured Sam, voicing his dissent again. "He doesn't seem like a stupid fellow. Don't you think he might be ready for such an obvious ploy?"

"Maybe not," argued Jake. "If you wanted to guard against such an attack, surely you'd chain us up?"

"Or, as we've seen, use magic to restrain us. He's not going to come down unready or unprotected. I'm sorry, guys, I just don't think it'll work."

"Let's vote," said Ben. "All those in favour of trying to escape?"

"Me," said Jake.

"Seconded," said Heather.

Ben took the decision. "I agree. Sorry, Sam."

"Fine," Sam huffed. "But when we're all spread out on the floor in sheer agony, don't blame me."

They waited for what seemed an eternity in the darkness of the dungeon. The steady 'plunk, plunk' of water dripped into the dungeon, a soporific noise that was in danger of sending them to sleep. Eventually, Ben heard approaching footsteps.

"This is it," he whispered urgently. "He's coming."

The four of them scrabbled into place, readying themselves, tensing every muscle in preparation to spring their surprise attack. Ben's heart was pumping hard, a thin sheen of sweat developing on his forehead. Jake had offered to be the first to jump Paleface, with the others falling in behind as quickly as possible. It was an offer that everyone had gladly accepted.

The footsteps came closer, growing louder as they slowly wound their way down the grimy steps. They stopped outside, and it seemed to take an age before they heard the clunk of the key being turned in the lock.

Gradually, the door creaked open, light spilling into the dim room.

"*Now!*" shouted Jake, leaping from his crouched position straight out towards Paleface. The others scrambled to follow him.

Paleface didn't even flinch. Jake simply rebounded off him and flew backwards into the dungeon as though he'd put his fingers in a plug socket. He careered into the others and sent them flying like skittles.

They all fell, banging their heads and arms painfully on the cellar floor, and lay wounded on the ground, groaning at the injuries inflicted.

Paleface walked into the dungeon, calm and collected. "An ambush, eh?" he sneered. "You obviously haven't learnt yet that it's completely useless to try and oppose me. It's a lesson you should learn, and learn well, before you meet Lord Blackwood." With that he threw his arms out and pointed his fingers at the four.

Lightning streaked from his hands, hitting each of them square in the chest. For several seconds, electricity coursed through their bodies, causing them to writhe on the floor in agony as the extreme voltage shocked them to their core. Paleface just laughed maniacally the whole time.

Ben clutched his head as it felt like his brain began to bubble in his skull and his eyes would melt. He had never felt so much pain in all his life. Right before he was about to pass out, Paleface stopped, and they all lay on the floor, their clothes smouldering, their thoughts scrambled.

"I hope you understand now that resistance is futile." Paleface grinned. "I would so hate to have to put you through that again." He licked his lips as he said it, daring someone to try and cross him.

Ben and the others staggered to their feet, groaning at their aching bodies. All defiance had gone from them, and they were ready to comply. None of them wanted any more of the treatment they just received.

Paleface looked at Ben, curling his finger to beckon him. "You, with me."

Ben looked at the others. "What about them?" he asked Paleface.

"They stay here. You come with me."

"Where?"

"Where do you think? You're going to see Lord Blackwood."

CHAPTER 11

Ben hobbled out of the dungeon. Paleface swung the door closed and locked Ben's friends up behind him; he was on his own now. He followed Paleface up the stairs and into the dim corridor. There was an aura of despair about this place that oozed from the dank, stone walls, a grotty-ness that spoke of a miserable existence for everything in the castle. They emerged from the corridor and crossed a cavernous space that echoed sadly with their footsteps. Reaching the other side, they began to climb some stairs, made of simple, rough stone initially, but the more they climbed, the more robust and ornate they became, until it was eventually a grand staircase made of marble. After what felt like an age, and with Ben exhausted by the climb, they finally reached the top. *This castle really is enormous*, thought Ben.

They came out into an antechamber made of huge sand-coloured bricks, where two further archways led off into other rooms. Its gothic look reminded Ben of a medieval church, built with such splendour that all who came would feel a deep respect for a higher power. The rest of the room was barren except for a massive painting hung on the wall to his left.

Ben instantly recognised it as a picture of Lord Blackwood; the striking figure was tall and clad in armour, no face visible beneath the shiny helmet, just two bright circles of fire. Holding a giant sword, he looked fierce and strong; no doubt the intended effect was to intimidate visitors.

It certainly worked on Ben.

"You wait here," Paleface wheezed.

Ben could do nothing but wait as Paleface rushed off through the arch on the left. A knot had formed in his stomach – he felt so sick and nervous he could barely stand.

Is this it? Am I going to die? said the scared little boy in his head. *If he wanted you dead you would be already*, said another voice, trying to reassure him.

Paleface had scarcely been gone a minute before he appeared again, beneath the stone archway.

"Lord Blackwood will see you now," he whined.

Ben took a deep breath, told himself to be brave and walked into the splendid throne room. Immediately he was struck by the opulence of the room – a grand space with swooping arches that soared majestically across the ceiling and huge colourful tapestries that hung on the walls. Fine, luxuriant rugs of gold, red and blue adorned the floor, and Ben realised with a shock that this was the first bit of colour he'd seen in the Shadow Realm. A huge hearth along one wall was ablaze with fire, casting flickering shadows across the room.

But Ben could hardly take it all in, for at one end of the room sat Lord Blackwood. He was perched atop a stone throne embedded with ruby-red jewels that sparkled dimly in the low orange glow of the firelight.

As Ben approached, Blackwood regarded him coolly, one arm propped under his chin, his fire eyes a weak ember.

Then, as he got nearer, a spark flew into them, turning them into a raging inferno. Ben's knees nearly buckled beneath him, but he tried to stay calm, to appear in control. His heart was hammering against his ribs and his palms were sweating, his stomach a bag of nerves.

There was no face for Ben to see, only a dark void surrounding two, perfectly round, roiling cauldrons of flame. Ben looked down at the floor, unable to meet Lord Blackwood's intense gaze. Blackwood looked Ben up and down, glaring fiercely, his eyes full of anger. When he spoke, his voice was loud and commanding, each word landing in Ben's brain with the weight of a knock-out punch.

"Tell me who you are."

Ben didn't know what to say, or even if he could get anything past his quivering lips. After a few seconds he received a clip round the ear in reprisal from Paleface.

"When his lordship asks you a question, you respond," shouted Paleface.

Ben rubbed his head, meeting the level stare of Lord Blackwood. "I'm B... Ben," he stuttered.

"Well, B-Ben," Blackwood said with playful menace. "You are not from the Shadow Realm, are you?"

Ben shuffled his weight nervously from one foot to the other. "No."

Lord Blackwood leant back, pulling a small dagger from his belt and toying with it threateningly. "Where are you from, Ben?"

The question unnerved him. Ben wasn't sure how much he should tell Blackwood. He had a sense it would be very dangerous to tell Blackwood what he really thought – that he was from another dimension.

"I... I don't know how to explain it..." began Ben.

Lord Blackwood clicked his fingers and Ben rose into the air, drawn towards him by some magical force. It was like his nightmares all over again, as he neared Blackwood's face and it consumed his world, the fire in those eyes growing hotter and brighter, until it was all that he could see. He was nose to nose with Lord Blackwood.

"Don't play games with me, boy," he hissed. "I could snap your neck with a click of my fingers, which I would enjoy, and won't hesitate to do if I think you are of no more use to me. Do you understand?"

Ben gulped and nodded. He could feel the heat from those eyes burning his skin, a furnace of anger writhing in his face. Then the invisible force holding him disappeared, and he crumpled to the floor.

"So," said Lord Blackwood slowly. "I'll ask again, and this time, give me a straight answer. Where are you from?"

Ben couldn't see much sense in trying to lie; it could be the last words he ever spoke. He tried to be as economical with the truth as possible instead. "I'm from the New Forest."

"The *New* Forest," said Blackwood, chewing the words slowly, rolling them around his mouth as if enjoying the taste of them. "And where is this *new forest*, Ben?"

"It's in Hampshire," he said, hoping it was enough of an answer for now.

Lord Blackwood considered this, before apparently reaching the conclusion that he was happy with this answer, at least for now. "Why are you here?" he said finally.

"I don't know," he pleaded, bowing his head. "I don't think I should be here. *We* shouldn't be here. I realise that now, and if you'll just let me and my friends go, then we'll leave and never come back, I promise."

A deep chuckling noise came from the void of Lord Blackwood's face, which seemed to shake the very foundations of the castle.

"Well, that would never do," he bellowed. "You've only just arrived!"

His fit of humour subsided, an unsettling softness entering his voice. "Tell me how you got here."

Ben wiped the sweat from his brow. "I don't really know. It just sort of happened. One minute I was stood in the New Forest, the next I was here." He was being deliberately vague and sensed that Blackwood knew this.

"But this isn't the first time you've come," said Blackwood, a threat carried implicitly for Ben to explain himself more.

"No," answered Ben. "I wanted to see if I could come back. If I could bring others."

"And you could."

"Yes." Ben hung his head in shame. "It was stupid."

"That remains to be seen. What aren't you telling me?"

"Nothing."

Lord Blackwood clicked his fingers, and Ben was lifted off his feet, rotated quickly into a horizontal position. He floated as straight as an arrow in mid-air for a few seconds, his arms forced above his head.

Slowly, Ben felt his body being stretched, as if he were on an invisible rack. As the rack tightened, his body was pulled further apart, his arms and legs groaning at the pressure to rip from their sockets. In a matter of seconds, it felt like his body was going to be torn in two. He screamed in sheer agony.

Blackwood laughed. "Why don't you tell me how you really got here?"

Ben could barely think straight, but he managed to splutter out his answer. "There's a portal between the two worlds. I can go through it."

Lord Blackwood's fiery eyes twinkled.

The stretching continued, and Ben grunted as pain fizzed throughout his stretched body. *This is it*, he thought, *I'm going to die right here.*

Lord Blackwood stooped down next to Ben's ear. "Hurt?"

Ben could only groan in affirmation.

"Want it to end?"

"Yes."

"Are you telling me the truth?"

"*Yes!*" Ben screamed.

Lord Blackwood straightened up and considered this. "OK." He clicked his fingers and Ben fell to the ground, released from the invisible rack he had been placed on. He instantly curled up in a ball, gasping for breath as his body clenched his extended muscles back together.

"You will take me to the portal," said Blackwood, replacing the dagger in its sheath. "And I will go through with you."

Ben just moaned.

"First, I'll speak to your friends." He motioned to Paleface. "Take him back, bring up the girl."

Ben could not protest. He had no strength left for anything. Paleface grappled him to his feet and pushed him out of the huge throne room. Ben hobbled along, following the miserable wretch back down to the dungeon. He was thrown back into the dank prison, where he stumbled and fell, half caught by the others, half tumbling over them.

They had no time to react when Paleface grabbed Heather by the hair and pulled her out of the dungeon, locking the door behind him. It all happened so quickly that Jake was still in shock and only reacted after the door closed, running to it and pounding his fists against the heavy oak.

"Leave her alone!" he shouted, but it was useless. Heather's screaming had already faded.

He turned back to where Ben had fallen to the ground. All concern had now gone from his voice.

"This is all your fault," he spat. "If they do anything to hurt her, I'll…" He let the threat hang, unsure how to end it.

Ben was still on the floor, stunned. He barely had the strength to stand, let alone argue with Jake.

Sam intervened. "Now calm down," he said, trying to appease Jake. "We all just agreed that we're in this together. Let's act like it, yeah?"

"It's easy to say, isn't it? But it's not your sister that's just been dragged off to face god knows what. Look at the state of Ben, it's obviously not all laughter and cake, is it? If she gets hurt, I'll kill him for bringing us here."

"Ben told us it could be dangerous, and you more than anyone still agreed to come. Arguing now isn't going to get us anywhere."

Ben felt incredibly weak. "I'm sorry, Jake," he managed to wheeze out.

Jake said nothing, still raging inwardly at his powerlessness.

There was silence for a moment before Sam spoke. "What happened?" he asked.

"He wanted to know why we're here. I told him the truth. That we didn't know."

"What did he do to you?"

"He… well, he had a rough way of checking that I was telling the truth."

"Like what?"

Ben told them about being stretched out in mid-air.

"Great," Jake cried. "So that's the kind of treatment my sister can expect."

Sam also started to pace about. "This is bad, really bad, guys. So bad."

"Thank you for that insightful commentary, Sam," snapped Jake sarcastically.

"Just calm down. I think he's mostly interested in me," said Ben, trying to sound more persuasive than he felt. "If you all corroborate my story, he'll know we're telling the truth."

"Oh, what do you know," Jake said irritably. "You're always so damned optimistic."

Heather was shaking as she was marched along the great hall towards Lord Blackwood, frightened for her life. It was so magisterial, so colourful and imposing compared to the rest of the place that she couldn't help but feel over-awed. Blackwood was sat on his throne at the end of the room.

She had never seen anybody quite so fierce and scary-looking in her entire life, his threatening presence filled the entire room, but then, she'd never seen *anything* like Lord Blackwood before.

He was as Ben had described, but she wasn't prepared for the hideous aura that Blackwood projected, those piercing, blazing eyes that radiated sheer wickedness.

She stopped nervously a few feet from Blackwood, who regarded her maliciously. She shrank away meekly from his gaze.

"Your name?" he snapped.

"H... H... Heather," she stammered.

"Why are you here, Heather?"

"We... we followed Ben here. He told us about the Shadow Realm, about how he could get here through a portal and that he wanted to bring us here. It was just meant to be a quick look, harmless, we weren't doing anything bad, I promise." She was speaking fast, blurting out whatever came into her head.

"I see," said Lord Blackwood, and sat silent for a while. Heather looked down the whole time, too scared to look into Blackwood's eyes. Finally, he spoke. "That's not what your friend... Ben... just told me."

Heather looked up in alarm. She had no idea what Ben might have just told Blackwood, and she felt a panic rising in her.

"He confessed to being an agent of the rebel Magus council, sent here in an attempt to dethrone me."

Heather was having palpitations. "That's not true," she wailed. "I don't even know what that means. Ben wouldn't have said that." She started to cry. She really didn't want to, but she couldn't help herself. "I just want to go home," she wept.

"I don't think there'll be much chance of that anytime soon." He paused, lapping up this pathetic girl's fear. "Maybe you don't know your friend quite as well as you think you do." He signalled to Paleface, who ushered the girl away.

She was sobbing uncontrollably.

She was thrown into the dungeon and caught by Ben, who asked her if she was OK. She nodded, tears still running down her face.

Jake swore at Paleface and for his troubles got yanked out of the dungeon and taken to see Lord Blackwood. Sam then realised he would be next and started to worry even worse than he had before.

"What did he do to you?" Sam said, fretting away.

"Sam, shut up," said Ben firmly. He continued to comfort Heather, who was still crying. "The last thing she needs now is to relive whatever just happened."

"It's OK," she said between sobs. "He didn't hurt me. Ben…" she began, and cut off.

"What is it?"

"He tried to say that you'd confessed to being some kind of rebel agent."

Ben blinked. "But that's ridiculous. I don't even know what that is."

"I know, but why would he say that?"

Ben didn't know what to say.

Sam coughed. "Could well be there are some rebels in this place opposed to his rule. He probably thinks we're working for them. Even more reason to have us killed," he finished glumly.

"Oh god, I hope Jake's OK," wailed Heather.

"He'll probably get on famously with Lord Blackwood," snorted Sam.

"Look, this is getting us nowhere," said Ben, stepping in. "We need a new plan for getting out of here."

Sam snorted again. "I'm all ears."

Heather spoke up. "We can't just force our way out; we'll have to try and trick him."

"Any ideas?"

"Well, I did have one…"

Over the next few minutes, the three of them devised a new escape plan and then waited patiently, in the darkness, for Jake to return.

Ben heard the footsteps first and started wailing and banging on the door. Heather joined him, screaming as loud as she could. They could hear the footsteps hasten down the steps to the dungeon, and within seconds they heard the key in the door. They stepped back as it swung wide open, blinking as the light poured in, stinging their eyes.

"What's going on in here?" Paleface demanded. Jake was behind Paleface, trying to peer over his shoulder.

"It's our friend. I think he's dead." Ben was breathless. "We've been hollering to get someone's attention, but no-one came."

"What are you talking about?" Paleface peered suspiciously into the dungeon.

"It's Sam – he fell over fifteen minutes ago complaining of pains in his chest. He's not breathing."

"Let me see," said Paleface, pushing past Ben and Heather. Ben saw the concern on Jake's face as he moved to come inside, but Heather forced him back and surreptitiously joined him in the corridor.

Ben followed behind Paleface, his heart racing. "Can you do anything?" he implored.

Paleface turned to face him and raised one of his white eyebrows. "And why would I want to do that?"

"I imagine Lord Blackwood will be pretty displeased if he can't interrogate his fourth prisoner."

The possibility of his boss being angry with him spurred Paleface into action. He knelt down beside Sam, who was lying perfectly still on the floor.

Ben didn't hesitate. He pushed Paleface hard, sending him sprawling over Sam and careering into the dungeon wall, where he bashed his head hard.

With Paleface bowled over, Ben grabbed Sam, helping him to scrabble to his feet, and threw him out the door. Ben dived through after him, rolling on the stone floor whilst Heather quickly pushed the door shut, turning the key that Paleface had left in the lock. It clicked into place, just as they heard Paleface shouting from inside the dungeon.

They looked at each other, feeling a surge of euphoria and fear at the same time, not quite believing the plan had worked. They were free.

CHAPTER 12

Ben was the first to snap out of the shock of the plan actually working, grabbing Heather's hand and running up the stairs, whilst exhorting the others to hurry up behind him.

He took the stairs two at a time, racing for the top, his lungs heaving with the effort already. Ben knew they didn't have much time to get out of the castle, that it wouldn't be long before either Paleface escaped or Lord Blackwood realised something was wrong. They needed to get out quick before that happened.

He hadn't thought too hard about the post-escape part of the plan, and it soon became apparent that it was not going to be as easy or straightforward as Ben hoped. Having turned right at the top of the stairs and raced down the tunnel they believed was how they'd come in, they soon reached a T-junction that no-one recognised. Both ways appeared identical, with long, gloomy corridors stretching off into the murky distance. Ben took a quick decision and turned left, and after a minute or two of running down the corridor, they found themselves in a small chamber with three wooden doors leading off in separate directions.

"Now what?" said Jake, as they skidded to a stop.

"I dunno," panted Ben. "We choose a door, I guess."

"This isn't the way we came in, is it?" said Sam, very matter-of-factly.

"No," replied Ben, peering back behind Sam. "I'm not really sure where we are." The castle was unnervingly quiet, the dim raging of Paleface now left far behind. The only sound was their heavy breathing.

"So, we're lost already?"

"No, we keep going until we get out. It's a castle, not a labyrinth."

"So which door do we go through?" asked Heather.

Ben felt the responsibility weigh heavily on him, that it was he who needed to decide. But what if he got it wrong? What if they just got lost, going deeper and deeper into the castle? But they needed to be quick, so he made his decision.

"This one," he said, and darted through the door to his left. The door opened to a squalid and dank corridor that had several small, heavy-looking wooden doors set into the wall along one side. Each had a little grille at face height, though the rooms behind were completely dark. Something about these rooms unsettled Ben, and they began to move forwards cautiously, as if they had all instinctively sensed the danger. About halfway along the passage they were startled into stopping by what they saw at one of the grilles.

A girl's face was pushed up against it, a look of panic etched into her face, her eyebrows raised in alarm.

"Hey!" she shouted. "Are you with the rebels?"

Ben looked at the other three, but they looked as blank as he did.

"Please," she implored. "You must help me."

Ben paused, unsure of what to say. "Who are you?" he asked eventually.

"My name is Sofiella." Her face was gaunt and unwashed, her long blonde hair cascading scruffily from her head, matted together and dirty. "Please, will you help me?" she begged. "I've been here for so long, a prisoner, and you're the first people I've seen in... well, I don't know how long it's been." Her sad eyes were a piercing blue, a down-trodden beauty shining from their depths. Ben felt mesmerised by her gaze.

"We… we don't know where we're going," he admitted.

She actually laughed. "I don't care. Please just get me out of here."

Ben jolted out of his stupor. "Yes… of course." He stirred into action, trying the door. "It's locked," he said to her, stating the obvious.

"I'm not surprised," she said. "This is a prison, after all." Her accent was posh, her voice soft. She looked not much older than they were.

Ben pushed and pulled at the door, his face darkening all the while. "I don't know how we're going to get you out." He looked at the others. "Any ideas?"

The other three shifted uneasily, looking around them.

"No, Ben," said Jake, after the uncomfortable pause. "I can't see a way of getting her out, and to be honest, at this point, I don't care."

"What?" blurted Ben, uncomprehending. "What do you mean?"

"We have to leave her," Jake said bluntly.

"But we should try and help," Ben protested. "She's just like us, only if we'd never escaped. Imagine that."

"But we haven't escaped yet, have we?" Jake said firmly. "And unless we get a move on, we're not going to."

Ben pushed his fingers to his temples and rubbed. He didn't want to leave Sofiella here, but what good were they doing standing outside her cell, procrastinating?

Sofiella appeared to judge that she was about to be left and grew desperate.

"*Please*," she beseeched them. "You have to get me out of here." She started to cry, pulling herself up desperately to the bars, shaking them vigorously. "Please don't leave me."

"We can't leave her to suffer like this," said Ben, staring at Jake.

"Can we force the door?" said Sam, in his first useful observation of the day.

Ben looked at it. "I suppose we can try."

"I'll give it a kick," Jake volunteered. "Stand back."

Jake stood in front of the door, steadied himself into a kung-fu stance and launched a ferocious kick at it. His foot rebounded off the solid oak, and he clutched at his foot, hopping around and groaning in pain.

"I guess that didn't work then," said Ben. "Maybe there's something we can use to force the door open."

They all looked around, but apart from a few spider's webs, the corridor was barren.

"Yeah," Jake snorted. "Of course there'll be a crowbar just lying around."

Ben looked at Sofiella, who was still peering expectantly at them through the metal grille. "I don't think we're going to be able to get you out," he said gingerly.

Ben could see her heart sinking. "But... but you must," she whimpered.

"We'll come back for you, I promise," said Ben.

Jake looked at his friend in shock. "You can't promise something like that, Ben, you won't be able to come back here."

Ben looked into Sofiella's big, blue, pleading eyes. "I'll find a way," he said. He pulled his gaze away from her and moved off, the others following him. Behind him, Sofiella started screaming at the top of her lungs and he winced; the racket she was making would no doubt attract attention.

He knew there was nothing he could do, no way to get her out, but it hurt him to leave her there. He just had to hope he could find a way to come back and save her.

Even as he thought it, he realised how hollow it sounded.

They ran on for a couple of minutes, twisting and turning down various corridors, not sure whether each new direction was bringing them closer to, or further away from, freedom. Many passages were pitch black, forcing them to slow down and hold hands, as much for comfort as to ensure they didn't lose each other. Those moments spent in the darkness were so lonely, so terrifying, they seemed to last an eternity. Eventually they would round a bend and there would be some light further on, throwing minacious shadows that crawled along the walls and reached out for them, like clawing black hands.

They kept running on, unable to find a way out of this maze, and they were beginning to get desperate when Ben rounded a corner and ran straight into a man, sending him rebounding backwards onto the floor. The stranger was first to react, drawing a dagger that was looped around his belt before Ben had even realised what happened. The man looked at Ben suspiciously, his eyes narrowing.

"Who are you?" he demanded. He had blond hair drawn back into a ponytail that fell to his shoulders, a few wrinkles etched in his face. He wore natural hemp clothing, which lent him a scruffy, peasant air.

A moment later, Manatang rounded the corner and stopped in shock behind the man.

"Ben!" he cried.

Ben was stunned. "M… Manatang?" he managed to splutter.

"Of course," said Manatang. He looked at the man, who still had his knife drawn. "Taegan, put your knife away. This is the boy we've come to rescue."

"Oh," said Taegan, relief pouring into his face, quickly followed by confusion. "Why aren't you in a cell?"

Ben looked between Manatang and Taegan, still in slight shock. "Oh, er… well, we escaped." He swept a hand across his sweaty brow. "You came to rescue us?"

"There's no time for explanations," said Taegan. "We've got to get you out of here, then we can talk."

"Ahem," said Jake, interrupting. "Would someone mind explaining to me what the hell is going on?"

"Guys, this," said Ben, motioning at the little monkey-man, "is Manatang. The one I was telling you about – who I met when I first came to the Shadow Realm."

Manatang pulled his finger from the ear he was picking and waved at them.

"I see," said Sam, stroking his chin. He leant over to whisper in Ben's ear. "Can we trust them?"

"Yes, I think we can," Ben whispered back. "Besides, do we have any other option?"

Taegan was getting impatient. "We need to go. We can't stand here talking all day in the middle of Lord Blackwood's castle."

"Well, thank god you found us," gushed Heather. "We were just running around all lost."

"We'll get you out," said Taegan, before nodding back down the corridor. "This way."

"No, wait," said Ben.

Taegan turned round in surprise. "What is it?"

"We've got to go back; we've got to go and help someone."

Taegan raised his eyebrows. "There's someone else?"

"Yes," said Ben. "She's locked up in a cell, and I promised I'd go back and help her." He looked Taegan straight in the eyes. "We have to go back."

Taegan sighed and muttered something to Manatang, who shrugged his shoulders in response.

"I'm not leaving without her," Ben said, feeling like an impetuous child.

Jake coughed and held a finger up to Taegan. "Just a brief moment, if you wouldn't mind," he said, turning Ben away from the others. "What are you doing?" he breathed. "We're trying to get out of here, we've got a very nice gentleman offering to help, and…" he whispered with a swift look at Manatang, "a strange, talking monkey. And you want to go back and waste more time trying to get someone we don't know out of a prison cell?" He paused, looking down the grotty corridor. "For all we know she deserves to be there; she could be a murderer."

"She's no such thing and you know it," scoffed Ben. "And I'm not arguing this. It's the right thing to do. Would you want to be left to rot in here?" The question was rhetorical, but Jake felt the need to answer it anyway.

"No, but—"

"Besides, I made a promise." Ben turned to face Taegan. "Will you help us?"

Taegan looked at Ben, considering him for a moment. "Doesn't look as if I have much choice now, does it?" He hooked his dagger back into his belt. "Which way is she?"

"Should be back this way, we haven't made too many turnings since we left her."

"Right," said Taegan, brushing past Ben and the others. "You best stay behind me as we go."

They started to run back down the corridor in the direction they had come. Ben sidled up next to Manatang.

"How did you know we were here?" he asked.

"I saw you and your friends get captured by Grimstone," replied Manatang.

"Grimstone?" said Ben, before twigging who Manatang meant. "We've been calling him Paleface."

"Well, I followed you to the castle and then alerted Taegan to what had happened. He launched a rescue mission."

"Not wishing to sound ungrateful, but couldn't you just have stopped us from getting caught? We've all been through some serious pain."

Manatang looked at Ben as if he were stupid. "Grimstone is a very powerful Mage, almost as strong as Lord Blackwood. There was absolutely nothing I could do to prevent what happened – far better I see where you were taken and come with backup." He looked glumly ahead. "And we're not out of the woods yet, so to speak."

Ben concentrated on finding the place where Sofiella was being held prisoner. Before long they were running past the doors in the walls with the metal grilles, and they slowed down.

"It's the second one up ahead," panted Ben, pointing at a door on the right.

Taegan slowed and approached the door carefully. There was no-one peering through the grille.

"Hello," Taegan called. "Is there anyone in there?" There was no response.

Ben was puzzled. This was definitely the same door. He decided to try calling for her. "Sofiella, are you in there?" He strained his hearing and could just make out some sobbing. "Can you hear that?" asked Ben, turning towards Taegan.

The look on Taegan's face was one of pure astonishment. "Did… you just say… Sofiella?"

"Yes," Ben said slowly, unsure if he'd done something wrong. "That's what she said her name was."

"Well, why didn't you say so earlier?" bellowed Taegan.

"I… I didn't think it was important," said Ben, but Taegan wasn't listening.

Taegan put his head to the grille and started yelling into the dark cell. "Sofiella!" he cried. "Are you in there? It's me, Taegan."

Jake caught Ben's eye and gave him a quizzical look. Ben shrugged his shoulders. He was as confused as anyone.

The sobbing in the cell had stopped, and Sofiella's faint voice came drifting out from within the darkness. "Taegan? Is that really you?"

"Yes," he said. "Get back from the door – we're going to get you out of there."

The others looked on expectantly as Taegan walked back from the door, turned sideways to it and charged.

"Careful," shouted Jake, just as Taegan slammed into the door and bounced off it. "…It's rather firm."

Taegan fell to the floor, dazed. Ben went over and helped him to his feet.

"Now what?" asked Ben.

Taegan looked at Ben with deep concern across his face. "I was hoping not to have to do this…"

"Do what?" asked Ben.

Manatang interrupted. "That's not a good idea, Taegan," he said. "We'll be exposed to him with no way of defending ourselves."

Taegan looked at him harshly. "If you've got another suggestion, I'd love to hear it."

Manatang looked down, dutifully silent.

"I thought not. I've got to get her out of there, and this is the only way."

"What's the only way?" Ben asked.

"I'm going to have to use some magic to open the door," Taegan said plainly.

Ben sighed in confusion. He'd seen enough of this world to know that magic here was possible and real, but that then begged a further question.

"Why didn't you just do that before?"

"Because it's the last that I've got, and if I use it up, we'll have no way to defend ourselves from any trouble on the way out."

"Ah," said Ben, not really understanding but sensing now was not the time to pursue the issue.

With a last troubled look at Manatang, Taegan closed his eyes and placed his hands out before him. He stayed like this for a couple of seconds before he started to shake violently, his face contorting with the effort and strain of performing the spell.

Ben looked from Taegan to the door, which didn't seem to be doing anything at all. Then, slowly, he saw the door start to shake, and the screws that secured the hinges started to ease their way out of the stonework, hesitantly, like worms emerging in the new dawn light. They plopped out on to the floor with a small, tinny clink.

Taegan dropped to his knees, exhausted, but the big heavy oak door stood perfectly still. Manatang sauntered up to it and called out to Sofiella.

"Stand back!" He pushed at the door, which slowly succumbed to the force of gravity with a loud groan as it fell inwards and slammed into the ground, shrouding everyone in a cloud of dust.

Taegan was recovering his strength quickly from the mental effort of performing the magic, and he got to his feet, cautiously approaching the open space where the door used to be.

"Sofiella?" he whispered into the dusty room. "It's OK, you can come out."

Nothing happened for a moment, but then a nervous-looking Sofiella appeared in the doorway. She looked dishevelled and emaciated, not much more than a bag of bones.

She looked up at Taegan with exhausted eyes, then rushed at him, throwing her arms around him and hugging him hard. "Oh, Taegan, you came for me!" she exclaimed, so happy.

"We have to get out of here, now," he said. "We've been here quite long enough already. Follow me." He set off hastily down the corridor.

Sofiella beamed at Ben, euphoric at her release, and Ben couldn't help but smile back at her.

"Come on," chivvied Manatang. "Get going."

Further introductions would clearly have to wait.

They followed Taegan down numerous twisting corridors and tunnels, apparently towards a 'back door' that Manatang knew about. Each minute that they continued to run through the castle, Ben grew more nervous. They pushed on through giant cobwebs and scrambled over broken walls, much of the castle having succumbed to the same decay that inflicted the rest of this blighted world. He wanted desperately to get home now, back to the safety and warmth of his family home, but there was still such a long way to go.

Lost in thoughts of home, Ben nearly ran straight into the back of Sofiella, who had stopped behind Taegan and Manatang. They had reached the end of another long passageway, which opened out onto a large courtyard.

"The back door is on the other side," whispered Manatang, motioning with his hand. "We just have to make sure that no-one is looking for us yet. We'll be totally exposed as we cross the yard."

Ben looked out across the square, which had fallen into disrepair, most of the walls now cracked and falling apart. In the middle was a disused fountain, covered in grey ash, decrepit with age like a geriatric elephant.

Along the top of the stone walls were ramparts, a ledge where long ago defenders of the castle would stand to protect it from aggressors. They were empty now.

Listening keenly, Ben couldn't hear a single sound, apart from the breathing of his puffed-out companions. Taegan raised his fingers to his lips, indicating that they should all be silent and that they should follow him across the courtyard.

Slowly, stealthily, they started to edge their way out into the open space. Taegan was constantly spinning, looking up and around the vacated courtyard, vigilant for any danger. When they approached the exposed centre square, he indicated they should all run for the other side and then bolted, expecting them all to follow. Everyone began to run as fast as they could, pumping their legs hard in this last desperate dash for freedom. After so much running already, Ben's legs were burning, but the adrenaline shooting through his system kept him going, pushing him on to reach the door. Out of the corner of his eye he saw Sam stumble, crashing to the ground like a ragdoll and yelping in pain. He wheeled round to help him back to his feet, dragging him up with all the strength he could muster.

Then disaster struck. To Ben it felt like he'd suddenly smashed into a brick wall that was covered in glue. They were all frozen to the spot, some of them in mid-air as they were literally caught in flight.

It was impossible to move, and Ben had the terrifying realisation that they'd been trapped, imprisoned by the same magic that Grimstone had used. But this was more painful.

"*Taegan!*" boomed Lord Blackwood from above them. Taegan was rotated by the force field now surrounding him, slowly pivoting to face his enemy. Blackwood was standing in an arched window frame that overlooked the courtyard, his hand outstretched and controlling them all. Even in the dim light, his metallic armour appeared to shine, reflections from nowhere glinting off the buffed iron.

Taegan's face contorted in pain as Lord Blackwood sent some unseen agony coursing through him.

"I've waited a long time to see you again." Blackwood's words oozed a maniacal glee. "I'm so pleased you dropped by."

Taegan couldn't speak, his mouth frothing with pain that he spat out in a tortured gasp.

"I can't say I'm at all impressed with your manners, though, helping my guests to leave without my permission." The words hung like daggers.

Ben looked on with an increasing sense of horror. They would never get out of here, not now, and in all likelihood, Blackwood would kill them for having the audacity to try and escape. He felt unbearably guilty in that moment, a tide of remorse sweeping over him as he struggled to acknowledge the truth: that his friends would die, and their blood was on his hands.

"And now, Taegan," said Lord Blackwood, raising his hands high, poised to strike, "I take the greatest pleasure in seeing you die."

There was a bang behind them as the back door they had been heading towards flew open, and a woman with long, blue, plaited hair came rolling in, as fast as a bolt of lightning. Before anyone could register what was happening, an arc of electricity came flashing out of her hands and struck Lord Blackwood hard in the chest, forcing him back away from the arched window.

They all dropped from his kinetic grasp, hitting the ground hard.

"Quick, *run!*" she shouted. They were up as quick as they could, Taegan regaining his wits sharpest to pick up and hassle everyone along.

Ben and the others ran faster than they had ever run before to the broken back door, funnelling through it like terrified sheep. The blue-haired woman shepherded them through, keeping an eye on the arched window, praying that Blackwood would not re-appear. She was all out of tricks and his return really would be the end.

The castle backed on to woodland, apparently marking the edge of the town they had travelled through on the way in. Waiting there was Taegan's transport: a cart with some animals that looked like horses but with strange heads, much rounder than a normal horse. He threw the four teens and Sofiella onto the back of the cart with consummate ease, hopping and twisting himself up into the driving seat in one easy, fluid motion. Manatang bounded into the back of the cart, and after a split second the blue-haired woman joined Taegan on the front bench.

"*Go,*" she screamed at him, looking back at the castle in abject terror. Taegan cracked the whip and the horse-like animals started with a jolt, quickly gathering speed until the woods around them were rolling by at a furious pace.

It was too much for Ben to take in; there were so many questions, though they felt trite and unimportant whilst they were still in danger.

The blue-haired woman turned round to them. "You'll want to find something to grab on to," she shouted.

Ben and the others scrambled around them for something to hold, though there wasn't much to grip in the wooden cart. Instead, they braced themselves against the sides, clenching their bodies in preparation for whatever was to come.

The cart hit a ramp and become airborne for a few seconds. Ben had the queasy and yet strangely pleasant feeling of weightlessness as gravity reasserted itself and the cart plummeted downwards. Instead of hitting the road, the cart fell right *through* it, landing with a sickening crunch that jarred and jolted the passengers. Ben looked ahead and saw that they were in a long tunnel that stretched out in front of them for miles. From what he could tell, the tunnel had simply been dug out of the ground, the walls nothing but packed earth, curving round in an oval shape. Its girth was impressive, comfortably taking the cart, with enough room for one to pass on the other side.

They sped on down the tunnel, occasionally careering down side passages that led from the main one, before joining other large tunnels. They seemed to make up a huge network, an underground labyrinth.

What struck Ben was that although there were many tunnels, none of them seemed to lead anywhere of interest. There were no doors or gates, just miles and miles of huge walls of dirt, flashing by as they sped further and further into the maze.

They kept going like that for a long time, until finally they began to slow down, coming to a stop in the middle of the tunnel, one that appeared just like all the others they had been through. Nothing appeared to mark this place as special. The rounded wall of dirt curved off up ahead, the gloom only lifted slightly by a dim, hazy light that came from the walls themselves.

"Where are we?" asked Ben.

Taegan ignored him. "Manatang." The monkey-man jumped to attention. "I'm going to have to ask you to open the doors, I haven't the strength."

Manatang muttered something but dutifully obeyed, hopping off the cart and heading towards the side of the tunnel. He put his hand against the bank of earth, saying a couple of words to himself. His hand burned brightly, a blaze of white light that Ben had to look away from. When Manatang had finished, he fell to the floor, unconscious. Taegan jumped off the cart and carefully picked him up, placing him into the back.

Ben looked at him with concern. "Is he going to be alright?" he asked.

"He'll be fine," Taegan growled.

Ben looked at the wall that Manatang had touched and was astonished by what he saw. Where there had only been earth and mud before, the outline of a huge wooden door was beginning to appear. As Ben watched, it grew in definition, getting firmer, stronger and more real. It was nothing short of... magic. Taegan went up to the door and heaved it open, the big door wide enough now for them to drive through.

"What is this place?" Ben asked in wonder.

Taegan raised an eyebrow, this time deigning to answer. "It's our home. Our rebel base."

CHAPTER 13

The doors swung open and Taegan geed the horse-like animals inside, their hooves thudding on the hard earth. A strong smell of smoke mixed with herbs and spices greeted them as they entered the base, reminding Ben of home and the lasagne his mother would cook.

The ceiling was low, but the room was wide and long, like an underground parking lot. Carts of different shapes and sizes were parked neatly on one side, and there were stables on the other. Ben counted five other carts but space for many more. Taegan pulled up into one of the empty slots, and he jumped off to untie the animals.

Ben looked around uncomfortably. The reception area was dusty and arid, a strange, hollow place that felt like it had been designed to be busy and bustling, but there was no-one else here now. The fires that burned on the walls cast ominous shadows that flickered and writhed like the souls of the damned. He looked round at his three friends, their haggard expressions showing trepidation and tiredness, which was exactly how he felt. He glanced at Sofiella, who was beaming a big smile, her blackened teeth visible under cracked lips. She looked happy, visibly excited at being free and coming home. He turned his attention back to Taegan.

"What now?" he asked.

Taegan dusted his hands off. "Now you come with us," he said gruffly.

Jake bridled at this rough answer, interjecting before Ben could say anything. "Now, hang on a minute," he said. "Who are you people?"

Taegan fixed Jake with a long, hard stare. "We're the people that just saved your sorry behinds. You should try a little gratitude."

Ben tried to defuse the situation. "We are very thankful, honestly," he countered. "It's just we're a long way from home, we don't know who to trust and it would be nice to know a little about who you are."

The blue-haired woman stepped off the cart then and took Ben's hand. "We are here to help you, I promise, but right now, you need to just trust us and come this way."

Her voice was lyrical, lilting up and down musically as she spoke, enchanting Ben with her words. Her skin was soft and pure, her eyes greener than an emerald sea, and he was quite smitten.

Jake was less impressed. "May we at least know your name?" he asked the woman.

"My name is Elena," she said demurely, giving a soft nod of the head to Jake, and he felt his anger instantly assuaged.

"There'll be plenty of time for questions tonight," she said finally, and started to walk with Taegan and Sofiella towards one of the doorways.

Ben looked at his friends, and an unspoken decision passed between them to comply.

They all jumped off the cart and followed behind. They were leaving Manatang on the cart.

"What about Manatang?" Ben protested, pointing back towards the lifeless man-monkey.

"He'll be fine," said Taegan.

"You can't just leave him there."

Taegan turned and grabbed Ben's T-shirt with a steady hand, holding his face only inches from his. "Do you know what's best for him?" he said angrily. "Are you an expert now in the recovery of magical animals from depleted thaumatology syndrome?" His anger relented and he let Ben go. "Of course you don't. He just needs to rest for a few minutes and then he'll be just fine."

Ben stood still for a moment, shaken. He hadn't expected such a fierce outburst, but he decided that it might just be better for him to shut his mouth for a while.

They were ushered through a door into a dank corridor that had no lighting. They stumbled on, only able to follow the silhouettes of the rebels, lit from a light source far ahead. They were quickly brought to a small room, which looked like a bedroom of sorts. It was poorly lit with a single candle, the first normal source of lighting that Ben had seen in the Shadow Realm. In one corner was a dingy bunkbed, and on the other side a small, grubby sofa. There were no windows and it felt stuffy: a gloomy, land-locked room.

"You lot," said Taegan, pointing at them all, "wait in here. We'll be back in an hour or so." He put his arm around Sofiella and led her away, who glanced back at Ben and offered a gentle smile just before the door closed. They heard a click as the door was locked.

"Another prison cell," noted Sam sombrely.

"It's a little brighter and more comfortable than the last one at least," said Ben, trying to look on the positive side.

Jake rolled his eyes. "Mate, it's a hovel under the ground."

"Well, yes," said Ben, forced to agree. "But I think we're safer here than in Lord Blackwood's castle."

"I don't think we can trust anyone," said Heather. She folded her arms and looked at the others. "What do we know about what's going on?" The boys were silent. "Nothing. For all we know they've just gone off to discuss how to kill us."

"They're hardly going to rescue us and then kill us," scoffed Ben.

"And we don't have much other choice, do we?" continued Sam. "We're just going to have to give them the benefit of the doubt. It's our only hope right now of getting home."

The mention of home made something click in Ben's brain, and a sudden panic took hold.

"What is it?" Heather asked quickly.

Ben did some hasty calculations in his head and grimaced. "Do you remember when I told you that time here seems to go slower than back home?"

"Yes…"

"How long would you say we've been here so far? Six, seven hours?"

"Hmm…" The realisation of where Ben was headed with this was dawning on the others.

"Well, I don't know what that might relate to on Earth, but it could be well over a day that's passed." Ben rubbed his forehead.

"And our parents will be going spare," Jake said, finishing the thought Ben had started.

"Yes. A few hours and they wouldn't notice. A day and they'll have called the police. However much longer it takes us to get home, we're going to be in some serious trouble."

Sam started to panic. He hated trouble. "We need to come up with a story. Something they'll have to believe, that makes sense of where we've been."

"Well, we can hardly tell them the truth, can we?" said Jake, sarcastically. "Sorry we've been missing for days, Mum, but we've been in another world, doing battle with an evil tyrant."

"I was just saying—"

"Well, don't, it's obvious we have to come up with a story. Now isn't the right time."

"OK, that's enough," said Ben, trying to defuse the rising tensions. "We need to stay calm, focussed and together. Jake, you're right. We need to think about how we can get back to Earth first. I think our best, perhaps our only bet is to try and convince Taegan to take us. Apart from anything else, we need their protection."

They all agreed with that.

"So, what do we do know?" asked Sam.

Ben shrugged. "We wait."

The mood in the camp was as gloomy as the room they were sat in, and time seemed to stretch out tortuously. Conversation wilted as each retreated into their own thoughts. Then there was a knock at the door. They all looked at each other.

"You expecting visitors?" joked Jake.

"Er... come in?" called Ben, feeling decidedly odd about inviting someone into their cell.

The handle twisted and the door opened a little. Manatang poked his head into the room.

"Manatang!" exclaimed Ben. "You're OK!"

"Of course I am," said Manatang, looking puzzled. "Why wouldn't I be?"

"Because you were unconscious when we last saw you."

"Oh... that. Well, doing magic tires me out no end these days. There's not much left of it, you see, so I try to use as little as possible, but it was necessary to open the door. Anyway, I'm rambling, how are you?"

Ben's politeness reflex kicked in before he had a chance to consider Manatang's words. "We're all fine – you sure you're OK?"

"Yeah, nothing to worry about. I was just resting." Manatang paused, looking around the room. In the candlelight his fur looked a dark ginger colour, untidy and shaggy. "So, you brought back others, despite my warning?"

Ben cast a furtive glance at his friends. "Yes, it... it was a mistake. We shouldn't be here."

"Damn skippy," hooted Manatang. "But now that you are, why don't you introduce me?"

"Of course," said Ben. "This here's Jake—"

"Howdy," said Jake, tipping an imaginary hat at Manatang.

Ben swept his arm towards Sam. "This is Sam."

"Hello," said Sam. Manatang tipped an imaginary hat at him, assuming this now to be a customary welcome. Sam laughed.

"And finally, this is Heather."

"Hi," said Heather, offering her hand towards Manatang, who took it cautiously, unsure of what to do. Heather shook it, and when she released it, Manatang looked at his hand, perplexed.

"Everyone, this, of course, is Manatang." Manatang bowed.

Ben lowered his voice to a conspiratorial whisper. "We need to get home, Manatang. Our families will be worried about us, and as long as we're here the more worried they'll get. Can you and your friends help us get home?"

Manatang chewed his lip. "I should imagine that's all they're talking about doing."

"You mean they're going to take us back?"

"Well, I can't see any reason why they'd want you hanging round here. Complete liability, you lot."

"We're not liabilities," complained Jake. Ben glowered at him to shut him up.

"That's great," said Ben. "When do you think we can go?"

"I don't know," said Manatang. "You need to eat first, and I'm sure the plan will be discussed at dinner. But that's not why I came to see you." Now it was Manatang who lowered his voice. "I just came to say that all four of you turning up here has really ruffled Taegan's feathers."

"We're sorry—" began Ben, before Manatang cut him off.

"But I promise you he does have your best interests at heart. He's concerned for your safety, not your feelings, and if he's a bit gruff, just don't take it personally. He's got a lot on his plate, and worrying about what your appearance here means is an added stress he doesn't need."

Ben raised an eyebrow. "What might our appearance here mean?"

Manatang screwed up his eyes, inwardly cursing his loose mouth. "Nothing, just ignore me. My point was that Taegan will do what's best for you, you'll see."

Ben wasn't going to be fobbed off so easily. "But our being here, our being able to come here through the portal means something, doesn't it? It's important somehow. Please, Manatang, if you know anything, tell me what it is," he implored.

"It's not for me to say," he said, turning his back on Ben. "Taegan will tell you as much as you need to know."

"But I know there's a reason for me being here – there just has to be," he pleaded. "What do you think it is?"

"I should go," said Manatang, walking to the door. "But remember what I said: Taegan is your friend."

Ben sighed. He was frustrated with Manatang, but he didn't want to take it out on him. He probably counted as his only friend in the Shadow Realm.

They waved at Manatang as he disappeared around the door and shut it. The lock clicked back into place.

"Is anyone else really freaked out by him?" asked Jake.

About half an hour later they heard the key being turned again, the door this time being flung wide open. Elena, with her fantastic blue hair, was stood there with hands firmly placed on her curvy hips.

"Right, you lot," she said in that soft, lilting accent. "Come with me."

She walked away from the bedroom quickly, and they all raced to keep up with her.

They wound their way deeper into the rebel base; a damp, musty smell filled their nostrils as they sank deeper into the fetid, underground air. The occasional flickering torch flame on the walls lit the way, barely illuminating the floor, which occasionally got boggy underfoot, their shoes sticking in the viscous mud.

"This place is a hole," murmured Jake.

Ben ignored him. A shabby-looking man shuffled past, barely paying them any attention as he suffered in his own private world. An old lady leant in a doorway as they passed, her gristly features set in a mucky frown. Ben smiled and said 'hello', receiving a stern glare for his troubles.

They crossed a larger hallway with a few wooden archways leading off, wood now underfoot to combat the mud.

"This must be the king's quarters," muttered Jake.

"Ssh," Ben admonished him.

He peered through one of the archways to the room beyond, which was long and wide, stretching off for maybe fifty yards. There were beds lined up against each side, the occupants of which were either lying still or sitting up and looking into the distance. A few hardy souls were limping slowly around, their grey, lifeless faces impassive. A lot of people were coughing.

"What is this place?" asked Ben.

"This is our infirmary," said Elena, without even looking. "Sadly, it's getting fuller by the day. We won't have anywhere to put the sick soon."

"Why are more people getting ill?" asked Heather.

But Elena didn't answer; she just kept on walking.

They stopped at an archway that had a door made of hanging beads, which Elena pulled back and held, gesturing for them to enter. The room they walked into was about the size of an average living room, with a small, unlit fireplace set into one wall and a sturdy oak table stood in the middle. Around the table were six chairs, each with a high wooden back with strange runes and symbols carved into them.

There were a few candles in this room to dispel the gloom, and Ben could see Taegan sitting at the head of the table. He looked in deep, contemplative thought, his brow furrowed with large creases and his mouth settled in a grim frown. His blond hair shimmered slightly in the soft light. He motioned to the chairs for them to sit down.

"Please, sit." His voice was calm, dulcet and yet determined in its purpose. Elena took her place next to him.

Not quite as grand as Blackwood's place, thought Ben as he sat down. *But a throne room, nonetheless – a place to conduct the business of war.*

The wood felt hard and uncomfortable, engineered to keep its occupant alert, on edge. Taegan didn't say anything for a long while, and Ben wondered whether he was meant to say something first. The silence was stretched and got so awkward that Ben cleared his throat, preparing to speak.

Taegan then spoke quickly and calmly, directing his question at Ben. "How did you get here?"

Ben blinked. He had his own questions but, remembering what Manatang had said, thought maybe he should answer Taegan's first, to keep him onside.

"We arrived here through a portal I found in the forest. The New Forest." Ben glanced at the others, and then added almost apologetically, "In England, on the planet Earth."

Taegan considered this for a moment, folding his hands in front of him. "And how, exactly, do you think you got here?"

"There's a kind of doorway, a portal between our worlds, out there in the woods. I'm sure I could show you it if you could take us back to the clearing."

"All in good time," murmured Taegan.

"Excuse me, Mr Taegan, sir," began Jake, in a polite tone that Ben knew meant a cheeky question was coming. "But would you mind telling us where the hell we are, *exactly?*"

Taegan began drumming his fingers on the table, regarding Jake coolly. "If my theory is right, then you are still on Earth. Just not your Earth."

"What do you mean?" asked Ben.

Taegan ran his fingers through his long hair, considering what to tell these children. "We have a legend here, in Sunea, that there was once a time when the early druids could travel between dimensions, that our earliest origins were from a nomadic tribe who would hop from world to world before they came here. To evade a fearsome enemy, so the legend goes, those druids decided to settle here, and over time the magic that enabled them to skip between dimensions was lost. I'm not yet sure how, but it may well be that you have stumbled upon a portal between our two worlds, between our dimensions. So, whilst this is not your Earth, it is *an Earth*; in some sense they're the same place, just different."

Ben nodded. It made sense to him – the portal was just that: a gateway to another dimension.

"What I'm struggling with is how you've been able to travel through such a portal. Inter-dimensional travel has long been studied by the greatest mages, and they were unable to master it, unable to siphon any truth from the legends. So, what I want to know is, how did you do it?"

"I'm not sure, really," answered Ben, truthfully. "It was an accident the first time. It just sort of... happened."

"Do you think you can travel through it again to get home?"

"I'd be certain of it. Since the first time I travelled through it's been getting easier to do."

Taegan considered all this in concerned silence, his fingers placed on his lips.

"Do you think there's a reason I can do it?" asked Ben eagerly. "Do you think it's important I'm here?"

Taegan frowned, pausing to choose his next words carefully. "Our world finds itself at a perilous crossroad. Its current path, the one which Lord Blackwood has forced upon us, has yielded the destruction of all that was good in Sunea. We cannot go on much longer like this; our world is dying, and if we cannot change its course, if we cannot salvage something from the ruin and decay above our heads, we shall all perish with it. The path to salvation is a long and winding one, but it begins with us vanquishing Lord Blackwood. That is our only objective, our only hope to save our world."

He paused to catch his breath. Elena instinctively laid an encouraging hand on his shoulder, which he grasped firmly.

"It is my belief," he continued, "that your appearance here is a serious danger to that objective, as much to our world as it is your own. I think it is imperative that we get you home, and to ensure you never come back."

Ben was stunned. *A serious danger?* He hadn't expected Taegan to say that; he was sure there was some other reason, some importance to him being here. Before he could say anything, though, Sam jumped in.

"Excellent," he enthused. "That's all we want too: to go home."

"To reduce the risk of re-capture by Blackwood, we will go under the cover of Galle's fog."

"Right... what's that?" asked Jake.

"It has come every week since the destruction of Sunea and prevents any magical activity whilst it is here. It represents our best chance of remaining hidden."

Sam coughed. "Er, did you say it only comes once a week?"

Ben suddenly realised what that meant. "But we can't stay here that long – we're already causing our families untold grief every hour we're here."

"Well then, you shouldn't have come, should you?" shouted Taegan, annoyed with their petulance. He breathed deeply to calm himself down. "We will help you get home, but this is non-negotiable. The fog is our only chance to get you to the portal safely. The good news is it will be here again within thirty-six hours."

Ben did some quick calculations in his head. That probably equated to a week on Earth. He hung his head in his hands, devastated at this delay. They were going to be in a *lot* of trouble when they got home.

"There's no other way?" asked Ben.

"No," Taegan said firmly.

Ben sighed. "We best get settled in then."

CHAPTER 14

Taegan shifted in his chair, clapping his hands together to indicate the discussion was officially over. "Now, we eat."

On cue, a young girl with mousy-brown hair that looked like it had never been washed, came in carrying a tray and plonked it down untidily in the middle of the table. On the tray was some hard-looking bread, a bowl of gooey stuff that looked a bit like porridge and some small, charred pieces of meat. *Better to not ask where that came from*, thought Ben.

She placed a jug down next to the tray, which sloshed with a red liquid.

Jake eyed the jug excitedly. "Is that wine?"

"Yes," grunted Taegan, already spooning some of the gruel and meat on to his plate. "Wine is pretty much all we have left to drink," he explained. "Bar the underground reserves of water. Nasty, stagnant stuff, that it is."

"The wine or the water?" Jake smirked.

"Both!" Taegan let out a gruff laugh, the first time they'd seen any sign of a sense of humour from him. The serving girl, having finished her duty with the food, turned her attention to the fire, shovelling charcoal into the grate from a bucket by the side. When she was finished, she curtsied nervously to Taegan and left without so much a glance at the visitors. Taegan eyed the fireplace and clicked his fingers. The charcoal lit instantly, the fire quickly ablaze and the room came alive with dancing shadows.

With Taegan apparently in a better mood, Ben thought it might be a good opportunity to get some of his own questions answered.

"Quite the place you have here, did you build it yourselves?" His tone was innocent, polite and enquiring only.

Taegan still eyed Ben suspiciously. "Some of it was here before us, but yes, we have built most of it ourselves since the war began. It's modest, but it suits our purpose."

"How many rebels are there?" Jake chipped in.

"Not enough," growled Taegan.

Ben changed the subject. "Where's Sofiella?" he asked.

Taegan raised an eyebrow. "She is resting. She's had quite an ordeal at the hands of Lord Blackwood."

Jake poured himself some of the wine, quaffed a bit, then pulled a sour face like he'd just drunk vinegar.

"Is she someone important to you?" Ben wanted to understand her relationship with Taegan, after he became so keen to rescue her once he knew it was her in the prison. He reckoned he was probably old enough to be her father, just, but doubted that was it.

Taegan waved a hand dismissively. "We go back a long way. No-one knew what had happened to her after the confusion of the great crash, but I had my suspicions Blackwood had her."

"Why did you not try and rescue her before?" queried Jake.

Taegan grew visibly irritated at the question, staring at Jake with murderous eyes. "You have no idea how much we risked rescuing you, do you? Lord Blackwood is extremely dangerous; he will kill any of us on sight. We didn't know where Sofiella was, and Blackwood has many castles in this land. I can't risk people's lives on a wild goose chase."

Jake looked down, chastened.

Taegan's face softened a little. "But it is good fortune that you helped us find her. I'm grateful for that."

Sam had been quiet so far, his arms crossed, but he was plainly confused now. "If it's so risky, why did you come to get us? Why bother if you're just going to send us home? What good is that to you? Why not just leave us to rot?"

Taegan chewed on a piece of meat. "As I said, I don't think your appearance from another dimension does anything except strengthen Blackwood's position. The best thing I can do is ensure you go home and never come back."

There was silence for a moment, before Ben leant forwards in his seat and spoke softly: "But what if we can help?"

"I beg your pardon?"

"What if we could help you defeat Blackwood?"

Taegan laughed again, this time a full, guttural belly laugh that echoed off the walls of the small chamber. After several seconds he began to calm down. "You? What could you do against Lord Blackwood?" he mocked.

Ben's shoulders dropped, his pride deflated. "I… I don't know. I just think there's some reason we're here, some way we can help."

"Do you know magic?"

"Well, no, but—"

"Then I fail to see how you can help." Taegan finished the sentence abruptly, turning his attention back to his food. Ben picked at his, trying a little of the gruel, which tasted like liquid ash, and some of the wine, which actually did taste of vinegar. He tried to eat as much as he could so as not to appear rude, as did Sam, but Jake and Heather didn't really touch theirs at all.

Taegan noticed this and grunted. "We used to have fantastic food, you know. Beautiful meat and sumptuous vegetables, seasoned with some of the most magical flavours known to history." A darkness passed across his face. "All that is gone now."

Heather shifted uneasily, the soft orange light of the fire reflected in her ginger hair. "What did the Shadow Realm used to be like?" she enquired.

Taegan looked at her, almost through her, as he looked back in time wistfully. "Sunea was a beautiful land," he began. "Bathed in glorious sunshine and flourishing with life, it was so colourful. One could take great pleasure from the simple things, like sitting down by the river, underneath the green canopy of the forest, and watching the fish swim by. But it was such a complex and wonderful realm too, with many cities that stretched from coast to coast. The provinces were united, but each had their own flavour, their own way of living, that one could spend many happy years visiting each and finding what treasures and delicacies were on offer." His eyes glassed over as he remembered a world that once was.

Most of the smoke from the fire was going up the flue, but the room was still filling with a hazy smog. Ben coughed. "Er, so what happened? Why is it now the way it is?"

A look of thunder struck Taegan's face. "Due to the relentless quest of Lord Blackwood to be the only power in the world." He sighed, stilling his rising anger. "Although, the truth is that even without Blackwood, the world was headed for ruin. He merely sped things up and enjoyed the ride."

"How so?" asked Heather, sympathy in her voice.

Taegan sighed. "It's a long story," he said impassively.

"It appears we've got quite a lot of time," she replied.

Taegan looked at her, blinking, as if deciding where to start. "We used to be a very powerful world," he said finally, closing his eyes in remembrance. "All of Sunea had basked in glorious peace for millennia and had built a magnificent economy fuelled by magic."

Ben was fascinated. "What exactly is this 'magic'? It's not something we have in our world."

Taegan put down his fork. "That is a complex question indeed," he said, putting his finger on his mouth and tapping. A silence passed for several seconds. "And not one I'm best placed to answer. Perhaps we will take you to our mage later and he can answer that."

Elena smirked, wiping her mouth with the back of her hands.

"What I can tell you is that the magic we had ebbed tirelessly into the world from the Driatic wells."

"The Driatic wells?"

"All of the magic that we use comes from, or at least came from, Driatic wells. They're a bit like the portal to your world, only these dimensional rifts are buried deep underground. Magic seeps into the world from them, providing a background radiation of magic that can be used by anyone. But there wasn't much of it, so it was used sporadically and only by those trained to harness it. Of course, there wasn't enough of it to keep the early mages thirst quenched, so they needed to find a way to tap into the portals, and that's what they did. They devised the Driatic wells, which allowed them to siphon off magic from these dimensional rifts in larger quantities. Only the mages had access to the wells, building vast monasteries over them to protect the wells from others, and so that only they could use the magic contained within. It turned them into powerful rulers of the districts they commanded."

"Sounds very feudal," Jake commented, as shadows flickered across his face.

Taegan raised an eyebrow quizzically. "They were powerful but fair. Under their leadership, local villages and their inhabitants prospered. However, over time, ordinary folk also wanted access to magic, which they felt they had a right to. They realised they could have a better standard of living if they could use the magic themselves, but the mages resisted because they feared losing their power, and the possibility that the magic would be misused. Eventually, in a bid to quell a popular uprising, the mages granted the right of 'Meritus veneficus' – the right for ordinary people to 'earn' magic. They surmised – correctly, as it happened – that if they forced people to work to get magic, it wouldn't be abused and would help to create a thriving economy. Within two hundred years, Sunea was transformed into a glorious string of wondrous cities, locked together in a magical economy in which personal ambition and hard work were rewarded with magical ability. This of course led to an easier life for all citizens, as they used magic to help them with everyday stuff, giving them more time to focus on other pursuits."

"Like what?" questioned Ben.

Taegan shrugged. "Whatever they liked – art, sport, making more magic. We were a free society in which creativity prospered."

"So, what went wrong?"

"Greed," said Taegan matter-of-factly. "Avarice, jealousy, whatever you want to call it. The system slowly went out of balance, and fewer and fewer people had access to more and more of the magic."

"That sounds a little familiar," said Ben, thinking of money and how the rich were getting richer back on Earth.

"Your world didn't end, though, did it? What started off as a great balancing of magical power from the mages to the common folk, had ended up putting it back in the hands of those who had all the power in the first place – the High Mages. Only this time, they had no need to quell popular opinion, as just enough magic was left over for enough people to get by. Those who couldn't get access to magic had a very harsh life indeed." Taegan sighed, recollecting the inequality of life in late Sunea.

He paused, studying the faces of the teenagers, who were all now rapt in his story.

"Lord Blackwood was one of those High Mages," he continued. "But whilst the others were happy to be part of a club that controlled most of the magic, he wanted it all."

"So how did he get it?" asked Ben.

"He didn't," replied Taegan. "His quest for power led him to fixate on an ancient amulet – the Star of Moirai – which was said to be what gave the first druids their awesome magic and their ability to cross dimensions."

"That's quite some amulet," Jake remarked.

Taegan fixed him with a steely look. "It is indeed; however, the legends surrounding its use tell us that one of the reasons the original druids stopped dimension-hopping was because the amulet had become unstable and that to use it again was to risk a terrible cataclysm. They put extremely strong spells around it to prevent it ever being used again, and ever since then the amulet and those spells have been protected by the order of the High Mages. There was no way they could allow him to have it."

"So why would Blackwood look to use it if that was the case?" said Ben, confused.

Taegan breathed in, wearying of this historic tale. "Because he didn't believe the legend. Or if he did, he hoped to be able to escape to another dimension, one where he could have all the magic to himself. He had grown rather demented, and no logic or reason could be used with him."

Taegan looked down, emotions playing on him as he remembered the painful, vivid past.

"Every High Mage had to willingly unlock their part of the spell protecting the Star in order for it to be used, but of course they all refused. The only alternative for Blackwood was to kill them all, to release the Star from their spells. A terrible war ensued that pitched Blackwood and those loyal to him against the High Mages. Killing a high mage isn't easy, and the war was bitterly fought – many of us believed that it was a war for the very life of this world. Alas, you can see for yourselves that we were right. Lord Blackwood has brought nothing but death and darkness to Sunea, and we've been locked in the same bitter struggle to defeat him for the last four years."

"So," Sam deduced, "the war was responsible for Sunea looking like it does now. But how? Did Blackwood get the Star of Moirai?"

"Yes," said Ben, picking up on what Taegan had said earlier. "You spoke of a great crash? Is that what happened when he tried to use it?"

"That was the... event... that turned this world to Shadow, yes. The Star was activated, and it wiped out life on a massive scale, plunging us all into eternal darkness."

"But you also said that the Star could be used to control magic in all dimensions," said Ben. "How come Blackwood is still here and not in some other dimension?"

Taegan looked at Ben through the smoky air for a few seconds, before tears sprang to his eyes and he blinked to wipe them away.

"Because Blackwood didn't use the Star," he said. "I did."

CHAPTER 15

There was a stunned silence, as Ben and the others stayed quiet, unsure of what to say. Taegan just sat there, softly whimpering and occasionally imbibing some wine. Eventually, Ben spoke.

"So… you used the Star?" he said carefully.

Taegan looked at him; the guilt and remorse radiating from his eyes was slowly replaced by defiance. "I had to," he roared. "There was no other choice. Blackwood had won; he had defeated the mages." He looked down, his voice softening. "Including my master."

"Did your master have the Star?" he asked.

"No," said Taegan. "But he was the last High Mage, and Lord Blackwood was on his way to murder him. He told me to go and sit with the Star, and that he would wait for Blackwood to arrive. His plan was to sacrifice himself to Blackwood, unlocking the last spell that protected the Star. He wanted me to use it before Blackwood could get there, to keep it out of his hands." He paused, a subdued grief bubbling up in his voice. "My master told me that the Star could only be used by someone who had a pure heart, but that there was still a considerable risk of it causing untold damage. So, I took along the only person I knew who had the purest of hearts… my wife."

Ben was surprised. "You wanted your wife to use the Star?"

Taegan recoiled at the memory. "You don't understand what it was like in those last moments," he wailed. "All was lost. If we did nothing, there was no chance for Sunea, none at all. We had to do something, anything, no matter how desperate it was, to keep control of our destiny." Taegan's shoulders dropped. "At least, so we thought."

"So, what happened?"

"My wife, Lenara, and I managed to reach the Star amidst the last convulsions of war between the mages and Blackwood. It really was the most violent and horrible time imaginable; the world was ending. We couldn't allow Blackwood to get his hands on the Star, or it would be game over – not just for us but for all other dimensions too. Lord Blackwood won, defeating my master, the last mage, and the Star was unlocked. We were there at the Star's chamber, Lenara and I, and I had hoped, in some way, to be able to use the Star with her, to have the Star's power penetrate into both of us." Taegan pinched his eyes. "Unfortunately, the headstart my master had bought us didn't last long, and Blackwood arrived. So, I had to tackle him to give my wife the precious few seconds she needed to activate it."

Taegan cricked his neck, closing his eyes and apparently forgetting anyone else was there.

Jake grew impatient. "And then what?"

"And then pain, death and destruction, that's what, on a scale that no-one could have imagined possible." He snorted. "I guess my wife wasn't as pure as I'd hoped."

Ben suppressed the inappropriate urge to laugh.

"So why didn't the Star work?" asked Heather.

"Oh, it did," Taegan growled. "My wife disappeared, I have no idea where, most probably to another dimension. And the prophecy about its use precipitating the end of the world came true. Look at the trees, look at the sky. This world is dead, and it was us using the Star that did it." Taegan held his head, grief-stricken and tired from the story. To his side, Elena rested her hand on his arm, trying to comfort him.

"The same would have happened if Blackwood had used the Star," she said, wheeling out an argument she'd obviously used many times before. "It's better he didn't get it."

Taegan looked up quickly, startling them, a renewed conviction in his eyes. "Lord Blackwood fights on; thus, we fight on. We do so in the hope that all is not lost forever, that one day we will defeat him, Lenara will return and the glory of Sunea can be restored."

Silence hung heavy and pregnant around the table. Ben still had questions, though.

"Why does Lord Blackwood have any power now, if you were able to prevent him from getting the Star?"

Taegan grunted. "He had already defeated the mages; removing the Star from his grasp just meant he couldn't have unlimited power. Now, though, he controls access to the last working Driatic well, which is buried underneath the monastery, here in Udon."

"Is that the name of the town?"

"No, that is Rumsea. Udon is our province. But that well is how he and his loyal cronies can still do magic, at will. In time, that too will fail, but I fear it will be too late to help us." Taegan sighed, scratching his chin. "We harvest what magic we can from the dregs left in the world. Scraps, really, that we hope to build together to have enough to stage a viable attack." Taegan sighed again. "We had to use half our resources to get you lot out."

Ben understood then why Taegan was so irate and gruff with them since their rescue – he'd had to use up valuable magic to save them. By coming here and getting caught, Ben had set the rebels back months, if not years. He felt awful.

"I'm sorry," he said.

Taegan looked at him contemptuously. "What's done is done."

Sam tried to stifle a yawn, stretching his arms as he did.

Taegan noticed and stood quickly, clapping his hands. "I think it's time for some rest. You've had a hard day." He touched Elena on the shoulder. "Can you show them back to the room for me?" It wasn't really a question, as he strode out of the room without so much as another word.

"Of course," she murmured. She really was rather strikingly beautiful, Ben noticed, curvaceous and lithe at the same time. He found himself unable to draw his gaze from her soft face; she winked at him when she saw him staring, and he looked away, red-faced. "Follow me," she purred.

She led them out of the room and back down the maze of corridors. They wound their way through the labyrinth, passing all sorts of different people, who stopped and stared in dumb amazement at the clean, young people. They had to step over one old and shrivelled man, who was resting on the floor, trying to snatch some sleep. He grabbed Ben's foot as he went past, shouting something loud and unintelligible at him. As Ben flailed and hopped around trying to keep his balance, Elena spoke to the old man in gentle, calming tones, until he let go, muttering quietly to himself. They continued shuffling along the dark tunnels until they reached the room they had been locked in earlier.

"Obviously this is our bedroom then," whispered Jake. "But still only one bunkbed."

"That's one more than a lot of the other people here," Ben whispered back, annoyed at Jake's lack of compassion. However, with room on the bunkbed for two, and one on the sofa, it did mean it was going to be an uncomfortable night for at least one of them on the floor.

Elena put her hand on Ben's shoulder, pulling him back towards the door. "Talk with me for a moment, will you?" she asked him.

The others looked at Ben with concern.

"I'll be fine," he reassured them, before Elena shut the door.

She was tall, at least six feet, so she had to stoop for him, resting her hands on his shoulders. Her eyes were a dazzling green, gleaming with an energy of their own, despite the low light.

"I just want you to know," she breathed, "that whatever Taegan says, I think that you are special, that you must be here for a reason." She turned her head, coyly, checking up and down the corridor, before looking back at Ben and tittering. "Who knows, maybe even the prophecy is coming true."

"The proph—"

Elena cut Ben off by placing a finger on his lips. "Ssh," she hushed. "Whatever your reason for being here, I'm sure all will become clear in the fullness of time. Until then," she said, leaning in and kissing him on the cheek, "rest well." She stood up straight and sauntered off, leaving Ben standing outside his room, confused and elated at the same time. He watched her disappear around the corner, before he opened the door and walked back into the grimly lit bedroom.

Three expectant faces looked at him.

"What was all that about?" asked Jake.

"You wouldn't believe me if I told you."

"Come on, don't hold out on us," he implored.

"She kissed me."

The other three roared with laughter. "Get out of here," mocked Jake.

"I did say you wouldn't believe me," said Ben, walking over to the sofa and lying down on it. "She also said that you should take the floor tonight."

He laughed back at Jake, who now stood perplexed and indignant as Heather and Sam scrambled for the bunkbed, Sam bounding up to the top bunk as Heather dived into the bottom.

Jake stood there with his hands on his hips, mild fury in his face. "Damn it," he muttered. His shoulders dropped. "At least give me a cushion."

Ben threw a cushion from the sofa at Jake, who fell backwards under the unexpected salvo. He landed in a heap on the floor and started laughing, sending impulsive high spirits coursing through the air.

It didn't take long for those spirits to fade, however, as they discussed the gravity of their situation. Their foray into the Shadow Realm had been nothing short of disastrous, yet they realised they were incredibly lucky still to be alive.

Ben blew out the candle, plunging them into an intense darkness that suffocated the urge to speak. He drifted into a fitful sleep, punctuated by terrifying dreams of Lord Blackwood coming to kill him in ever more violent ways. Each time he would wake up sweating, reaching out in the dark to protect himself. Fortunately, he didn't scream or shout, so his suffering was kept hidden from his slumbering friends, but it was one of the longest and loneliest nights he had ever endured.

The door creaked open in the morning and Elena crept in with a candle, placing it on a table by the bunkbed. The soft orange light flickered playfully on the walls, waking the four of them slowly, groggily.

"Morning, all," she chirped. She was wearing what appeared to be a hessian sack, although it had been tailored to fit. Her blue hair was un-plaited, hanging freely in waves around her torso. "Did you sleep well?"

It was an endearing question, one that gave Ben a reverberating pang of homesickness; how he wished he was back in the safe fold of his parents' embrace.

"Fine," said Jake, responding when no-one else did, "for a floor."

Elena looked embarrassed, glancing at her feet. "Yes, apologies about the accommodation we can offer. We don't have a lot of space or beds, unfortunately…"

"It's absolutely fine," said Ben firmly, shooting a reproving glance at Jake. "We're the ones who have inconvenienced you, not the other way around. We shouldn't be here at all."

She broke out into a smile. "Well, you're here now, and I'd like to be a good host, so we've got breakfast for you. I'll give you ten minutes to get yourselves straight and then I'll come back to get you."

"Thank you," said Ben quickly, cutting Jake off from saying anything else.

She smiled at Ben and left, closing the door behind her.

Elena knocked on the door ten minutes later, although with no running water it had only taken them a minute to get themselves straight, the en-suite being only a bucket in the corner. She opened the door and beckoned them to follow her, which they dutifully did.

She took them a different way to where they'd gone the evening before; this time the tunnels led gently upwards, until they came to a wide corridor with giant oak doors set into the far side. They'd been pushed right open to reveal a cavernous dining area, where row upon row of wooden tables wove their way up and down the length of the hall. A head table sat proudly on a raised platform at the far end of the hall, flanked by candelabras. It was all quite medieval and rustic. *And rather convivial*, thought Ben.

Despite the large seating arrangements, the tables were only about a quarter full, most of the inhabitants of this underground base sitting close to the head table. The general hubbub and good-natured banter dimmed into a hush as the four kids appeared at the door.

Ben gulped. It was like something out of a Wild West film. There must have been over a hundred people in there, all now sitting quietly and looking directly at them. The silence was over-bearing, like the heavy peace of a cathedral in prayer. Ben felt the hot gaze of all those eyes upon him, and the redness of embarrassment creeping across his face.

Elena shepherded them in and there was an explosion of hushed whispers and pointed fingers. Ben detected a distinct excitement buzzing in the air of those careful conversations – an undercurrent of joy at their appearance, rather than the distrust he had expected. Feeling slightly buoyed, Ben took his seat at the table that Elena indicated, where a shabby-looking man and a thin woman both sat, dressed in ragtag clothes. He tried a sympathetic smile, earning only a blush from the woman and a frown from the man.

His breakfast came and wiped the smile off his face; delivered by another young girl, no older than eight or nine, she could do no more than place the bowl of gruel and water in front of Ben before running off, shy and abashed. He looked at the gloopy soup and suspect glass of water, hoping and praying he would be back home with some soft toilet paper before any of this made its way through his system.

Elena was looking at him expectantly, waiting for him to wolf down his breakfast. Ben took a few careful mouthfuls before setting his spoon down as the bile rose in his throat. He managed to contain himself, until Elena had busied herself with another man further down the table. He sighed and pushed the gruel away, his stomach rumbling.

"Something wrong?" asked Sofiella, as she sat down next to Ben.

"N… No," spluttered Ben. "I just… feel a bit ill."

"Oh dear, you should have some food," she said, concern in her voice.

"We would if there were any here," muttered Jake from across the table.

"Pardon?" said Sofiella.

"I'll be fine," said Ben loudly, cutting across Jake. Ben hadn't known if he'd see her again, but now here she was, and Ben began to feel butterflies in his stomach. She'd got cleaned up, her long blonde hair now bouncing softly down around her shoulders, her skin delicate and smooth. Her piercing blue eyes studied him keenly, and he began to feel himself lost in them.

She took his hand, and Ben thought he might faint.

"I just wanted to thank you, personally, for what you did for me."

"Oh, it was nothi—" Ben tried to interject.

"It was extremely brave," she said, lowering her face to peer up at him. It made her look very cute. "If you hadn't come back for me, I would still be languishing in that cell, and not long for this world." She looked down, sadness overcoming her. "Unfortunately, I don't think this world has long either."

Ben squeezed her hand. "We'll make it better again."

Sofiella looked back at him, sorrow plain in her eyes. "Your optimism is commendable, Ben. But you don't understand what's going on here. How could you?" She touched him on the shoulder and stood up. "Have a safe journey home."

"But…" started Ben, but she was already walking off. Ben sat there, feeling impotent and entirely useless. He was just a burden, a nuisance to this world, and all he'd really achieved was to put his friends, as well as the occupants of this world, in danger.

The feeling was still there, though, deep in his bones, that he *could* help, that there was a purpose for his being here. Trans-dimensional travel doesn't happen every day, he reasoned, so there *must* be some reason why he could do it, why he was here.

But how could he help? He couldn't do magic, so what use would he be against such a powerful enemy?

"You look very glum," said Heather as she sidled up to Ben, a smile on her face in an effort to cheer him up. Her freckles had receded dramatically in the bleakness of the Shadow Realm.

Ben somehow summoned the energy to smile back. "I just feel so… stupid," he sighed. "Coming here, putting you all in danger, and for what? To go straight back home with our tails between our legs, and probably get the mother of all groundings even if we do get home."

"Of course we'll get home," she said soothingly. "And I, for one, am very glad you brought us here."

"You are?" he said, surprised.

"Sure." She nudged him. "It cleared up whether you were crazy or not, didn't it?"

They both chuckled, but the cloud still hung heavy over Ben.

"What on Earth are we going to say when we get home?" he said in exasperation.

Heather put her arm around him, slightly awkwardly, and tried to give her best reassuring look. "Let's get home first. Then we'll get through it like we always do – together."

At that moment Taegan walked into the room, his chiselled jaw set with an iron purpose. Scanning the room quickly he found the four of them and strode over, sitting down briskly.

"The good news," he said, foregoing any niceties, "is that it appears Galle's fog is coming in a little early. We should be good to go in an hour."

"But that's excellent!" Sam chimed.

"I haven't told you the bad news yet."

Sam's smile dropped instantly. Ben shifted uneasily in his seat.

"Which is?" asked Ben.

"We're getting reports from our outposts that Blackwood is mobilising every minion he can to be on the lookout for you. I think he'll guess our plan is to use the fog as cover to get you home. I think it's likely he'll be waiting at the portal for us to make our move."

Ben had to agree; there was no way Blackwood wouldn't have the portal site under surveillance.

"So, what do we do?" asked Jake.

Taegan raised his eyebrows and let out a sigh. "We walk into his trap."

"What?!" yelled Sam, so that everyone in the room who had been pretending not to listen to their conversation dropped the pretence and stared straight at them.

"Keep your voice down," he hushed. "We're going to have to create a diversion at the portal site, something that will distract Blackwood long enough for you to get back through to your world."

"And how do you propose to do that?" asked Ben.

Taegan looked down. "I don't know." He started rubbing his hands together nervously. "What I do know is that this will be our only chance. When the mist comes early it doesn't tend to stay very long. We'll have a couple of hours tops before it lifts, and we'll be vulnerable to him again."

They sat there, contemplating what Taegan was proposing. Jake piped up first. "Why doesn't Lord Blackwood know where we are now?"

"We're able to throw up a protective shield around the base that conceals its presence. The magic is based on our research of Galle's fog. It does cost us quite a lot in magical resource, so much so that we have several individuals whose sole purpose it is to gather magic just to keep the shield going. Needless to say, without it, we wouldn't last very long."

"This Galle's fog," began Ben, "it will protect us from Blackwood?"

"It gives us a chance," replied Taegan.

"And we only have this one chance to get to the portal?"

"Yes," he sighed.

Ben thought for a moment. "Let's do it," he said, looking to the others for support. They all nodded their heads, though fear was etched in their faces.

Taegan stood up abruptly. "Good, because it wasn't a question."

He turned sharply and marched out of the dining room, leaving them to the remains of their horrible breakfast.

"Look on the bright side," said Jake, "at least you won't have to face much more of this food."

"It's not the food I'm worried about facing," Sam said, laughing nervously. "It's the evil sorcerer infatuated with catching us that worries me most."

Ben didn't say anything. He felt their fear too; in an hour or so they'd be leaving this place to walk into a trap. The prize for success was getting home. Failure would bring capture by Lord Blackwood, a lot of pain and, in all probability, death.

He had never been so scared in his life.

CHAPTER 16

Trying to while away the next hour was one of the most painfully long and uncomfortable experiences of Ben's life. They had returned to their bedroom to await the summons to leave, and now they were just sat around, barely saying a word to each other, their nerves frayed and burnt at the edges. It was excruciating torture. Ben decided that as it was his fault they were here, he should at least try to say something.

"I know it's pretty scary, guys, but I think we can do this. We've got the cover of the fog, and there's a plan to distract Lord Blackwood. We just have to do our bit and get through the portal, but we have to stay close – we have to stay together."

Heather and Sam managed a feeble smile, though Jake looked disdainful.

"Do you really believe we can make it?" he sneered.

"I have to, what's the alternative?"

Jake just grunted.

"We need to be together on this, Jake. We're not going to get home otherwise."

Jake exploded. "Of course we're not going to get home. We're walking straight into a trap, and you think that idiot out there can protect us? You heard him, Blackwood has unlimited power here, and what have we got? Nothing. Just a bunch of pathetic rebels and a talking monkey."

Jake's outburst ended and a harsh silence settled over the group again. Ben was about to reply, to try and talk Jake round, when Heather spoke.

"You're so selfish, Jake," she said, standing up to her brother. "At least Ben's trying to stay positive, keep our spirits up. All you can do is snipe. Taegan didn't ask for us to come here, to use up half of his magic to save us and then risk his life to get us home, but here we are and still he's trying his hardest to help. And all you can do is call him an idiot. Shame on you, Jake." A smouldering look in her eyes dared him to make some retort.

He didn't oblige, merely folding his arms and looking away defiantly. *He really can be a stubborn git sometimes*, thought Ben.

A knock came at the door, and they all looked at each other. It was time.

"Let's just get ourselves home, shall we?" said Ben, as Sam opened the door to Taegan.

"You ready?" Taegan asked.

"As ready as we'll ever be," mumbled Jake as they filed out the door after him.

Within moments they were back out to the holding garage where the horse-type creatures and carts were tied up. Ben noticed now how thin the animals were, their bones bulging out beneath wasted muscles. He felt a pang of sadness for them; their future was grim, with just survival on scraps and working until they dropped to look forward to.

Ben slowed down as they neared the cart that had brought them in, but Taegan continued to stride on past. He turned around when he saw them lose pace.

"What are you doing?" he barked.

"Are we not taking the cart?" asked Jake.

Taegan laughed. "No, I'm afraid not, sonny. We'll be walking today; it's not far and it'll be safer."

Taegan continued towards the door where three other people were standing waiting, coming to attention as Taegan approached.

"Must be some goons," Jake whispered. Ben ignored him.

There were two men and one woman, but Elena wasn't there.

Taegan embraced his brethren, then turned to Ben. "This is Aaron, Cleedon and Katarina. They are the small task force I've put together to help get you home. If they ask you to do something, you will do *exactly* as they say, without question." Taegan looked firmly at Jake. "Do you understand?"

They all nodded, nervous energy mixing with their escalating fear.

Sensing the mood, Taegan changed tack, managing to smile at them. "Don't worry, we're going to get you home." He looked squarely at Ben. "And once there, you're never going to come back, are you?"

"Absolutely not," said Sam immediately. Ben didn't answer. He knew he should agree, should promise that he would never return, but something stopped him. He couldn't put his finger on it; he certainly didn't want to come back, but he wasn't ready to admit that he never would, either.

"Good," said Taegan, eyeing Ben suspiciously. He then looked over the top of him, raising his eyebrows at an approaching figure. "Ah, excellent, Manatang, you're here."

Ben turned around, pleased to see the warm eyes of his monkey friend. "Manatang!" he cried. "You're coming with us?"

"Yep. Couldn't let you leave without saying goodbye, could I?"

"As a magical creature of the realm he also represents some extra insurance against any meeting with Blackwood," Taegan interjected.

Ben was confused. "How so?"

Manatang answered, "Magic naturally charges within me much faster than the humans, so I've already got back everything I used yesterday. Taegan asked me to come along to provide some additional protection."

"But you fainted when you used your magic yesterday. What happens if you faint in front of Lord Blackwood? You'll be helpless," he exclaimed.

Manatang looked down, not answering.

"No more questions," said Taegan. "We need to get moving." Ben was deeply dissatisfied but kept his mouth buttoned, putting his trust in the rebels.

The journey topside was quicker than the route they'd taken to get here. They walked only a hundred yards or so down the dusty tunnel that led from the base door before they stopped abruptly. Ben watched as Taegan walked up to the wall, inspected what appeared to be a hairline crack, and then, to Ben's astonishment, simply carried on walking, right though the wall. The other rebels motioned for him to follow, and it was only as Ben got closer that he saw it was an optical illusion; there was a passage set back almost imperceptibly into the wall, which blended in perfectly with the rest of the tunnel. Ben followed Taegan, sidling into the thin passage and was immediately plunged into darkness. Groping around and slowly shuffling forwards, he nearly tripped up when he stubbed his toe on a step. He blindly followed the sound of Taegan's footsteps upwards, until he reached the top and bumped into the back of him. Ben could see a very dim semi-circle of light just ahead of where he stood.

"Where are we?" he breathed.

"We're in a hollowed-out tree trunk," Taegan whispered. He stooped down to the hole, peering out to check the area. He turned back to the others.

"It's all clear. We can't normally use this exit except in the fog – it's too close to the base. But it's much closer to the site of your portal, therefore perfect for a quick journey."

Taegan went first, lying flat on his belly and wriggling through the small hole. Manatang went next, and then Aaron indicated that the four of them should go. Ben went first, his hands squelching through the wet mulch and mud on the floor, and within moments he was standing outside again in the Shadow Realm.

The gloom was now suffused with a thick dense mist, making it impossible to see more than a few feet. Ben began to worry about the journey. Visibility was so bad that they wouldn't know if they were about to run into Blackwood or one of his henchmen until it was too late. Or what if one of them got separated from the others? They might never be found.

Ben was contemplating this as everyone else made their way through the tree trunk. Heather stood up and shivered; Jake bounded up next to him.

"Blimey, it's a bit foggy, isn't it?" he exclaimed.

"Ssh," whispered Taegan. "The fog affords us visual cover from Blackwood and his slaves, but that doesn't mean they can't hear us. We must all stay very quiet. Cleedon, Katarina and I will fan out in front, with Aaron bringing up the rear in a diamond formation. Manatang will stay with you."

With the plan in place, Taegan and the other two walked off into the gloom, and a moment later Manatang started walking after them.

"Well, come on then," he said, turning around. "We don't want to lose them."

"I already have," muttered Sam, but they fell into step, walking two by two with Manatang a pace ahead.

They had been walking for about ten minutes when they heard a sound like a bird screeching. Manatang put his fist in the air and they all stopped instantly, keeping dead still and listening carefully.

Ben's heart was in his mouth, the fog pressing in from all sides, suffocating him with claustrophobic zeal. Manatang was on full alert, clearly scared, which didn't help calm Ben's nerves at all.

A rustling sound started to emanate from in front of them, the sound of steps crunching over the dead loam, and they were coming directly towards them. They all instinctively crouched, expecting an attacker to come flying through the mist any second.

Then they heard a familiar voice.

"Halt, you're surrounded." It was Taegan, addressing the approaching person. "Who goes there?" he said firmly.

"Taegan?" replied a soft, disembodied voice. "Is that you?"

There was a pause. "Akmar?"

"Yes, 'tis I."

There was another pause, this time pregnant with fury. "Come here," hissed Taegan.

Ben saw four figures emerge from the mist only yards away – the three rebels and an old man dressed in a robe.

"What the hell are you doing here, Akmar?" demanded Taegan.

"It's Galle's fog," Akmar said, his eyes blinking. His tone was neutral, his voice tired. "I was making my weekly pilgrimage to the henge."

"I told absolutely everyone to stay in the base. Why are you defying me?" Taegan was apoplectic, his face red and his neck throbbing.

Akmar looked shocked, not expecting this attack. His fingers curled around the staff he was holding, hugging the wooden pole close to him as if to hide behind it. "I didn't think you meant me. I always make my pilgrimage."

Taegan rubbed his forehead, not saying anything for several seconds.

"We nearly put an arrow through you, you fool. When I give an instruction to everyone, it is to absolutely *everyone*. Do you understand?"

Akmar looked down, cowed. "Aye," he said softly. His eye caught Ben's, and they opened wide. He looked back up at Taegan, his face contorted with questions. "Is that—"

"Those are the guests we're taking home, yes," said Taegan quickly.

Akmar dropped to his knees in front of Ben and grabbed his face, looking deep into Ben's eyes. Ben squirmed, trying to release himself from the old man's grasp, but he was stronger than he looked. Akmar then looked up to the sky, closed his eyes and breathed deeply for several seconds. Ben stopped struggling, aware that something odd was going on.

Akmar brought his face back down and looked at Ben calmly. Long, grey straggles of hair were plastered across his face, damp from the fog. The voice that came from Akmar was suddenly deeper, stronger than it had been before. "If the boy leaves, it will be the end." The words hung in the air.

"He's going," Taegan said abruptly. "It's not safe for him to remain."

Akmar stood back up and levelled his stare at Taegan. "True," he said, conceding the point. "But the legend is clear, as it was before, and look what happened then."

Taegan's patience deserted him. "Go back, Akmar, before I do put an arrow through you."

Akmar stood still for a moment, before nodding solemnly and turning to go. He put his hand on Ben's shoulder as he passed. "Stay safe, young man, and good luck. You're going to need it." He wandered off into the mist, disappearing in seconds, leaving Ben thoroughly bemused.

"Who was that?!" he blurted.

"That," said Taegan, pointing at the thin air where Akmar disappeared, "is our crazy old mage."

"What did he mean by 'it will be the end'?"

"I'm afraid he's gone quite mad and talks nonsense, so it's best to just ignore him. Come on, we need to keep moving."

Ben's mind was burning with questions, but he didn't push it. Akmar had poured more fuel on the fire and yet still he couldn't get any straight answers. Why did everyone have to be so damned mysterious in this place?

He mooched along beside Manatang, the creature who had offered him the most comfort and friendship since arriving in this strange world, and tried to focus on the task at hand. A moment later a giant shape loomed out of the fog, a tall, ominous oblong standing sentry by the side of the path. As he got closer, he saw that it was a huge stone and that there was another one a few feet further on. Resting atop these two huge rectangular stones was another one, making an upside-down 'U' shape.

Ben gawped at it open-mouthed.

"What is this?" he hissed to Manatang, who had walked a few feet on.

"That is nothing," he whispered very quietly, furtively looking around and trying to grab Ben's hand to pull him away. "We must keep going."

"No," said Ben firmly, pulling his hand from Manatang's grasp, who looked shocked at this outburst.

"Please," he whispered urgently, "keep quiet."

"Then tell me what this is," Ben demanded.

"It looks like Stonehenge," said Sam, the others now crowding around. Aaron had also now walked into the back of them and made a strange noise, like a bird call.

Ben looked at Sam. "I can see that it looks like Stonehenge, and I want to know what on Earth it's doing here."

"This is just our henge," said Manatang, shrugging his shoulders. "There are many like it; it is where the mages like Akmar come to worship."

Before Ben could ask any more questions, Taegan came barrelling out from the mist, a demented look on his face.

"Why have you stopped?" His voice was quiet, but suppressed rage hissed and fizzed in it. A vein boiled on his forehead.

"These stones, they look like a place in our world, a place called Stonehenge. I... I was surprised to see them," he offered meekly.

Taegan's eyes were bulging. "I don't give two hoots what you see – you could see your mother here for all I care, but you don't deviate from the plan. We keep moving, and we do so in formation, OK?"

Taegan moved off immediately, precluding any chance for debate, muttering and cursing under his breath, and they all set off to follow him. Ben glanced round to see the giant stones fade into the fog. *More questions I'll have to bury*, he thought ruefully.

They kept walking like that, in silence, for about half an hour, when suddenly Manatang stopped, and they piled up behind him.

Taegan appeared out of the mist in front of them, on full alert like a spooked meerkat. He hunched down, drawing everyone near to him, and urgently whispered some instructions. "We're not far from the portal site, so it's extremely likely that Blackwood and some of his men are waiting nearby. Me and the others are going to scout round, see if we can find out how many there are, and then we'll come back." He pointed decisively at Ben and the others. "You will all stay here, and not, repeat *not*, make a single sound," he frothed.

Ben and the others nodded their agreement. The next few minutes seemed to stretch out forever, with nothing to see or hear except the grey around them, nothing to pre-occupy them except their own dark thoughts about what was to come, whether they were going to get home or get themselves killed.

And what would happen to the rebels who were left here if they did get home? Ben hadn't thought about it before, but now the thought struck him: he realised that they would be lucky to escape with their lives. They were potentially making the ultimate sacrifice to get him and his friends home. He offered a silent prayer to Taegan and his rebels, thanking them for their courage.

Then Taegan was back, motioning for them to quickly come to him, and there was no more time for brooding.

The adrenaline pumped as they walked over to him, Ben's stomach fluttering with the sudden natural rush.

Taegan whispered quickly again, "He must have spread himself thin, as we can only find tracks for him and one other sentry, who appears to be guarding the other side of the clearing from here. That means that Blackwood is probably in the middle of the clearing. Aaron and Katarina are going to create a diversion that hopefully both of them will rush off to check out, but if not, Cleedon will make a secondary diversion on the edge of the clearing that Blackwood will have to move for. We need to be ready to go for the portal at that exact moment." He turned to look Ben directly in the eye. "Do you think you can get back through the portal, first time?"

"We all need to make sure we're touching each other, but sure, I can get through," Ben said, more confidently than he felt. What if he couldn't find the portal? It had been a day or so now – what if he had lost his ability to sense it?

He put the thought out of his mind. He had to find the portal again or all would be lost. Blackwood would catch them, lock them up, and Taegan's sacrifice would be for nothing.

Taegan held up his fist, and they slowed, picking their way through the forest carefully, treading lightly. Ben began to see the faint outline of the clearing up ahead, and he caught his breath. He could hear his own heart pounding as the blood rushed around his head. It was beating so loudly he was sure it would give them away.

He looked at the others and saw only fear in their wide, white eyes. Ben extended his hands for Heather and Sam, who took them, grasping tightly, their lives depending on the close contact. Jake placed his hands on Ben's shoulders, completing the awkward formation.

There was a loud crack and a yelp on the other side of the clearing, as Katarina and Aaron created the first diversion. Taegan paused, listening intently. A second loud bang off to the left made them all jump, and they realised this was Cleedon, making the second diversion to lure Lord Blackwood away from the portal.

They couldn't see a thing, but Taegan urgently signalled for them to go, before he jumped up and ran round the edge of the clearing, disappearing from view.

This was it. They were on their own, and it was time for action. Ben put his head down and charged.

CHAPTER 17

Ben couldn't see much as he surged into the anarchy of the clearing, his world filling with shouts and cries, bangs and booms. He felt Heather's hand stiffen and he squeezed it tighter in response, urging them all on with the force of his movement. He mustn't lose contact with anyone; they all had to be touching when he went through the portal, or they would be left behind.

They stumbled on, feeling as if they were running through treacle soup, as Ben began to feel the portal, the hairs on his arms standing on end from the electricity coursing through the air. All he wanted to do was hurl himself through that rip in space-time, to get there before Lord Blackwood got them.

He allowed himself to hope, to think they were going to make it, just as a loud noise to his right startled him. "*No!*" he heard Taegan scream.

Ben turned to look whilst still running towards the portal, a feeling of dread rising in the pit of his stomach. Through the mist he could see the outline of a large figure moving towards them, and he knew they were in trouble. It was Blackwood.

"Move!" he cried to his friends, pulling them towards the portal as fast as he could. Sam and Heather screamed as they made their frantic dash, but it seemed that Ben's momentum would get them there before Blackwood reached them.

Then disaster struck.

Jake's grip loosened as Ben advanced, his fingers holding on to Ben's shirt by friction alone. Panicking, Jake tried to lunge forwards to regain his hold, but he slipped on the moist mud and instead completely lost touch with Ben's shoulders. Ben's heart dropped as he realised he faced a grim choice.

Let Blackwood catch us or leave Jake behind.

Neither were good. He made a desperate last play.

"Grab my foot," Ben shouted as he jumped headfirst towards the portal, kicking his feet out for Jake to seize. Jake leapt, reaching out desperately to try and touch Ben's foot. He connected just as Ben's face touched the dimensional rip. Time slowed to a crawl. The pain of being squeezed through dimensions was coming, but a sweeter pain Ben could not imagine. It meant they were going to make it home.

Ben watched the chaotic scene of the clearing in almost infinite peace; the smoke and explosions ringing all around him were freeze-framed and removed from his existence, as if he were viewing a photograph. Then, from the corner of his eye, he saw Blackwood, and the picture became one of impending horror. In his desperation, Blackwood had thrown himself towards Jake, his eyes of fire raging with fury, arms reaching with a drastic madness as he battled to stop them leaving.

The last thing that Ben saw before the world went 'pop' – beyond the frozen, screaming face of Jake, who was clinging on to his foot for all his worth – was Lord Blackwood's hand connecting with Jake's ankle. Then the world disappeared; he was squeezed into the space of an atom, his body and soul compacted through an event horizon.

It took a moment for Ben to realise that he had travelled through the portal; the stress of trans-dimensional travel had been much harder that time. Lying on his back and breathing heavily, he allowed himself to slowly recover and let his eyes adjust to the sunlight now pouring into them.

Then he sat bolt upright as he remembered the last thing he saw. He looked to his left and saw only Sam and Heather, still nursing themselves on the floor. He swung his head round to the right and had his worst fear confirmed, although not in the manner he expected.

Lying next to Jake on the floor, gasping for breath, was a wretchedly thin, wasted man, who looked like he hadn't had a good meal in months. He was naked, his wrinkled skin wearing him like a dishevelled coat. Ben's stomach turned at the sight.

This can't be Lord Blackwood, surely?

Jake was up first, shrieking at the naked old man next to him. "What… who… is that… thing?" he yelled, pointing at the heinous apparition.

"I… I think that's Blackwood," said Ben.

"What—" he blurted, disbelievingly. He was cut off from saying anything further as the old man regained his senses and bounded up.

He eyed them all suspiciously, saying nothing, keeping his distance from them whilst weighing up his surroundings. He looked down at himself, at his droopy, wrinkled, arms and legs, and was repulsed by what he saw. He looked back at them, and although the fire was gone from his eyes, they still burned with malicious intent.

There was a stand-off, neither party sure of what to do.

"Ben," Jake whispered. "We could totally take him down. Look at him, he's old and frail, we might never get a better opportunity to kill him."

"We're not going to kill him, Jake," said Ben, a little shocked at his friend's ruthlessness.

"Why not? He'd kill us, and you'd be doing Taegan a massive favour."

"Look at him, he's a defenceless old man. Are you going to do it? Because I couldn't."

Jake folded his arms, unhappy. "I bet you this is our best opportunity to end it now. We'll regret it if we don't."

"We might regret killing him more. Besides, he's hardly a threat as a weak old man, is he?"

"Don't forget he knows how to do magic," added Sam.

Ben squinted, looking at the old man and considering Sam's words. "No, I don't think he can do magic here. If that were true, he'd have done it by now. I reckon he needs that Star thing to do magic in this dimension, and that's not here, is it?"

Blackwood spoke then, his voice high and reedy, sending shudders down Ben's back. "Astute young boy, aren't you, Benjamin? There is one slight flaw in your thinking, however. I've bet my life on the fact that the Star is here, in your dimension. But good luck with killing me – you'll have to catch me first."

With that, Lord Blackwood turned tail and ran, surprisingly fast, like a cat let loose after being swaddled in a towel. He looked quite a sight: a thin, naked old man running at full pelt through the forest.

"And now he's getting away," Jake muttered.

"Well, that's mucked it all up, hasn't it?" parped Sam. "Go to a dead world, bring back its evil ruler, set him loose on Earth. Good work, everyone."

"Look on the bright side," interrupted Heather. "We're home. I didn't think that was going to happen half an hour ago."

Ben didn't say anything; he was brooding on what Blackwood had said.

"The Star," whispered Heather. "What if it is here? If Lord Blackwood gets his hands on it, he'll be able to do magic. He'd be invincible; no-one could stop him. Imagine the destruction he could cause."

"*If* the Star of Moirai is on Earth, that is," said Sam. "It might not even be here."

Jake threw his hands up in desperation. "I bet it is here – he's not going to have risked his life for nothing, is he? We should have stopped him then; that was our best chance." He pointed at Ben. "And you let him go."

"Oh, stop being so melodramatic," sniped Sam. "He's a naked old man running around a forest. How far do you think he's going to get before being picked up by the police?"

Ben looked up then, the force of the idea hitting him like a steam train. "That's it," he exclaimed. "We don't have to stop him at all," he said, jumping up excitedly.

"What do you mean?" asked Sam.

"We've got to give an explanation for where we were the last few days, something that's plausible, right?"

"…Yes," the others slowly agreed.

"And if we've been away for as long as we think we have, the police are probably already involved, yes?"

"A cause for great excitement," said Jake.

"But if we say we were kidnapped by a man and give the description of Blackwood, then the police will have to look for him. If someone sees him running around and report him, they'll tie the two together and bingo, we've got ourselves an insane, naked, child-kidnapping, criminal maniac. We won't have to look for him at all – the police will do all the work."

Jake was nodding his head vigorously, as was Heather, but Sam looked worried. "That's going to involve telling some pretty big lies," he whined.

"Would you rather tell them the truth?" Ben asked flatly.

"Well, no, but…" Sam began, knowing he couldn't win this one.

"Stop being such a loser, Sam," said Jake, already returning to his usual self now he was back on terra firma. "There's a bad man on the loose, we need a cover story – it all fits perfectly." Jake winked at Ben, sealing his approval of the idea.

"OK, well let's get our story completely straight then," said Ben. "We'll likely be asked about it in minute detail."

They spent the next hour going over the details of their

'kidnapping'. They tried to cover every angle and loose end, so the story was believable but also so they couldn't be nailed down on specifics like location or timing.

Feeling incredibly tired and hungry, they began the long walk home.

Ben started to get nervous when they turned down his road and he saw the police car outside his house.

"How long do you reckon it actually *has* been?" asked Sam.

"I'm not sure," replied Ben. "But I think we're about to find out."

They'd barely turned the corner when a police officer jumped out of the car and ran towards them, speaking urgently into a radio holstered on his shoulder. They all froze, unsure of what to do.

"Just stick to the story," Jake hissed quietly through his teeth.

"Hey," shouted the policeman as he neared them. "You there, stop."

It was a completely irrelevant command to give; they already had.

The policeman ran up and stopped in front of them, a little out of breath. He was quite tubby. "You are them, aren't you?" he wheezed. "You're the missing kids?"

"Yes," Ben gasped, starting up his act. "And you must help us, we've only just managed to escape."

The policeman's expression immediately softened. "It's alright, lad, you're safe now. Come with me, your parents will be mighty relieved to see you."

At that moment, Ben's front door burst open and his mum came rushing out, followed closely by his dad. A second police officer appeared behind them, apparently the one radioed by her partner.

"Ben!" his mother shrieked, running up to him and grabbing him tightly, enveloping him in the biggest hug he'd ever had. "Thank god you're safe."

He returned the hug warmly, and suddenly his emotions got the better of him and he began to cry, the sheer joy at being home overcoming him.

Sam, Heather and Jake waited patiently to one side, when one of the officers came to his senses. "Quick, Jane, go and tell the other parents that they've turned up safe and where we are. We'll all go into Mr Freeman's house to calm down and have a bit of a chat to the kids." He motioned to everyone. "Let's go inside and have a cup of tea. You must have been through so much."

Ben nodded meekly, not finding it hard to agree with the statement despite the lie that was emerging. His mum was still gripping him tightly, then holding his face and looking deep into his eyes, kissing him softly. "Oh, my baby, we were so worried," she said.

"Mum!" Ben said, teenage embarrassment quickly overriding all other emotions. "Please don't call me that."

It was too good an opportunity for Jake to pass up. "Don't worry, babe, we won't mention it," he whispered in Ben's ear as they were herded into the house.

Ben walked in through the door and felt a wave of relief crash over him as the familiarity of home washed through his senses: the lavender aroma permeating the house from an air-freshener plug-in, the elaborate tangled vase wrought in blue glass that his mum kept on a table in the hallway, the TV as it murmured the news softly from its speakers. There was a feeling of distance and safety from the Shadow Realm that being home brought.

As they sat down for tea and biscuits he felt a raw confidence flow through him, his determination steeled that he must weave the lie he was about to tell, that there was no other option. The policeman, who had identified himself as PC Coppertop, fished a notepad out of his pocket, carefully turning the pages until he got to a clean one.

"OK," he said, exhaling loudly. "Why don't you tell us, in your own words, what happened?"

That seemed quite an expansive question, and Ben remembered the first rule of lying: don't say too much. Over-elaborate and you run the risk of saying something you later contradict or, worse, can't remember. People tend to be succinct and to the point when telling the truth.

"We were kidnapped in the forest and held against our will." He stopped, part of the strategy for not over-elaborating. PC Coppertop nodded, encouraging him to continue. "It was an old man. He threatened us with a knife," he said, warming to his story. "He grabbed Heather and told us he'd kill her unless we went with him. We didn't know what else to do, so we followed him." He paused, eyeing how this was being taken in. The policeman was busy scribbling away, whilst Ben's parents looked horrified.

"You poor, poor things," his mum muttered softly.

The pause gave the policeman time to ask another question, a tactic Ben then used repeatedly to try and appear a bit shell-shocked and disorganised in his responses.

"And where did he take you?"

"He bundled us in his van, where he handcuffed, gagged and blindfolded us. We had no chance to call for help – we were scared he would hurt Heather." He looked at Heather for effect, before dropping his head into his hands. "It was terrible."

"Where did he drive you to?"

"We don't know. It seemed like he was driving for a good hour or so. Eventually we were led from the van into a house and down some stairs. When he took our blindfolds off, we were in a room… it might have been a basement… but it was more like a prison cell. We were forced to sleep and eat in there for god knows how long. We were so scared, we thought we'd never get out."

"Did you see your captor?"

"He would come and give us food and water, trying to chat with us. We pleaded with him to let us go, but he only laughed."

"And what did he look like?"

Ben looked up to his left, pretending to think about the kidnapper but actually remembering how Lord Blackwood had looked when they came back to the New Forest.

"He was very thin, but quite tall. About six foot, I would say. He had a very tired and hollow face, lots of wrinkles. He must have been about seventy, if not older. But unnervingly strong – when he was handcuffing us, we struggled a bit, but he kept us firmly in place." Ben paused to sip some tea, getting into his stride. "He had fairly long grey hair, no beard or anything."

"We'll have to put you with our photo-fit guy, if that's OK?"

"Sure," said Ben, adding a quiver to his voice.

"How did you all escape?" The question was to them all, but again Ben answered.

"One day he came in and tied us up again, blindfolding and gagging us, and generally being quite rough. He seemed really upset about something, shouting at us for no reason. He marched us up the stairs and out of the house. He shoved us into his van and just started driving. I was terrified he was going to kill us."

"Do you know where he drove to?"

"No, the van stopped and we were pulled out, our blindfolds ripped off. We were somewhere in the middle of the forest, but it was nowhere any of us recognised. He was holding the knife again, laughing and saying that he was going to kill us." Ben nodded at Jake. "It was Jake who saved the day. He managed to knee him and kick him unconscious. We were then able to take the keys for the handcuffs and run off. We didn't look back."

"You left the man there?"

"Yes."

"But you don't know where this was?"

"Well, eventually we found a road to Bramley, which was four miles away, and we'd already been going a good few miles. We ran most of the way, although we had to walk after a while, we were too tired. So, it must have been somewhere round there."

"Good, good. If you think you can stand it, we'd like it if you could help us identify the area."

"We'll do what we can." He paused, then sniffed for effect.

The policeman shifted uneasily in his chair. "Is there anything else you can recall? Any other details which might help us at this point?"

Ben considered the question for a moment and then answered in the negative.

Sam coughed. "Er, there was no way for us to tell how many days we were kept in his basement. How long were we gone for?"

PC Coppertop shifted his collar nervously. "You've been missing for a week, lad."

A stunned silence settled on the room. *A whole week?* Ben couldn't believe it. His parents must have been through hell.

At that moment they were interrupted by animated chatter coming from the street outside. All the other parents were descending en masse, desperate and frantic to see their children.

They burst in through the door with vigour and intent, not wanting to believe what they'd heard was true until they saw it for themselves. But the kids were there, finally home after the terror of their disappearance, and there was a hectic few minutes as they embraced emphatically, hugging and kissing their children for all they were worth.

The kids felt a bit embarrassed but overcome by the experience they'd been through; they mostly just soaked up the emotional reunion with their parents.

After a few minutes of tearful greetings and, making sure everyone was alright, Ben's parents remembered the police were still there.

"Is there anything else you need at this point, Officers, or can we let the kids get some food and rest?" asked John Freeman.

The policeman tapped his pencil on the notepad, trying to think of anything else they needed. "No, I think that's all for now, but would you mind dropping by the station around four o'clock this afternoon? We'd like to get a photo-fit done of the criminal as soon as possible, whilst it's still fresh in the mind."

John Freeman deferred to his son.

"That's fine," said Ben.

The commotion quietened down as the others left with their parents. Jake raised his eyebrows at Ben as he walked past, a signal that carried a huge number of different meanings. 'Looks like they bought it', 'we've still got trouble', 'see you later' were just three of the possible meanings that Ben took from it.

Once everyone was gone, Helena Freeman started making even more of a fuss of Ben than she had before.

"We were so worried about you," she said whilst plumping the cushion behind his head. "We had no idea what had happened, and when the police found your bikes but not you, we feared... we thought..." She put her hand to her mouth, starting to cry again, unable to finish her sentence.

"I'm sorry, Mum," Ben said, guilt punching him in the stomach.

"Don't be sorry, darling, it's not your fault. We're just so happy you're back safe and sound."

"It's good to be back..." he said, his voice cracking.

She held him then, tears running down her face. "Look at me," she said after a minute. "You've been through so much, and here I am, the emotional wreck." She stood up then, fussing around him, tidying by his feet.

"Mum," he appealed, "please stop fretting. I'm fine." It was unconvincing.

She stopped abruptly, looking at him blankly for a second. "Of course," she said after a moment. "I'll get you some food. What would you like? Cheese on toast?"

Ben felt hungry but also too sick to eat right now. "I think I'll just go to my room and get some rest." He stood up quickly and shuffled out of the room, unable to look at his parents; if he did, he felt sure they would see right through him to the lies he was telling.

He ran upstairs to his bedroom, threw himself onto his bed and fell asleep almost immediately, exhausted.

A couple of hours later, his mum knocked on his door and walked in, carrying a steaming bowl of tomato soup.

"I thought you could do with something like this," she said, smiling. She'd been crying; her eyes were puffy, and the crow's feet that nested around them looked ten years worse.

Ben sat up, propping himself up with a pillow. "Thanks."

She gave him the tray and perched herself on the side of the bed. "I just had a call from the police station," she said. "They've had a report of an old man running into a garden and stealing clothes off a line. They want to bring forward the photo-fit to see if it's the same person that took you."

Ben evidently looked quite shocked, as she added, "They want us to go now."

"Right," said Ben. Just as he'd hoped, Blackwood had been spotted and the police were linking the two together. Although events were moving along according to plan, Ben felt nervous. The story was becoming a juggernaut, too big to stop and out of control.

She stroked his hair. "I just want you to know that your father and I love you very much."

"I love you too, Mum."

Helena moved the soup aside and cradled her son, wanting to protect him now as she'd been unable to before. "You've been through a lot, Ben. It'll take a long time to come to terms with what you've been through, and we just want you to know we're here for you. If there's anything you want to talk about, you know you can talk to us. We're on your side."

Ben nodded but kept his mouth shut. There was so much he wanted to say, so much he needed to tell his mother, but he couldn't. There was no way to tell the truth without sounding crazy. So he bottled it up inside, praying he could keep a lid on his roiling emotions in the pressure cooker of his mind.

The old man pulled his hood over his head, enveloping his face in shadow, giving him the aura of fear he needed to pull off this feat. The rain drizzled down at both ends of the underpass, the night sky dark and foreboding. He was cold, and he shivered as he felt the blade hidden in his pocket, as though touching it would somehow make him feel warm. The weapon was the only thing keeping him alive right now; it was his protection, and his only source of income.

It won't be for long, *he kept telling himself. This hardship was a means to an end, a test he must endure to get what was rightfully his. This weak, pathetic body was a stopgap, a part-time inconvenience that would give way to greater things once he had achieved his goal.*

He heard the footsteps approaching and readied himself at the corner of the subway. Each mugging was a risk; you never knew who was coming round the corner. Someone brave enough and tough enough to challenge the knife could be the last person that Gregovir Blackwood ever fights.

Gregovir brandished the knife as the couple entered the underpass, their enjoyable Friday-night date destroyed in an instant.

"Give me your wallet," said Gregovir, in the toughest voice he could. He struggled not to cough, trying to hide his ailments and face, to keep the illusion of a tough criminal going.

The man looked him up and down, trying to assess his choices, although they were clear. Give over the wallet and move on, or stand and fight. His girlfriend clutched his arm and whispered to him to hand it over. The reluctance on the man's face was clear, and for a moment it looked like he would react angrily, attempt to snatch the knife. But he didn't, instead opening the wallet and giving Gregovir his cash.

"You're not having my cards," said the man.

Gregovir didn't want or need the cards, and he snatched the cash quickly, turning tail and running as fast as he could, as though he were the one mugged.

I'm the lord of another world, *he thought,* reduced to this, a petty criminal. *He wasn't sure how much longer he could stomach it, the hunger, the cold, the pain. But he had a plan, and he had to see it through. He had to get money to live here, in this world, and achieve his aims.* But it won't be too long now, *he thought.* No, not too long at all.

CHAPTER 18

The next morning was grey and insipid, the rain seeping melancholically down from the heavens above, rending the world wet and miserable. It was not a day for going back to school, so Ben just turned over in his bed and furrowed himself further beneath the duvet.

Yesterday they had gone back to the police station to give a formal statement, and for a photo-fit to be made of Blackwood. So far, the police had believed everything the boys had said – their stories corroborated each other and there was no real reason to doubt them. All of which only made Ben feel worse at the lies they were telling – they were all so readily believed. He desperately wanted to tell the truth but knew that there was nothing to gain from doing so. No-one would believe him; in fact, they'd probably just think he'd gone crazy. There would be more questions about what did happen, and worst of all, the police might stop looking for Lord Blackwood.

He could hear his parents speaking about him downstairs, wondering what they could do, what they could say to try and make things better, but there was nothing they could say or do. Ben curled up in the warm darkness of his bed, trying unsuccessfully to get back to sleep. At least here in his cosy bed he felt snug and secure, cocooned away from the harsh reality outside. He found his mind wandering towards Blackwood, how he might have coped with his first night on Earth, whether he'd been cold and hungry, and if he felt frightened and alone. Ben certainly hoped so.

He got up later after his dad had gone to work and moped around the house whilst his mum busied herself with her crochet. He sat down to munch through a bowl of cereal, and a semblance of normality began to settle over him. If he tried hard enough, he could almost believe that the past few days hadn't happened, that there was no danger from Lord Blackwood and that it was all just a figment of his overactive imagination. Almost.

His mum came over to the kitchen counter. "How are you feeling now, love?"

Ben shrugged his shoulders. "I'm OK." He really didn't feel that OK.

"You gave us a real fright, you know."

He couldn't look his mum in the eye. "I'm sorry..." he mumbled.

"There's no need to be sorry, Ben. I'm just glad you're back with us. I think we need to be extra careful until the police catch this lunatic, that's all."

"Don't I know it," he muttered. Then with an encouraging smile he asked, "Is it OK if I go to see Sam today?"

"Well, I'm not sure," Helena began.

"Only I think he took the whole thing pretty badly," Ben interrupted, "and I think it would be good to be there for him."

His mum frowned for a moment, before breaking into a smile. "OK, love, that's very thoughtful of you." She gave him a little kiss on the forehead.

Rain pattered softly on the ply-board roof of the treehouse in Sam's back garden, as the four of them sat on blankets strewn around the floor. Occasional gusts of wind blew falling leaves in through the window, where they spun frantically through the air before landing on the floor with a gentle slap.

Ben's fringe played delicately in the wind, rustling against his forehead. He tapped his fingers against his mouth. "The facts as we know them are that Lord Blackwood is here but can't do any magic so is currently harmless," he stated.

"But how do we know that?" challenged Sam, playing devil's advocate. "What if he gets hold of the Star?"

"I can't see how that's going to happen," chipped in Jake. "There's no evidence it's even here."

Heather looked dubious. "We need to plan as if it is, to think about what we're going to do to defeat Blackwood before he gets it."

"I can't see how we're going to be any better at finding him than the police are," said Sam. "I think we should just leave it to them."

Jake pursed his lips, deep in thought. "What if we take another tack?" he began.

"Like what?"

"Rather than looking for Blackwood, why don't we start looking for the Star?"

"That's actually not a bad idea, Bro." Heather smiled.

"But where would we start?" asked Sam. "We don't even know if it's here on Earth."

"Maybe we could start by looking for the woman who brought it through?" offered Heather.

"Or just run some internet searches for 'The Star of Moirai'." Jake smirked.

Ben listened to all this and came to his conclusion. "We know so little about the Star or the person who brought it here, it's going to be like trying to find a needle in a haystack. I don't think Blackwood is going to find it easily either, and sooner or later he's going to make a mistake and be picked up by the police. I think we just wait for that to happen – let them do their job."

Jake and Heather shared a look that suggested they weren't so happy with this plan, whilst Sam agreed.

"Can't we at least try to find the Star?" implored Heather.

"That Star has already destroyed one dimension; I think it might be better left unfound." Ben's expression suggested he wasn't budging. "The best thing we can do now," he continued, "is keep our eyes and ears open to anything that might help the police find him."

"Like keep lying to them?" sniped Jake.

Ben ignored him. "Blackwood may well try and come back for one of us; he might think we can help in some way, and he won't think twice about hurting us. Just be on your guard, OK?"

The putrid stench of human scum filled Gregovir's nose; it was all he could do not to be sick. Remnants of society were scattered around him in the small, dingy flat, a base where the homeless and criminals could squat and hide. It reeked here, more than the normal smell that Gregovir found disgusting in common places. No, it really was a hive of revolting people, but he had to stay here to keep himself off the streets and off the police radar.

Life was difficult here; there was no doubt about it. He went from crime to crime, trying to scrape enough together to eat and to buy a gun. The denizens of this squalid place said they could put him in touch with the right people, but it would cost him big. At least a thousand pounds. But he didn't care; he needed the gun for the next stage of his plan. He was weak here without it, too weak, and he didn't like it.

The smelly man next to him was slumped over, apparently asleep or passed out. His head lolled and he fell across Gregovir into his lap. Gregovir was repulsed, pushing the man off him and jumping up, outraged at his suffering in this world.

"Look at you all," he spat, to the uninterested bums in the flat. "You're all worthless, hopeless, vile scum." A fury was taking over him as he talked, a great revulsion at this weak and desperate world. "You're all pathetic creatures, a useless shower of feeble flesh and bone. You have no idea of how strong I am, how much I should be lording it over you, ruling and crushing you all in my iron grip."

A couple of the less inebriated squatters were regarding Gregovir with mild interest now and nudging others, sharing a smirk.

"If I had my way, you'd all be dead!" screamed Gregovir Blackwood, before he started to cough, great hacking coughs that had him bent over and unable to breathe.

"Looks like you'll be dead soon enough, mate," joked one of the vagrants, and the others all laughed.

Gregovir, barely recovered from his coughing fit, could scarcely believe it. These imbeciles, these tramps and beggars, were all laughing at him. The injustice of it, the fact he couldn't just mutter some spell and kill them all there and then sent him into a frenzy. He seethed with rage. His blood boiled around his veins; his body thundered with anger.

And in the middle of it all, he felt something. A small spark, a quiver in the atmosphere that spoke of an untapped energy, hiding just out of reach. It was something he hadn't felt in this dimension before, something he didn't think existed here, but now he realised it did. Something he just had to tap into, and everything could be his. Magic.

The days passed without any further word on the whereabouts of Lord Blackwood; it was like he'd vanished off the face of the Earth. Ben couldn't understand where he might be hiding, given he didn't know anyone or have any way of supporting himself. His faith in the original vision that the police would find Blackwood was beginning to waver, and the lack of any news was troubling him. But as the days wore on, life began to return to normal.

They had gone back to school and been treated like mini celebrities. Everyone just wanted to find out what had happened to them, to know as much as they could of the gruesome details. There was little in the way of sympathy, although the bullies did at least lay off, sensing it may not have been the best of times to pick on the kids that got kidnapped. Ben was uncomfortable with lying to so many people and would play down what had happened, not really wishing to talk about it. But Jake relished the opportunity to tell the story, weaving it into conversation at every opportunity, using it to try and impress girls and slowly embellishing it with each re-telling to make himself sound both hero and victim.

After another day in the spotlight, Ben and Sam were sat together on the bus on the way home. Ben was lost in idle thought as the bus pulled out of the school gates, the bushes and trees opposite blurring beyond his reflection as he gazed into nothing. A figure suddenly caught Ben's eye, forcing his focus back to the real world. Someone was stood behind one of the old oak trees, but in a flash, he was gone. Ben strained his head to try and get a further look, but it was no good; he couldn't see them anymore. He whipped back round to Sam.

"I think I just saw Lord Blackwood," he whispered urgently.

"Where?"

"Just by the school entrance, back there."

"Really?" said Sam, craning his neck to look back at the receding bank of trees.

"Well, I can't be sure, we went by so quick, but I think so, yeah."

Sam frowned. "It seems unlikely he'd stand outside the school gates at home time, mate."

"I know, but I'd swear it was him."

"Why do you think he'd come here?"

"Maybe he's keeping tabs on me, finding out what my routine is?"

"It would be incredibly risky for him to come to the school."

"He might not know how risky it is, or he might be getting desperate?" Ben speculated. "He might be running out of time, so he's more willing to make his move."

Sam scratched his chin. "It's possible, but we don't actually know it's him you saw back there."

Ben sighed. "True."

"Do you think it might be about time we started to look for the Star ourselves?"

"Maybe I should tell the police that I saw him at the school?" he said in reply, ignoring the question by posing his own.

"But you don't know whether you did see him, do you?"

Ben looked deflated. "No," he conceded.

"So that would just be more lies, wouldn't it?"

"Yes," he was forced to agree.

"So..." Sam said encouragingly, "maybe we should begin looking?"

"You've changed your tune, haven't you?"

"I think it just might be time to concede that plan A isn't working out as we'd hoped, and perhaps we should start doing something about it ourselves."

Ben bit his lip, still not convinced. He was worried that if they went looking, they might well find the Star, which could be exactly what Blackwood wanted. They might inadvertently help it to fall into his hands. All he wanted was the police to find Blackwood and put an end to this whole sorry saga. Why hadn't they caught him yet? Ben turned away and looked out the window. Hedges and trees sped by in a blur, the setting sun flickering behind them, lighting up the sky a beautiful deep crimson red. He wished he'd never found the portal or gone to the Shadow Realm. He just wanted this to be over.

"He can't be having any luck finding the Star," he said, turning back to Sam. "As soon as he tries to surface, the police are going to catch him. Let's just keep a low profile for a bit longer, yeah?"

Now it was Sam's turn to sigh. "Fine," he said, though it was clear he thought it was anything but.

The thin, frail old man sat under the bridge, the river rushing around him as he meditated. He sat cross-legged, naked, semi-submerged by the water, and tried to feel the flow of liquid over his skin. It was cold, and he was already beginning to feel the illness inside him, kept at bay for so long, but gathering strength as he lost his, and he knew he did not have much time. Every effort must be made to locate the amulet, but the magic required was too much; it would take half a year to store up enough from the puny amounts available to him.

He let his fingers dip, touching the surface of the water, and tried to concentrate on the magic within the river. The constant flow was the best chance he had to energise with enough magic to give him glimpses – the glimpses he needed to make his next move. He closed his eyes and tried to empty his mind, focus on nothing but the here and now. He felt the energy flow into him, and he searched, searched for the boy.

Where are you?

Then, an image of a house, the boy. Mum and Dad. Mum...
Gregovir's eyes flew open.

Got you.

Ben sat down with his parents for his evening meal, the atmosphere still subdued by the spectre of what had happened. Even the light from the faux chandelier seemed dim.

"Has there been any news from the police?" Ben asked, as nonchalantly as he could.

"Nothing I'm afraid," said his dad, peering at him from behind his glasses. "I spoke to them today, and they're going to make another appeal for information, get his face on the news, that sort of thing. But they're worried he's fled the area, perhaps even the country. They may never find him."

Ben chewed on his lamb and considered whether to say anything about the bus ride home. His parents would of course insist he told the police, and he wasn't even sure if he had seen Lord Blackwood. His mind could have been playing tricks on him.

"I can't believe they haven't found this horrid man yet," said Helena. "It makes my blood boil to think he's still out there, having done what he's done. What is this world coming to?" As had happened many times over the last few days, a tear formed in his mother's eye, but she managed to hold herself together this time. "If I ever get my hands on him..." she said, trailing off.

"I'm sure the police are doing all they can," said John, trying to reassure his wife. He had such a calm manner, it would sometimes seem that he didn't care enough, so slow was he to anger.

"Well, they're not doing enough!" his mum suddenly yelled, exploding with fury.

Ben sat there, slowly pushing food around his plate. The conversation was becoming familiar now, emotions still running high. They'd rail against the lunatic kidnapper, the police for not finding him, against themselves and society in general – anybody but him. And in the middle of this, Ben would sit, a huge fraud. The guilt he felt was pushing him over the edge. He wanted to tell his parents everything, to expose the big fat lie he'd foisted on them, to ease his pain at putting them through emotional hell. But he couldn't say anything; how could he? No words could explain what had happened to him; no sane person would believe the tale he had to tell. So, all he could do was sit there and listen to their sense of injustice whilst he bottled up the guilt, trying to keep a lid on the fizzing genie inside that was desperate to escape.

Ben finished his dinner and was about to excuse himself from the table when his dad placed his hand on his mum's and a serious expression glazed over both their eyes. Ben groaned inside, for he knew this was the preamble to an uncomfortable talk.

John Freeman spoke first, his brow creased with wrinkles, his wispy hair frazzled. "How are you doing, Ben, really?" his father asked slowly.

"I'm fine," replied Ben, shifting uneasily in his chair.

"Me and your mother are concerned about you, about the effect that… all this… attention has had on you. It's perfectly understandable that you should feel confused, and angry, and all manner of things that we can't really imagine. But we want to try and help you – we don't want to see you moping around all the time."

"I'm OK, really," Ben began, but he was cut off by his mother.

"We just thought it might be good for you to speak to someone, and it might be easier for you, if you felt embarrassed talking to us, to speak to someone else. Someone professional."

Ben couldn't believe what he was hearing. "Are you saying I should see a shrink?"

Helena looked at her son with her soft, hazelnut eyes, radiating compassion and love. She reached out for his hand, but he pulled it away. She looked hurt.

"A psychologist, Ben. We just think it might help you get what's happened…" she paused, looking for the right words, "out of your system."

"I don't believe this. I've not gone mad or anything, I'm fine," he protested.

"No-one's saying you're mad. It's just that it can sometimes help to talk about a traumatic event, to get things off your chest, you know?"

"Why won't you listen to me? I've told you I'm fine, I don't need to see a ruddy head doctor!"

"There's no need to raise your voice, Benjamin," his father said firmly.

Ben sprang to his feet, knocking his chair backwards. "But you're not listening to me! There's nothing wrong with me, I just want to put it all behind me, OK?" He stomped out of the room and up the stairs, leaving his parents to frown at each other.

That night he went to bed more miserable than ever, just hoping, praying, that tomorrow it would all end – that Blackwood would be caught, and this nightmare would be over.

It was night time and Ben found himself alone in the woods. A dark and sinister tree towered over him, thrashing wildly in the howling storm as rain smashed into the gnarled bark. Ben pushed wet hair away from his eyes, struggling to see through the lashing rain. A flash of lightning illuminated the tree for a brief second, just long enough for Ben to see the figure standing amongst the branches, looking down at him. The flare faded, plunging the world back into darkness, but his pulsating heart told him what he didn't want to know. Lord Blackwood had found him.

Two fearsome circles of fire erupted in the black tree, bright and raging in the maelstrom, and Ben understood instantly that he was beaten, that he must die. Blackwood jumped down, the Earth shaking as he landed in front of Ben, his metallic armour gleaming in the moonlit rain. In one swift, fluid motion he grabbed Ben by the neck and lifted him up so that he was eye to eye with the monster, his world once again engulfed by flames.

"Do you like my new suit?" he boomed.

Ben croaked, unable to speak.

"The Earth was kind enough to provide the magic for me." He laughed a long, hollow laugh. "And soon I will have all the magic... all the power... and there is nothing you can do to stop me."

As Lord Blackwood snapped his neck like a twig, Ben woke up, sweating and clutching his throat, gasping for air. As his eyes adjusted to the dark, he realised that there was a figure sitting on the end of his bed. He recoiled in horror and screamed.

It was several seconds before Ben registered the shushing and soothing noises that his mother was making, to try to calm him down, and he stopped shrieking. His heart was going ten to the dozen.

"Mum!" he yelled. "You scared the bejesus out of me."

"I'm sorry, Ben," she said, stroking his brow. "It's just I could hear you were having a bad dream and I wanted to comfort you."

"Well, you didn't do a very good job, did you?" he said, letting out a little laugh.

"Sorry." She laughed too. "It must have been a pretty bad dream?"

Ben remembered Blackwood with his powers, how his neck had snapped so easily, and shuddered. He placed his hands round his neck unconsciously, checking it was OK.

"It was... nothing. A silly nightmare."

"It didn't sound like nothing," she pressed. "You might feel better if you tell me."

"By re-living my nightmare?"

Helena breathed in deeply, her brow tensing and creasing as she considered her son. Her eyes were inquisitive, knowing.

"Who's Lord Blackwood, Ben?"

The question came like a hammer blow to Ben's stomach. How did she know that name?

"What... what do you mean?"

"Lord Blackwood – you were talking in your sleep and you said that name. It's an... unusual name."

Ben's mind was reeling as he thought of something to say. He couldn't think of anything clever, so he just shrugged his shoulders. "I dunno. Must have been in my nightmare." He could feel a new line of sweat beginning to appear on his forehead, saw his mother's eyes twitch as she registered the lie.

"Ben, I'm your mother," she began calmly, in a way that troubled him deeply. "I know you like no other person on this Earth does, and I can tell when you are holding something back from me." She held his face and looked him square in the eyes. "Whatever it is, you can trust me."

Ben looked into those deep brown eyes and felt so hopeless, so unfathomably out of his depth that he was desperate to confide, to tell his mother what had happened, and stop the lying. But what would she think? How could she possibly believe the tale he had to tell? His face fell away from hers.

"I... I can't," he stammered. Tears welled in his eyes.

"Oh, Ben," she said, kissing the top of his head. "You can tell me anything, and I'll always be on your side. Always."

"You wouldn't believe me even if I told you," he defended weakly.

"Why don't you try me?" She smiled, adding, "You know I believe all sorts."

It was all the encouragement he needed in his parlous state of mind. He took a deep breath.

"What I told the police... about the kidnapping," he said, stumbling over the words, struggling to find the courage to say each one. "It... it wasn't quite... true."

"O-K..." Helena said slowly, awareness dawning that this might be bigger than she had imagined. "What do you mean?"

"We weren't kidnapped."

"Oh, lordy." She hung her head in her hands for a moment, breathing in strongly to quell the rage that was rising within. "Well... what did happen then? Who's the poor man the police are chasing?"

"That, um, well, that's Lord Blackwood."

Helena's eyes narrowed, her expression telling Ben that she was beginning to think this was another lie. "You're not making a lot of sense, Ben."

"I did say you wouldn't believe me." Ben studied his hands, feeling stupid now.

"I haven't said I don't believe you." Helena grasped her son's hands in his. "But you have to tell me everything – how else will I know the truth?"

Ben looked at her again, his heart beating fast as he nodded, accepting he must tell her everything. He paused to summon some courage.

"Lord Blackwood is from another dimension."

Helena's eyes widened in surprise. "What do you mean, another dimension?"

"I found a portal to another dimension, a place called the Shadow Realm, although it used to be called Sunea," he gabbled.

"Oh, god," said his mum, pursing her lips and looking towards the ceiling, trying to stop her eyes from tearing up. She composed herself and looked back at Ben.

"Well, you really best tell me all about it now," she said. "Considering I'm from Sunea too."

CHAPTER 19

Ben was silent for several seconds, blinking as if blinded by sunlight, the weight behind his mother's words taking their time to sink in.

He cleared his throat. "Do you want to run that one by me again?"

"I'm from Sunea, Ben. I know it's an awful lot to take in, and you'll have a lot of questions, but right now, it is absolutely imperative that you tell me everything that happened."

"But... what... how?" he spluttered.

She held him firmly by his shoulders. "You need to go first, then I'll tell you everything. What happened to you in Sunea?"

"I can't believe it," he said, shell-shocked.

"Well, believe it," she said, unusually hard. "You need to focus and tell me what happened."

It took a few moments for Ben to come out of the shock he was feeling and begin his story, starting with the moment he first found the portal. He laid it all out for her – his dreams and subsequent forays to the Shadow Realm, and then telling his friends and their decision to go through to the Shadow Realm together.

"We didn't know what we were getting ourselves into," he cried. "I should never have taken them with me."

"It's OK," his mum said sympathetically. "I'm not surprised that's what you all did – you lot go everywhere together."

Ben told her how dark and dead the world was, and about their capture by Lord Blackwood and being held prisoner in his castle. He explained how they'd escaped, and then been helped by Taegan and Manatang. Helena gasped at the names.

"You met Taegan?" she whimpered.

"Yeah, he's kind of like their leader. Do you know him?"

"You could say that…" she muttered.

Ben carried on his story, finishing up with their efforts to come home through Galle's fog and how Blackwood managed to come through the portal with them.

Helena stood up as if a firecracker had been lit under her. "So, the old man…?"

"Really is Lord Blackwood, yes."

Helena's eyes widened in terror. "This is bad," she cried, shaking her head. "This is really, really bad. Terrible."

"That's why we told the police about him, so that they could conduct the hunt. We wouldn't know where to start."

Helena looked rueful. "I've got a pretty good idea of where he'll start."

"Where?"

Helena sighed. "It's pretty likely he'll try and find me."

"Because you're from there too?"

Helena scratched her forehead. "Because I know where the Star is." The incomprehension must have been written on Ben's face, because she added, "I brought it here, Ben."

The truth slammed down on him so hard he felt winded. "You…" he gasped. "Of course… *you* used the Star."

"Yes."

"And that means you were Taegan's wife."

Tears sprang into Helena's eyes. "Yes," she sobbed.

Ben couldn't believe what he was hearing, his reality exploding as he struggled to come to terms with what his mum was saying. Helena cried for a few minutes, letting the emotion pour out, as Ben sat there trying to digest it all. Somewhere outside a fox shrieked and a dog barked in reply. The curtain fluttered on a puff of wind. It was his mum who pulled herself together and spoke first.

"So Sunea is ruined?" Tears were still running down her face.

Ben realised that his mum couldn't have known what happened after she activated the Star. "I'm sorry, Mum. It's all dead."

"How did it happen?"

"Taegan said it happened just as the mages foretold – when the Star was used."

Helena slumped into Ben's swivel chair, her face ashen with grief. "We thought we were saving the world," she whispered. "Instead, we ended it. I ended it."

Ben clasped his mum's hands. "You can't blame yourself, Mum, things would have been a lot worse if Blackwood had got hold of the Star. It was the right thing to do, despite the terrible cost. You had to take that chance." Ben stopped in his tracks as he suddenly realised the enormity of his error. "Oh god, what an idiot I've been! I've led Blackwood right to it, haven't I? If he finds the Star, it'll be all my fault for bringing him here. What have I done?" he sobbed.

His mother put her arm around him. "It's not your fault, Ben. You've been placed in the middle of all this by me. I should have told you about my past before; I just didn't know where to begin. But don't worry, we won't let Blackwood get the Star. I was sent here to protect it, and that's exactly what I intend to do."

"All the sacrifices that have been made," he bawled, "all that you've been through to keep it safe, and I've undone it all. I've put everyone in danger." Ben hung his head and cried, whilst his mother comforted him.

"We won't let him win," Helena stated. "We can't."

Ben felt a strange relief wash over him as he sat there being comforted by his mother. His whole world had just altered; the fact that his mother not only believed him but was now actively on his side gave him a new sense of optimism. The guilt he had been feeling lifted from his shoulders, and he felt that the burden of responsibility was now shared; he was no longer alone. His mother's determination also imbued him with purpose, and he felt a renewed sense of urgency to act.

"Where is the Star?" he asked.

"In a safe place," she said calmly. "I cannot tell you where, Ben; it would be too dangerous should Gregovir find you."

"Gregovir?"

"That was Lord Blackwood's name."

Ben was taken aback – he hadn't really considered that Blackwood had a name, a history as a man, but it made sense. Taegan had talked of him as a High Mage, bent on power, but he was still just a man before Sunea fell to Shadow.

"But surely I should know, just in case—"

"No, Ben." It was firm, and he knew he couldn't argue with the ice-cold logic of his mother, despite the intense desire he had to know where it was. It passed as another million questions formed in his mind.

The first one bubbled out of his mouth, unbidden.

"How come I can travel there? I mean, without the Star?"

Ben's mum ran a hand through her hair, contemplating her son, almost as if she were seeing him for the first time.

"There's never been anyone quite like you, Ben. You're half-Sunean, half human; your DNA is from both dimensions. Maybe that's what allows you to slip between them."

"But why there, why now?"

"You say this portal is in the forest?"

Ben nodded.

"It could be that you found the place where I came through when I used the Star. It obviously unleashed some very powerful magic that ripped between our two dimensions, sending me here whilst destroying my world. Perhaps that scar never healed, and as a child of both worlds you were able to sense it."

Ben looked at his Greenpeace poster, his mind racing through the incredible story. "What happened when you got here, Mum?"

Helena exhaled lightly, her heart lamenting a life that never was. "When I arrived, I was completely and utterly alone, with no idea where I was or what had become of the land I left. I had no way of supporting myself, and for several years I eked out a living working menial jobs, cleaning and the like. It was only when I met your dad a few years after I got here that life began to get easier for me. I had by then begun to accept that I would never return to Sunea, and I started to let go of my previous life, of Taegan. Your dad saved me, and I love him dearly, Ben, you must know that. And we love you too — none of this changes that."

"I love you too, Mum."

There was a warm pause before his mother continued. "On some level, I think that I always knew something like this must happen, that the past would come crashing in to the present and I'd have to tell you the truth." She paused, allowing herself a rueful smirk. "I didn't think it would be because you would travel between dimensions and bring back my arch-enemy, though."

Helena's face soured as she reflected on her life past, painful memories coming back that had been pushed into a dark place for a long time.

"Taegan..." she began softly. "How is he?"

"A little gruff," replied Ben before remembering this was the man his mum had once loved. "He's in remarkable shape, considering what he's got to put up with."

His mum smiled.

Ben's eyes lit up as he had an idea. "I could take you there," he enthused. "You could go back to see your home, to see Taegan."

"I don't think that's a good idea, Ben." She cast a forlorn look out of the window. "It sounds as though much has changed, and I'm not sure I could bear to see it."

"Although..." he began, before thinking against it.

"Although what?" pressed his mum.

"It's just," Ben began delicately, "time runs slower in the Shadow Realm than it does here. We were only there a couple of days when we were missing, but a week passed here. Only a few years have passed there since you left."

Ben opened his mouth to say more but caught the sad look in his mum's eyes that said she fully understood what this meant. She was now old, whilst Taegan was young.

"I think that I'm happy to stay in this dimension now," she said, attempting a smile and stroking his hair.

There was a long pause. "I can't believe this," Ben said finally. "Would you ever have told me?"

"I'm not sure how I could. I thought so many times of telling you, but face it – you wouldn't have believed me, would you?"

"Probably not," agreed Ben.

"I kept taking you to Stonehenge, wondering if you'd feel anything."

"Oh yeah," chimed Ben, remembering the giant stones he had seen in the Shadow Realm. "What is it about Stonehenge? We saw one in the Shadow Realm, and I couldn't quite believe my eyes."

"I couldn't quite believe it either when I saw Stonehenge here for the first time. I'm not sure what it all means, to tell you the truth, but I do know that Sunean henges were built many thousands of years ago by the High Mages, in the same way druids here on Earth built Stonehenge. I don't have anything to base this on, but I've theorised that they could have been trans-dimensional communication portals – some way to speak or travel between our two dimensions, perhaps by a magic now lost to us."

Ben had seen too much weird stuff to dismiss the theory out of hand, like he would have done before. Anything was possible now.

"Mum, have you ever heard of the prophecy?" he asked, innocently enough.

Helena gave him a queer look. "Why do you ask?"

"It's just…" He paused, struggling to find the right words for the next sentence. "Some people mentioned it in the Shadow Realm, and I just wondered what it is." He hoped he sounded casual and not like someone who thought that maybe the prophecy could relate to himself.

Her eyes searched his, piercing beneath his facade of nonchalance. "You're nothing to do with the prophecy, Benjamin," she replied emphatically.

"No, no," protested Ben, but his pride was deflated. "I don't think I am – I'm just curious."

"Good, because all these problems started when someone began to believe they were the chosen one."

"You mean Lord Blackwood?"

Helena sighed. "Yes. The prophecy was divined in a series of ancient essays written by Alberos, one of the Highest Mages who ever lived, over two thousand years ago. He set down his teachings and beliefs on how life should unfold in Sunea. They're interesting and, of course, highly significant historically, but they aren't the most reliable guide to the meaning of life, and they weren't widely read. It was only after Gregovir took such an interest in them that most people then heard about the prophecy."

"What does the prophecy say?"

"Alberos wrote of a chosen one who would lead Sunea into a new golden age, being the most powerful mage who ever lived. Gregovir believed it to be himself, which led to his obsession with the Star and his quest to possess it. You can see the problem the prophecy created – it became both self-fulfilling and self-defeating."

"I'm not sure I understand?"

"If we didn't have the prophecy, Gregovir wouldn't have thought he was the 'chosen one', he wouldn't have raised such merry hell trying to get the Star and none of this would have happened. Sunea would probably still be alive and well today."

Ben was pensive. "Taegan said that Sunea was suffering even before Lord Blackwood came along."

Helena looked sad. "It's true – there's no point denying that our greed as a society had overcome the planet's natural ability to provide us with magic. A war over resources was, I suppose, inevitable." Tears sprang to her eyes. "It's just the good guys lost."

"I'm sorry, Mum," said Ben, hugging her again. He had been so caught up in his own story, he'd forgot his mum had just found out she had lost her whole world – everything she had sacrificed had been for nothing.

"Oh, don't be sorry for me," she said, wiping the tears from her eyes. "I've got you and your dad now. Be sorry for Sunea."

"I am."

A new resolve entered Helena's eyes. "First, we've got to think about how we find Blackwood. If he gets hold of the Star, there's no telling how much devastation he could cause. It may well wreck the Earth in the same way as Sunea."

"Do you think he could find the Star?"

Helena narrowed her eyes. "Sooner or later, it is inevitable."

"So, what should we do?" The question was phrased so innocently that his mum pulled him to her, hugging him and resting her chin on his head.

"We must find him before he finds us, and we must kill him."

Ben gasped. He had never imagined his mum could harbour such thoughts. "Kill him?"

Helena's resolution would not waver. "Yes, Ben, it's the only way to stop him. And if what you're saying is right, it's our best chance to rid Sunea of his evil too."

Ben knew she was right. If they could stop Blackwood here, whilst he was weak, then not only could they save the Earth but they could offer Taegan the chance to rebuild Sunea, exactly as he wanted.

"Yes," he said, nodding slowly. "We must kill him."

Helena stood up then, moving to the window and pulling back the curtains to look out at the pale glow of the garden as it bathed in the moonlight.

"There's something else," his mum began, blowing her nose. She turned back to look at Ben, struggling to find the words, her eyes welling up.

"What is it?" Ben said softly.

"I made a huge mistake," she said, bursting into tears. Ben got up and hugged his mother, trying to calm her through her cries. "I was young and scared," she sobbed. "I didn't know what else to do. I don't know how you'll ever forgive me."

Ben was alarmed at his mother's words; whatever it was she was trying to tell him was clearly very important to her.

"It's OK, Mum, you can tell me," he reassured her.

But then a reedy voice rasped from the doorway, making them jump.

"So nice to see you again, Lenara."

It was Lord Blackwood.

CHAPTER 20

Helena and Ben jumped up, their hearts suddenly pumping adrenaline through their bodies at this dangerous intrusion.

Lord Blackwood was standing in Ben's bedroom doorway, a knife in his hand and a furious anger in his eyes. He looked like a homeless person: bone-thin, with an ill-fitting shirt flapping around his chest and brown corduroy trousers which finished well above large, cracked leather shoes. His face was sallow and pale, and appeared tinged with illness. He ran his hands through his dank, thin grey hair.

Ben might have laughed at his appearance were it not such a serious situation. They were trapped in the room, with nowhere to run. Ben needed a weapon, but there was nothing close to hand. Then he remembered that he'd been given a baseball bat by his dad a few years ago, which was now in his cupboard. He just needed a way to get it without Blackwood attacking him first.

Blackwood looked them up and down, breathing in their fear and enjoying every ounce of it.

"John?" shouted Helena, trying to call her husband.

"I'm afraid he's... indisposed."

"What have you done to him?" Panic was edged in her voice.

"Let's just say he's not going to wake up for a little while."

"If you've hurt him, I'll kill you," said Helena, mildly hysterical.

Blackwood flung his head back and laughed, a high-pitched howl like a wailing coyote.

Helena's patience snapped. "What do you want?" she spat.

Blackwood played with his knife, touching the tip to his fingers. "You know perfectly well what I want, Lenara." Helena shuddered to hear him say her old name. "But first I would like to say thank you to your son. So considerate of him to bridge the gap between our dimensions and lead me directly to you."

Ben scowled at him.

"We won't let you have the Star, Gregovir," said Helena.

"You don't have a choice," he rasped. "You can either tell me where it is or I kill you."

"Clever as you are, Blackwood, there's rather a large flaw in your logic: if you kill me, you'll never find out where the Star is."

"That's not entirely true," said Blackwood, unable to disguise his sneering delight at knowing something they didn't.

Helena narrowed her eyes but said nothing.

"You really don't feel it, do you?" he said, after a pause.

"Feel what?"

Blackwood laughed. "Well, why would you?" he mocked. "You're just the daughter of a tradesman, and not a very good one at that."

Fury entered Helena's eyes, but still she said nothing.

"A High Mage like me, on the other hand..." He twirled his hand as if to indicate his brilliance.

"What are you talking about, Gregovir?"

"Magic, Lenara. It's here, on Earth, just like it is in every dimension. There's not much of it, just a small background amount, but I can feel it charging within me; such an *energising* sensation, don't you think?"

"You don't look very good on it," she said sourly.

"I'm saving it all for a particular spell. I'm sure you can guess what I might use a locating spell on? Once I have the Star, I'll have all the magic I need."

Helena narrowed her eyes. "You're bluffing, Gregovir, you wouldn't be here if you could find it imminently. Even if what you say is true, I reckon you've got a few weeks before you can charge up enough magic. The police will have you by then." She hoped she sounded more confident than she felt.

"I wouldn't count on that, my dear. I'd say two to three days at most. But I grow tired of waiting and thought I might offer you a deal for your co-operation."

Helena snorted. "You think I'd co-operate with you? You're quite deluded, Blackwood."

"It's Lord Blackwood to you." His voice was cold, calculating. "And the deal on offer is you tell me where the Star is or I kill your son."

Helena instinctively shielded Ben. "You just try and touch him," she threatened.

"Then tell me where the Star is."

"I can't give you the Star. I don't have it."

"Do you expect me to believe that?"

"I threw it over the side of a boat, into the sea. The English Channel, to be precise."

Blackwood's smug grin faltered. "You wouldn't dare," he said, unsure of himself for once.

"Of course I would," she said defiantly. "Much better that than the alternative of you turning up here one day and claiming it for yourself. Looks like the shrewdest move I ever made."

Lord Blackwood's temples twitched, the blood almost visibly boiling in his veins. "You stupid woman!" he shouted, lunging at her with the knife. As he did so, Helena knocked Ben out of the way behind her and brought her hands up to protect herself.

Blackwood slashed across her, making a deep cut along her forearm. She screamed as blood spattered onto the floor and Ben's bed.

"I'll kill you," raged Blackwood, flipping out completely. Helena managed to grab his arm to prevent him from stabbing her further, and they struggled furiously against each other.

Ben, having been flung to the floor by his mum, regained his senses and made a dash to the cupboard to retrieve the baseball bat. He turned to face Blackwood, who had now gained the upper hand over Helena. As Ben swung the bat back, Lord Blackwood plunged the knife through Helena's dressing gown and into her chest.

A stifled scream escaped her lips and she crumpled to the floor.

Ben's bat smashed into Blackwood's midriff a moment later, and he was knocked backwards, rolling over the bedroom floor, dropping the knife. He shrieked and held his stomach where he'd been hit.

It all happened so quickly that Ben didn't initially register what had happened, but seeing his mum stricken on the floor, he quickly went to her, stooping down beside her.

"Mum, are you OK?" he gasped.

She was breathing fast, her eyes wide in shock. Ben put his hand to her chest and when he brought it away, it was coated a crimson red. She was bleeding fast. He turned towards Blackwood, rage building inside him uncontrollably. Blackwood was picking himself up; on seeing Ben with the bat and murder in his eyes, he turned and fled.

"Come back here!" screamed Ben, following him out onto the landing before a groan from his mum forced him to let Lord Blackwood go and return to tend his mother.

"You're going to be OK, Mum, I promise," he said, kneeling next to her. "You need to keep pressure on this wound. Can you do that whilst I call for an ambulance?"

His mum nodded weakly. Ben wasn't sure she could, but he had to leave her to grab his phone and call for help.

He ran to the bathroom to grab a towel, dialling '999' on his mobile as he did so. He balled up the towel and placed it against the entry wound, applying pressure to try and stem the heavy flow.

He urgently explained the situation to the call handler and then just waited, cradling his mum in one hand whilst holding the towel in the other.

"You're going to be OK, you're going to make it," he said, sobbing through his own words. She looked as white as a ghost.

"Listen to me, Ben," she croaked. "I might not make it—"

"Don't say that," Ben interjected. "You're going to be OK."

"Listen," his mum pushed on insistently, "you need to get Taegan. You need to bring him back here, to Earth. Tell him Lenara asked him to come."

Ben blinked, taken aback by the request. "Why?"

"Just promise me, Ben. He's the only one who can help... the only one who can... who can..." Her eyes started fluttering as she found it hard to breathe in the air she needed to speak.

"Mum!" shouted Ben, alarmed and upset. "Stay with me, Mum."

"Ben," she whispered, stroking his face with her hand. "I love you."

"I love you too, Mum," he sobbed.

Her eyes quivered shut.

"No," he shouted. "You can't leave me, Mum, not now."

Ben checked her pulse and her breathing; she was still alive but fading fast. He could hear the sirens from the ambulance getting closer, rising in volume as they neared his house.

He leapt down the stairs and wrenched the door open, rushing out to the paramedics and imploring them to come quickly.

"Where is she, son?" asked one of the paramedics, a kindly-looking man with a touch of weariness which suggested he'd seen too much in his many years on the job.

"Upstairs, in my room, first on the left." The paramedic looked at Ben quizzically before pushing past him into the house.

The second one strode in next to Ben, asking him what had happened.

"She was stabbed. He came into the house and attacked us," Ben shouted, on the verge of insanity.

The second paramedic, a woman in her forties, then used her radio to call for police backup as she ran up the stairs to his bedroom.

Ben was right behind her. "Is she going to be alright?" he fretted.

"I think her lung's collapsed," said the male paramedic. "Please keep back and give us space to work."

Ben stood back, watching, crying, as the paramedics worked on his mum, apparently stabilising her enough to transfer her to the ambulance.

"We're going to take her to the hospital now. You can come with us, but you're going to need another adult to meet you there. Is your father around?"

Oh God – Dad! In all the pandemonium, he had completely forgotten about him. He raced down the landing and burst into his parents' bedroom. His dad was lying unconscious on the bed. Ben stood in the doorway, shocked and unsure of what to do. He was vaguely aware of one of the paramedics pushing past him and stooping over his father, checking him over and shining a light into his eyes.

After a moment he turned around. "He's going to be OK, son, he's been knocked out, but he'll be OK. I'll stay with him until he comes round and send him to the hospital. You get in the ambulance with your mother."

Ben swayed on his feet, his mind a hazy blank. What was he supposed to do now? How was he meant to deal with this? His shocked brain was struggling to compute the situation, leaving him in a haze of white static.

"Go on, son, join your mother. It's OK."

Ben blinked and finally nodded. An approaching police siren jogged him out of his reverie, spurring him into action. He ran back out into the cold night air.

A few neighbours were now standing at the end of their driveways, craning their necks to see what was going on. Ben ignored them and hopped into the back of the ambulance. It sped off, sirens blaring, towards the hospital.

Ben was slumped in one of the plastic chairs in the relatives' room when his dad arrived, bursting in through the door. He looked haggard, ten years older.

"Ben!" he exclaimed.

Ben jumped up to hug him. "I'm so sorry, Dad," he sobbed.

"It's OK, it's not your fault, son. How is she?"

"I haven't heard yet," Ben said, pulling himself together. "They had to do a chest drain; her lung had collapsed."

His dad slumped himself in a chair at this news, holding his head in his hands.

"How are you feeling?" asked Ben, after a few silent seconds.

"Apart from a banging headache, I'm fine. To be honest I'm not sure what happened. One minute I was fast asleep, the next I felt a searing pain in my head and then I woke up to a policeman telling me that my wife and son were at the hospital."

Ben wasn't sure what to say about what had happened, so he stayed silent, a terrible mix of sadness and guilt raging within him.

"I can't believe this is happening," John Freeman said quietly. It was clear he was placing the blame on his own shoulders. Ben had never felt so low. He was about to try and tell his dad the truth when a doctor in scrubs came into the waiting room.

She paced over to where Ben and his dad were standing. "Mr Freeman?" she enquired.

"Yes, that's me. Do you have any news about my wife?"

"The good news is she's stabilised, so the immediate danger is over." The look in her eye told John Freeman that there was bad news coming too. "One of the complications from pressure building on the lung was to push the heart to one side, which induced a cardiac arrest. We managed to restart the heart and it's settled into a nice stable rhythm, but I'm sorry to have to tell you that your wife is in a coma."

John Freeman rocked on his feet, the colour draining from his face, his shoulders slumping. He fell back onto the chair and put his head in his hands.

Ben felt numb. He couldn't believe he had nearly lost his mum, and worse, it was all his fault. It was his persistence on going to the Shadow Realm that had led Lord Blackwood back here to his mother, who had given up everything to try and protect the Star of Moirai. He'd not even been able to defend her from the feeble old man Gregovir Blackwood had become.

The doctor let the news sink in for a moment and then carried on. "We believe that she will regain consciousness in time, but unfortunately we've no idea when that might be."

John looked up at the doctor, ashen. "Right..." he stuttered. "Can we see her?"

"Shortly. The surgical team are just finishing up and she'll be transferred to ICU. You'll be able to see her there."

John Freeman didn't say anything, so Ben thanked the doctor and she walked off.

They waited half an hour until another doctor came out and said that they could have ten minutes with her. They followed the doctor down to the intensive care unit, pushing through the big double doors that sealed the unit, pausing to wash their hands with alcohol gel.

Then they saw her there, lying in one of the bays. She had a tube running from her mouth to a machine that was pumping air into her lungs, and several other wires and tubes were protruding from her body. She looked white, a phantom apparition, with a weak and fragile grip on life.

Despite this, the look on her face was serene, as though she had found peace amidst the turbulence.

His dad's hand sought his then, grasping it firmly. "We have to be strong through this, Ben. We have to be strong for your mother." His eyes were red.

Ben thought for a moment, coming to a rapid decision. "Dad, did Mum ever mention 'Sunea' to you?"

"What's Sunea?" asked his dad, bemused.

"Never mind," said Ben, deflated. Helena had obviously never shared her secret with her husband, deciding instead to keep the past buried. He wasn't surprised. His dad would probably have thought his mother had truly gone off her rocker if she started saying she was from another dimension.

The truth must have been an incredible burden on his mum, to keep it secret for so long, hidden from those she loved most. All the visits to Stonehenge made sense now: it was the one place that would have reminded her of home. Perhaps there, she could feel close to those she had loved, sense them just behind the dimensional curtain but beyond perception. Invisible and untouchable, like ghosts.

Ben battled against the sadness welling up inside of him, but it was too much. He couldn't face to see his mother like this, lying there with a machine breathing for her, when it was all his fault. He excused himself from his father's side and left the room. How on Earth had he managed to cause such a mess?

As if on cue to remind him of just how much turmoil he had created, he saw two police officers round the corner, heading down the corridor straight for him. One of them turned to the other and said, "That's him," and Ben's first instinct was to run. But that would have been an astonishingly stupid thing to do, so he remained rooted to the spot as they approached.

"Ben Freeman?" asked one of them.

"Yes," Ben replied warily.

"Where's your father?"

Ben motioned behind him. "He's in there with my mother."

The officers shared a look. "We need to speak to both of you. It would probably be best if you're together."

"Why?"

"We need to take a formal statement, and you need to be supervised by a legal guardian to do so."

"Oh." Ben realised he was going to have to lie quite heavily to the police again, and he wasn't sure he could cope with it this time.

Ben plonked himself down in a plastic seat, and a couple of minutes later his father emerged from ICU, bleary-eyed and shocked. He didn't seem to register the police at first.

"Mr Freeman?" one of them ventured.

John was startled out of his trance and looked at the police officers in surprise.

"I know this is a difficult time, but we'd like to take a statement."

He sighed. "I really don't know what I could tell you – I was unconscious the whole time."

"Well… it's really your boy we need to speak to," said the second officer.

"Oh, right," sighed John Freeman.

"Yes, but you need to be present too. We wondered if you could come down to the station."

"Why can't you take it here?"

"We think it would be more appropriate down at the station."

"But why?"

"It's just standard procedure, for any knife-related incident, for us to interview down at the station, that's all."

"Interview? You said a statement before… oh, I get it," said John Freeman, understanding dawning in his eyes and anger rising in his voice. "You think Ben did it. You want to interview him as a suspect."

Ben was extremely alarmed at this development. "That's not true!" he shouted. "It was Lor… the old man." Ben had nearly said Lord Blackwood. "He came back to get to me but got my mum instead!"

The police officer stretched his hands out. "Both of you, calm down," he ordered. "No-one is under suspicion of anything right now; we just need to ascertain the facts, and the hospital is not the right place for that." The policeman straightened out his visibility jacket. "I understand that it's hard for you right now, but if there is someone out there that we need to catch, the sooner you can give us the information, the better."

That argument registered with John Freeman, and he quickly acquiesced. "Yes, of course, sorry. We'll follow you down there, shall we?"

Thirty minutes later, Ben was sat awkwardly on a hard plastic chair in the police station, his dad next to him. DCI Wainwright was opposite, the introductions already over. He was a middle-aged man, reasonably trim but with a heavy, hard face. He had mousy-brown hair with grey patches just above the ears, but he wore it short and sharp. He was dressed in a grey suit and carried himself with an air of authority.

"Right," said Wainwright, clapping his hands. "Let's get started." He leant towards the recorder. "This is DCI Wainwright interviewing Benjamin Freeman, thirteen years of age, attended by his father John Freeman. The time is four thirty am, October twenty-eighth." He leant back from the recorder and folded his arms.

"I'm up to speed, Ben, with the background of your case, so why don't we begin with what happened tonight?"

Ben scratched his head, shuffling uneasily in his chair. "Well, my mum had come into my room to comfort me... I was having a nightmare. The next thing we know, the man who had kidnapped me was standing in the doorway, threatening us with a knife."

"What did he want?" asked Wainwright.

Ben hadn't really thought this part of the story through, knowing only that he couldn't tell the truth, so he said the first thing that came to mind. "He said he'd come to tie up the loose ends, to finish me off."

Wainwright raised his eyebrows. "Pretty gutsy move when you think about it. He could have no idea if the police would be there."

John Freeman thought that was crass and said so. "Maybe you should have been, considering my wife is now lying in a coma."

Wainwright coughed apologetically. "Yes, I'm sorry about your mother. It's awful that she's fallen victim to this maniac. We wouldn't have normally put a car on in this situation, but that's going to change now. We're stepping up security on you and all of your friends until we find and catch this man."

"That's something at least," John muttered.

The plastic clock on the wall ticked intrusively, slicing the silence into ever-lengthening seconds.

"So how did your mum get injured?" asked Wainwright eventually.

"She was trying to protect me," said Ben, bowing his head in guilt. "It was all such a blur. He'd said he wanted to finish me off, so she got herself between us. There was a struggle and I... I tried to help. I got the baseball bat from my cupboard, but it was too late. By the time I managed to hit him with it, he'd already stabbed my mum."

"Do you have any idea where he may have gone?"

Ben shook his head.

Wainwright considered this, coming to a quick decision. "OK, I think we can't do much more here. I'd suggest you get yourself on home and get some rest – you won't be able to see your mum until tomorrow anyway. We'll have a marked car parked outside the house – any problems or you're getting jumpy, make sure you speak to them."

Ben's dad stood up. "Thank you, Detective," he said, shaking his outstretched hand. "Please keep us informed on your manhunt. We don't want any of the other families to have to go through this pain."

Wainwright nodded. "We'll be doing our utmost."

In the car on the way back home, Ben and his dad sat in silence, both contemplating the events of the past few hours.

"I'm sorry, Ben," said John, breaking the quiet. "I should have been there to protect you."

"It's not your fault." Ben sighed, looking out of the window at the black night. There were a few dark clouds scudding across the starry sky. "It's all mine."

John Freeman took a hand off the steering wheel, clamping it on to his son's shoulder. "You must never think that, Ben. You're a victim in all this, just like your mother. If I could get my hands on the man who did this…" He trailed off, leaving the threat hanging idle.

Ben decided not to say anything; he wasn't sure what good it would do to confess now. His mum's revelation had been a game-changer, and he couldn't tell his dad a secret that his mum had gone through so much to keep hidden.

They passed the panda car that was now keeping a watchful eye over them and pulled into their driveway. Ben wondered if Blackwood would be stupid enough to return with them there. He doubted it; so far, he had proved wily and resourceful.

He got out of the car, standing up and stretching out his aching limbs. He shivered; the night was cold, and a frost had formed on the lawn. The moon shone down, giving the garden an otherworldly bleakness as everything turned ghostly white. In that moment Ben saw the desolate and blighted world of the Shadow Realm, re-created here on Earth, and the memories of that awful place rushed back.

If Lord Blackwood got the Star, the Earth would go the way of Sunea and be plunged into a dark and dismal nightmare from which there would be no dawn. He couldn't let that happen. The responsibility was his, and his alone, for stopping Blackwood.

Blackwood had said he could charge up with magic on Earth without the Star and in a couple of days would have garnered enough to use a locating spell to find it. He may have been lying, but that was a risk that Ben could ill afford to take, so he needed to act quickly. There was precious little time to lose.

They'd made a promise to Taegan not to return, but everything had changed now. His mum had told him he needed Taegan's help, and he felt pretty sure that if he didn't do something drastic, it would be too late.

There was nothing else for it. He would have to return to the Shadow Realm.

CHAPTER 21

Ben and his dad ate breakfast in silence; there really wasn't much to say. Ben played with his Marmite on toast, turning it over in his fingers, hardly eating any of it. He was shattered, having barely slept a wink, kept awake by visions of Lord Blackwood attacking his mother, his mind preoccupied with plans of revenge.

Rain pattered softly on the window as he considered how to get back to the Shadow Realm. He needed a plausible excuse to give his dad, something that wouldn't raise his suspicions. He was unlikely to let his son out of his sight after what had happened to his wife.

Ben chewed his fingernails as he anxiously worked through his options, trying to figure out the best excuse that would give him enough time to get to the Shadow Realm, find Taegan and bring him back. He thought he would need at least an hour there, a period of time that would swallow four to five hours on Earth. If he was delayed for any reason then it would begin to get late here, potentially turning his father into an even bigger emotional wreck.

His phone vibrated; it was a message from Jake:

M8, herd bout ur ma, rly soz. U wanna meet?

Ben wondered if he could use Jake for cover, tell his dad he was going around there for the day, which would give him enough time to go to the Shadow Realm. He messaged back:

Thanks. Are you able to cover for me today?

His dad looked up from his paper. He disapproved of using phones at the table, but it seemed churlish to reprimand Ben this morning.

"Who's that?" he asked, as casually as possible.

"It's Jake," responded Ben. "I'd like to meet him at his house. We're, uh, just going to hang out and stuff."

"OK. Maybe I should call his mother, just check that's alright."

Ben shifted uneasily in his chair. "Er, there's no need, Dad. He's already run it past his mum. It's no problem."

"After everything that's happened, I think it would be a courtesy to his mum, don't you?"

Ben didn't want to push it further and raise suspicions. His phone buzzed again; Jake had replied with a one-letter answer:

Y?

Ben pursed his lips and quickly wrote back, as his dad went to pick up the landline:

Dad going 2 phone ur mum, put him off, tell him Ill b @ urs & we're just hanging out.

Ben finished writing and sending the message about ten seconds before his dad had finished finding Jake's home number and dialled it.

John Freeman rocked on his feet a little nervously as he waited for the other end to pick up. It finally did, and Ben was treated to a one-sided conversation.

"Hello, is that Jake?"

A small pause.

"John Freeman here – can I speak to your mother?" Another pause.

"Well, do you think she could ring—" John Freeman was cut off by something Jake was saying.

"Yes, it is about Ben coming over." A much longer pause.

"Well, that does sound nice." John started to twirl the telephone cord with his finger.

"And she's OK with that? She wouldn't prefer the family to be alone?"

John listened as the question was answered.

"OK, good – yes, pass her my love too. Goodbye, Jake."

John Freeman put the phone down, a pleased smile on his face.

Ben had to hand it to Jake: whatever he had said to his dad had worked a charm.

"So everything's OK?" he asked.

"Sure, just make sure you're home for dinner. I'll probably go to the hospital shortly if you want to come. I can drop you round Jake's later?"

"That sounds good."

His mobile buzzed again:

U O me. Wots goin on?

Ben excused himself from his table and went to his room, to avoid his dad getting any more suspicious. Once he'd shut himself away, he composed a message back:

If I tell you, you must promise not to tell anyone.

The reply came back almost immediately:

K

Ben shot back instantly:

I'll send a message on the group. Need to speak to all about Shadow Realm.

Ben sent the next message on a group that contained the four of them; he wanted to find out what they all thought about his mother's revelation:

Ben: Hey everyone, I guess you all heard about Blackwood attacking my mum?

Hev: Yes, so sorry to hear about that, are you OK?

Sam: yeah, sorry mate

Ben: I'll be alright, thanks

Jake: So what's up, what do you need to tell us?

Ben: My mum told me that she was from Sunea yesterday

Sam: What?!?

Hev: !!! Explain?

Jake: That's unbelievable

Ben: She was Taegan's wife. She was the one who brought the Star here.

Sam: This is all too much to take in

Hev: So the Star is here on Earth then? Do you know where?

Ben: No, she didn't tell me before we were attacked. She did tell me that I should go and get Taegan though

Sam: I think that's a good idea. Taegan will be able to deal with Blackwood much better than us

Jake: No way, we can take Blackwood. We just need to find him.

Hev: We should start looking for the Star, make sure we find it before Blackwood.

Ben: We might not have much time.

Sam: How do you mean?

Ben: Blackwood said that there was a small amount of background magic that he was able to charge up with, here on Earth. He said that in another day or two he'd have enough to find the Star.

Sam: What?? That's terrible news... what will we do if he gets it?

Ben: We have to hope it won't come to that. I'll go and get Taegan, and we'll go from there

Hev: Won't it be perilous to go back?

Ben: I don't know. I'm hoping that with Blackwood gone, it'll be less dangerous.

Jake: Let me come with.

Ben: No, I've put you in enough danger already. I need to do this myself

There was no reply for a little while then, and Ben thought he had upset his friends. Eventually he got a reply:

Sam: Just come back safe OK. I don't fancy it being just me and Jake against Lord Blackwood.

Hev: And me!!!

Jake: We can take him!

Hev: Good luck Ben. Come back quickly

Ben: I intend to. Thanks guys. It means a lot to me to have your support.

Jake: oh stop it you're embarrassing yourself

Ben: LOL. I'll ping you when back.

Ben put his phone back in his pocket and joined his dad downstairs for the drive to the hospital.

It was a horrible grey day, matching perfectly with Ben's darkening mood and growing fear for what he must do. On the journey into the hospital, he saw a homeless man slumped in the shelter of a doorway, and for a nervous, flickering second, he thought that it was Lord Blackwood. But it was just his agitated mind playing tricks on him.

He found himself wondering where Blackwood had gone after his violent incursion to their home, where he was spending his time during the days that meant the police couldn't find him. It was clear that Blackwood was resourceful, else he wouldn't have been able to avoid detection for so long. Ben cursed himself for having put so much faith in the authorities. He'd wasted valuable time that he could have spent looking for the Star or Lord Blackwood. Now he only had a couple of days to force the issue, to make sure he defeated him.

They pulled into the hospital car park, and his thoughts turned back to his mother. He allowed himself to think his mum might be better now, imagining a scene where he walked into the hospital to find her sat up in bed, radiating her beautiful smile, embracing him and holding him close.

He stepped out of the car and felt the drizzle on his face.

"Grim, eh?" offered his dad.

"Yeah," agreed Ben, pulling his coat up around his neck.

Reality deflated his foolish daydream as they walked into ICU, and he saw his mother again, lying immobile on her bed. Needles and tubes were coming out of her at all angles, the life-support machine that breathed for her the only barrier between this world and the next.

They both stood there for a few minutes, holding her hands and mumbling soft regrets and wishes.

Having composed himself a little, Ben turned to his dad. "Dad... would you mind if I had a few minutes alone with her?"

His dad looked a little hurt. "You don't have to be afraid of saying anything out loud to her in front of me, son."

"It's not that, it's just... when she was stabbed, she looked so scared. I was too late in defending her, I took too long to get the bat. I feel like I failed her."

His dad looked at him with soft eyes.

Ben continued: "I think it would just help me to spend a few minutes alone with her. I dunno, it's probably silly, but I feel like I need to ask for her forgiveness."

John put his hand on his son's shoulder. "You don't," he whispered. "But I understand. I'll go and get us some coffee, eh?"

Ben nodded, and his dad retreated from the ward.

Ben just looked at his mum for several seconds, not really knowing where to start. Her pallid, ashen face offered no help, no encouragement, no emotion.

"Mum... I don't know if you can hear me, but I want you to know that I'm really sorry. I've been monumentally stupid in all of this, not understanding from the beginning what's been going on. But I understand now; I know what needs to be done. I'm not going to let him win, Mum. He will not take from Earth what he has taken from Sunea." He paused, looking around nervously in case anyone was listening, but no-one cared what he had to say. Only the rhythmic clunk and hiss of air from the life-support machine was making any noise.

"I'm going to go to the Shadow Realm and bring back Taegan, like you wanted. We're going to kill Lord Blackwood and sort this mess out once and for all." He stopped to look at the heart monitor, hoping – almost expecting – that he might elicit a response from her. It didn't change. It just carried on beeping its monotonous symphony.

"Anyway, I'm going this afternoon, and I wanted to tell you. I don't know why, you can't hear me, it's all a bit stupid, really." He studied his fingernails briefly, rubbing his hands together anxiously. "I'll bring him here if you like. Taegan, I mean." He touched her forehead gently, leaning over to kiss her on the cheek. "When you wake up, Mum, we'll all be free from this nightmare. Lord Blackwood will be dead and Sunea will be free once more. I promise."

He squeezed her hand, and for a millisecond he was sure he felt her squeeze it back. He jumped up, looking from her to the monitor, praying to see signs of movement. But there was nothing.

His dad walked in then, holding two cups of coffee. "Nurse says

I'm not supposed to have these in here, but it'll be OK as long as we're extra careful."

"OK," said Ben, taking the coffee cup from his dad's outstretched hand.

They slurped their coffee together in companionable silence.

Later that morning Ben was back at home, furiously packing things for his journey back to the Shadow Realm. He wanted to be prepared for every eventuality, but he was equally indecisive on how he would use things there. Should he take a torch? Or would it attract undue attention? Should he take some food for the rebels, or might that bring out those savage beasts in the forest? He decided in the end to pack only the bare minimum so that he could move quickly. He wouldn't have long once there.

The thing he most wished he had was a gun, but there was no way for him to get one. He might stand a chance then against the magic of Blackwood's henchmen. He settled instead for a large chopping knife he stole from the kitchen and his baseball bat.

He slung the bag over his shoulders and crept down the stairs. He placed the bag just outside the front door so that he could collect it in a moment, then went back through to the lounge where his dad was sat on his leather chair, staring silently into space.

"Dad?"

His dad jumped, startled back into the real world by Ben's presence. "Are you off then?"

"Yep, I'll aim to be back around 5–6pm."

"OK."

"Will you go back to the hospital?" he ventured.

His dad looked blank for a moment but then recovered. "Yes," he said. "Yes, I think I will." He paused for a second, then added, "Be careful, son."

"I'm only going round the corner, Dad. Don't worry about me." Guilt stabbed at him as the lie left his lips.

"I know. It's just... I couldn't face it if anything else happened to you." His dad started to cry then, and Ben felt his heart sink. He went to his dad and hugged him – there was nothing more he could do, really. His dad sobbed for a minute before pulling himself together.

"Go on, you get going. Try and have some fun, god knows you need it."

Ben kissed his dad on the cheek. "I'll see you soon, Dad."

Ben backed out of the room hastily, not wishing to waste any time. He was going to need every second he could get when in the Shadow Realm, so he rushed outside, picked up his backpack and set off, walking quickly.

The journey to the clearing was uneventful. The weather had brightened up and it was turning into a very pleasant day, the sky a deep and clear blue, and the sun warm for this late in the year. The forest was at peace, basking in the unexpected sunny afternoon.

This was at complete odds with how Ben felt inside. His stomach was churning, his nerves were racked with fear and guilt, a nauseating combination. He was about to re-enter the Shadow Realm, something he'd promised not to do when he left but which had ironically become inevitable once Blackwood had hitched a ride back to this dimension with them. A sense of foreboding was rising inside of him, and it felt strange against the backdrop of such a beautiful day – it served to remind him of everything he was now battling to save. He couldn't let the fate of Sunea become the fate of the Earth.

Ben crept towards the clearing, keeping a keen eye out in case anyone was around. As he neared the clearing, he felt the atmosphere change around him. It was a familiar feeling by now, but it had also changed slightly. Not only did the atmosphere feel charged, somehow he felt as if it were charging him as well. The aches, pains and tiredness of the last few days ebbed away, to be replaced by a vim and vigour that put a spring in his step.

The effect of the portal was certainly more pronounced than it had been the first time he'd accidentally found it. Now it was as though his body was in tune with the portal, to the dimension beyond it that he now knew was a part of him, a part of his genetic make-up.

Whatever it was, he felt energised, emboldened to take on the quest before him. He took a deep breath and strode purposefully through the clearing, promptly vanishing into nothing at the centre.

CHAPTER 22

Ben popped into existence in the Shadow Realm, standing in a ghoulish copy of the clearing he had just disappeared from. He crouched down, listening intently for any noise. He pulled his knife out, waiting for his eyes to adjust to the oppressive gloom, for the dim light to slowly lift the world into view.

It was a very strange, unnatural kind of light, coming as it did from the trees and bushes around him. He wondered if it could be some form of radiation left over from the apocalyptic event that had happened when his mum activated the amulet, but that wasn't a comforting thought, so he tried to banish it from his mind.

He made his way to the edge of the clearing where he could take cover. There didn't appear to be anyone, friendly or otherwise, watching the portal site. He looked at his watch. He had gone through at midday, and now the clock was ticking, working against him. He had to find Taegan and convince him to come back to Earth with him within an hour, or too much time would pass on Earth, and he'd be in a whole other world of trouble.

He knew he would have to throw caution to the wind and strike out quickly to find the rebel base; he couldn't afford the luxury of stealth. He had to assume that the lack of anyone keeping guard over the portal site was a good thing, that maybe Lord Blackwood's support had melted away when he disappeared, and that it would be relatively safe for him to walk through the forest. He didn't really have any other choice. He just hoped he didn't come across one of those snarling Kraw beasts again. He took a deep breath, trying to calm his racing heart, and set out, taking long, quick strides.

Within fifty metres he began to realise the folly of his plan. When they had trekked through the forest before it had been extremely foggy – Galle's fog, Taegan called it – and they'd relied entirely on the rebels. Now that he had no-one to guide him, he could be hopelessly lost in minutes.

He remonstrated with himself for having acted so hastily. *What an idea this was!*

Ben looked around, caught in two minds. Should he call it quits and go back to the clearing whilst he still knew where it was, or forge on and risk getting lost? A slight gust of wind kicked up, rustling the leaves on the floor, the boughs of the trees groaning and creaking as they swayed lightly. Something hooted above him.

Then he had a flash of inspiration. The knife. He could use it at intervals to mark a route back to the clearing. If he felt at any point that he wasn't going to find the base in time, he could just follow the markings back, like his own version of the breadcrumbs from Hansel and Gretel. *Just as long as I don't end up in anyone's cooking pot*, he thought with a rueful grin.

Feeling pleased with himself, he etched an arrow into the nearest tree, pointing the way back to the portal site. The arrow glowed on the tree, the scar on its bark bleeding a soft, blue light. It stood out in the dark world, which Ben was uneasy about, as it effectively advertised the site of the portal. But it was necessary, and at least it would make them easier to see if he needed to get back quickly.

He pressed on, stopping every hundred yards or so to mark another arrow on a tree.

He carried on like this for about half an hour – walking along, marking an arrow, making his way further and further into the forest. He shivered, noticing the cold suddenly, as if an icy gust had suddenly blown through his body, and stopped to get a fleece out of his backpack. He was just about to pull it over his head when he saw something that made his heart sink.

It was an arrow etched into a tree.

He rushed up to it and rubbed it, disbelieving that it could be one of the arrows he had only just made. But of course it was, and it meant that he'd just spent the last half hour walking around in a circle.

He slumped down against the tree and held his head in his hands, realising that he was failing. He was wasting too much time, the gloom of the Shadow Realm testing him more keenly than he thought it might. He now only had half an hour left, and he was still no closer to finding the rebel base.

He rocked his head back against the tree, closed his eyes and breathed out a deep sigh. He really didn't know what he was going to do. He listened to the sounds of the Shadow Realm, though there were few. The shuffle of something foraging through the mulch and loam; a slight whistling of the wind as it danced through the treetops.

And then something else – something that sounded like... humming?

Ben strained his ears, his heart racing as he struggled to make out the sound. He got up and started to creep towards where he thought it was coming from, nervous and alert for a trap. It was definitely humming, and he hoped that whoever or whatever was making the noise would turn out to be friendly. He could certainly do with catching a break. The strange humming and his pulsating heart began to mingle in his head, creating a rhythm to his fear, like the beating of a war drum. His footsteps were careful, and his eyes peeled wide for danger. Then, rising like a monolith out of the gloom, was one of the stones of the Sunean henge.

The similarities between here and Stonehenge were striking; the formation and the way the stones had been assembled were almost exactly the same, as if they'd been built by the same hands.

Ben peered into the circle of rocks and saw someone perched on his knees in front of the centre stone, a silhouetted figure against the shadowy darkness. He looked to be praying, humming in a deep tone as a form of incantation and occasionally touching the stone in front of him. Relief flooded through Ben as he realised who it was.

"Akmar!" he shouted.

Akmar shot up and whirled round, his long grey hair swishing behind him, picking up his stick and brandishing it as a weapon.

"Oh, it's you," he wheezed, lowering the stick and clutching his heart, breathing heavily. "You gave me the fright of my life!"

"That was the fright of your life?" said Ben sarcastically. "You live in the Shadow Realm!"

"Yes, well," muttered the old man. "You know what I mean."

Ben's expression softened. "Sorry to startle you, I was just so pleased to find someone I knew."

"What are you doing here anyway?" Akmar began looking around nervously. He looked dishevelled and emaciated, as if on some religious fast where he couldn't eat or wash. "Have you brought Lord Blackwood back with you?"

"No, but he is the reason I'm here. Blackwood is in my world, where he intends to get his hands on the Star of Moirai."

Akmar's hands flew to his mouth and he took a sharp intake of breath.

"If he does," continued Ben, "it'll be the end for my planet. I need to find Taegan." He looked Akmar directly in the eye. "Can you help me find him? I don't have long."

Akmar shook his head and stroked his beard, as if he couldn't believe this extraordinary turn of events. Eventually his eyes widened, and he lifted his head to look back at Ben. "Don't you see what this means, my boy?"

Ben shook his head, not caring for the distraction.

"I was right all along. Everything I have told Taegan was bang on the magic, but he wouldn't listen, oh no," said Akmar, wagging his finger.

"Right about what?" sighed Ben, exasperated with the change in subject.

"That you come from the dimension the amulet was sent to. It was protected there, safe from Lord Blackwood's grasp, but now it transpires that by sending you back, we've put it all in jeopardy." He threw his head up to the sky. "Oh, these are woeful tidings indeed."

Ben was losing his patience. "Listen, I need to find Taegan. Do you know where he is?"

Akmar brought his eyes back down from the sky, to look plainly, almost blankly, at Ben, as if he had never seen him before.

Ben's patience snapped. "Well?"

"Aye, I'll take you."

"Excellent, then can we please hurry up about it?"

"I can't run, if that's what you're after," said the cantankerous old man.

"No, but I need to get going now. How far is it?"

"About half a mile, not far."

Ben looked at his watch. He reckoned he had about twenty-five minutes, plus a little bit of contingency before his dad started to get worried. That didn't leave much time at all.

As they walked, Akmar told Ben about what had happened after Blackwood had gone. Most of Blackwood's 'loyal' servants had quickly vanished into hiding, with only Grimstone maintaining a stronghold at the castle. A strange kind of ceasefire had broken out, with people able to come and go freely, but one that felt unreal, as if they were in the eye of a storm.

It did mean there was no need to be quiet and cautious.

"Where did your henge come from?" asked Ben, keen to understand the importance of the site.

"It's been around since the dawn of time," said Akmar, waving his hands majestically. "It's written that the very first mages built it, and several others like it across Sunea, as temples to magic. For thousands of years, practitioners of magic would come to worship at these temples, to pay their thanks to the god of sorcery and to learn and discuss with fellow mages how best to use their gift." Akmar furrowed his brow. "Alas, as magic became commoditised and sold on to ordinary folk, the henges became less and less relevant. People realised that they had nothing to do with the ability to perform magic, so they just didn't see the need to go. But of course, it's not all about being able to *do* magic; it's also about *how* it should be done, and that's something they don't teach at school." He looked off into the distance. "I'm probably one of the only people still alive who worships at the henge."

Ben looked at the old man, his expression forlorn as he considered his lost past. "There's a similar place in my home world, called Stonehenge, not too far from where I live."

Akmar raised an eyebrow. "Really? That is interesting. I wonder who put it there?"

"I was kind of hoping you might know the answer to that one?"

"I can't really say I do... some of the earliest legends we have talk about a band of dimension-hopping druids, but there isn't any evidence that any of the writings are true. Although, I suppose you may have just provided some of the first!"

Ben decided to try his mother's theory on Akmar. "Do you think it could be a communication device? You know, between dimensions?"

Akmar scrunched up his face. "I doubt it, I think we would know about it by now if that were the case."

"But you said yourself so much gets forgotten through the ages, like who built them, so why not what they're really for?"

"I suppose in theory, it might be possible. But whatever it is they used to do, I don't think they do it anymore. It's been too long."

Ben scratched his chin. "It's just I've been curious about the similarities between our dimensions, and if there had been some sharing of culture through this portal, on whatever level, it might help explain some of them."

"What similarities?"

"Like the fact we both speak English—"

"Sunean," Akmar interrupted.

"Whatever," Ben pressed on. "The fact that we're both human – I mean, could all these things happen by chance?"

"It certainly is peculiar. But you should also remember, Ben, that there are an infinite number of parallel dimensions, ours being but two of them. There will be a great number of similarities and differences between all of them and what we consider our own reality. Ours might be far apart in some respects, but in others may be much closer than we could ever imagine." Akmar gestured with his stick that they were nearly at the gate to the rebel base. "None of which I think point to good tidings. I fear we may be entering an endgame for our two dimensions – a magical event of awesome proportions. A lot of the old writings certainly seem to be coming true in recent years."

"Like the prophecy?"

Akmar tapped his chin. "It is most interesting." He motioned at the base of the massive tree they were now standing by. "We're here. After you."

Ben scurried down onto his front and wriggled through the wet leaves into the gap between the tree and the ground, groping his way through the hole. Akmar followed shortly behind him, and once he'd struggled to stand up, he banged his staff on the ground, lighting it up like a torch.

"Cool," said Ben, impressed by the magic.

Akmar shrugged. "It's not much – I used to be able to send a blaze of light brighter than a thousand candles from this staff; now it's just a dull glow. There's not a lot of magic around these days. It's better than nothing, though – it's absolute murder trying to make it down these stairs without a light."

Ben could now see the stairs leading down just beyond his feet, steep steps that swiftly receded into the darkness beyond.

They made their way down gingerly, the steps slippery from the recent fog, the moisture of which had soaked into everything. Akmar explained how the fog was now one of their major sources of water, as they descended into the caverns underneath the forest.

The light from Akmar's staff didn't really penetrate the gloom here, and Ben couldn't see more than a few feet in either direction.

Then a voice from the darkness called out, "Halt, who goes there?"

"'Tis I, Akmar," said the old man.

Ben thought he recognised the voice. "Taegan, is that you?"

"Who is that?"

"It's me, Ben," he called out into the dark. There was a pregnant pause.

"What are you doing here?"

"I came back to get you," he announced happily.

A figure moved out from the darkness and into the soft light. Taegan looked concerned. Ben was so happy to see him he almost flung his arms around the big man to give him a hug but caught himself just in time.

"What do you mean, come and get me?" His tone was harsh.

"Lord Blackwood," Ben said, slightly breathlessly. "He's on Earth, and he's trying to find the Star of Moirai."

"Aieee!" cried Taegan, putting his head in his hands. "All that effort and sacrifice for nothing." He looked at Ben, anger in his eyes. "Why did you ever have to come here?" he shouted. Ben withered under his ferocious glare.

"I... I..." he stuttered.

"Things have been calm here since Blackwood left – good, almost. We've been able to start planning for a better world."

Ben paused, unsure of what to say.

"Maybe you should have just stayed at home."

"But if Blackwood gets his hands on the Star, it'll be the end for all of us."

Taegan sighed, fed up with the problems he kept being brought. "And do you think he has a chance of finding it?"

"He says that in two to three days he'll have enough magic to cast a spell that will find it." As an afterthought he added, "That's probably a few hours from now, in your time."

Taegan considered this, scratching his stubbly face. "Well then, why have you wasted time coming back here? Why not just deal with him yourself?"

Ben hesitated; he had one rather large grenade left in his arsenal, and he felt it was time to use it. "My mother... she said I should come and get you."

"Your mother? Why would she say that?"

"Because she was the one who brought the Star to Earth." Ben gulped, struggling to formalise the truth into words. "She was your wife... you called her Lenara." The grenade was thrown; it just needed to detonate.

Taegan's face screwed up, his instant reaction one of denial. "No... that's not possible." He looked Ben up and down. "You're what – twelve, thirteen? My dear Lenara departed this dimension but four years ago."

"I told you, it seems that for some reason time goes slower here than in my dimension. I assure you, as hard as it may be to believe, the woman you sent back to protect the amulet, your wife, is also my mother."

Taegan shook his head, refusing to believe the truth. "It can't be true; you must be mistaken. She wouldn't have... she can't have..." Taegan began to lose control. "You must be from some other dimension, and Blackwood is with you and nowhere near the Star."

Ben remained calm. "If that were true, how would I know her name?"

Taegan looked at Ben with mistrust. "I must have told you."

"Think back – you never said her name to me. But she did. And now she needs your help. We need your help." Ben looked around. "And I could do with it pretty darn quick."

Taegan slumped against the wall, struggling to take it all in. "My Lenara, she's really there? She's really your mother?"

"She is. Except she's in a bad way right now. Blackwood tried to kill her; she nearly died right in front of me. She's in hospital now." A tear sprang to Ben's eye as he thought of his mum. "She's in a coma."

"A coma?"

Ben wasn't sure how best to describe it. "I guess it's like being asleep, but you can't be woken up. It's not good."

Taegan slammed his fist into the wall. "How dare he hurt my Lenara?" he yelled.

Ben jumped, shocked by the sudden outburst.

"The last thing she said to me was that I should come and get you, that only you could help."

"She said that?"

"Yes."

"That only I could help?"

Ben nodded.

Taegan blinked twice, bewilderment etched in his face. "I'm not sure why only me; that doesn't make any sense."

"That's what she said."

"I'm not sure what she means."

"Fine," sighed Ben, looking at his watch. "Will you come anyway?"

Taegan took no time in coming to a decision. "I will come back with you," he declared. "We will find Lord Blackwood, and when we do, I will kill him."

"Good," said Ben. "Because I really have to get back now, or I'll be in so much trouble I'll be grounded for a year."

"OK, I will round up some people and get some things."

"There's no time; we need to go right now." The urgency in Ben's eyes seemed to convince Taegan.

"I will be back in a minute." And with that he turned tail and bolted off down the corridor, already yelling instructions that Ben couldn't make out.

Akmar's staff went out then, plunging them back into darkness. "Uh-oh," he said. "Looks like I've run out of magic." He turned to Ben. "Well, this is where you and I part ways, my young friend." He placed his hand on Ben's shoulder. "Good luck."

"Thanks," said Ben, unsure of what else to say. A pang of sorrow flickered through his chest that he might not see him again. "I'll come back," he called after Akmar. "Once we've defeated Lord Blackwood."

"I think that might be unwise," the old man replied, shuffling away.

Ben remembered his torch then, fishing it out and turning it on, but Akmar had already disappeared. Taegan came rushing back with Elena, her blue hair glittering in the torchlight, like tinsel on a Christmas tree.

Elena gave Ben a hug before he knew what was going on. "I'm so relieved you're here," she said. "We were worried when Blackwood disappeared with you, about what he might do to you all."

"He doesn't have any powers in our dimension – yet. We need to find and stop him before he can get his hands on the Star."

"Of course." She released Ben from her grasp. "I'm pleased we have the opportunity to finish this."

"First we need to get out of here."

Taegan was eyeing Ben with suspicion. "Have you discovered magic, young Ben?" he asked slowly.

Ben didn't understand what Taegan meant at first, until he realised he was staring at the torch. "Oh no, this is just a torch. It produces light, but, er, without any magic involved. I'll bring you back loads if we can just go now?" he said impatiently.

"I'll lead the way," said Taegan, scrambling off up the stairs. Ben was thankful to have Taegan back in control. He was a tetchy and surly soul, but he was a good leader. They raced up the stairs after him, quickly squeezing out from under the tree and setting off across the Shadow Realm at a good pace. Ben was happy – they'd be at the portal site in no time at this rate.

They began the journey in tense silence, but Ben was buzzing with an undercurrent of excitement as he knew he'd be home soon. The Shadow Realm was still, almost too still, as if it was trying to throttle Ben's buoyant mood with oppressive quiet. The only sound was their footsteps, a quick, rhythmic crunching of the dry leaves underfoot. Suddenly Taegan stopped, coming to a halt so fast that Ben crashed into the back of him. Taegan turned, putting a finger to his lips, his eyes wide in fear.

Ben's heart raced. He didn't know what the problem was, but he knew if Taegan was scared, he should be too. Then a deep, menacing growl came ripping through the forest, a sound that Ben recognised instantly.

"Oh, heck," he muttered, knowing that this was the same noise as the vicious, snarling beast that had attacked him on one of his earlier forays into the Shadow Realm. Taegan and Elena joined hands in front of Ben, whispering urgently.

"We use a joint incantation, a shock bolt," Taegan ordered. Elena nodded in agreement. They could hear the smash and crash of the creature as it began its charge through the trees.

Ben could see the animal's outline now, as it swept towards them through the gloom. The two rebels began muttering under their breath, a bright ball of light engulfing their hands and crackling there momentarily, before shooting out towards the beast. For a brief second the horrid creature's features were illuminated from the ball of fire: huge, sharp teeth bared in a vicious wolf's face, its body as large and heavy as a rhinoceros. The surge of energy hit the animal square in the head, and it roared in agony as it was knocked backwards. The rebels themselves were blown off their feet by the force of the impact, landing in a crumpled heap on the floor.

The animal whimpered on the ground, clearly stunned but still very much alive. Ben watched in amazement and terror as the thing slowly began to regain its senses, even making a wobbly effort to stand up. It wouldn't be long until it recovered, and then he'd be in serious trouble. He moved to Taegan to try and wake him, slapping and shaking him, desperately trying to rouse him, but he was out cold. He looked over at Elena, who was in the same condition.

The beast was now standing, shaking its head to try and clear the fug from the blast. It turned to look at Ben, refocussing its rage squarely on him.

He gulped.

The animal growled a deep, guttural roar that rolled around the trees and shook the ground he was standing on. It dropped its head and charged. There was no point in running; Ben wouldn't get further than a few paces before the Kraw caught him and ripped him to pieces.

Adrenaline surged through his body, as a primal instinct for survival kicked in. He was on his own, and unless he did something, a quick, gory death was bounding towards him.

Something took over. An energising surge began to work its way through his body, from the bottom of his feet right up to the top of his head. His skin felt electric, his muscles bobbling and rippling as the energetic charge went through them. He felt stronger, more alive and more powerful than he ever had before.

But he couldn't control it. The charge built to an unbearable level, roiling within him like he was strapped to an electric chair. The pain pulsated through his body as white-hot needles scraped and stabbed at his skin. Ben was terrified; he felt like he would be blown apart. He threw his head back and screamed as the force within him built to a final, apocalyptic level.

The beast jumped towards him, its sharp claws ready to strike, and at that moment the energy exploded out of Ben in all directions, a rapidly expanding and powerful dome of bright electricity, crackling and shining a fluorescent blue in the gloom of the Shadow Realm.

It hit the thing mid-jump, sending it flying backwards and slamming into a tree, where it fell to the floor, dead.

The rebels, rocked by the explosion passing over their bodies, came round, dazed and confused.

Ben fell to his knees and heaved. He wasn't sure what had just happened, but he didn't feel good. Had that blast really just come from him? He looked at his hands and felt nothing; no charge, no energy, nothing. He just felt shattered.

Taegan and Elena were getting to their feet now, alert again to the danger the animal posed. They spotted it lying inert against a tree and instantly relaxed, assuming it was their magic that had killed it.

"Are you OK?" asked Taegan, helping Ben to his feet.

Ben had no time to process what had just happened, or how. "I… I'm fine. A little shaken, perhaps."

"We were lucky there; a Kraw is a very difficult beast to take down. We'll just have to hope we don't run into any more; we won't have any magic left to fend it off."

Ben nodded. He didn't know what to say, what words to use to explain what had happened. He wasn't even sure he knew what did happen, so he stayed quiet.

"Let's keep moving," said Elena, pointing the way.

The clearing was quiet – calm, and unknowing of its pivotal role in this battle across dimensions.

"OK," said Ben. "You both need to hold on to me as we go through. And it's going to hurt – a lot."

They signalled their assent and moved towards Ben.

Just then they heard some shouting and crashing from the forest around them.

"Not again," Ben cried.

Taegan held an arm up. "This is different," he said.

They strained their ears, trying to hear what was approaching. It sounded like shouting voices, still distant but rapidly approaching. Then they looked at each other in surprise; it was Ben's name.

"That sounds like Sofiella," said Elena.

Then a different voice, shouting for Taegan.

"And that's Manatang."

"We're over here," shouted Ben, moving away from the clearing to find them.

Sofiella and Manatang appeared from the gloom a few moments later, panting, and took a second to regain their breath.

"What are you doing here?" asked Taegan.

"We just needed to see Ben," said Manatang. "Wish him good luck." Manatang gave Ben a hug, catching him off guard. Ben stiffly hugged him back, finding it strange to be hugging a monkey, his fine hair surprisingly soft. As they hugged, Ben felt a slight repeat of that charge rising in him, and Manatang pulled back, giving him a curious look.

The moment broke when Sofiella came and took Ben's hand. "Good luck, Ben," she said, giving him a peck on the cheek. Ben went red, which he hoped no-one could see in the murky darkness. "The entire Sunean people are counting on your success." Her blonde hair shimmered nebulously in the dull light.

"Thanks," said Ben, smiling. "Not much riding on it then."

"I also wanted to give you this." She handed him a small round bracelet, made of two strands of silver that wove around each other in a double helix pattern.

"What is it?" asked Ben.

"It's a charm bracelet – I made it. It was kind of my thing... before the war. It'll help keep you safe."

"Uh, thanks," stuttered Ben. He failed to see how a bracelet was going to keep him safe, but he slipped it over his wrist anyway so as not to cause offence.

"Now if you will excuse us, we really must be going." Ben grabbed Elena's hand and Taegan's, and told them both to breathe deeply.

Sofiella and Manatang watched as the three of them walked towards the middle of the clearing, saw the faces of the two rebels stiffen in shock as Ben pulled them towards the portal, and then, as if by magic, they disappeared.

CHAPTER 23

They landed with a bump in the New Forest.

Ben, who by now was used to inter-dimensional travel, got up immediately and surveyed the scene. The rebels were in a sorry state: Taegan swore breathlessly as he tried to lean up on his elbows but failed, the effort proving too much, too soon. Elena lay on her back, heaving life-giving air into her winded lungs. In the light of day they looked terrible, their faces etched with dirt and worry, their tatty clothes worn and tired.

The sun was getting low now, but Ben breathed a sigh of relief. If he was home before sunset, he figured he'd be OK. He fished his mobile out from his pocket and called his dad, just to let him know that he would be home within the hour.

His dad sounded vacant, distracted by his own melancholy, which was hardly surprising given everything that had happened. The fact his dad was at home presented Ben with a new set of problems: he wasn't too sure what he was going to do with the rebels now they were here. He could hardly take them home to meet his dad.

He finished the call and hung up. Taegan and Elena had now recovered and were stood up, staring around them with their mouths open.

"It's all so... beautiful," said Elena.

Taegan drank in the sunshine, gulping down the freshness and vitality of the forest in all its glorious colour. "It used to be like this in Sunea, Ben," he said. "Such simple, outstanding beauty. Everything so vibrant, so *alive*. Lord Blackwood destroyed all that with his greed and thirst for power." He placed a hand on the bark of an oak tree, rubbing and patting the solid, knotty wood, feeling its strength. "We must prevent him from doing the same here."

Ben nodded. "We need to find him first."

"What is that?" asked Elena, motioning at his smartphone. Her blue hair glistened in the early evening sunlight.

"What, this? It's a phone." As soon as Ben said the word, he realised they wouldn't know what it was. "Er, it basically allows me to speak to other people, wherever they are."

"Wow," said Elena. "That's some impressive magic."

"Oh, it's not magic," began Ben, laughing softly. "It's..." But then he couldn't explain it easily. A quote he'd heard once came back to him about how, to a primitive audience, any sufficiently advanced technology would be indistinguishable from magic. To the Suneans, who had relied on magic to make their lives convenient, much of the technological progress on Earth would seem like magic.

"Never mind," he finished meekly.

Taegan breathed in deeply, enjoying the fresh air of the forest. "Ben, this planet, your home, is magnificent. I am pleased that Lenara came here and found it to be a good home in which to raise a family." For a moment, Ben thought Taegan might shed a tear, but he kept it together.

"Well, the forest is a nice place. But the world isn't all great, you know, we have many of our own problems," said Ben.

"Maybe so, but at least you have this to save. What is left in the Shadow Realm to salvage...?" Taegan trailed off, and no-one answered. They didn't want to face the truth, which was that there was nothing.

"Well, shall we make tracks, eh?" suggested Ben, finally.

Ben hoped that they didn't come across anyone on the way home. The rebels stuck out like a sore thumb in their dishevelled and ragged hemp clothing. The first thing he would have to do when he got back was sort them out with some new clothes. A bath wouldn't go amiss, either.

They wandered out of the clearing and over the brow of the small hill which led down to the main track they'd take back to the village. A stunning vista of the forest lay before them, the setting sun sparking the sky alight in pastel orange and blue, the canopy of the trees ablaze with gold and amber. They walked for a bit in silence before Ben noticed that Elena was crying.

"What's the matter?" asked Ben.

"I'm sorry," sniffed Elena, wiping her eyes with her arm. "It's just to see the sun again after all these years, it's a little... overwhelming. It's warm, and light, and fresh, and everything that was so beautiful about our planet. I'm just mourning what we've lost." She looked melancholic and lost in that moment, and Taegan put his arm around her.

"If we can defeat Blackwood, maybe we can rebuild Sunea," Taegan said, trying to lift her spirits. She touched his hand, grateful for the support.

"Thank you," she said to Ben, to his great surprise. "Thank you for bringing me here so I could see this. We must prevail over Blackwood. It is our fault that he is here, and we must put it right."

"It's not your fault," said Ben glumly. "It's mine. If I hadn't gone to the Shadow Realm, none of this would have happened. My mum would still be safe and so would the amulet."

"Don't be too hard on yourself," she began. "You didn't know what you were getting yourself into. It was us who sent your mother to this dimension with the amulet, setting off this whole chain of events. It is our dimension that burst into yours, so you see it is our fault and we must make it right."

"Well, we're in it together now," offered Ben with a smile.

"And let's not forget," said Taegan, "that the situation may be to our advantage. It will be much easier to kill Blackwood in this dimension, whilst he's defenceless."

They continued walking for a while in silence, and Ben began to muse on another point. "What do you think actually happened to your world?" he asked.

"Nobody really knows," answered Taegan. "We assume that the Star set off some catastrophic magic that broke our reality, that maybe we were yanked out of our own, proper dimensional space and placed somewhere else. Almost like we got put in the pocket of another universe, where there is nothing, just cold and darkness." A deer that had been grazing nearby was startled by them, bounding off into the forest.

"Many of our finest mages tried to answer the question before they perished of illness, but to no avail. I still hope one day we can restore our world to the way it was, but I don't know if it's possible."

"And you've never seen the sun, or the moon, or the stars since the day the Star was used?"

"No, all we have now is the fog and the gloom, and the strange light that comes from the land itself."

"You've no idea what that is either?"

"No, but we are grateful for it. Without it we could not see at all."

They walked along in silence for a while as Ben mulled this over. It stood to reason that Sunea had once been just like the Earth, orbiting the sun in space. Could it have somehow dropped out of the physical universe into some strange kind of other dimension? Ben knew that the answer to that was well beyond his sphere of expertise, but it was an interesting notion.

They were nearing the main road now, and Ben was conscious about how the rebels looked, with so many cars going past. But they had to cross it, so he was just going to have to hope that no-one paid them much attention.

What he hadn't thought about was the reaction of the rebels to the thunderous, mechanised chariots that zoomed past at high speed. At once scared and intrigued, Taegan was about to walk out in front of a van when Ben only just managed to pull him back.

"Stop!" he shouted. "If it hits you, you'll be killed."

"What are these things, Ben?" Taegan said. "They move like they are possessed by Devilius himself."

"They're cars," he replied. "And they're very dangerous. You need to be careful around them." Elena and Taegan stood at the roadside, mouths agape as they watched the cars race past. "They help us to get around, much faster and further than a horse can."

"Are they magic?" asked Taegan.

"Not quite," said Ben, pulling a face to cut this wasteful chatter out. "We need to cross the road, and we do it when I say, OK?" The chastened rebels nodded, and Ben waited for a few cars to pass until there was a gap in the traffic. "OK, now," said Ben, pushing the rebels across the road ahead of him.

Ben took a shortcut and raced along an overgrown path that led down past the estate to behind his garden. He peered over the fence, trying to see where his dad was, but there was no sign of him. He breathed a sigh of relief.

"OK, this is my house," said Ben.

"It's amazing," interjected Elena.

Ben looked at his modest house and shrugged. "I'm going to hop over the fence and make sure the coast is clear. I'll come back for you and try and smuggle you into the house. Just wait here for five minutes, understood?"

"Yes," said Elena.

"When do we look for Blackwood?" asked Taegan, impatient to begin his quest.

"As soon as we can get you out of those conspicuous clothes and we've discussed a plan." Ben rubbed his forehead. "Please just stay here until I come back for you?"

"Of course," Taegan promised.

"Good," said Ben. He checked that the coast was still clear and then scrambled up and over the fence.

He dashed around the side, smoothed down his hair and entered the house via the front door.

The house was silent apart from the grandfather clock in the hallway that dutifully ticked each second by, emphasising the passage of time yet also stretching it to infinity. Ben's heart was pumping fast, his hands sweaty.

"Dad?" he called out, timidly.

Some rustling from upstairs. "Is that you, son?" his dad shouted down.

Ben silently cursed. "Yeah, I'm back from Jake's."

"Excellent, I was just going to head down to the hospital to see your mother before doing dinner, if you want to come?"

It was phrased as a question, but Ben knew he would be expected to go. He had to get himself out of it somehow.

"Um… no thank you," he called back. "I need to have a shower and do a bit of homework before school tomorrow." The lies tumbled from his lips, and with each one the knot in his stomach grew tighter.

A pause, which expressed all the disappointment it needed to. "OK," said his dad. He was coming down the stairs now. Ben finished taking off his shoes and met him at the bottom. "But you don't have to go to school tomorrow if you don't want to." John Freeman put his hand on his son's shoulder and looked at him through tired, shabby eyes. "You've been through an awful lot, and if you need some time off, I'm sure the school will understand."

"Sure, thanks, Dad." Ben tried to smile naturally, unsure he was pulling it off.

His dad wandered into the kitchen, away from his son. "What homework do you have anyway?" he asked nonchalantly.

"Sorry?" Ben spluttered, trying to delay an answer.

"The homework you have to do – I just wondered what it was. I'm sure I could write you a note to the teacher to get you out of it."

Ben wasn't sure whether his dad was probing him for the lie or was genuinely trying to help. He said the first thing that came to his mind. "It's a history project we've had for a while, on Stonehenge. To be honest, I'd quite like to just spend an evening getting at it, doing something normal and boring, if you know what I mean?"

His dad gave him a lopsided smile, and a wetness sprang into his eye. "Sure, son, I know what you mean. Shame your mother's not here, eh? You know how much she loved Stonehenge." His face crumpled and he looked like he was about to lose it completely. He took a deep breath and pulled himself together. "I'll leave you to it."

His dad walked past him, gave him a kiss on the top of his head, picked up his car keys from the sideboard and opened the front door.

"I'll see you in about an hour or two," he said, closing the door behind him.

Ben couldn't believe his luck. He waited for his dad to pull out of the drive before going back out into the garden.

"OK," he whispered over the fence, "we're good to go."

Taegan popped his head up over the top, bobbing there as if disembodied for a moment. Then he vaulted the fence in one swift movement, like a panther springing into action. Elena followed Taegan promptly, and Ben quickly ushered them into the confines of the house.

"First things first," declared Ben, "I reckon you could do with some food and clean water."

The excitement in the rebels' eyes was palpable. They drank the water down thirstily, amazed at the clarity and the way it appeared from the tap.

"I can see that yours is an ingenious civilisation," said Taegan. "You have found a way to overcome basic needs within your home. We must seem like terrible savages."

Ben handed Taegan a peanut-butter sandwich. "No, I think if you saw how we let people live in parts of our world, you would think that of us," he sighed. "I'm very lucky to live here in England, where I have a nice home, good food and clean water. In many parts of the world, people live in huts and they can barely scrape enough together to feed their children. We have some terrible poverty and huge inequality between the rich and the poor. So you might well think of us as the savages."

They finished their sandwiches, and, duly refreshed, Ben set about stage two of his plan. He pulled clothes out of his parents' wardrobe, whilst running baths for them both. Twenty minutes later they were bathed and dressed, Taegan in his dad's jeans and T-shirt, Elena in a floral dress belonging to his mother. When she returned from the bathroom with it on, Ben blushed. She looked quite stunning, and his crush on her was complete. He knew it was like having a crush on a teacher, one he could never act on, but he couldn't suppress the feelings all the same.

"You think I look OK?" she purred.

Ben spluttered a 'yes' before looking away, embarrassed.

"What now?" she asked. "How do we find Blackwood?"

Ben looked at Taegan, hoping he might have an answer. But Taegan had picked up a photograph of his mother and was looking at it dolefully. Ben went to his side.

"She looks so much older," Taegan whispered, not taking his eyes from the picture. Ben saw it was one from last summer, when they'd gone to Bournemouth beach. It was a windy day; her hair was flapping madly, and she was struggling to hold on to her hat. "I can't believe it's been a lifetime for her."

"She's been a fantastic mum," said Ben, hoping these words might somehow console him. It was still strange to Ben that his mum had meant so much to Taegan and he to her. He seemed so different from his dad. Taegan stroked the photograph gently, his melancholy painful to witness.

"Can we go and see her?" Taegan asked, so softly that Ben didn't quite hear him.

"I beg your pardon?"

"I was hoping we could go and see her. Lenara."

The floorboard creaked as Elena rocked on her heels.

"She has a new name here; it's Helena," said Ben. "But yes, we can go and see her."

Taegan broke out into a smile, running his hands nervously through his hair.

"Not 'til tomorrow, though," added Ben. "We need to come up with a plan for dealing with Lord Blackwood. He could have enough magic to find the Star very soon."

"Do you have any bright ideas?" asked Taegan.

Ben sighed. "I was rather hoping you might."

CHAPTER 24

Ben, Sam, Jake and Heather sat with the two rebels in the windy treehouse, debating their next steps. They hadn't got very far. So far, they'd been distracted by Ben showing pictures of his mum and Stonehenge, Sam showing them the world from space, and Jake a video of a cat surfing, all on their smartphones. The Suneans marvelled at it all, bemused and enthralled in equal measure.

"Right," began Ben, clapping his hands together. "Enough distractions; let's get down to business. How are we going to find and kill Lord Blackwood?"

There was a moment's silence.

"Shouldn't we try looking for the Star as well?" asked Heather.

"I still can't believe you're a child of both dimensions, dude," hooted Jake.

"It's pretty cool," said Sam, looking almost reverentially at Ben.

"So, did your mum tell you where the Star was?"

"Unfortunately not; she thought it would be too dangerous if I knew. After Blackwood attacked us, the only thing she told me was to get Taegan and bring him here. She said he was the only one who could… do something, but unfortunately she slipped away before she could tell me what."

"Well, Taegan," said Jake rather forcefully. "What is it that you can do that no-one else can?"

Taegan stared hard at Jake. "I think she might have thought I'd be able to use the star to defeat Blackwood, but I don't know, really," he said calmly.

"Wonderful," Jake remarked.

"So where do we start?" asked Elena.

Silence descended on the treehouse again as they all tried to think. The wind whistled as it rushed through the leaves, portends to a gathering storm.

"We could try and smoke him out," volunteered Jake.

Ben arched his eyebrow quizzically. "What do you mean?"

"You know, 'smoke him out'," repeated Jake. "Like they say in America."

"O-K," said Ben slowly. "How do we do that?"

"I'm not really sure." Jake's shoulders dropped. "I think it means we make it hard for him to hide."

"I don't wish to rain on anyone's parade," interrupted Sam. "But it's not like the police haven't been looking for him this past week. That manhunt must have been stepped up since the attack on your mum," he said, looking at Ben. "I can't see how we can put any more pressure on him than the police are currently doing. And look how far that's getting them."

"Isn't it strange how they haven't found him yet?" said Ben. "Where do you think he could be hiding?"

"My guess would be he's squatting somewhere, keeping very low until he can charge up enough magic to do what you said," replied Jake.

Heather stirred. "We do know how to apply pressure a bit more keenly, though, don't we?"

"How do you mean?" asked Ben.

"Well," she said sprightly. "We know what he wants – the Star. Maybe we can flush him out by pretending we've found it."

"How would we do that?"

Heather faltered. "I... I'm not sure."

Jake snorted. "Well, that'll work then."

Taegan cleared his throat. "To catch Lord Blackwood, we need to think like Lord Blackwood. Where would he stay? How would he get food and water?"

Sam piped up then. "He's used to taking things from people, so he'd probably try and do that. I don't know how – maybe he'll try and rob people, take their money, that sort of thing?"

"OK, and that means he'll need to be round people, somewhere he can be anonymous."

Ben nodded. "He'd need to be in a city. Southampton is the closest one."

"And maybe he'll find somewhere to squat," said Sam. "If he sees other lowlifes doing it, he'll just join them."

"OK, this is good," said Taegan. "I think you may be right. You said he was charging with magic?"

"That's what he said when he broke into our house. He said that there was still background magic here on Earth, that he was able to use it."

"If that's true, he just needs to play a waiting game, eek out time for a while. It's interesting, though, I can't feel it. Can you, Elena?" She shook her head. "Granted, I only made it to level five during my magus trials, and Blackwood is a High Mage, but there must be very little magic here, if any at all."

"So do you think we have more time?"

"I cannot say for sure. There may be techniques for distilling magic that Blackwood knows that I don't. There must be magic in some form here, else the Star would be worthless anyway. Some of the things I've seen in this world are magical enough, in a sense."

"It's not magic; it's just science," said Ben.

"Perhaps your science is just a version of our magic."

Jake rolled his eyes. "We're not getting very far, are we?"

"There may be something in the idea of flushing him out by pretending we have the Star," said Ben, flashing a supportive look at Heather. "We could pretend that we've found it, or at least know where it is, and try to lure him out."

Jake laughed sardonically. "That's never going to work."

Ben was getting a bit disgruntled by Jake's negativity. "Do you have any better ideas?" Jake was silent. "'Cos I don't hear any. Maybe this one's worth a try?"

"How's he going to know that we've got it? He's smart enough to know that if we did have it, we wouldn't broadcast the fact, so I just don't see how we can a let a fugitive in hiding know we have something that we don't."

"Well, we need to think of something."

Jake sniffed but said nothing more. They sat for another hour trying to think of ways to find and deal with Blackwood, going round in circles but managing to come up with little. In the end they decided on nothing more than having the others search Ben's house for clues regarding the location of the Star, whilst Ben and the rebels visited his mum in hospital.

Feeling a little dejected at their lack of a plan, Ben checked his watch and, seeing that it was already 8pm, called time on the evening. Whatever tomorrow held in store for them, it was bound to be a long day.

Taegan and Elena would sleep in the treehouse this evening – for this Ben and the others had already brought sleeping bags and provisions.

"Enjoy your slumber party!" Jake laughed, as he made his way down the rope ladder.

Sam shook the rebels' hands warmly, telling them how pleased he was that they'd come back to help them face the threat of Lord Blackwood.

Heather wished them a good night's sleep and scuttled off after the others. Ben was last down.

"Just don't leave until we come back for you in the morning. The last thing we need is for you to attract the attention of Sam's parents and get the police round here."

"Sure," said Taegan. "Don't worry about us, we won't make a sound. We're very focussed on the task at hand." He pursed his lips. "This is an historic moment for our world, Ben. We have the chance to end a war that has raged for many years."

Ben nodded. "Thanks for coming back – we couldn't do it without you."

Taegan grunted and waved him off, but Ben caught an almost imperceptible smile behind the gruffness.

He clambered down the swinging ladder, where he wished his friends a good evening and headed home.

Ben slept as the sun rose over the New Forest that morning, birds greeting the first light with gleeful song. There was a slight frost on the ground; the first chills of winter were on the way, and the world seemed calm and peaceful. There was no inkling in that pleasant dawn as to the events that might come to pass, no idea amongst its inhabitants that their lives and the entire future of the Earth hung in the balance. If Lord Blackwood got hold of the Star, the destruction and horror that he could unleash was unimaginable.

Ben twitched as his alarm came on, which began quietly at first before building to a crescendo. He awoke and slammed his hand onto the snooze button, rolling over and burying his head under the covers. Then his mind flooded with the memories of yesterday, the urgent need to find Blackwood waking him up quicker than having a bucket of cold water thrown over him. He clambered out of bed, threw on his dressing gown and jumped down the stairs.

It was important not to rouse his father's suspicions, so he followed his usual routine: having breakfast, getting washed and changed, then saying his goodbyes.

"You sure you don't want to miss school and come and see your mum? I'm sure I can clear it with them."

Ben couldn't tell his dad that of course he wanted to see his mum and was actually going there later with her ex-husband. So he had to keep lying. "I just think I've missed too much school already, and it would be good for me to get back into it. I'll stop by the hospital afterwards."

"OK," his dad sighed, giving him a hug and a kiss. "I'll go after lunch and see you there?" Ben nodded. "You stay out of trouble."

Ben's plan for missing school wasn't subtle; having wandered down the road a little towards the school bus stop, he jumped behind some bushes and hid. A few minutes later he saw the bus trundle past, full of kids, and disappear off round the corner. Shortly afterwards, his dad pulled out of the driveway and drove past. Ben glimpsed his father's face, which looked tired and shabby, a shell-shocked man with a heavy weight on his mind. Ben wished he could do something to make his father feel better, but there was nothing.

Once the coast was clear he emerged from the bushes and went back to his house, changing quickly into jeans and T-shirt, before setting off for Sam's. When he got there, Sam had already retrieved the rebels from the treehouse, and they were all sitting at the kitchen table having breakfast.

"Good morning, all," said Ben. He looked at the rebels. "Did you sleep well?"

"Yes, we did, thank you," said Taegan. "Those sleeping bags are excellent for keeping warm."

Ben smiled. "You can keep them if you like."

Taegan grinned as if this was the most magnificent piece of charity he'd ever known.

He joined them at the table and nabbed a piece of toast, whiling away the time until Jake and Heather arrived by chatting idly with the rebels about the wonders of kettles and teabags.

Ten minutes later they arrived. Ben had expected Jake to make some lame joke, but he didn't seem to have the chutzpah for it this morning, which was strange.

"You alright, mate?" Ben asked him. "You don't look so good."

"Charming," Jake shot back. "As it happens, I didn't sleep so well. Had a dream that Lord Blackwood was roasting me on a spit."

They finished their breakfast and got their things together, determined to make a quick start.

"Right, let's go and see my mum then," said Ben. "You guys alright to get going without us?" His friends nodded in unison.

Taegan hopped towards the front door, clearly excited and agitated at the same time to be off to see his old love. They didn't talk as they left the house and walked through the village towards the bus stop. Ben suddenly became horribly aware that he was something of a minor celebrity in the village now and, worse than that, was out and about with two strange adults. Most of the locals just stared, although some did ask if he was OK. A smile and a nod, or a cheerful reply, was generally enough to keep any interested parties off his case for now. But there was no doubt that news of this would get back to his dad, and when it did, he would have some rather difficult explaining to do.

They strode through the mazy lanes of Lyndshaw until they reached the main road and the bus stop to Southampton, where they were the only ones waiting. Ben studied the bus timetable intently, checking his watch and then returning his stare to it, before eventually coming to his conclusion.

"Five minutes," he said brightly.

He leant up against the wooden shelter, putting his hands in his pockets. "I think you should prepare yourself, Taegan, for the fact that my mother is quite different from the Lenara you knew."

Taegan nodded.

"She built a life here, you know, and none of that should change."

It took Taegan a moment to grasp the nettle, but after a moment his face stiffened, his eyes firm but fair.

"I'm not here to take your mother back, Ben, or change her life. I just wish to see her; my eyes have been starved of her beauty for so long…" He trailed off and looked away.

Ben remained silent. He found it hard to imagine Taegan and his mum had ever been… together. It felt like just knowing it was being grossly disloyal to his dad, let alone taking Taegan to see her. Ben wondered if this was a big mistake, but it was too late to back out now; the bus was coming. They boarded, with Ben paying for the two rebels. He took his seat behind them and yawned, realising just how tired he was. His body was aching, so he settled in and looked out of the window for much of the journey. At least the rebels had stopped being amazed at every little thing and were trying to blend in.

Finally, he'd been able to buy it. And not a moment too soon. He'd felt the disturbance in the balance of magic and knew that others from Sunea had crossed over. He'd have to act decisively or risk being defeated. He studied the gun, turning it over and feeling the cool metal against his skin, the reassuring weight of it in his hand. His hand a little shaky now, his grip on his physical presence slipping all the time. He would have to find them now; there was no time to lose. He meditated, once again feeling the magic charge slowly in him. But he'd been saving up for a little while now, and the visions came quickly. A hospital. A blue-haired woman. And him.

He tucked the gun in his trousers, covering it with his ragged shirt, and strode purposefully out of the squat.

It took about forty-five minutes to reach Southampton General Hospital, the bus depositing them a couple of minutes' walk away. Ben was anxious, fearing how Taegan might react when he finally saw his long-lost wife, much older than his memory of her and in such a bad way. She'd sacrificed so much to try and save Sunea, and yet it had been for nothing. It was ironic that moving on with her life and having a family had led to her old life catching up with her.

They entered the hospital by the south entrance, hoping to attract as little attention as possible. The hospital was a grey and uninspiring building, built in the sixties as part of the great social project's initiative, which had left so many cities across Britain scarred with concrete architectural disasters. Inside, the hospital was clean and reasonably modern, brightly lit and with freshly painted pastel-coloured walls. There was modern art hanging up and flower vases potted around, creating a warm, inviting atmosphere, rather than clinical and cold.

They dodged their way down the bustling corridors towards the intensive care unit. They burst into the reception area, and Ben bounced into a young nurse. He spun round to apologise, only the words got caught in his throat when he realised who it was.

"Natalie?" It was the woman who had given him a lift home from the Forest when his bike had been ruined by the school bullies.

Natalie looked at him quizzically for a moment and then recognition lifted her smile like a spring dawn. "Ben," she exclaimed. "Fancy seeing you here."

"You're a nurse?" he asked.

"Yes, I did tell you that," she replied.

Ben went bright red. "Of course," he spluttered. "I just didn't expect to see you here, on this ward."

"How come you're here?" she asked, and then on appraising who he was with: "Is this your mum and dad?"

"Oh no, they're not my parents," he said, motioning at Taegan and Elena. "They're…" Ben suddenly realised he'd have to be careful about what he said here. "…they're family friends. We've come to see my mother."

Natalie looked shocked. "Your mum is in here?"

"Yes," said Ben, sadly. "She was brought in the other day."

"Who is your mum?" Natalie asked softly.

"Helena Freeman."

Natalie moved towards Ben, placing a hand reassuringly on his shoulder. "I'm so sorry, Ben. It was an awful thing that happened. I hope it is of some small comfort to you that I have been assigned to her, and I have been doing my very best to keep her comfy. There's something about your mum, Ben, that makes me think everything's going to be OK; she exudes a strength that I can feel when I'm near her. She's a fighter; she'll pull through this."

Ben looked into the depths of her perfect brown eyes and tried not to cry. The last thing he wanted to do was cry in front of Natalie. "Thanks," he whispered. "Can we go and see her now?"

"Of course." Natalie beamed. "Although, I'm sorry, the rules are there can only be two visitors at a time. I'd love to let all three of you in but I'm only a trainee, and I'll get busted out of here by Sister quicker than you can say superbug."

"It's OK, I understand." Ben looked at Elena. "You wait here, I'll go in with Taegan." Natalie's eyes locked with Taegan's then, and she felt a strange sensation come over her. It was like she had been on a moving escalator that stopped with her on it, jolting her and making her nervous at the same time. She shivered and tried to let the feeling pass.

"This way," she ushered, leading them through to where Ben's mum was before leaving them to attend to her duties.

The smell of disinfectant washed over them as they entered the ward. Ben saw his mother lying there just as she had the previous day, the spectre of death chilling her face, her features still there but her soul temporarily departed.

He looked at Taegan, whose own eyes were stoic and unyielding of emotion. Taegan walked over to Helena and ran his fingers across her brow, pushing the hair back off her face. He stood there for several moments, not moving or saying a word, head bowed as he touched her face.

"I'm so sorry," Taegan whispered.

Ben watched her for any reaction, but there was none. Taegan just continued to stand there, and it was a moment before Ben realised that Taegan was crying. It was a tender and caring side to Taegan that he had not seen before, and he realised then just how much Taegan had sacrificed too. He had given up his own wife to try and save his world, and yet it had all been in vain. The fact he was still going, still fighting for his cause proved just how much determination and iron will the man had.

Ben went to join him by his mother's side. She looked peaceful yet brittle, like a porcelain doll. The heart monitor played a soundtrack of constant beeping, reassuring whilst also a stark reminder of her fragility.

"I can't believe this is her," Taegan said, sadness tinged in his eyes. "She was still so young when she left, so full of verve and passion." He bowed his head. "I can't believe it's come to this."

"She's been a great mum," said Ben, in some way trying to comfort Taegan. "And she still had passion. She wanted to save the world, make people realise the path we were headed down was unsustainable. Of course, I never realised she'd had actual experience of a world on its knees," he mused. "Puts a new slant on some of her more radical ideas."

Taegan smiled, patting Ben on the shoulder with his big hands. "It sounds like she has a fine life here, Ben."

Ben began to feel a little nauseous so turned to get some water. As he passed the heart monitor, he suddenly bent over double, clutching his stomach, a vicious stabbing pain knifing his insides. Feeling like he was going to be furiously sick, he spun round, looking for a bin, dizzy and disorientated from the pain.

He held his head, afraid he was about to pass out as spots danced across his vision. Then the pain changed, a growing sensation beginning in his stomach, like a ball of electricity that was gathering power and mass. The feeling quickly spread through his whole body, encompassing him in blind agony as the energy thrashed around within him. He flung his arms out involuntarily, smacking his hand into the heart monitor, which seemed to earth him, sending a massive spark flaring out of his fingers and into the machine. The charge and pain were instantly drained, all fired out in that one bolt.

An instant later his mother received the jolt, her eyes flying open in shock, her back arching up violently. She gasped for air in a muted howl of anguish, as she frantically fitted on the bed, her mind reeling under the bright glare of the hospital lights.

"Lenara!" shouted Taegan.

"Mum!" cried Ben, stunned and confused as to what was happening.

Helena was writhing, her eyes spinning wildly and uncontrollably. They would try to focus but then roll again. Taegan and Ben held her hands to try and calm her down, making soothing sounds to try and reassure her that it was OK, that she was safe.

A moment or two later, she softened, the rigour of the shock easing from her body, and she began to settle. Her eyes stilled, focussing on Taegan before widening in bewilderment.

"Taegan?" she croaked, uncertainty and fear entering her voice.

"It is I, my love, do not panic," said Taegan, grasping her hand firmly.

"Where am I?" she said, her eyes heavy with confusion. "Am I dead?"

"No, my love. You are alive. Your son is here."

Her head lolled to the other side, and she saw Ben and smiled. Ben smiled back behind welling tears. He couldn't believe his mother had come back to him. But then he saw her eyes begin to roll, and he realised he was losing her again.

"Mum!" he cried.

She could barely speak, but she leant closer to Ben, trying to say something before she lost consciousness, her voice hoarse and weak. Ben hovered above her, holding her face and pleading with her not to leave him again.

With her remaining strength she pushed her lips up towards Ben's ears and breathed only one word before she slipped back into her coma.

"No!" shouted Ben. "Don't go, Mum." But it was too late. Her heart slowed to the rate it had been before, and just as quickly as she had come back to him, she was gone.

Ben sat on the bed sobbing, his despair crashing out of him in huge waves, so much so that Taegan was moved to place an arm around him. It comforted him a little, and he grabbed on to Taegan, letting out all the rage that he was feeling against the world, against both worlds, but most of all against Lord Blackwood.

A few minutes later he calmed down and stopped crying. Taegan waited for Ben to compose himself and then escorted him back outside. Ben and the two rebels emerged into the windy autumn morning from the hospital, bracing themselves against the biting cold. Taegan now asked the question that was clearly bothering him.

"What happened back in there, Ben?"

"What… what do you mean?" he parried.

"When you touched that… thing," Taegan began, "lightning leapt from you. It brought your mother back to life."

Ben looked at his hands. "I don't know," he said eventually. "I don't know where that came from. It… it just kind of charged within me, and I had no way to control it." He hung his head. "I'm not normal."

Taegan ruffled Ben's hair. "That's a good thing in my book," he enthused. "Who wants to be normal?"

Ben didn't say anything.

"Has that happened before, this charge thing?" asked Taegan.

Ben nodded, looking up, and decided then to tell Taegan the truth. "It happened in the Shadow Realm – when we were being attacked by that creature. You'd both tried to kill it, but it didn't work; the Kraw was barely stunned, and you were knocked unconscious on the floor." Ben paused, running his hand through his brown, tousled hair, working out how to relay the strange happenings that came next. "I was on my own. It happened then, as the animal charged at me; I felt the same build-up until it exploded out of me, killing the Kraw. I didn't tell anyone because… well, because I didn't really know what to say."

Taegan eyed Ben long and hard then, folding his arms and breathing out heavily. "Sounds like you can do magic," he conceded, eventually.

Ben looked up keenly. "Do you really think so? Do you think that's what it is?"

"Well… I don't really know. I can't detect any magic in this world, but if Blackwood can, then maybe there is. And perhaps that's what you're channelling."

"And maybe because I'm from both worlds, I can do magic in both?"

Taegan smiled. "Now that really would be something special." There was a moment's silence then, as Taegan looked off into the distance. Finally he looked back at Ben, his eyes sad yet grateful. "I'd like to thank you for bringing me here, Ben. You can't imagine how hard it has been not knowing what happened to my wife after she activated the Star. I did of course hope and pray she was safe, but that's quite different to knowing it. I'm pleased she was able to move on and have a life."

Ben nodded.

"And at least we know she's still there, after your little stunt. She'll come back to you, one day. I'm sure she will."

"Thanks," said Ben.

"What did she say to you?" asked Taegan.

Ben cocked his head to one side. "I think she said, 'Stone'."

"What do you think she meant by that?"

"I don't know. But let's reconvene with the others and see what they think."

They began to walk across the hospital car park, back towards the main road. Morose concrete buildings stood in drab sentry against the greying sky. Ben checked his phone to see if any of the guys had left a message, but there was nothing. He jumped as a voice addressed them from behind.

"Hello, Benjamin."

Ben recognised the raspy voice at once. He whirled round to see Lord Blackwood, thin and wretched, snarling at them from a few metres away. In his hand was a gun. *How on Earth did he get that?* thought Ben. Taegan was already moving towards him.

"You best tell him to back off," said Blackwood, waving the gun. "He doesn't know what these things can do."

Ben thrust his arm across Taegan's chest. "Don't," he commanded. "The gun can kill you."

Taegan narrowed his eyes. "More of your magic," he muttered, but he stopped.

"Where did you get a gun from?" shouted Ben, hoping someone might hear him.

Blackwood laughed. "It's amazing how easy it is to procure things in this world if you're quite prepared to be a criminal. I saw that you'd brought back my good friends here and knew I had to take extra steps to protect myself." He shot Ben a menacing glance. "I know more than you think about this world, Ben, and how to get what I want. I also know how feeble humans really are, and that you would have to bring Taegan here to see his *beloved* wife," he sneered.

"No-one needs to get hurt here, Gregovir," said Ben, trying to sound calm and authoritative. He noticed a small twitch from Blackwood when he used his real name. "Let's just stay calm and talk this through."

"Ha," spat Blackwood. "*Talk this through?* What's there to talk about? You and your pathetic chums are only still alive so you can help me find the Star."

"I thought you didn't need our help, Gregovir," said Ben, his mouth running away from him again. "I thought the *Great Mage* could find it by himself."

Lord Blackwood narrowed his eyes. "I grow tired of waiting; the magic in this place is puny. The whole place deserves to be demolished if you ask me. Nothing but useless, wretched humans, who can't even do magic." Blackwood began coughing violently, a horrible, hacking sound like a choking dog.

Ben watched and an understanding dawned on him. "You're ill," he said. "And without your magic to preserve you, your health is deserting you."

Blackwood wiped his mouth with the back of his hand, small flecks of blood smearing across his skin. "Shut up," he demanded.

"You're going to die here, Gregovir: a long, slow death without one ounce of power."

Blackwood cocked the gun, pointing it directly at Ben. "I'm going to give you one chance to help me."

Ben gulped. "I'll never help you, Gregovir."

Lord Blackwood flashed a wicked smile. "I think you will. You see, you have a choice here, Ben: either you tell me where the Star is or I'm going to kill you and all your friends. It's quite a simple choice, really, so what's it going to be?"

Ben's heart was beating fast; the situation could easily spin out of control, but he tried to remain defiant. "You think you know about this world, but you really don't, do you? If you did, you'd know you're already number one on the most wanted list around here. How do you think the police are going to react if you start shooting innocent people at a hospital?"

Blackwood snorted. "You think there is innocence here? This whole place is vile and corrupt. There is only power, Ben, and those who have it, and those who don't. When I get my Star back, I will have it all, and when I do, this world will pay a steep price for the actions of your mother."

Taegan stepped in. "It's not your Star, Gregovir. It never was."

Blackwood was unimpressed. "You've got five seconds, Ben, or I shoot Taegan. Tell me where the Star is."

Ben looked down. He didn't know where the Star was. How could he stall Blackwood now, what could he say?

"Five."

His mind raced, but there was nothing.

"Four."

"He can't tell you where it is," said Taegan. "Because he doesn't know."

"I don't believe you. Three."

Ben looked at Taegan, who appeared calm. He didn't know how he was staying so composed.

"Two."

Ben began to sweat as he saw Blackwood's finger exerting pressure on the trigger.

"One."

"OK, OK," he said, his heart banging in his chest. "I'll tell you where it is."

Blackwood eyed him suspiciously but stayed his finger.

"Where?" he demanded.

Taegan looked at Ben with astonishment, amazed that he might know where the Star was and shocked that he would consider telling Blackwood. The rebels couldn't understand why he still wielded such power when he was stood there looking so frail and puny.

Ben continued to try to stall for time. "My mother..." he stammered. "She hid it, she wanted to protect it."

"Spare me the details. Where is it hidden?"

Ben stuttered and then his mouth fell open. The realisation hit him like a sledgehammer to the face. His mother's clue... it was so obvious now. He knew exactly where the Star was.

And Blackwood had seen it too, seen the understanding smack Ben in the eyes and now he could smell how close he was to his dream.

"*Tell me where it is!*" he screamed, pointing the gun back at Ben.

Elena decided she had taken all she could of this stand-off. She jumped towards Blackwood, like a cat pouncing on its rodent prey.

"*No!*" cried Ben, but it was too late.

She hadn't even got close before Lord Blackwood adjusted, swung the gun round at her and pulled the trigger.

CHAPTER 25

Ben instinctively recoiled, ducking away from the blast of the gun. Time seemed to slow down, his senses heightening so that he saw everything in freeze frame. The shocked, pained face of Elena as she fell backwards to the floor. The red blood that was seeping from between her fingers as she clutched her stomach. The grim face of Lord Blackwood, twisted in a sneer of contempt, and now training his attention and gun on Taegan.

Without thinking, Ben flung himself through the air, dive-bombing towards Blackwood. He connected with Blackwood's midriff just before he could pull the trigger, fiercely rugby tackling him to the ground. The gun fell out of Blackwood's weak grip and skittled away across the tarmac.

Blackwood fought dirty: kicking, gouging, spitting and biting, flailing his limbs about until a knee connected with Ben's groin, sending him rolling away and clutching himself in agony.

Some doctors were making their way out of the hospital, shouting and pointing as they ran across the car park towards them. Lord Blackwood scrambled to his feet, sprinting off to evade capture. He'd disappeared round the corner before Ben even realised he was escaping.

Taegan was holding Elena, who was moaning softly on the floor, her life force visibly draining away before their eyes. Her skin was sheet-white, and her eyes were rolling in their sockets. Further chaos descended as the two doctors reached them, issuing orders and shouting to each other. Ben felt like everything was washing over him, a tide of confusion and pain that he couldn't fight, as if he was having an out-of-body experience. His brain was entering shock and wouldn't process what had just happened. *How has Blackwood done this again? How is he always one step ahead?*

Elena was losing a lot of blood, and the doctors were on her immediately, administering as much first-aid as they could before they attempted to move her inside. Taegan refused to let her go, cradling her as she lay there dying in his arms.

Ben snapped back into the moment. "You have to let them do their work," he beseeched Taegan. "They can save her life."

Taegan looked blankly at Ben, his own face nearly as pale as hers. Ben pulled his arm, pleading with him to let her go, and finally he acquiesced, all fight slumping out of him.

A couple of orderlies appeared with a trolley, and Elena was gently moved on to it.

One of the doctors turned to Taegan. "You need to come in and wait for the police to arrive," he said. Taegan was in shock, ashen and unresponsive, so Ben nodded. They meekly followed the orderlies into the hospital and were shown where to sit in the waiting room. Elena was taken out of sight into the operating theatre.

Ben knew they only had a few moments to decide their next move.

"Listen," he whispered urgently to Taegan. "We can't stay here. I'd say we've got two to three minutes max before the police turn up and we're in a world of trouble. Shootings don't happen every day in Southampton, and there'll be a *lot* of questions, especially given my involvement. And you won't turn up on any database anywhere, which is not good, believe me." Ben glanced around nervously.

Taegan just nodded, staring ahead vacantly.

"In short, we get out of here now or we risk losing any chance we have of finishing this."

"What about Elena?" asked Taegan, his words slow, the shock refusing to leave his system.

"I think we have to leave her. If we don't get out of here, we won't be going anywhere for a long while, and Blackwood will get the Star."

Taegan frowned. "I can't just leave her here."

"It's that or spend a long time in jail. There's no time to procrastinate; we have to act, now."

Taegan dithered.

"Look, I think I know where the Star is," declared Ben. "We've got to go and get it now, before Blackwood finds us again."

Taegan turned to look at Ben, the fug starting to clear. "You know where the Star is?"

"Yes," Ben replied. "I think I know what my mum was trying to tell me."

Taegan breathed in deeply, his resolve and strength visibly returning. "Then we must get it before Blackwood does. Do you think he could know where it is?"

Ben frowned, a look of concern spreading across his face. "There's every chance he'll figure it out soon."

"Where is it?" asked Taegan.

Ben could hear sirens approaching. "We must go – *now!*"

He grabbed Taegan by the arm and made a break for it. They barged their way out of a side door and sprinted as fast as they could away from the hospital, ducking down side streets and weaving through alleyways. Ben couldn't really believe it had come to this: on the run from the police, in the grim and drizzly surroundings of the city, with a scruffy rebel from another dimension. After about five minutes, they stopped to catch their breath, hidden from sight behind a skip. Ben bent over double as he heaved air into his lungs.

"So," said Taegan, recovering quickly. "Where is it?"

The sun was attempting to peek out from behind a grey cloud, creating a rainbow that sparkled faintly behind a nearby high-rise. Ben squinted, regaining the breath he had lost, admiring the rainbow, an illusion that proved that just because you could see something, it didn't mean it was there.

"It was rather obvious from the start, when you think about it," he said with mystique.

"Oh, yes?" said Taegan, raising an eyebrow.

"Yes. She's hidden it at the one place where she would have felt it connected with her own world, a place she could visit with almost ceremonial frequency. It's at Stonehenge."

Having explained his plan to get there to Taegan, Ben needed to speak to his friends.

"I wouldn't tell them where the Star is," warned Taegan. "It's the best way to keep it safe. If Blackwood gets to them, he'll hurt them to extract the information."

Ben nodded, aware of what was at stake.

"I need to warn them that he's got a gun."

He dialled Jake first, but it went straight through to voicemail. Ben cursed, hung up and tried Heather.

The phone rang for a couple of seconds and then she answered, breathless.

"Heather?"

"Yes..." she wheezed.

"It's Ben. Are you OK?"

"Hi, Ben." She gulped down some air. "Not really, I've been running around trying to find Jake."

"He's missing?" said Ben, alarmed.

"He went outside to take a phone call, and after about ten minutes I went to find him and he wasn't there. He's disappeared, Ben, and now I can't get hold of him." Her voice sounded like it was about to crack.

Ben tried to calm her down. "I'm sure he's fine, Heather, just stay calm."

"What if Lord Blackwood's got him?" she croaked.

"Well, he'd have to be pretty fast, seeing as he's just shot Elena in Southampton."

"*What?*" she yelled. "Elena's been shot?" A moment's pause. "Wait – he's got a gun?"

"Yes," Ben said quietly. "I'm ringing to warn you. I don't suppose anything has happened to Jake, but we need to get hold of him."

"Oh my god, I'll keep looking." Another pause. "Is Elena going to be alright?"

"I… I don't know," he admitted. "Taegan and I had to flee the scene. The doctors had just taken her in to the operating theatre." He sighed. "She didn't look good."

"Oh, Ben," she moaned. "This is getting completely out of control." Ben thought he could hear her crying.

"It's coming to the endgame," he said, trying to boost her resolve. "I can feel it. We just need to see this through. I've got a plan, but I really need to speak to Jake, so if you see him, can you get him to give me a call?"

"Yes, but… what's your plan?"

"I think it's better if I don't tell you."

"Oh," she said, clearly deflated. "Well, good luck then."

"Thank you, Heather. I really don't know how I'm ever going to make this up to you all."

"I'm sure we'll think of something," she said playfully, and rung off.

He tried Jake again but frowned when it went straight to voicemail. He decided to leave him a message.

"Jake, it's me, Ben. I hope you're OK. Heather's worried about where you are." He paused. "Listen, I really need to speak to you – I need your help. Please call me when you get this message." Another pause as he considered whether to say any more. "I think I know where the Star is."

He ended the call and looked at Taegan, who was arching his brow quizzically.

"What?"

"I thought you weren't going to share anything with your friends?"

Ben shrugged. "Jake's my best mate. And I *really* need him to call us. I didn't say where I think the Star is."

"I think best keep it that way, eh?"

"OK." Ben felt like a sulky teenager, being told off for a misdemeanour. He dialled Sam, speaking only for a few moments with him, having a shorter version of the conversation he'd just had with Heather. He would go out and join the hunt for Jake too.

Ben rang off from Sam but kept looking at his phone, willing it to ring with all his might, for Jake to call him back. It stayed silent. For good measure, he sent a text off too.

"What now?" asked Taegan.

"We keep moving," said Ben. "We can't afford to let the police find us."

After about twenty more minutes of weaving through the side streets of Southampton, Ben heard his phone ringing. He fished it out of his pocket and looked at the display. It was his dad.

Ben gulped and, after a moment's hesitation, answered.

"Hello?" he said meekly.

"Ben?" came a gruff voice from the other end of the line. "Where the ruddy hell are you?"

"I'm just… with my friends."

"Don't lie to me, Ben. I've just had a phone call from Inspector Wainwright, trying to get hold of you. He said you were involved in a shooting at the hospital. Now you're going to tell me what's going on, right now."

"I'm sorry, Dad." Tears sprung to his eyes. "I can't tell you; there's too much at stake."

"Ben, please, think about this for a moment – your whole future is tied to the decision you make right now." He sounded like he was holding back tears. "I know that I've not been there for you enough these last few weeks, that I've been unable to protect you and your mother from harm, but I'll be damned if I'm going to let you throw your life away. We can sort this out. You just need to let me help you. Tell me where you are, I'll come and get you, and we'll go and talk to the police."

Ben sucked in air and lifted his shoulders, trying to make himself feel braver than he actually was.

"I'm sorry, Dad, I can't do that. You just need to trust me and know that I'm doing this for Mum. I love you." He pressed 'end' and switched his phone to vibrate. He wanted to turn it off but couldn't risk missing Jake's call.

The phone immediately began vibrating, but this time the number was unknown. He pressed 'accept'.

"Hello?"

"Ben, this is DCI Wainwright. Don't hang—"

Ben pressed 'end' as quickly as he could. Would the police be able to trace him by his phone? He didn't know for sure, though it sounded plausible.

"C'mon, Jake," he muttered to himself.

"Can we walk to the henge?" offered Taegan.

Ben sniggered, amused at the naivety of the comment amidst the darkness of his thoughts. Then his phone buzzed again, and he whooped with delight as he saw that it was Jake ringing.

"Where have you been?" he shouted down the phone.

"Sorry, dude," replied Jake, as nonchalant as ever. "My phone ran out of battery, so I had to cruise on home to put it on charge."

"You could have told your sister; she was freaking out when I spoke to her. You're such a clown sometimes."

"I don't need this abuse," mocked Jake. "I rang you because you said you needed some help. You said you had found the Star?"

Ben turned his back on the stranger who walked past at that moment and began to whisper into the phone.

"We've got an advantage here, Jake, I know where the Star is, and I can go and get it. But I don't have much time – I'm on the run from the police."

"What? Why?"

"Somehow Blackwood found us at the hospital, and he had a gun. He shot Elena."

"Oh my."

"Me and Taegan had to run from the scene, but I think Blackwood knows I know where the Star is, and he could come for any of us next."

"It's all getting a bit out of hand then," Jake said casually, in the understatement of the year. "But I'm not sure how I can help?"

"I need to borrow your brother's motorbike."

Ben heard a sharp intake of breath over the line. "There's no way, dude, uh-uh." Ben could hear Jake's head shaking. "He'd never let me have his bike. It's his pride and joy."

"I'm not suggesting you *ask* him for it—"

"I can't steal his bike, Ben; he would kill me. And I don't mean that in a figurative sense. I mean he would quite literally kill me. More than that, he'd enjoy it."

Ben sighed. "Jake, I'm not asking for this lightly; this is actually a life-and-death situation, not just for us but for the whole world. We can deal with your brother later, but right now we've got a chance to get the Star before Blackwood and finish this whole madness once and for all. So will you please, pretty please with a cherry on top, go get your brother's bike and meet us at the bowling alley in twenty minutes?"

"Well, where's the Star then?"

"I think it's best if you don't know."

"I disagree. If you want me to take you somewhere on my brother's bike, I'm going to need to know where."

Ben bit his lip. "Actually, I kind of need you to leave the bike with us so that Taegan and I can go."

"What? So you want me to drive the love of my brother's life into Southampton, which is tantamount to committing suicide, so that you can ditch me and ride off to save the world? Sometimes, Ben, you're a really bad friend."

Ben smiled; he knew that Jake was just taking the mickey now and that he was on board. "Come on, Jake, I've got the police after me, and I need to turn my phone off. Will you be there?"

Jake let out a big sigh. "OK."

"Yes! Thank you, Jake, you won't regret it."

"Hmm, I rather think I might," he said, and rang off.

Jake chewed his fingernails for a good few minutes after his conversation with Ben had finished. He knew he was going to get into so much trouble with his brother if he took the bike, but then he'd just promised Ben, and he was in a huge amount of trouble already.

"Sod it," he muttered. He dived into his brother's room to find the keys. It was a stroke of fortune that his brother had caught the bus into college that day. Something about needing to revise on the way in. He walked out to the garage, hoisted up the big metal door which screeched along its ageing tracks and eyed the brawny hog appreciatively. Shaking his head in dismay at what he was about to do, he walked over to the bike and sat astride it, putting the key into the ignition. It felt good to sit on the beast, powerful, like he owned the world. He was about to turn the key when he heard a cough from behind him.

"Going somewhere?"

It was Lord Blackwood, and he had a gun to his sister's head.

Ben and Taegan made it to the Megabowl complex with a couple of minutes to spare and saw Jake come roaring into the car park. Ben really wished Jake could just make a quiet entrance for once in his life, but it seemed like he was hard-wired to announce himself wherever he went.

With the helmet on, Jake was anonymous on the bike; no-one could tell he was underage. When he pulled up alongside them and took it off, he drew one or two funny looks, mostly from mums and dads who must have thought he looked young to be riding a motorbike. Ben could only hope they would dismiss it.

"Thanks for this, Jake, I really owe you one."

Jake stayed sat on the bike as Ben approached, looking nervous.

"I've been thinking, Ben," he began.

"Yes…?"

"I think I deserve to know where you're taking my brother's bike."

"And I told you, I don't think it's a good idea for anyone to know."

"I'm sorry, Ben, I'm going to have to insist upon it as a condition of having the bike."

"Why?"

Jake threw a hand through his hair to ruffle it. "Say something goes wrong and you two have an accident, or something happens that's bad when you find the Star. Don't you think someone else should know where you are? We could say if you don't call me in three hours, I know something's gone wrong and can ride in with the cavalry."

"Like a backup plan?"

Jake flashed a smile. "Exactly."

Ben sighed, hunching his shoulders. He had to admit it did sound like a good idea.

He looked at Taegan, who just shrugged his shoulders to indicate it was Ben's call.

"OK, well, we're heading to Stonehenge."

"Stonehenge? The Stonehenge?"

"Do you know of another one?"

"No," scowled Jake. His face moved through several contortions of understanding over the next few seconds. He tapped his chin. "Of course," he muttered. "It makes so much sense. It's the one place on Earth that would have reminded your mother of home. How did you find out?"

"My mum woke up in hospital and told me."

"Your mum's awake?" said Jake, surprised. "She's out of the coma? But that's great news."

"She only... came out of it momentarily. She fell back into it after she told me."

"But that's great – well, not that she's back in the coma. But that you know where the Star is!" exclaimed Jake.

A group of giggling girls burst out of the Megabowl, rolling along the pavement, holding their hands in front of their mouths and tittering as they passed the boys.

"So can we have the bike now?" asked Ben.

"What? Oh, oh, yeah." Jake paused for a moment. "You will be *really* careful with it, won't you?" He stroked the bike as if it were his own.

"Don't worry about us," Ben reassured him as he hopped on to the bike and passed the spare helmet to Taegan, who looked at it with utter mistrust. "You just worry about Blackwood."

Jake nodded but said nothing. He held his hand out, upturned to the heavens. He could feel the first spits of rain splashing onto his skin. "Looks like rain," he warned. "Don't go too fast."

Taegan had now climbed suspiciously aboard the bike, with his helmet on. Ben just grinned back at Jake and flipped his visor down.

He gave the bike two revs, engaged first gear and released the clutch. Ben had hoped he would ride off confidently with smooth acceleration, but because of his passenger's nervousness and inexperience, he only managed a jerky, fitful start where he nearly lost balance several times.

Jake watched them off, shaking his head before reaching for his phone.

"OK, they've gone," he told Lord Blackwood.

"And do you know where they're going?"

"Yes."

"And…?"

"You let my sister go first. I want to know she's safe," demanded Jake. There was a sigh on the other end of the phone.

"Fine, I've let her out."

"I need to be sure."

"Oh, you will be. I'm coming round the corner to pick you up right now."

As Ben sped along the A36, wind rippling his jumper, he grinned at the cleverness of his plan. The helmet was the perfect disguise – no-one was paying them any notice, just a couple of regular people out for a ride on their bike. After a wobbly start, Ben had got used to the bike quickly, the time spent learning how to ride proving to be one of the most useful evenings he'd ever spent with Jake and his brother.

The tarmac glided beneath the wheels, as the trees and bushes whizzed by in a blur of speed. The feeling was exhilarating to Ben, liberating from the shackles that his life had become in the past few weeks. *If I come through this without dying or going to jail,* Ben thought, *I'm going to have to get myself one of these bad boys.*

"Enjoying the ride?" he shouted back to Taegan.

Taegan just grunted, which Ben couldn't interpret one way or the other. The tight grip that Taegan was exerting on Ben's midriff suggested that he wasn't too happy about the transport.

The journey to Stonehenge was relatively swift and mercifully without incident. As they powered down the A303, the giant stones heaved into view, like a proud ship over the horizon.

Ben heard Taegan gasp.

"Impressive, aren't they?" shouted Ben, above the roar of the bike.

"This is no mere coincidence."

"Quite," agreed Ben. He pulled into the car park, easing the bike into a space as far away from prying eyes as he could. Taegan dismounted first, pulling his helmet off and shaking his long blond hair. Ben swung his legs over the bike and hopped off, easing his helmet from his head and itching his scalp.

"I am not surprised Lenara chose this place to hide the Star. It would have made perfect sense," said Taegan.

Ben disagreed. "I've been thinking about it, and I think it's a terrible place. It's obvious, really, and anybody from your world would gravitate towards it, sooner or later. It's the one place that, given time, Blackwood would have found with or without magic. So it's the worst place to hide the Star. I mean, I feel a bit dumb for not realising it sooner myself."

Taegan turned his big, sad blue eyes on Ben. "Your mother is an emotional person, Ben. Don't forget she had lost everything from her previous life – this would have been the one place where she could feel connected to her past. Don't be too hasty to judge."

"Well, it certainly explains why we were dragged here so many times," he muttered.

They were wandering towards the entrance gate when Ben started patting his pockets furiously.

"Oh no," he fretted.

Taegan stopped walking and looked round at him. "What is it?"

"I've not got any money. I don't know how we're going to get in."

"Why not?"

"Because we have to pay to get in."

"We can't just go in?"

"No, we have to pay to do pretty much anything in this world. It's called money, and it makes the world go round," said Ben sarcastically.

"Magic makes the world go round," said Taegan, ignorant of Ben's tone.

"Whatever," sighed Ben. "We need a way of getting in there."

"Is there another way in?" asked Taegan.

Ben blinked. "I don't know," he said. "I'll just have to see if I can blag it."

"What does that mean?"

"Just follow my lead," said Ben, marching off towards the entrance.

He approached the ticket booth, which contained a portly older lady. She had a scowl on her face that could freeze hell.

This won't be easy, he thought.

"Hello there," said Ben, as breezily as he could.

"Yes?" came the curt reply.

Ben pointed at his face. "I don't suppose you remember me?" The ticket lady just raised an eyebrow suspiciously.

"It's just I've been in there, with my parents, and I came out to get my uncle. I thought you might recognise me?"

The woman's scowl just grew deeper.

"So I was hoping you could just let us back in?"

"Do you have your ticket?"

"Um, no," admitted Ben. "I think my dad has got it in there."

"What about him?" she drawled, pointing at Taegan. "Where's his ticket?"

"He, uh, ah, I think my dad's also got his ticket too."

"So you came out to get your uncle, but without the tickets you'd need to get back in?"

"Yes," said Ben, blushing slightly.

The woman sighed. "It's eight pounds to get in, do you want to buy two tickets?"

Ben's smile tightened. "Sorry, but I don't have any money. Can you not just let us in?"

"Doesn't your... uncle... have any money?" she said, looking Taegan up and down.

"No, he doesn't," Ben sighed. This really wasn't going very well at all. He put on his most pleading face. "Is there any way, any way at all, that you can just let us in? We've come a really long way, and we just want to see the stones. I need to get back to my mum and dad."

The sour-faced woman was unmoved. "They don't pay me money to let people in for free. Now, please move away, you're holding up the line."

Ben wanted to explode with anger, he was so infuriated with the woman. Taegan pulled him aside.

"I have another plan," he intimated.

"OK, what is it?"

"We just need to get in there and find the Star, right?"

"Yes."

"So what if we jump the railing and make a break for it? It's a pathetic barrier, it would be easy to get over."

"That's not really the point," began Ben. "There'll be security, and we'll get caught and chucked out."

"But if I can keep security occupied for long enough, then you can get in there and find the Star."

Ben dropped his shoulders. It was a terrible idea, but they didn't have a lot else to go with right now.

"OK, let's do it," he sighed, mentally adding yet another item to his long list of broken laws.

CHAPTER 26

Taegan had vaulted the barrier before Ben had any chance to change his mind. He was forced to scramble after him, leaping the security gate, a rush of adrenaline and fear surging through his body. He could hear muffled cries from the box office as his legs took him away from the entrance, his feet pounding the concrete as hard as they could in his bid to reach the stones. He hoped that security was a bit inept here and that they might stand at least some chance of reaching the henge before several burly guards descended upon them.

He was puffing furiously as he ran under the flyover, Taegan already a good twenty yards ahead of him.

"What are you going to do when we're in there?" he shouted between breaths.

Taegan looked back at him. "You just concentrate on finding the Star," he said, noticeably calmer and even-breathed than Ben. "But don't use it," he added as an afterthought.

"What happens if I use it?" yelled Ben.

"The legend states that only those qualified to use the Star can control its power," Taegan called back. "I doubt that covers you."

They emerged from the subway below the road, the ancient site looming into view. Ben shuddered as he got closer to the magnificent stones, their significance to him multiplied a million times now he knew about their counterparts in Sunea. The strong, old stones stood reverentially in their circle, dilapidated by time but no less powerful a sight for that. He could feel the history permeating this place, almost sense the druidic ceremonies that would have been practised at the stones, hear the chanting of the mages as they worshipped. Could his mother be right? Could this once have been a portal to another dimension?

The stones had been wrapped in mystery for millennia now, their true purpose shrouded by the mists of time. How could he ever tell people that the same Stonehenge existed in another dimension, where magic was a currency and the fight for control of it had destroyed the world? He wouldn't believe it if he hadn't seen it himself.

"You go round the back," barked Taegan. "Lose yourself in the crowd."

Ben peeled off to the left as Taegan ran round to the right. Glancing behind him, Ben saw a flash of luminescent jacket coming through the subway and knew it wouldn't be long until security was with them. He ran as fast as he could round to the back and joined up with a pack of kids on a school visit, hoping to blend in. He saw that Taegan had stopped quite close to the front, the security guards closing in on him. Ben hoped he knew what he was doing.

He hadn't had to think about his own task for too long, and where he should look for the Star. He knew the answer in his bones. His mother would have wanted to lay the Star to rest in only one place, where it could be relatively safe from being found, and where it would feel at home: in the middle of the stones. How his mum ever got it in there, he had no idea. *Perhaps at a summer solstice*, he mused. However she did it, Ben felt certain that was where it would be. Which just left him with the tricky task of how to recover it without anyone noticing him going in.

So far, all the security had focussed on Taegan, with his distinctive blond hair and 6'5" frame, he was easy to spot in the crowd. Now that he'd got the security team to concentrate on him, Taegan decided it was time to put his plan into action. He nodded at Ben, took a deep breath and sprang over the fence that separated the gravel path from the stones. He ran towards the stones, bellowing a primeval, guttural roar that became one word: 'Sunea'.

People stopped and started pointing, shouting towards the man who had clearly gone insane. Security began hopping over the fence too, running towards Taegan in a bid to tackle him before he could get to the stones and cause any damage.

Taegan reached the middle of the site long before they got to him and then started hopping about, doing a jig. He looked completely mad, yipping and yelling as he bounced around on one foot, his hands lifted towards the sky as if in prayer. Ben had to smile – it certainly was one hell of a diversion, though his stomach lurched when he realised that it meant he had to act, and now. He swept his gaze left and right; people were pointing at Taegan, some laughing, some looking shocked, but all of them were slowly shuffling away from Ben, towards the entrance side, where they could get a better look at the spectacle. The tough-looking security guards had now encircled Taegan and were moving in.

Taegan roared as the first security guard launched at him, an attempted rugby tackle that was nimbly brushed off. An expert at close-combat fighting, within seconds he'd floored another guard, but there were too many of them and they soon had hold of him. For his part, Taegan writhed and squirmed, shrugging men off as others came to help those who were struggling to restrain him. It was going to take at least five of them to carry him off, which they now endeavoured to do. Taegan shouted and screamed as he was carted away, encouraging the other visitors to move further round to the front of the site and, importantly, away from Ben's position.

This is my chance.

Ben was about to jump the fence when he heard something in Taegan's voice change. It went from being the cry of an embattled madman to one of desperation and anguish. "I'll kill you, Blackwood!"

Ben's blood froze. Lord Blackwood was here.

His heart sank. A million thoughts and questions clouded his mind. How could Blackwood be here? How could he have known so fast where to come? It was the second time he'd turned up unexpected and outwitted them today – what on Earth was going on?

Ben snapped himself from these thoughts. The task at hand was even more urgent now, and he didn't have any time to waste. He hurdled the fence and ran across the open space, stooping as low as he could whilst maintaining speed. He snuck round one of the larger outer stones, pressing his back up flat on the other side. His heart was hammering in his chest, his breathing shallow and fast, and he forced himself to calm down, to keep quiet and listen. He could hear Taegan still howling, straining at every sinew to fend off the guards and rise to face Lord Blackwood, to mete out some summary justice to his bitter enemy. No-one appeared to have seen Ben make it into the stones.

He darted in further towards the middle, trying to find a place that couldn't be easily spotted from the outside, eventually tucking himself up behind one of the central stones. He moved his head round the cold, grey monolith, peeking out towards the entrance area. He saw Taegan being carried away by four guards, all holding an arm or leg each, with him writhing madly. He was snarling and screaming off to his left, where Ben assumed Blackwood must be.

Ben moved round to the other side of the stone to see if he could get a better view. His heart jumped as his worst fears were confirmed. There in plain view was Blackwood, looking frailer and older than he had only a couple of hours ago. He was grinning sardonically at Taegan, enjoying watching his nemesis so close and yet so futile in his efforts to stop him.

Ben cowered back behind the slab, not knowing what to do next. He was breathing hard, adrenaline coursing through his blood. If he started to look for the Star, he would be seen by someone from the outside. And what would Blackwood's next move be? *Think, Ben.*

He would know that Ben was here, and the Star too; he might even assume that it's in the middle. Even if he didn't, once he'd cracked that Ben was nowhere else to be seen, it would be clear to Blackwood where he was hiding.

Ben's mind bubbled. He was so close, and yet it seemed he was further away than ever from winning. He didn't know what to do, and every second that passed felt like an eternity. The whole future of the world was at stake, and Ben knew he was in way over his head. He needed backup.

He pulled his phone out of his pocket and browsed through the recent calls, finding DCI Wainwright's mobile number. He was going to have to involve the police now; he needed their help to catch Blackwood. And he had to do it before the Star could fall into Gregovir's hands, otherwise they would never get him. Ben gulped as he pressed 'call'. He knew he would be in a world of trouble, but he had to do it. There was no alternative now.

The phone rang for a few seconds, before there was a click and Wainwright came on the line.

"Hello?" he demanded.

"Inspector Wainwright?" whispered Ben.

"That's right. Who is this?"

"This is Ben Freeman."

"Ben!" exclaimed Wainwright, quickly followed by, "Where are you?"

"I'm at Stonehenge."

A pause. "You better start talking."

"I need help. The man who kidnapped us, the one who attacked my mum and shot Elena, he's here and he's trying to get me again."

"Christ! Why are you at Stonehenge?"

"Does it matter? Will you send some officers?"

"Yes, just hold tight. Where exactly are you?"

"I'm hiding in the stones."

"You're *what*?!" spluttered Wainwright.

"I had to hide," said Ben matter-of-factly. "Inspector?"

"Yes?"

"How is Elena?"

"I take it that's the name of the victim?"

"Yes."

Inspector Wainwright sighed. So many unanswered questions. "She'll live."

Relief flooded through Ben's body, his hands shaking as he digested the news. *She's going to be OK.*

"Thank you," whispered Ben, pausing to add: "Please hurry." He ended the call, leaving Wainwright no opportunity for further questions.

He listened intently for a moment; the commotion from before had died down. Ben assumed that the security men had got Taegan under control and moved him away; he was on his own now.

He didn't expect what came next.

A single gunshot thundered through the fledgling calm and sent the entire site into pandemonium. Screaming women and children started running in every direction, men shouted orders that Ben couldn't make out, but in one chilling second Ben understood that he had lost, that Lord Blackwood was going to take control of the site, kill anyone who stood in his way and find the Star.

Ben felt sick to his stomach. There was nothing he could do against a lunatic with a gun. He could hear the stomping shoes of people running to leave, a clamour of voices as panic gripped those rushing to escape. Lord Blackwood was thoroughly enjoying himself. Ben could hear his reedy voice above the hysteria of the crowd, exhorting them with banal statements to make themselves sparse. Before long everyone had gone, bar a couple of hardy security men who had stayed behind in an apparent effort to talk him down.

"Just put the gun down, mate," Ben heard one of them say. "You don't need to do this; no-one's going to hurt you."

"You want to leave as well," snarled Blackwood.

The security guards didn't heed the warning, continuing to address him. "Whatever is it you want – perhaps we can help?"

"Can you give me the whole world?"

"Huh?"

A clap of thunder boomed as Blackwood shot one of the men. Ben heard a scream and a soft moan. His mind imagined all sorts of horrors.

"Leave," said Blackwood calmly.

"You're crazy!" shouted one of them.

"Do you want to be shot too?"

"No, we're going, don't shoot." There was more groaning and huffing as Ben heard the security guards shuffle away, leaving him, he assumed, totally alone with Blackwood.

He was sweating profusely and he felt overwhelmed. How could he hope to win now?

For a moment, everything was quiet. A surreal sensation came over Ben, like deja-vu, even though this was clearly something that had never happened before. The wind rustled through the grass, and the stones imposed their powerful aura over him, calming him, somehow giving him some of their stoic strength. This was no time for giving in.

That was when Ben felt it. It began as a slight ringing in his ears, a harmonic sound that seemed to be coming from around him, from the stones themselves. A deep, pulsating, beat began to thrum through his body, and he looked urgently around, unsure where this unknown beacon was coming from.

Lord Blackwood's high, screechy voice punctured the swelling noise. "I know you're in there, Ben," he taunted. "I think it's about time you surrendered to me."

Ben laughed bitterly, trying to bide some time. He realised that, somehow, he could sense the Star, that it was near and sending a signal, as if it wanted to be found by him. He instinctively felt that it would be near to the centre stone, the symbolic heart of the henge.

"If I come out, you'll shoot me. I'm not stupid, Gregovir." He hurried to the centre stone, ducking down behind it.

"Well, maybe." Blackwood laughed. "But there really is no way out for you now. I've won, Ben, I'm going to own the Star, I can feel it. It knows that a new master is at hand; it's calling out to me."

"What makes you think it's not calling out to me?" shouted Ben. He could feel it beneath him now, emanating from underneath the ground. He ploughed his hands into the soil, digging for all his worth.

"You're nothing, Ben, an unfortunate child of two dimensions, sent to help me fulfil my destiny by reuniting me with my birthright. You've done that ever so well, there's no need for you to get in the way now."

"I'll never let you have the Star, Blackwood." The words were strong and brave, coming from somewhere that Ben didn't know existed inside of him. He scrabbled through the dirt and mud, frantically burrowing down to find what he knew lay beneath the soil.

"Don't be stupid, Ben, you've got no choice." Blackwood's voice was much closer now; he was heading towards the stones and Ben was running out of time. His fingers struck something solid, something cold. He dug around the edge madly, hoping that it wasn't just a rock, working it free from its earthly grave. He felt euphoric as he heaved the dirty, muddy box out of the ground and scrabbled to pull the lid off. Years of being underground, caked in mud and moist from rain, had caused the lid to stick firmly. Ben furiously tugged at it, desperate to get inside before Blackwood reached him.

"Come out, come out, wherever you are," called Blackwood menacingly.

Ben finally got the lid off and lifted the Star of Moirai out of the box as Blackwood rounded the first stone.

Ben saw Jake first, and confusion poured through his mind. Why was Jake here? What was going on? Why would Lord Blackwood have him? Jake had gaffer tape around his hands and over his mouth, forcing him to breathe wildly through his snotty nose. Blackwood had one arm locked around Jake's neck, his free hand holding a gun against his head. Jake's eyes were wide, frightened and puffy from tears. His gaze locked with Jake's, and he saw the pure fear chasing through the ghostly white of his eyes, and Ben understood. Blackwood had got to him and forced him to tell all.

Lord Blackwood saw what Ben had in his hand, and there was a brief, tense stand-off, each side weighing up their options. Ben thought he saw a split-second of doubt in Blackwood's expression before greed twisted his face into a perverted sneer.

"Don't come any closer," yelled Ben. "I've got the Star, and I'm not afraid to use it." Ben looked at the small amulet he held in his hand, dulled from years spent underground in a tin, and couldn't believe it was one of the most powerful things in the universe. A small golden star suspended in an egg-shaped silver lattice, it looked like a lot of fuss over nothing.

"You don't even know how," spat Blackwood. "Give it to me before I shoot your friend in the head."

The Star was beginning to feel hot in Ben's hand, as if it were getting excited at the prospect of being used again. "You shoot him, and I'll use it. I swear, Gregovir, you hurt him, and you'll regret it."

Blackwood sighed, bored of the game already. "Think about it, Ben. The Star ruined a whole world because someone unqualified tried to use it, all to keep it from its rightful owner – me."

"That's not true," shouted Ben. "It was your stupid quest to possess the Star that caused all this to happen in the first place. You forced my mum to do what she did because if they'd let you have it, then you'd have destroyed Sunea anyway."

"No, Ben, you are mistaken. I can control the Star; I would have brought a new golden age to Sunea. But instead those stupid rebels threw it all away by trying to use the Star themselves, and look what happened. And that's what'll happen now, if you use it. This horrid little planet will die, just as assuredly as Sunea did."

Ben gripped the Star tightly, trying to ignore Lord Blackwood's lies, but doubt gripped him. What if he did use it now? Taegan had warned him not to use the Star, so what if it did destroy the world, just as it had done on Sunea?

The gun was still pointed at Jake's head.

"So I'll tell you what, Ben," Blackwood said, a smug smile on his face as he saw Ben's determination waver. "You give me the Star, and I let you and your friend here go. The alternative is I shoot Jake, and you activate the Star destroying the world. Which is it to be?"

Ben looked at Lord Blackwood, his disgusting face crowing in anticipated victory, and at Jake, who was barely keeping a grip on sanity. Anger swelled within him: anger at being in this situation once again, with Blackwood having an upper hand that he couldn't see how to overcome. He didn't think he could really use the Star, but it was the only weapon left in his arsenal. Neither could he hand it over to Blackwood; the Earth was just as assuredly condemned to destruction if he did.

Then he heard them in the distance – *police sirens.* They were coming! If he could hold out a bit longer then the police would get Blackwood, and Ben wouldn't have to do anything.

Blackwood heard the sirens too, and his gaze hardened, his eyes darkening as his determination steeled.

"Give me the Star, now." It was an order that was hard to disobey, Lord Blackwood's voice compelling him to comply.

He breathed in deep, puffing his chest up to draw in as much strength as possible. The fate of the world was tied to this decision. "No," he said, his voice cold but his head sweating like he was in a furnace.

"Fine," sniffed Blackwood. "You just killed your friend."

An invisible signal passed between Ben and Jake then, an

instantaneous message sent between best friends. Jake elbowed Blackwood in the ribs, ducking as he did to avoid being shot. The slight advantage in timing was crucial, as Blackwood staggered backwards and Jake was able to free himself of his grip, lurching to the right and rolling away.

Seeing Jake break away, Ben moved to the other side, aiming to get clear of Blackwood's range. If he could keep the Star away from Blackwood just a little bit longer, then he would have won.

But Blackwood was too quick. He'd been surprised by the deftness of Jake's attack, but he still had a gun, and it didn't take much conscious effort to aim and shoot.

The gun boomed as Blackwood fired, the crack of the shot reverberating around the giant rocks. The bullet hit Jake in the shoulder, pitching him forwards and twisting his weight at the same time, so that his body pirouetted in mid-air before he slammed into the ground. His head cracked against a rock, knocking him out cold.

Ben screamed, not wanting to believe what had just happened. He wasn't given any time to react before Blackwood swung his aim round onto him.

"Stop," he commanded.

The fight left Ben. He began to sob for Jake, who was bleeding heavily from the gunshot wound, a crimson red staining his T-shirt. He turned to face Lord Blackwood, the Star of Moirai hanging limply from his left hand.

"I haven't got time for these games, Benjamin." Lord Blackwood spoke slowly, each word entombing itself into Ben's brain. Ben could see the flashing lights of the police cars, screeching down the A303 now – in just a couple of minutes they'd be here. If he could only hold out for a couple more minutes, then the nightmare would be over. But Blackwood knew this too, and he was bound to act before then. He needed the Star, and he needed it now.

"Please," whispered Ben. "I need to help my friend. Let me help him, he could die."

"The Star, Ben. Give it to me."

Ben was shaking, his palms sweaty with the fear of what was to come, but his resolve was iron.

"No."

Blackwood broke out into a little grin, showing Ben his black-stained teeth, their decaying rancour giving the impression of a slug crawling across his lips.

"Then die." Lord Blackwood aimed the gun at Ben and fired.

CHAPTER 27

Time slowed down to an imperceptible crawl.

The bracelet on his wrist, the one given to him by Sofiella when he left the Shadow Realm, began to itch. Yet he couldn't move to scratch it, his arm feeling like it was encased in concrete. He was a statue, a helpless bystander to real-time events.

The bracelet grew warm, glowing an amber yellow as the thin metal began to heat up. It got hotter and hotter, flashing bright orange and searing his flesh as it powered up. Ben screamed within the confines of his mind, unable to make a real sound, as exquisite pain permeated his entire body, his wrist feeling like it was being sawn off. What was the bracelet doing to him?

He saw a flash of fire spurt out of the gun as Lord Blackwood squeezed the trigger and the bullet came spinning out of the barrel.

Ben couldn't move, no matter how hard he tried; he was rooted to the spot directly in the path of the bullet. In a moment it would tear through his body and likely kill him. The bracelet was reaching a zenith now, as bright as the sun and so painful he wished his arm would drop off. Suddenly there was a hurricane of noise as everything sped up again, the bullet regaining full speed and slamming into his chest, knocking him backwards off his feet.

Ben saw Blackwood's smug face as he fell, his repulsive mouth contorted into the wry grin of victory. Ben hit the deck with his eyes still open, aware of Blackwood moving towards him, stooping to pick up the Star, eyes ablaze in victory. He said something, his lips moving, but Ben couldn't hear the words. His failure was abject and complete; Lord Blackwood had won. Blackwood walked off quickly in the direction of the central stone.

The only thought that ran through his mind ran as he lay there, dying, was, *I'm sorry, Mum.*

Gasping for breath, waiting for the grim darkness of death to claim him, Ben began to realise that his breathing wasn't getting shallower; it was becoming deeper, the pain in his lungs easing rapidly. It was like being winded – extremely unpleasant to begin with but quick to wear off. He touched himself on the chest where he had felt the bullet strike and brought his fingers up in front of his face.

There was no blood.

Ben rolled onto his side and looked down at himself. He was completely unharmed.

The bracelet.

It had disappeared off his wrist. It must have protected him from the bullet, some form of magical defence. He rubbed his chest, offering up a silent prayer of thanks to Sofiella. With the bracelet gone he assumed he was out of help now, that he was alone against Blackwood.

He staggered to his feet, wobbling sluggishly from side to side like a drunk, his balance still off after the force of being shot. Ben could no longer see the police on the road, so he hoped they were arriving in the car park now and would be pouring into the site at any moment. Blackwood had his back to him, palms resting atop the centre stone. He looked calm, like he was meditating.

Lord Blackwood began to laugh maniacally, his shoulders rising and falling in a wild frenzy. Ben felt a chill sweep through him.

"I can sense you there, Ben, you know. I don't know how you

survived, but I don't care. You're too late. Behold," he said, lifting up the small star-shaped necklace, "the power of the Star of Moirai!"

"Stop!" shouted Ben, hoping there might be some last chance to reason with the madman.

Blackwood curled his lip into a sneer. "Stop? Sure thing, Ben. I'll just put this back and we can all go home, shall we?" He laughed, dangling the Star from his hand. "You are full of excellent ideas, aren't you?"

Ben didn't mind the sarcasm, as he could see the armed police making their way to them from the entrance. A helicopter suddenly screamed across the sky above them, circling viciously around the stones.

"You're too late, Gregovir!" shouted Ben. "You should give up. The police are here, and they will shoot and kill you if you threaten them."

That sneer again. "Oh, I'll do more than threaten them, my dear boy." He lifted the Star up, placing it over his head and around his neck. "I'll positively murder them."

The effect was instant, as if out of a movie. Storm clouds gathered above Stonehenge and a violent wind picked up, so that leaves and litter were whipped up in the turbulence as the Star exerted its power. Thunder and lightning crackled above their heads, the air thickening with the static charge of electricity.

Lord Blackwood roared as the magic poured into him. As it did, his frailty and age receded, each passing second delivering strength and youth into his tired bones. Ben looked on, too shocked to move, as Blackwood grew powerful in front of his eyes.

Ben saw the police shouting through a megaphone, but he couldn't hear them over the deafening wind. He waved his arms at them, trying to get them to understand the danger they were in, to tell them to move away. But they couldn't hear him; they weren't even looking at him. They were sitting ducks for Blackwood now.

Blackwood threw his hands up into the air and two huge bolts of lightning came streaking down out of the sky, lancing into each hand. Ben watched as the lightning crackled into him and saw his eyes once again light with fire.

Ben gulped. Here was the terrible monster of his dreams – his nightmares – made real on Earth. There was no chance for any of them now.

The magic filled Lord Blackwood with fizzing malevolence, his whole aura demonic and alive with evil intent. He thrust his hands out, energy surging out of them and arcing its way through the air to smash into the helicopter. It exploded in a groaning fireball of metal, spraying deadly shrapnel down onto the ground below.

Ben dived for cover as the popping noise of gunfire rang out, the police having no other option now but to bring this psycho down. Ben wondered if they could believe their eyes – what would they make of a man who could shoot lightning from his hands?

Bullets ricocheted off the stones around Ben, deflected his way from those aimed at Blackwood. Fourteen armed police were all firing at Blackwood, but not one single bullet was hitting him. They continued to shout their instructions, confusion levels escalating higher and higher, but with no other plan than to continue shooting at the seemingly invincible man. Ben put his hands over his ears as the cacophony of noise erupted all around him.

Inside the bubble of his force field, Lord Blackwood was laughing, enjoying the attention of the police officers. He was merely toying with them, letting them try their best to take him down, but he was effectively invincible now. The Star of Moirai had shown him how to utilise the magic hidden within the Earth, to give him mastery of this long-forgotten resource, and he knew exactly how to use it.

Ben realised it had suddenly gone quiet. Only the sound of the rain pattering against the stone could be heard; the police had stopped shooting. He looked from around the stone he was lying behind and saw Blackwood take in a deep breath, lift his arms up wide to command the sky and begin to murmur mystically.

Slowly, the police surrounding Lord Blackwood were lifted into the sky. Confused shouting and screaming erupted from the officers; wild cries of anger and fear rang through the air.

Blackwood carried on calmly reciting his incantation, pushing the officers upwards with little more than the motion of his arms. They hung suspended fifty feet in the air, like puppets being played by a new master. Then in one sudden, sickening motion he threw his arms down to the floor and the officers were flung hard into the ground.

Screams were extinguished; terror silenced by death. Ben gasped, shocked by the casual death of so many people. He realised in that moment what Lord Blackwood's power truly meant, what his failure to stop him had unleashed. It was suffering on a grand scale, for all those he would hurt and for those affected by the pain he caused. The friends and family of those police officers, who at this moment had no idea of the hurt they were about to endure, whose broken hearts could never be repaired; their grief was on his hands.

Ben knew that Blackwood would continue to hurt others, to plunder, maim and kill anyone who stood in his way, as he sought to bend all life to his will. It was an unbearable thought, and it was all his fault; he'd failed to stop him.

Ben retched, vomit spraying the ground beneath him. Rain spattered down his face, causing his vision to blur, as tears mixed in and flooded away down his cheeks. He breathed hard, his chest rising and falling rapidly. Then his thoughts seemed to clear, a surge of defiance building within him as one single thought crystallised in his mind.

No more.

Blackwood could not be allowed to cause any more anguish and misery in his megalomaniacal quest. Ben wouldn't let him.

He stood up from behind his stone, feeling strangely calm – relaxed, almost. It was like he was having an out-of-body experience. He knew he should be feeling fear, that his actions were not those of a sane individual, but he had given control of his body over to instinct.

He could feel the Earth, sense the ebb and flow of the mystic energy of this site, of the massive flux of power happening right in front of him as Lord Blackwood played with the magic of this world.

He understood at that moment what magic was. What, in essence, it was, everywhere.

Energy.

The rebels had been impressed because humans had harnessed energy in the form of electricity and used it to power a strange and wonderful world filled with technology. But Ben understood now that electricity was part of the magic of the world, part of the energy it possessed, part of the fibre of the entire universe's being. The earth was part of it, a living and breathing, seething mass of energy.

Lord Blackwood was using the Star to channel that energy in a way that no ordinary mortal could do in this dimension. But Ben understood something else in that moment.

He was no ordinary mortal.

He was the son of two worlds, created by parents from different dimensions, his DNA a unique mix blended in parallel universes. He was able to bridge the divide between the dimensions and had seen that he could be a conduit for magic in both. He might not know how to control it, but he knew that he didn't need the Star to perform magic on Earth, and that within him he possessed the strength to take Gregovir Blackwood on.

He had to try. The Earth would be doomed if he didn't.

He took a huge breath. "Gregovir," he shouted. "Stop!"

Blackwood was facing away from Ben, surveying the damage he had caused, feeling pleased with his work, when he heard Ben's cry. He turned round slowly, pausing, almost comically, with one eyebrow raised.

"I'm not sure how you're still alive," he sneered. "But I don't mind the chance to finish you off again, this time good and proper."

"Just try me," Ben shouted back nonchalantly. His tone surprised Blackwood, sending a wave of uncertainty across his face.

Blackwood threw his arms up, pulling in energy from around him. Ben looked on, his nascent sense of the energy shifts allowing him to see what was going on; the energy gathering in Blackwood's hands looked like a small feverish ball that glowed an intense white.

Ben could sense it was a lot of magic, enough to fry him to a crisp, but his problem now was how to stop it coming his way. With no training in how to deal with magic, Ben was reliant on instinct alone. He concentrated hard, attempting to manipulate this flow of energy, trying to understand how Blackwood was bending it to his desire. Ben could sense that the energy was somehow being conjured in the space around Blackwood, as if he were converting the energy out of thin air. He focussed, trying to understand how he was doing it, to understand where the power was coming from. The glowing white orb was a fizzing, spitting shower of sparks now, and Ben realised he was out of time, as Blackwood sent the swirling bolt of lightning towards him. Ben could feel the fireball moving through the air, his mind instinctively pushing back against the maelstrom of energy as it raced towards him. It struck him square in the solar plexus, sending him hurtling thirty feet backwards through the air, until he slammed into the ground, skidding to a stop in the mud.

He held his ribs and chest in agony where it had impacted, his clothes blackened by the scorching heat. He could barely breathe, but he was alive, somehow. Something had prevented the energy from dissipating entirely through his body. He guessed every atom would have been vaporised if it had.

No-one was more surprised than Blackwood, who couldn't believe that the kid was still alive and intact. It was one of the most fearsome attacks he could muster. No-one on Sunea would have survived that attack if they didn't have enough magic to summon a deflection spell.

Blackwood narrowed his eyes as he looked at Ben, writhing around in pain on the floor. Could it be possible that the boy could do magic, here on Earth? If that were true, he was far more interesting than he had previously realised. As a foe he needed to be extinguished. But as a friend?

Ben saw Blackwood coming for him and instinctively knew this was the end for him. That hit had completely taken the wind out of him, and despite his understanding of Blackwood's power, he feared that he was no match for it. He tried to get up but couldn't, his body refusing to co-operate. He was a sitting duck for Blackwood now. The rain kept battering down, soaking him wet through, the water running down his hair and into his eyes. Ben took several deep breaths, trying to find some energy reserves from somewhere.

Energy.

That word again. It could mean so many different things in different circumstances, but Ben could suddenly see the whole cycle of it – the symmetry that the universe was imbued with. Energy was constantly being converted from one form to another, from food to kinetic, from heat to light. It was never lost – only *changed.*

He pressed his face against the wet grass, trying to feel the energy in the world, in the raindrops splashing on his skin. Time slowed down as it had before, as the energy all around him came alive and danced through his mind. He began to perceive the tiny elements of matter that existed that he could bond with, that he could convert into energy. *Magic.* He tried to draw on it, to bring it into his body and fill his tank up. As he did, he began to feel that warm glow inside of him, the unmistakable buzzing feeling he'd had before, the sensation of electricity pulsing through him. He could feel himself getting stronger, the energy pooling within him, swirling inside of him, his mind on fire.

Lord Blackwood sensed this too, shouting at Ben and preparing another spell. Ben thrashed around on the floor as the energy built up to incredible levels again, levels he knew he could not control.

The magic pulsed out of him in one go; energy pushed indiscriminately in all directions, catching Blackwood as it exploded outwards, sending him flying against one of the stones. Blackwood lay there stunned for a moment, rocked by the raw energy Ben had sent at him.

Ben tried to sit up. His use of magic had been crude and had tired him out. He knew he wouldn't be able to do that again anytime soon, so he needed a new plan.

But Blackwood was up quickly and marching over to him, and Ben could barely lift his arms. Blackwood kicked Ben back down, his face slapping into the mud. He grabbed Ben by the hair, yanking his head up and causing Ben to scream out in pain. He put his grim face inches from Ben's, snarling in his ear. "You are full of surprises, aren't you?" he spat. "I can see I'm going to have to finish you off the old-fashioned way."

Lord Blackwood grinned as he pulled his jacket to one side to reveal a knife.

"You know, in some ways, I have to respect your durability. You could be quite a powerful mage, given the chance. But what you have in talent you lack in skill. You need a teacher, someone to guide you, to show you how to master the magic you command. Think about it. We could be an awesome team, Ben, if we joined forces." Blackwood placed the knife on Ben's neck. Ben felt the cold steel nipping at his skin, the blade razor-sharp. "You think you know what happened, don't you? You think that I ruined Sunea and that the rebels are the good guys, that everything is black and white. The rebels have done things that would shock your soul, Ben. All I ever wanted was to build a Sunea that was powerful, that prospered and would last another thousand years. But the rebels destroyed that dream when they selfishly used the Star, sending our world into Shadow."

Ben tried not to listen, sure that Blackwood would only be feeding him lies. But maybe the world did exist in shades of grey, rather than good versus evil. Perhaps the rebels did cause the downfall of Sunea. Ben only really had the rebels' word of what had happened.

"We could build that prosperous world together, Ben," continued

Blackwood. "Think about it, the power you would have; anything in the world that you wanted would be yours. We could do it, Ben; you could be at my right hand, the most powerful lord within my kingdom." Blackwood pressed the knife into Ben's neck, drawing a bit of blood to emphasise the nature of the 'offer'. "All you need do is submit to me. Agree that I am your master and end this pointless war, once and for all."

Lord Blackwood's words danced in his ears, seductive and hypnotising at the same time. He could feel his mind falter, his senses placed into a trance by a different kind of magic, one that placed greed and power before respect and love. But he cleared his mind, remembering Gregovir Blackwood's methods and how he tried to get what he wanted. The way he'd tortured him and his friends, had knifed his mother in cold blood and shot Elena. He was an evil, nasty piece of work, no doubt. Ben gulped as he built up to his last act of defiance.

"I'll never join you, Gregovir."

Lord Blackwood shrugged. "Then you must die."

"Not if I've got anything to do with it," came another voice, startling Blackwood. He looked round just in time to see Jake's foot before it connected squarely in his face.

Jake whooped as he felt the contact, Lord Blackwood spinning round from the force of the kick, dropping the knife. He continued his melee attack with another kick aimed right in his gut.

"This one's for my sister! And this is for Ben's mum! Didn't know I was a black-belt, did you?" screamed Jake, as he rained kick after kick into Blackwood, who was too stunned to defend himself and, after two or three more heavy blows, was sent flying through the air, landing in the mud with a heavy thud.

Ben looked on, amazed and bemused in equal measure, still unable to stand. He tried to call out to Jake, but his voice was failing him. He saw Jake stoop to pick something up, then stand triumphantly over Lord Blackwood.

Gregovir Blackwood regained his senses quickly, his blurred vision coming into focus to see the figure of Jake stood over him. He pulled his hands up to attack him with a spell, but nothing happened. No lightning bolt came shooting out of his hands, and he felt no power within him. He scrambled at his neck for the Star. It wasn't there.

"Looking for this?" said Jake, dropping the Star from his hand and dangling it above Blackwood. The dark clouds that had raced in when Lord Blackwood had drawn on the Star's power began to break up, sunlight cascading down through the gaps to illuminate the henge. Blackwood blinked in the bright light, squinting against the image of Jake above him.

He reached in vain for the Star.

"Ah, ah, ah." Jake laughed as he placed his foot lightly on Blackwood's chest. "I don't think you'll be getting your hands on this again." Jake looked at the Star, admiring its beauty. Small, delicate, perfectly formed – a simple gold star balanced within a golden oval thread. He couldn't believe that so much power resided in such a simple object. It began to resonate with him, to fill his mind and soul with nefarious whisperings, an irresistible call to power. "In fact, I think I might just keep this for myself," he murmured. "See what all the fuss is about." He looked Lord Blackwood directly in the eye and added with as much venom as he could: "And I'm going to start by killing you."

Ben couldn't quite make out what was going on, but he assumed that Jake had managed to disable Blackwood – it looked like he now had him pinned to the ground. He breathed a sigh of relief, thanking god for Jake's last-minute intervention.

He tried to call to him, his voice hoarse and barely able to travel the distance.

"Jake. Jake!"

Jake looked up suddenly, as if snapping out of a trance. "Ben!" he called back. "Are you alright?"

"Yes, I'm OK. How are you?"

"I'm alright, Ben. I'm going to finish this off now. It should never have got this far; we nearly let Blackwood win. But I can make it right – I can see this through."

Ben didn't like the sound of this. "What do you mean?"

"I can be special too, Ben. It doesn't have to be just you. I can help, I can do it. It wants me to do it."

Ben tried to stagger to his feet, sensing that something was about to go disastrously wrong.

"Don't get up, Ben, don't come any closer. I'm going to do this; I'm going to make it right."

Understanding dawned on Ben. "Don't do it, Jake," he shouted. "I'm telling you, do not put the Star on. It would be a huge mistake."

Jake laughed. "Oh, really? And why is that?"

"You won't be able to handle it. No-one can; it only exists to destroy. If you activate it, you could be killing the Earth as surely as Blackwood would. Just give the Star to me and we can wait for the police backup to arrive."

Jake snorted, dark thoughts clouding his mind. "I knew it. You just want the Star for yourself. You're the only one who's allowed to be *special*. Well, you're not going to get it, not this time. I'm going to make this right, Ben, but I'm going to do it my way."

"Jake," Ben shouted. "Listen to yourself. That's not you speaking – it's the lure of the Star. Just throw it over to me and this'll all be over."

"No," said Jake, as he slipped the Star over his head.

Ben stood, frozen in time, mouth open in horror. Rain hung in the air, refusing to submit to gravity. Lord Blackwood lay on the floor, a beaten and old wrinkled man, his face screwed up in loathing. All of this, Jake observed, every nanosecond stretching into infinity, and he felt the power of the universe envelop him. At first, it felt nice, like stepping into a warm bath. Then his body tingled, as the temperature began to creep up, and his skin started to protest at the scorching heat. His mind flickered to the image of a lobster being boiled alive. Was it right, this pain? The sensation of power flooding his body was swiftly replaced by fear. His brain felt like it was about to explode through his head, bubbling and boiling in agony. His soul screamed in silence, unable to share space with all the energy that was pouring into his body. The last thing he saw was a dazzling bright light before everything winked out, to a deep, dark, inky black.

Ben witnessed Jake put the Star on and bellowed out to him, but it was already too late. Jake was lost in an explosion of white light that blinded Ben like the flash from a nuclear bomb, forcing him to shield his eyes.

For a moment, all the sound in the world was sucked out of existence, as the Earth held its breath.

Then a roar began to build around Stonehenge, a rumbling that started deep in the ground but got louder as it reached a crescendo of crashing noise that smashed against the stones. The white flash was fading, and Ben saw that Jake was now just a black shadow, an imprint gouged in space where he had once been standing. A giant beam of light erupted out from his silhouette, shining up towards the sky.

The light pulsated, beating like a heart as it pumped pure energy into the sky. Then the streaming light bent in mid-air, winding its way back around towards the ground and smashing into the Earth in the middle of the stones.

Ben watched in wonder as the place danced with vitality, the stones that had lain dormant for thousands of years coming to life, bathed in a blue haze that purred and buzzed. A droning sound began to emerge from the cacophony that surrounded him, slowly getting louder. It sounded like monks chanting on their way to prayer, a low chorus of holy singing.

It built towards a climax, and Ben felt his skin prickle. It was like he was near the portal again in the forest. Could it be? Were the Star and Stonehenge combining, here, to open a portal to another dimension?

The haze grew, in size and definition, until it became a bright, blue dome of energy, surrounding and encompassing the henge with throbbing, seething power.

Ben could still make out Jake's shadow in the middle of it all, a black hole where his body had been, a silhouette cut in the same position as it had been when he had placed the Star around his neck.

The blue hemisphere of energy covering Stonehenge contracted in, bringing itself to a dazzling white singularity that hung over the centre stone for the briefest of moments, a beautiful reminder of everything that was magnificent and momentous in the universe.

Then it exploded outwards, knocking Ben flat back down on the ground as the energy within it was released. Before he blacked out, he managed to lift his head, looking into the fading light, and saw the disappearing shadows of Lord Blackwood and Jake as they winked out of existence.

CHAPTER 28

The sun was setting over a cool and crisp autumn evening in Lyndshaw. Ben, Heather and Sam were sat in the treehouse, deep in reflective discussion over the recent events.

It was three days since the incident at Stonehenge, and this was the first time they'd had an opportunity to get together away from the studious glare of the police and their parents. Ben was just finishing up giving them the full story.

"The last thing I saw before blacking out was them disappear," he said pointedly.

Heather looked sad. "So he's definitely gone?"

Ben frowned, placing his hand softly on her arm. "I'm sorry, Heather. I tried to stop him using it."

She began to cry.

"It can't have been long before I woke up again," Ben continued, "because the police backup hadn't arrived yet. I went to the spot where Jake had been standing and found this." Ben dug his hand into his pocket, pulling out a small gold object.

"Is that—" gasped Sam.

"Yes," interrupted Ben. "It's the Star of Moirai." He'd given the Star a polish, and now it sparkled in the dipping sunlight.

"I told the police it was just a piece of my mother's jewellery, something I'd been carrying since she had gone into hospital, and they lost interest in it." He held it up so they could all inspect it. "But this is, of course, what all the fuss has been about." The trio were silent for a moment, letting it sink in. The Star of Moirai hung on the end of a thin, metal chain, spinning slowly in the dying light. It consisted of two oval bands of silver, which intersected to create a lattice about the size of an egg. In the middle, hanging by two links of golden thread, was a small, five-pointed star, with a brilliant, aquatic green gem set into the middle of it. It was hard to believe that such a small item could hold within it so much power, to bend men to its will, to destroy planets and dimensions.

"And you think that the others disappeared at the same time as Jake?" asked Sam.

Ben looked down, the pain of learning about what had happened still raw. "Yes, I think so," he said, breathing in deep. He had only learnt later that day when he was taken to the police station for questioning that it wasn't just Jake and Lord Blackwood who had disappeared when the Star was activated. So too had all other Suneans on Earth: Taegan, Elena – and his mother.

One moment she had been lying in her hospital bed, the next she wasn't. The staff and the police didn't know what to make of it, apart from assuming she'd somehow been kidnapped. Ben couldn't tell them the truth. It would do no good; they wouldn't believe him. He still went numb every time he thought about it, which was all the time.

He hadn't said anything to his dad about what really happened, although he'd wanted to so many times. When he saw the depths of depression his dad was plumbing, his heart sank, and he just wanted to be able to confide in him and in some way bring relief, or at least the truth. But how could he? His dad would never believe him. The truth wouldn't make the agonising pain any easier; in fact, it would probably just make it worse.

"Where do you think they are, Ben?" asked Heather.

Ben looked up from his thoughts, purpose clarifying in his face. "I think they were transported back to the Shadow Realm. You should have seen the light show when Jake used the Star. Somehow, Stonehenge acted as a bridge, a gateway between the two dimensions, with the help of the power from this thing." Ben looked at the Star in disgust and put it back in his pocket.

"But that means—" started Sam.

"That my mum is back there too, still in a coma," said Ben, finishing Sam's sentence. "And Elena also, in her delicate state." He held his head in his hands, hoping beyond hope that somehow, they were alright, that Taegan had acted swiftly and been able to help them. The alternative was too distressing to think about.

"That's awful, Ben, I'm really sorry," Heather said, putting her hand on his knee. They comforted each other for a moment, united in their grief for lost family.

"Have you seen the latest in the local?" asked Sam.

Ben looked up, blinking away the formative tears. "No. Why?"

"Here," said Sam, giving his phone to Ben. "They don't know the truth, of course. They're still going with the line that your mum was kidnapped and that the incident at Stonehenge was the work of a lone, crazed gunman."

Ben took the phone and scanned the article, where a picture of his mum was featured under the headline 'Snatched from hospital'. He scrolled through, barely taking in any of the information, which was all just hypothesis, itself based on a lie. But a name he saw slapped him in the face, forcing him to read the article seriously. His face darkened as he continued reading, his hand covering his mouth as he took in the news, scarcely able to believe it could be true.

"What is it?" asked Heather, with some trepidation, having seen the change on Ben's face.

"It's Natalie," breathed Ben.

"Who's Natalie?" Heather and Sam chimed at the same time.

"She's missing too."

"Yes, but who is she?" asked Sam, exasperated.

"She was my mum's nurse," he said, talking slowly. "It says here that she hasn't been seen since my mum went missing. The police would very much like to talk to her, so if anyone has any information as to her whereabouts they should get in touch."

Sam and Heather looked at each other. "What does that mean?"

"I'm not sure," mused Ben. "She could have been nursing my mother and caught up in the vortex that took her back to the Shadow Realm."

"You really think she could have been taken there too?"

Ben shook his head. "I don't know," he sighed. "But she went missing at the same time, so it's a possibility."

"And all because Jake tried to use the Star," muttered Sam. "Why would he do it?"

Ben pinched his eyes. "The Star exerts an influence that can be hard to resist. We shouldn't be too hard on him. We mustn't forget that without him, we would have lost. He saved my life at the end, and all of us, for that matter, from Blackwood. He couldn't understand what would happen if he used the Star any more than the rest of us."

"So the question is, what are we going to do about it?" asked Sam, puffing his chest out.

Ben looked Sam in the eye, seeing his friend's determination, and smiled. He knew he could always rely on them; it gave him the strength to carry on.

He looked at them both earnestly, audacity sparkling in his eyes. "The only thing we can. We're going to go back to the Shadow Realm and we're going to get our family back. Then we're going to kill Lord Blackwood."

Heather and Sam looked scared but eager to help.

"How?" asked Heather. "Blackwood is too strong in the Shadow Realm – our best chance to defeat him was when he was here; we can't win on his home turf."

Ben had been wondering how to tell his friends this without them thinking him crazy. He decided to just dive right in.

"I can do magic."

"*What?*" they both shouted in unison.

Ben held his hands up. "It sounds mad, I know, but I wouldn't be here now if there wasn't something in me that could do it. I think it's to do with my parents coming from both dimensions." Ben looked down, his expression sheepish. "I think I might be the chosen one."

"The chosen one?"

"Predicted in Sunean legend as the one who would return to lead his people to the promised lands." Ben studied his fingernails and dusted his cuffs. "I may well have the responsibility of the entire Sunean planet on my shoulders."

"Well, you're bearing it remarkably lightly," joked Heather. "But you're quite serious about this? You think you're this... chosen one?"

"I don't really see how it could be anybody else."

"Mmm."

Sam had been quiet up to now. He was eyeing Ben suspiciously. "So... can you do magic now?"

"Well, I'm not sure. It's funny, I can feel it around me and could see Blackwood using it when he had the Star, but I don't really know how to control it. The times I've done it so far, it's just kind of... happened, like an involuntary reaction to being in danger."

"Right," said Sam, suitably unimpressed.

"I don't know how to explain it. It's like there's magic in the air, an energy that can be harnessed. That's all it is, really, just energy."

"Energy?" said Sam, sceptical. "Like new-age stuff?"

"Not really, more like real energy, the stuff that makes up the building blocks of all of us – you know, matter, atoms, the universe. There's a lot of energy around, and it's just a question of how it's harnessed. Mankind has understood the invisible forces at work in our world through science, manipulated energy and bent it to our will with technology. The Suneans have done it with magic. It's just a matter of perspective, really."

The trio sat in quiet contemplation for a moment.

"And the Star?" asked Heather. "What will you do with that?"

"I'm going to destroy it. It should never be used again by anyone. There isn't a living thing in the multiverse that isn't in danger from it."

"How will you destroy it?" asked Sam.

"I'm not sure," said Ben, wrangling his hands, wanting to reach out for his friends. "I'm hoping we can figure it out together?"

They didn't need to say anything. Heather slipped her hand into his, and Ben knew he could count on his friends. It seemed to Ben in that moment that friendship was another form of magic – a bond between people that couldn't be seen, or touched, but a bond nonetheless that provided immense strength, a strength that men like Lord Blackwood always underestimated.

Ben knew it would be hard, that it would be dangerous to go back to the Shadow Realm, but he had no choice. He owed it to Heather and Jake, to Natalie, and to Taegan, Elena and the other people of Sunea. But most of all he owed his mum and dad. He had to put his family back together.

His preparations would begin tomorrow, but for now he just sat with his friends, watching the sun set and the light slowly drain from the world. Tomorrow, his quest to free Sunea and make the sun rise over that ruined land once more, would begin.

For writing and publishing news, or recommendations of new titles to read, sign up to the Book Guild newsletter: